CW01509367

The Girl
who wasn't
Good Enough

Liz Wainwright

Book One of the Lynda Collins Trilogy

Elizabeth Wainwright asserts the moral right
to be identified as the author of this work.

This novel is entirely a work of fiction.
The names, incidents and characters portrayed in it are entirely
the work of the author's imagination.
Any resemblance to actual persons living or dead,
events or localities is entirely coincidental.

Loveday Manor Publishing

ISBN-13: 978-0957227903
ISBN-10: 0957227906

DEDICATION

For Glyn
And
Our wonderful family

CONTENTS

ACKNOWLEDGMENTS

With special thanks to Jane Rushforth for proof reading
and for convincing me I could write a novel .

CHAPTER ONE

Lizzie Luck was in need of a good wash, she'd no knickers, and she was a bit sticky from being in the company of a half-eaten Mars Bar. Miss Bates paused and stared for a moment at the tiny doll, made from scraps of wool and cotton, and with a silly expression on its face. Then she slapped the 1961 GCE history O level exam paper down on to the desk in front of Lynda Collins.

Miss Bates wondered if she should confiscate the good luck mascot but decided she would prefer not to touch it. Barbara Bates didn't like getting her hands dirty. She didn't like Lynda Collins either, but seeing the fear in those usually defiant blue eyes caused the Geography teacher to have a rare, almost sympathetic thought. In her opinion, to have any hope of passing these exams Lynda Collins would need all the luck she could get.

Lynda knew she'd failed the Geography exam, but she was hoping to pass this one. She'd stayed up till two o'clock in the morning revising in bed, the faded pink satin eiderdown wrapped round her shoulders to deflect the draught from the disintegrating sash window. Her parents, Ray and Doreen Collins, had taken over the tenancy of The Black Bull in Milfield in 1956. They had no experience of running a pub, or anything else for that matter, but Ray, a swarthy, swaggering 'man's man' had managed to wheedle the favour from the brewery owner's son, one of his drinking pals from his days in the army.

It wasn't a big favour, the Black Bull was in a downtrodden part of town where the loss of jobs in the cotton mills had shoved many families into hardship. The grime layered pub was still popular with the hard-up local population but, like its customers, had been getting shabbier by the day.

Sunshine was a stranger to the male preserve of the tap-room, the windows faced away from the sun most of the day and the window panes

1

were, in any case, usually too dirty to let it in. The grey stone- flagged floor was littered with sawdust and cracked spittoons, and was brightened only by the reflected flames of the coal fire which was the pub's big attraction in the winter. The seating consisted mainly of wooden backed benches screwed to the walls and coated in layers of varnish and nicotine. There were two long slate-topped tables for playing dominoes, and half a dozen round, heavy cast iron tables you couldn't easily knock over in a brawl.

The snug, with its faded burgundy plush seats and a wood and frosted glass screen which kept out the draughts, was the warmest room in the building. It was treasured by the wives whose husbands were kind enough to let them come and enjoy a Pale Ale with their women friends. But the best room, in Lynda's opinion, was the piano room.

The thinly padded benches behind the oblong tables along two of its walls were not very comfortable, and neither were the stools grouped round the smaller tables in the centre of the room, but the upright piano, bequeathed to The Black Bull by a former customer who had got away from Milfield and made a bit of money, gave the well-worn room and everyone in it a bit of life.

The happiest times Lynda could remember were in that room, with everybody singing old music-hall songs as well as the Guy Mitchell and Doris Day hits, and clearing a space for her to stand and sing solos. There'd been a row about it of course. She remembered Madge, her grandmother coming into the crowded bar to rescue her from pulling pints.

'Come on, Lynda, they're asking for you in t' piano room. Come and give them a song.'

'Can I, Mum?'

'Yes, but wait till your Dad's come back up from the cellar.'

'She can go now, I'll serve till Ray gets back – how long does it take to tap a barrel? He'll be having a fag and a sit down, I bet.'

Doreen had stepped aside as she always did for her mother-in-law, and Lynda had been about to escape to the piano room when her Dad emerged from the cellar.

'Where do you think you're going?'

'They want me to sing in the piano room.'

Ray's smile was twisted with sarcasm. 'Are they going to pay you?'

'No. But neither are you!'

'You're stopping here. And less of your lip!'

'Are you not paying her?' Madge stepped between her son and his daughter.

'No.'

'What do you think you're playing at? If she's working, she gets paid.'

Doreen, as always, trying to keep the peace, explained quietly, 'He gives her a bit of extra pocket money.'

'I'm not talking about a couple of bob spending money, Doreen, I'm talking about wages. Not even t' bloody mill owners got away with what you're doing, Ray!' Madge snatched a ten shilling note from behind the bar and shoved it in Lynda's hand. 'That's toward what you're owed, love, and from now on, she gets paid, or else!'

So grudgingly Ray had started to pay his daughter a few pence an hour, and Doreen tried not to resent and envy yet another demonstration of her mother-in-law's power over her husband. Any influence Doreen had once enjoyed in Ray's world had faded as soon as he'd returned home after learning the meaning of mortality on the beaches of Normandy. Ray had vowed to make damned sure he enjoyed life to overflowing from then on, and not necessarily with his wife.

When Ray and Doreen Collins had moved into The Black Bull the brewery representative had talked about money for modernisation, but so far all that had been funded was a freezing cold bathroom and more efficient pumps in the bar. Lynda, sixteen, and long ago hardened to the realities of life in a family where talk of money always led to a row, reckoned she knew nearly all there was to know about running the pub now. It didn't help her progress at school, of course, spending so much time serving pints but as far as Ray was concerned, exams weren't as important as making sure the takings were high enough to keep the brewery from shutting the place down.

The pub would have been a lot more profitable if Ray, who liked to be popular, had been less flamboyantly generous when in the company of his 'drinking pals' - both male and female. In contrast to this, he could also be very tight-fisted, as his wife and daughter knew too well. All the time he was growing up Ray had been embarrassed and annoyed that, because of his father's poor health, it was his mother who'd been the main wage-earner and had managed the money. All his friends' families were run in the traditional way; the men had control over their wages and consequently their word was law. Ray had decided many years ago that when he married he would make sure he had that power.

The amount he paid Lynda, on a strictly hourly rate, was a fraction of the money he handed out to her brother. Terry was only a year older than Lynda, but he did less work and yet received more appreciation, and affection, from his father. Lynda knew she wasn't being treated fairly and so, with only a little hesitation, she secretly topped up her 'wages' with three-penny bits, sixpences and the occasional half-crown from the piles of coins laid out on the shelf beneath the bar before opening time.

She didn't regard it as stealing; to her mind it was money she'd earned serving drinks, washing glasses and filling up the shelves with Britvic Fruit Juices, Babycham and bottles of Guinness. Lynda, when she thought about it, resented having to help herself because her Dad was too mean to treat her fairly.

She remembered how he used to spend money on her when she was a golden curled little girl who adored her Daddy; but as soon as she learned to answer him back when he was unreasonable Ray had stopped buying her even a bar of chocolate. So Lynda took what she could, and was pretty sure God would forgive her; after all, the money was going to a good cause - she was saving up to leave home.

There was an old black cast-iron fireplace in Lynda's bedroom, another of the promised 'modernisation' jobs still waiting to be done. It was on a ledge up in the chimney that Lynda hid her cash in a tin box, and it was mounting up nicely. She'd not spent any of the money she'd been given for her sixteenth birthday. There'd been no celebrating, of course, not in the circumstances.

Summer seemed to have developed a habit of flaunting its sunniest, most enticing, strawberry-laden days during the weeks of school exams. This was one of the hottest days this year, and at Milfield High School for Girls the sunshine had already streaked into the silent gymnasium, smoothing its warmth along the varnished wall bars. Specks of dust hovered above the tables and chairs positioned in strictly spaced, cheat-resistant rows below the coils of hanging-strength rope.

Lynda watched Miss Bates shuffling along the polished parquet floor in her black, tightly laced old maid's shoes, her grey flannel skirt flapping wearily round her lumpy calves. She couldn't imagine the cold-eyed woman ever having been a teenager. Well, Lynda thought to herself, she wouldn't have been, not in her day. Teenagers were the new breed of youngsters and the stuck-up people were dead worried about them. Glad to switch her mind away from the exam, Lynda smiled for a moment as she thought about making a name for herself one day among this new generation that was going to turn the world into a different and much more exciting place.

Sometimes, she thought, it was great being sixteen. Looking in the mirror gave her the confidence of knowing she looked all right, even though her clothes were the cheapest you could get. She had blonde hair which curled itself casually over her shoulders and a figure that made boys turn and gawp when they passed her in the street. Lynda ignored their wolf-whistles, and to tell the truth was embarrassed by them. She and her best friend, Jean Clayton, had read the grubby 'Facts Of Life' booklet which had been surreptitiously passed around in the third form, but had postponed thinking about its contents in any detail. It was romance they were interested in, falling in love and having a big white wedding. And Lynda had already met the boy she was going to marry; his name was Daniel Heywood.

She'd fallen in love with Dan, a few months ago, the first time she saw him at an end of term football match between the Technical High School and the Grammar School. Terry was in the team, so she and Jean had used it as an excuse to go and survey the gathering of local male talent. Dan had been in the Grammar School team with his friend John Stanworth, who, with his dark brown, long lashed eyes and deep quiff of thick black hair, was the embodiment of the 'tall dark and handsome' women's magazine cliché. Jean had a crush on John Stanworth, and at the end of the match she dragged Lynda over to stand with the rest of the girls who had swooped towards him and other members of the team. Jean knew the boy standing next to John and, keeping hold of Lynda's arm, pushed her way into the centre of the group.

'Hiya, Sid.'

'Oh, hello, Jean.' Sid looked down kindly at the thin girl in the faded, handed-down dress. 'Been watching the match?'

'Yeah.' Jean smiled briefly at him before fixing her flutteringly wide-eyed gaze on her quarry. 'That was a great goal, John. Your name is John, isn't it?'

'Yeah, John Stanworth.' Even as he nodded he was already looking over Jean's sparrow brown head at Lynda's golden hair.

'What's your name?'

'Jean Clayton. I'm a friend of Sid's.'

'She lives on our street,' his team mate informed him, giving John enough knowledge to make him feel sorry for Jean there and then.

'Nice to meet you, Jean. And . . .?'

Reluctantly Jean introduced Lynda, who smiled but was more interested in the solidly-built, sandy-haired goal-keeper who was speaking to him.

'See you tomorrow, John.'

'Aren't you coming round to Bob's? He's invited us all for a drink.'

The goal-keeper shrugged his broad shoulders with a glance which aimed his apology at Lynda as well as his friend. 'Can't. Got to go home. Sorry.'

John shook his head as he watched his friend hurry away.

'Who's that?' Lynda asked.

'Dan Heywood. My best mate.'

'The Heywoods who own the cake shops?' Jean asked, open-mouthed.

John could see that both girls were impressed, and so continued, 'Yeah. They live in that big house on Wellington Road. Geoff Heywood's a friend of my Dad's. He's offered me a job but I had to turn it down.'

'Why?' Jean, who came from a family not popular among local employers, was in awe at the idea of refusing the offer of a job.

'I'd already got an electrician's apprenticeship at Earnshaw's,' John announced proudly, and then raised his hand at his team-mates who were shouting at him to follow them. 'I've got to catch up with them now. You two go to the Saturday dances at the Carlton, don't you?'

'Yes,' Jean answered eagerly.

'See you there sometime, then.'

'Yeah! See you!' Jean waved enthusiastically even after he'd started to run towards his friends.

'Oh, Lynda, isn't he smashing?'

'He fancies himself too much for my liking. I prefer his mate.'

Jean was very relieved.

'Dan Heywood? I think he fancied you.'

'Do you?' Lynda smiled at her friend and felt happier than she ever had in her life.

She remembered that feeling of happiness and hung on to it like a lifeline as she struggled through the exams and the long hours at the pub. Dan hadn't asked her out yet, but she'd seen the way he'd looked at her and knew he had fallen in love just as she had. She dreamed of their first date almost every night.

During the next weeks and months the two teenagers took every opportunity to contrive a blushing encounter in Alexandra Park, or in town, outside one of his father's three baker's and confectioner's shops. They somehow didn't manage to go to the dances on the same Saturday nights, mainly because Lynda always had to work, so they rarely came within touching distance.

When they saw each other on the opposite side of the street, Dan's lack of confidence made his legs turn to lead and Lynda was still obeying the 'rules of courting'. Rule number one was that girls didn't make themselves cheap by making the first move. Anyway she'd worked out that Dan wouldn't think it was fair to distract her from her exams, so was probably waiting till they were finished. So it wouldn't be long now before they got together and started the romance of the century.

She knew there might be problems, of course, because of his mother, Ellen Heywood, a haughty looking woman whom Lynda had seen occasionally in town, getting into a sleek black Daimler. Bit by bit, she managed to gather information about Dan and his family from customers, and from her Mother, who wasn't keen to talk about the subject, but told her that the car had belonged to Mrs Heywood's father.

Lynda had even caught the bus to the high class part of Milfield and walked past the Heywood family's home, Kirkwood House. It was an imposing, dark-stoned Victorian mansion which had also belonged, until his death the previous year, to Alexander Buchanan, Geoff Heywood's autocratic father-in-law. In accordance with the terms of the Scottish banker's will the house now, in law, belonged solely to his only child, Ellen Heywood, but in spirit it remained her father's possession, just as she did.

It went without saying that Ellen Heywood would forbid her son to fall in love with a girl whose mother used to scrub the floors of the Buchanan residence. Lynda had faith, though, that such class prejudice could be charmed away. From experience, Lynda had learned to trust her intuition; she just knew that Dan was only waiting for the right moment, and the courage, to ask her for a date. She was so sure that Dan Heywood was the man she would marry that she had eventually even confided her dream to her mother, not long before she died; but she was taken aback at her reaction.

'Dan Heywood?'

'Yes.'

'Oh.'

Doreen Collins, by then a frail, worn out ragdoll, with tired eyes set in the grey hollows of her pale little face, had stared at her daughter in silence for a moment, and then asked.

'Can you not find somebody else?'

'No. I've got this feeling, Mum, I can't explain it, but he's the one.'

'The Heywood family aren't our sort.'

'I know, they've got money. But that's not why I want Dan.'

'I know it's not, love, but I hope you'll change your mind. Geoff Heywood's all right but Dan's mother would make your life hell. She's a Buchanan, and takes after her father. Dan Heywood's not for you.'

'He is.'

Doreen Collins was again silent, struggling to make a hard decision.

'You remember I told you I used to work at Kirkwood House, cleaning for them when you were a baby.'

'Yeah. So what?'

'They put the fear of God into me, her family. They wanted nothing to do with us – and she still doesn't because there's something I know about the Heywoods.'

'What?'

'It's a secret and you must promise me you won't tell anyone, ever. Promise.'

So Lynda made that unbreakable promise and listened to the secret that didn't seem important at the time.

Lynda had made up her mind not to be afraid of Dan's mother; there was no doubt in Lynda's mind that the adults of Mrs.' High and Mighty' Heywood's generation, with their snobbery and prejudice, were on their way out. The confidence of being part of the modern new generation, and her anger at the way Ellen Heywood and her father had treated her mother would give her the courage to stand up to the old witch. And Lynda had already been trying out teenage rebellion. For example, she thought it was rubbish that she was now old enough to wash glasses in the pub, but not old enough to drink, so she quietly helped herself to half a pint of lager and lime whenever she felt like it. Her Mum had always obeyed rules, done as she was told without question, and Lynda had seen what kind of a life she'd had.

Doreen Collins had talked to her daughter more during the last few weeks of her illness than in all the years of Lynda's childhood. She'd told her about the tough life she'd led, working on her grandparents' farm where she and her mother, Elsie, were treated more like servants than family.

Little Doreen Bradshaw had been conceived out of pity and guilt; the pity Elsie Bradshaw, had felt for her husband, Robert, condemned to be shipped back to France in 1917; and the fear and guilt she felt about a mad moment of lust she'd shared with a married man only a week before her husband's unexpected return home on leave.

A year later Robert Bradshaw had been killed, leaving his wife, young son and new baby daughter to live as unwanted dependents on the Bradshaw farm which was eventually to be inherited by Robert's pig-headed younger brother. Elsie and her children were required to be grateful every day, and Doreen had been taught from early childhood that to survive she had to be obedient and to make every effort to please people.

She had pleased Ray Collins one weekend in Blackpool in 1939, a treat paid for by her brother Len, who'd already started making a bit of a name for himself as an early recruit to the R.A.F. Ray Collins had been smitten by the innocent, pretty young girl who was as different from his mother as anyone could be, and who instantly adored him in a way his ego could not resist.

He'd taken her back to Milfield with him, found her a job and lodgings and ignored his mother's disapproval. He loved defying his mother, making her prove to him again how special he was. When Ray received his call-up papers, Madge Collins gave up trying to persuade her beloved only child to change his mind about Doreen Bradshaw, and let him, as usual, have what he wanted.

Miss Bates' dispassionate voice cut through the nervous silence.

'You may begin.'

Lynda touched Lizzie Luck, and fought back tears as she silently prayed to her Mum for help. The poor scrap of a doll had been her mother's. Lynda had dug it out of the bottom of Doreen's sewing basket when she was a child and had claimed Lizzie Luck as her friend and mascot. It was only last November that Doreen Collins had given her last regretful little smile to her daughter, only two weeks before Lynda's sixteenth birthday.

Lynda would never forget that smile and, as she'd walked behind her mother's coffin in the ancient graveyard overlooking the Pennine hills, Lynda had vowed that she wouldn't go through her life having regrets like her mother had. She'd get out of Milfield, move up in the world. She would make damned sure she'd have a good time, and above all, have her own money.

These flaming exams were part of all that. You had to have qualifications these days. Her brother, Terry, hadn't been bright enough to go to the Grammar School but had got a place at the new Technical College. Terry was lazy, like his Dad, and had not seen the importance of doing any work at school until it was too late. He knew he'd been lucky to get the chance to train as a mechanic at Goodwin's – thanks to his uncle Len.

Feeling guilty at emigrating to Australia and leaving his sister to a life which he knew wasn't going to be happy, Doreen's brother, Leonard

Bradshaw had come to pay her one last visit. Doreen had been very worried about Terry, who was having trouble getting a job, but had had enough of working in the pub for his Dad, whose moods were becoming more and more unpredictable.

So Len, using his carefully acquired R.A.F old boys' accent and manner, had persuaded the local garage owner to take on his nephew as an apprentice. Len had also sent Doreen money later when his business had started to do well, but Ray had quickly asserted his right to apply the 'all my worldly goods' vow to that.

Lynda had surprised everyone; she had passed the eleven plus exam and won a place at the girls' grammar school. She'd walked on air for a few hours the day the results were announced, in spite of the realisation that she'd thus been condemned to wear the itchy brown woollen uniform of Milfield High School for at least five years. And here she was at the end of those five years, sitting her Ordinary Level General Certificate of Education exams, the first step to higher education and a whole new world. That was what she wanted more than anything, a chance to be somebody special, join the people with good jobs and smart clothes.

Except for Grandma Collins, who'd briefly enjoyed boasting about her grand-daughter being selected to go to Mifield Girls' High School, no-one in the family had seemed particularly pleased. Ray wasn't really interested, and Doreen's first instinct when she heard the news was to worry about what the uniform would cost, and about Terry being jealous. Terry had been annoyed that Lynda had done better than he had, and even now would be relieved if his little sister didn't pass these O level exams, but he'd also feel guilty.

Lynda knew she'd definitely failed Latin and would be lucky if she scraped through French. She just hadn't had the time to revise for any of her subjects because her Dad had needed her to keep the pub going. Playing the landlord and over-generous host behind the bar of the Black Bull, Ray Collins had kept quiet about the fact that it was his wife who had dealt with the money and the weekly order for the brewery, as well as more aspects of managing the pub than he liked to admit, even to himself. When Doreen died Ray had panicked and then quickly started to depend on his daughter to take over her mother's unappreciated duties. Lynda had said nothing at first but had begun to challenge Ray when his demands threatened to take over all the time she needed to revise.

'I've got to have time to do my schoolwork, Dad,' she'd told him as she began to wash the dirty glasses stacked up by the sink in the bar. 'They're important, these exams.'

'You worry too much. You'll be all right. I'm only asking you for a couple of hours.'

'Oh, yeah, like the couple of hours last night that started at six and went on till closing time. You'll have to get a barmaid. Joan Dawson was asking me the other day if you needed any help.'

Ray had laughed as he'd humped a crate of bottles onto the bar.

'It wouldn't be any help having her behind the bar, her face would put anybody off his beer, and she's got armpits like a bag of rotten onions.'

Lynda stopped washing glasses, and stood facing her father.

'Well, you'll have to get Terry to help out more. It's not fair. I want my O-levels.'

Ray had ignored her, of course, but sometimes Lynda felt she would explode under the pressure of the resentment which for so long had been building up inside her. She had few illusions about her Dad, and had also worked out that Grandma Collins knew she had spoiled her only child; but no-one, not even Lynda, would dare tell her that.

Madge Collins had kept quiet about her son's imperfections when Ray had brought little Doreen Bradshaw home to meet her and Alfred, the husband who had proposed to Madge just after she had resigned herself to remaining an old maid. Madge had been annoyed that Ray had chosen this wide-eyed young girl who hadn't a penny to her name, but, as shrewd as always, she consoled herself with the knowledge that Doreen would do as she was told and give them no trouble.

Having met some of the hard-faced, flighty pieces her son had been trying his manhood out on before he met Doreen, she'd decided in the end that this quiet little thing might turn out to be her best option as far as daughter-in-laws were concerned. In fact, Madge had been very careful before the wedding, and had not let slip any hint that her son wasn't cut out to be the strong, hard-working husband her future daughter-in-law had thought she was marrying. She'd felt sorry for the girl later, and had always been silently grateful that Doreen had not complained to her about Ray as most women would have done.

Question One was: 'Describe and discuss the causes of the 1789 French Revolution'. 'Thank you, God! Thank you, Mum! Thank you, Miss Lydia Mansfield, clever-guessing History teacher.' Lynda gripped her Parker fountain pen, Grandma Collins's birthday present, and began to write at a breakneck pace. She'd show them, she'd show all those tight-lipped, sniffy teachers that looked down their noses at her second-hand school uniform and broad Lancashire accent.

When the two hours of unnatural silence were over Lynda was one of the first through the door, desperate for some fresh air and dying to share her relief that the questions she'd revised had come up.

'What did you think, Elaine?'

Normally Lynda wouldn't have spoken to, or been acknowledged by top of the class swot Elaine Tattersall.

'Not too bad.'

Lynda gritted her teeth at the diffident response that meant darling Elaine was expecting to get a Grade 1. Oh, yes, Tatty Sal was definitely going into the sixth form, and then perhaps even Cambridge if they could push her hard enough.

Lynda noticed that Elaine didn't bother to ask what she had thought of the exam but walked away quickly to the main entrance to join the small select group of friends who were going for lunch at the Waring's detached house opposite the school. Not for Sandra Waring and her cronies the crowded, clattering surroundings of the school dining room where the air was heavy with the stench of stewed cabbage.

Lynda was starving. She looked back through the slatted wooden doors to the gym. Where the hell was Jean? Miss Bates had got her. Some of the exam candidates had omitted to replace their chairs tidily under the desks, and Jean Clayton and Christine Greenwood had been dragooned into making sure everything was in regulated perfection ready for the next victims of the education system.

Lynda sighed as she saw Jean shuffling around with her head bowed as she moved chairs into the correct positions. Jean, in spite of obviously not being very strong, had an air of always hoping to be noticed, and so she was often picked on for jobs like that. It drove Lynda mad to see how willingly she would comply, as if she was flattered to have been chosen. She was almost bobbing a curtsey to Basher Bates as she finished the task and heaved open the door. Lynda grabbed hold of her arm. 'Come on, we'll miss seconds!'

The two girls sped down the corridor, their knees knocking together as they walked as fast as possible without being accused of running. They'd glanced over their shoulders and seen that Miss Bates was standing at the end of the corridor, watching and waiting for an excuse to call them back.

'Did you answer all the questions?' Lynda asked her friend breathlessly.

'No, only three and a bit.'

'You did the one on the Causes of the French Revolution, though, didn't you? I told you it'd come up.'

'Yeah.'

'Did you remember the Gabelle?'

'What?'

'The salt tax. I reminded you about it yesterday.'

'Oh, no,' Jean moaned in despair, 'I forgot that one.'

Jean paused only to tuck her straight, wispy hair behind her ears before shovelling her way through the stringy beef stew and mashed-up potatoes and carrots on her cold plate. Her habitually anxious brown eyes stared sorrowfully at the greasy glass salt-cellar. Jean ate carefully, she couldn't risk spilling any food down her white blouse and brown cardigan. They had been loaned to her by her cousin Angela, after much bullying 'persuasion' had been delivered by Jean's mother, Shirley, to the younger of Stan Clayton's more fortunately married sister.

Lynda, who always ate faster than her friend, returned in triumph from the canteen serving area. She watched for Jean's reaction as she placed two dishes of jam roly-poly pudding and custard on the Formica table.

'Just got there in time.'

'How did you manage to get two?' asked Jean who beamed like a child receiving a special gift.

'Mrs Cooper was serving, and I told her I liked her eye-shadow.'

She'd also told Mrs Cooper that the second pudding was for Jean Clayton, and this had had more influence than the flattery. Mrs Cooper had once had the misfortune to live down the street from Jean's parents and knew how little food was shared out in that household. Dorothy Cooper felt so grateful that she'd managed, through her marriage to a man who had a reputation as a good worker, to move out of the slum area locally known as 'The Clough'.

The rented accommodation for most of the population of Milfield consisted of rows of small, slate roofed terraced houses built in the nineteenth century for mill workers. They had been built of golden sandstone, but you'd never have guessed. Their walls had long ago been blackened with the soot from coal fires and industrial chimneys, so that from a distance the cobbled streets looked like thick lines of charcoal drawn close together on sheets of grey paper. There were hundreds of such narrow streets in Milfield, but none had a reputation for thieving and rough living to match the lawlessness of The Clough.

Milfield High School for Girls was several miles away from The Clough, or indeed any of the streets of terraced houses. It had been built only a few years ago as Milfield's share of Harold McMillan's prime ministerial 'never had it so good' Great Britain. Its smooth concrete walls were so often washed a drab grey-brown by the rain that its pupils had christened it Strangeways, after the Manchester prison, but the new school was looked upon with smiles of great satisfaction by the wealthier residents of the town.

The men of parochial ambition who inhabited the Town Hall had thought they were being both careful, financially, and 'modern-minded' when they accepted the plans for a two storey E shaped building with a flat roof, hundreds of metal framed windows, and even a gymnasium! This magnificent building was declared, at a ceremony given a photograph and a full page of praise and acknowledgements in 'The Milfield Express'. It was assumed that the girls who passed the eleven plus examination would be mainly from a middle-class background, but the true socialists among the town's dignitaries had hoped that a fair number of girls from the working class majority in the town would also manage to get places. As it turned out, there were surprisingly more 'clever' working class girls than had been anticipated, but this would make no difference to the vision of the headmistress, Miss Forsyth.

There was no doubt in her mind - a mind which rarely permitted itself any variation of thought - that the girls of Milfield High School would be young ladies who clearly belonged to the more refined strata of society. She was content to look out of the window of her study and fix her horizon along Gainsborough Avenue. This was where her girls came from, the road they walked along every morning before entering the gates of her school. This was their world, the avenue of detached and semi detached houses adorned with a careful geometry of lawns and colourful margins of well-tended roses, snapdragons and alternating cushions of blue and white alyssum. It was a comfortable vision, but an incomplete one as it blocked out the other world which was the all too real and grubby provenance of some of the pupils.

Miss Forsyth was determinedly unaware of the home circumstances of these working class girls. She had, she would admit, heard the name of one of them, Lynda Collins, and knew that she had a reputation for being bright but rather too outspoken, and altogether not well brought up. What she didn't know was that this pupil, and her much quieter best friend, regularly sought refuge in a forbidden corner of Miss Forsyth's educational establishment.

The bell rang to signal it was time for afternoon registration, and reluctantly Jean and Lynda stacked their empty dishes on to a trolley and wandered out of the canteen. This time they took the longer route to the classrooms, enjoying the sunshine in the gardens which were part of the vision of an environment suitable for the young people of a well-to-do county.

'Shall we test each other on our 'Hamlet' quotes this afternoon?'

'Yeah, if we can get the store-room.'

Both Jean and Lynda had told their parents that they weren't allowed to go home early from school after the exams. This was true, but only because the privilege hadn't been requested. A form had been issued for parents to give permission for their child to go home from school once they had finished their exam, but Lynda and Jean had made sure they'd lost that particular piece of paper. They both knew that in their homes they would be given neither the time nor the peace and quiet to do any revision.

Jean and Lynda hid in the toilets next to the cloakroom at the end of D corridor until ten minutes after the first of the afternoon lessons had begun. When the corridors were silent they quickly made their way to the English department store room on D floor. Pupils were forbidden to enter these store-rooms without permission, but Lynda and Jean had, in their need for a space in which to study, adopted the English store-room as their refuge. This small, narrow room was filled with old and new copies of novels and plays considered suitable for the education of young ladies, or selected for study by the Examination Board. The books were arranged on the overflowing shelves, or stacked up on the floor. Some recent arrivals were still in their large sturdy cardboard boxes and Lynda and Jean had dragged two of these boxes to the far end of the room, so that they could read by the daylight which managed to force its way in through the small frosted-glass window.

They spent the first half hour quietly reciting to each other the quotes from 'Hamlet' which Lynda had noticed Mrs Leighton had paid particular attention to in her lessons. Lynda was astute enough to realise that Mrs Leighton had studied past papers and made an educated guess at what aspects of the play might be taking their turn, in one form or another, in this year's English Literature examination. Lynda loved the idea of taking a gamble on such guess-work, she loved the sense of risk, and the chance of, for once, being ahead of the game.

When the bell rang to signal the end of the first 40-minute period, Jean started anxiously watching the door. Sitting hunched and still, their hearing sharpened by the danger of being discovered, they listened to the sound of their fellow inmates hurrying to their next lesson. They heard their muffled voices as, shuffling in single file along each side of the corridor, they enjoyed a few moments of free speech, or even laughter, before being pinned down in submissive rows in front of chalk covered blackboards.

The two friends had just begun silently trying to memorise passages from 'Pride and Prejudice' when they heard the door-handle rattle. They held their breath, Jean terrified, Lynda trying to think of a plausible reason for their being there. Susan Robinson, a small, spindly-legged first-former staggered in with a pile of ancient copies of 'David Copperfield'. Some of the books slid from her grasp as she gazed wide-eyed at the two fifth-formers. Lynda stood up, and fixed the small creature with a steady, commanding look.

'What do you want?'

'Nothing,' Susan stammered. Miss Hargreaves just wanted these out of the way.'

She glanced down at the three books she had dropped, and wondered if she dared take her eyes off Lynda long enough to retrieve them.

Then she stopped being nervous; she'd remembered that she'd come across this older pupil before. Lynda had been the one who'd come to her rescue on her first day when, in a shadowy corner of the school grounds, Susan had been selected by a group of third-formers as one of their 'new girl' victims. They'd unfastened the buttons of her gymslip so that it had slipped from her shoulders, and were wrenching off her carefully knotted tie when Lynda had marched up and made them scatter.

'Well, pick those up, and put them all on the shelf where they belong. It's that one, third up on your left.' Lynda had a detailed knowledge of the contents of the store-room, English literature was her passion, but not one she'd admit to anybody except Jean, who shared, and marvelled at, all her dreams.

'What's your name?'

'Susan Robinson.'

'Right, Susan. You won't be telling anybody at all, will you, about us being in here?'

The girl smiled and shook her head. 'No, I won't tell.'

'Cross your heart and hope to die?'

'Yes.'

'OK. Skedaddle.'

The tiny creature scampered through the door but didn't forget to close it silently and reverently behind her.

Jean never ceased to marvel at Lynda's ability to take charge of situations like that.

Lynda watched the door closing. 'Poor kid.'

'She was the one you helped out on the first day of term.'

'Was she?'

'Yeah.' Jean smiled at her friend as they'd both been reminded that was how their friendship had started, when Lynda had rescued Jean in the schoolyard at infant school.

'Right, we've got another hour. Do you want me to test you on some quotes?'

'No, I haven't learnt any properly yet. Ooh, I'll be glad when it's Friday and these exams are over. I've failed most of them, I know I have.'

'You haven't. Don't give up, Jean. Nobody gets anywhere by giving up.'

'My Mum's already put my name down for a job as a machinist at Marsden's. She keeps asking me when the last day of school is.'

'You should have told her to see if they had a job for her instead. You've told her you've got exams on Friday, haven't you?'

'Yes.'

Jean hated telling lies, but she'd finally realised deception was the only way she could grab a little life for herself.

'Stop looking so worried. Just get ready for school as normal and then come round to my place. I've found a skirt and a little jacket that'll fit you – you can't celebrate the end of the exams in school uniform. We'll have a great time, fish and chips at Duckworth's and then 'South Pacific'.

'Oh, I can't wait. Everybody says it's a fabulous film. But are you sure . .?'

'I told you, it's my treat, and it'll spoil it if you keep worrying about the money. Just tell your Mum that my Grandma's invited you round. She won't dare argue with my Grandma.'

Jean smiled at the truth of that. Madge Collins wasn't afraid to tell people what she thought, and even Shirley Clayton wasn't bold enough to answer her back. When Doreen had died Madge Collins had resolved to honour her daughter-in-law's memory in any ways she could, and one of those would be doing what she could for Jean Clayton.

Doreen Collins, perhaps recognising her own childhood in little Jean Clayton's air of wistful resignation, had always welcomed Lynda's timid friend into the ramshackle warmth of the kitchen at the Black Bull. To protect Jean's pride, she had constantly invented excuses to give Jean what small treats she could. Madge Collins had noticed these small acts of kindness and now also tried to find small ways to help the girl, though privately she thought the only way Jean could get rescued from her family was for her to find a good man to look after her. She wasn't bad looking, though nothing like Lynda, of course, but she might drop lucky one day.

Jean loved musicals and the thought of going to see 'South Pacific' on Friday was helping her through what was a tough week. There had been even more rows than usual at home, and last night her Dad had knocked her mother across the living room. Luckily her brother, Dennis, hadn't been in, otherwise there'd have been another fight. Dennis got exasperated with his mother but didn't think his Dad had a right to hit her. He ignored Jean, just as his father did, but sometimes would buy an ice-cream for her sister Marilyn. Marilyn, five years old and already, according to her mother, 'a right little madam', had just started school and Jean usually had to dash away as soon as the bell rang at four o'clock and go and collect her because her mother was 'too busy'.

Jean was conscientious about getting to the infant school on time but today she found Marilyn already standing at the school gate. As soon as she spotted Jean in the distance, she began a wailing of such volume and intensity that the children hurrying through the gates were putting their fingers to their ears. A teacher spotted Jean and hurried forward, anxious that the older sister should immediately remove the embarrassment of this unfortunate, but nevertheless excessively noisy child.

'What's the matter, Marilyn?'

The only response was a wide eyed stare accompanied by the shuddering intake of air which preceded another loud howl.

'There was an incident in the playground. Your sister's undergarments,' the teacher paused delicately, 'the elastic needed replacing.'

'My knickers fell down. And they all laughed!' exclaimed Marilyn indignantly.

'Oh, heck.' Jean didn't laugh.

'Please ask your mother to make sure her underwear is kept in good repair, and, perhaps washed a little more frequently.'

Jean felt herself shrivel in the heat of the humiliation which overwhelmed her.

'Yes, Miss,' she mumbled before taking Marilyn by the hand and hauling her away to hurry home along the rows of thin terraced houses whose front doors opened straight onto the narrow streets.

Jean was careful to choose a route along the cobbled back streets. This was partly to avoid meeting anyone who might call out to Marilyn and start the hysterics off again, but also because the owners of the shops had a habit of watching from their doorways and grabbing hold of Jean to tell her to remind her parents that they owed them money. Jean hated getting home from school. Four thirty felt like the start of another working day. She was the one who, every afternoon, had to clean up before her Dad got home from work. Then she had to prepare the vegetables and if possible cook the meat for the following day. That was after she'd done the pile of washing up of course.

Jean's mother, Shirley, was still bottle-feeding the youngest child, Peter, and constantly asserted, in many a slanging match with her husband, Stan, that her life was hell. There was no way she could look after him and his kids, do all the housework and cook meals. And what's more, she was damned if she was going to kill herself trying. Shirley Clayton specialised in doing the minimum amount of work with the maximum exhaustion, and took it for granted that Jean would do the rest of the housework when she got home. Shirley's evening was taken up with putting the two youngest children to bed before getting ready to accompany her husband to the pub.

Doreen Collins had never argued with the Claytons but they knew she had disapproved of their way of living, to the point of seeing the need to offer a refuge to their daughter. One evening, after they'd had more drinks than they could afford, Shirley and Dennis had suggested to Doreen that perhaps she was inviting Jean to the pub as unpaid help, and owed them some money. Doreen had not spoken a word in response, but the quiet judgement in her steady look had managed the almost impossible feat of making the Claytons feel embarrassed.

As a consequence, Stan and Shirley had crossed The Black Bull off their list of favourite pubs. They now usually went to The Fighting Cocks a few streets away from their house. The landlord there lusted after Shirley and would let the Claytons have a few free drinks in exchange for Stan playing dominoes in the tap room, and remaining carefully unaware that the landlord was in the back room showing his appreciation of Shirley's soft, well-rounded warmth.

That evening Jean worked even harder than usual, and even offered to set her mother's hair in curls to make sure she was in a good mood before telling her about Friday.

'Mum, Lynda's Grandma's invited me round on Friday, straight after school.'

Shirley paused in the act of passing another grubby pink plastic curler to her daughter, 'Straight after school? What about Marilyn?'

'Will you go and get her? Please, Mum.' Jean saw Shirley's down-turned mouth and called in reinforcements, adding, 'Mrs Collins says we have to have a treat as a reward for working hard for our exams.'

'Oh, does she?'

'Yeah. It's to make up for Lynda not having a treat on her birthday. You know, because it was just after her Mum . . .'

'Yes, all right, all right, I know all about that!' Shirley was terrified at any mention of death, and suddenly, with a rare stirring of guilt, she remembered that Jean also hadn't had any treats on her birthday.

'Lynda wants to take me to the pictures and for a Knickerbocker Glory afterwards. She'll pay for it all.'

'Where's she getting that sort of money from?'

'It's what her Dad pays her for helping out.'

'Oh,' said Shirley, staring guiltily at her unpaid helper. 'Well, Ray Collins must be making a packet out of that pub.'

'Can I go? Please, just this once.'

Shirley's feelings of guilt tipped the balance. 'Yeah, I suppose so, but you'll have to be back by 9 o'clock for me and your Dad to have our Friday night out.'

Lynda didn't have any trouble getting permission, because she didn't ask for it. She'd recently got into the habit of telling her Dad what she was going to do, she'd realised it was the only way to hang on to some freedom. He didn't like it, and she didn't always get her own way, but this was one of those times when Lynda reminded him so strongly of his mother at her most determined, that he knew that he'd be wasting his time to try to argue.

Madge Collins had tried to insist that her grand-daughter be named Margaret after her, but Doreen had begged that her child be given the pretty, fashionable name of Lynda. Madge had agreed in the end, but she took care to influence her grand-daughter's development as much as possible; she wanted Lynda to grow up as strong and independent minded as she was. Madge was a tall, heavy-boned, intimidating woman, with a loud, forthright way of speaking which had impressed all the young girls who had worked under her supervision at the Victoria cotton mill.

It had been Madge's experience that no-one looked after you, so you had to look after yourself, and she was relieved and pleased when she saw Lynda learning to fight for what she wanted. Madge, ever the realist, also knew that Lynda's good looks would prove to be an advantage to her. Madge was less happy when she remembered whom Lynda resembled.

Madge's flighty and much younger sister, Amy, had managed to inherit – no-one was quite sure where from - golden hair and a very desirable figure. It hadn't taken Amy long to work out that these attributes could be made use of to facilitate her escape from Milfield. At eighteen she'd run off with a married man, but the affair had ended when the war began and he'd been called up to join the navy. Amy had trained as a driver, and from then on she'd had a marvellous time, especially when the GIs came on the scene.

She had only come back to Milfield once to visit her bossy, lip-pursing sister Madge. That was in 1954 when Amy had, she reckoned, finally achieved respectability by marrying a widower. He was quite a bit older than she was, but had plenty of money to make up for the age difference. With her new husband in attendance, Amy had turned up one day to show off her rings and smart new clothes to everybody in Milfield and then, having proved they'd all been wrong, she had said goodbye again and forgotten about them.

Lynda didn't forget Amy, though. She'd been only nine years old when Amy had come back on that 'flying visit' and given her a beautiful bride doll and a frilly pink taffeta party dress. She'd soon grown too tall and well-rounded to fit into the dress but had cried when it had been sold to help pay for a new winter coat. Lynda had never understood why her mother and grandmother had disapproved of the dress, even though they'd let her wear it on special occasions.

She could still picture Amy as she had seemed then, a beautiful and glamorous creature, like a Hollywood film star. She also remembered, although she hadn't understood the jokes at the time, that her auntie had had a sense of humour which made women blush and men smile. Amy was rich, confident, successful and adorable. She was the kind of woman that the nine-year old Lynda had dreamed that she, too, would one day become.

That Friday evening, as she and Jean emerged from the sunshine paradise of 'South Pacific' and back into the dusty, grey cobbled streets of Milfield, Lynda thought about her now more detailed dreams. It wouldn't be long before she took her first steps into that future. Now that the exams. were over she was fairly confident that, in spite of all the problems, she would have scraped the five O-level passes needed to qualify to stay on into the sixth form. Somehow she'd stick it out at that horrible school and get two or three A-levels. Then she'd start her career.

She wasn't quite sure what career yet, but it would be something glamorous which would allow her to travel abroad, to go to Paris at least once a year. It was going to be exciting, her future. Her poor Mother had had enough disappointments to make her give up hoping for anything. Lynda was determined that her life would be different, it would be what she wanted, not what other people made it.

After the delights of the ice cream, jelly and glace cherries that made up Milfield's version of a Knickerbocker Glory, the two girls set off to walk to the bus station. They were silent for a while, both sad that their day-out was almost over. Then Lynda glanced up at the hills beyond the town and saw that a beautiful pink and gold sunset had spread itself across the evening sky. Suddenly she felt part of that golden world and, linking arms with Jean, she made her dance with her along the street, singing the bits they knew from the wonderful 'South Pacific' songs.

Lynda had danced away from Jean and was performing a loud and suggestive rendering of 'Honey Bun', belting out the line, 'Get a load of Honey-Bun to- nigh ite!' when she crashed into someone coming round the corner. She lost her balance and instinctively clung to the man to steady herself.

'Sorry,' she gasped, laughing as she looked up to see whose arms were holding her.'

'Lynda!'

Never had her name been spoken with such longing.

Dan Heywood felt his whole body move to kiss her passionately, and she would have let him. It was what she wanted, he saw it in her eyes, but he let his fear and embarrassment take over and move his body away from hers. Without daring to look back, and with tears of frustration in his eyes, he walked quickly out of sight before he could make even more of a fool of himself.

Lynda stared after him, willing him to turn round and smile, and walk back to her. Jean, knowing how Lynda dreamed of Dan Heywood, came to stand quietly beside her.

'Was that Dan?'

'Yeah.'

'I thought for a minute he was going to kiss you.'

'So did I.'

'Are you sure he fancies you, though?'

'Of course he does. You should see the way he looks at me whenever we see each other. You know, 'Across a Crowded Room!' she sang.

'You'd think he'd have stopped to talk to you.'

'He's shy, that's all. He doesn't chat everybody up like John Stanworth does.'

Jean, who was still hoping John Stanworth would 'chat her up' her one day, wasn't pleased at that comment.

'I think you're wasting your time, waiting for Dan Heywood. He's too posh for you.'

'He's not!'

'He didn't even say anything to you.'

'He said my name.'

'He's not interested, Lynda.'

'Oh, he's interested. Ooh, you should have felt the big wave of heat between us.'

Jean tugged at her arm. 'Come on, we're going to miss the bus.'

They were both silent again as they travelled back together on the grimy, draughty, rattling Number 10 bus. Jean was depressed at having to go back to her shabby, comfortless home after being in a tropical paradise. Lynda didn't want to talk, she didn't want to let her mind move away from what it had felt like to be in Dan Heywood's arms.

She knew for sure now that she would give up her dream of being a fashion model, or an air-hostess, or the owner of a luxury hotel in the South of France – a fantasy which had come together after watching Cary Grant and Audrey Hepburn films. She was in love, and would give up all those careers without a single regret, as soon as Dan Heywood asked her to marry him.

CHAPTER TWO

'Lynda. Where the hell have you been?'

'To see 'South Pacific', I told you, Dad.'

'You didn't.'

'I did, on Tuesday.'

'Well, get your coat off, and get behind this bar, I need to go down and change a barrel.'

'Where's Lorraine?'

'She's not on tonight, she's doing Monday dinner time instead.'

Lorraine Garvey was the new barmaid Ray had taken on two weeks ago, more for her looks than her ability to work out the right change for her customers.

'But I do Monday dinner time.' Lynda wasn't going to lose that Monday morning shift, it was the quietest time of the week in the pub.

'You won't be here.'

'Why not?'

'You'll be at Heywood's, their Belmont Road shop. I've fixed you up with a job there. You start on Monday, half past eight.'

'A holiday job? But you need me here.'

'I need you to be earning some money. It's permanent, not a holiday job, Lynda.

I chatted up the woman who runs the shop, told her you were looking for work. She mentioned it to Geoff Heywood, and he said he'd take you on as soon as you'd left school.'

'But I haven't left school, I told you, if I pass I'm going to stay on and take my A levels.'

'Don't be daft!' He turned to greet a regular customer. 'Hello, Nathan. The usual?'

Nathan Oldfield, who'd enjoyed quietly watching the life around him for over sixty years, nodded and began to dig around in his trouser pocket for the price of a bottle of Guinness. He observed with interest that Lynda was pale with anger and glaring at her father.

'Dad, I'm not going to work in a bloody cake shop, I want to stay on and go to college.'

'What you want and what you get are two different things. And watch your language!' Then, seeing that Lynda was standing her ground, and Nathan was getting ready to enjoy a fight, he added more quietly, 'We'll talk about it later.'

And they did talk about it; they also shouted about it, and Lynda yelled and sobbed, but it made no difference. There just wasn't the money for her to stay on at school, Ray told her, and anyway, it wasn't as if she was going to pass any exams, was it? He was wrong about that; Lynda got her five O level passes.

Annie Fielding, the manageress of the Belmont Road shop, was a pretty little woman in her forties, with dark, neatly curled hair and eyes that twinkled without her knowing it. Her husband, Malcolm, was a clerk at the town hall and would have been happy for his wife to stay at home and keep house, but when they'd striven in vain to have healthy children, Annie had decided she needed a job. And whatever Annie wanted to do was all right with him. He was proud that Geoff Heywood had put her in charge of the Belmont Road shop, and trusted her to run it in her own way.

It was terrible that morning in August when Lynda learned she'd passed enough exams to entitle her to a place in the sixth-form. Annie knew the results were being announced that morning and had no hesitation in allowing Lynda an hour off to go to school, get the results and tell her family.

When Lynda came back Annie observed that her eyes were swollen from crying and in her kindly way asked what was wrong. Lynda explained, Annie congratulated her on her exam results, but didn't comment about Ray Collins's unwillingness to change his mind. Instead she just quietly substituted a cream cake for the jam tart which was usually given to the Heywood shop staff as a treat, to go with their sausage roll or cheese and onion pasty, at lunch-time.

Dan Heywood arrived at the shop just after two o'clock, having volunteered to deliver the batch of tea-cakes which Annie Fielding had requested. As soon as he'd heard Lynda was working at the Belmont Road shop Dan had found some reason to call in there at least twice a week. His Dad, Geoff Heywood, was amused to notice his son eagerly volunteering to be the one to deliver goods to the shop, and guessed the attraction was Lynda Collins. He'd not made any comment, though, he wouldn't want to embarrass Dan, who reminded him so much of himself. Geoff, when only a couple of years older than Dan, had chased around all over town just to get a glimpse of

Ellen Heywood. She'd ignored him, and at times he'd been in despair, but in the end she had, reluctantly, become his wife. Geoff only hoped that Dan would also get the girl he wanted, though he knew that if it was Lynda Collins he chose he'd somehow have to find the courage to battle against his mother.

Dan, encouraged by Lynda's smiles and willingness to chat to him, had been building up his confidence and was ready, just about, for this opportunity. Like Annie, he observed that Lynda was miserable, but tact and subtlety were, like a lot of the nineteen-year old's inter-personal skills, as yet not highly developed.

'What's the matter, Lynda? Has somebody been upsetting you?'

'No.'

'Oh, is it your O level results? Did you not pass? Don't let it bother you, I failed half of mine.' Remembering his mother's furious disappointment, he winced a little as he admitted that.

Lynda tilted her head back with pride. 'I passed five, including maths.'

'Flippin' heck, that's good going.'

'I know, but it makes no difference to my Dad. He still won't let me go back to school.'

'Oh. That's a shame.'

'Yeah.' She looked away, trying to hide the tears that were overwhelming her again. Dan's mind was racing, was this the chance he'd been waiting for ever since that night he'd held her for a brief but heart-stopping moment? He paused, took a deep breath, looked over his shoulder to make sure Mrs Fielding wasn't around, and very hesitantly put his arm round Lynda's shoulders. He held his breath and could have shouted for joy when she didn't move away but looked at him with those Doris Day blue eyes of hers that he dreamed about every night. Drawing on all the, mostly imagined, experience he had of girls, Dan recognised that this was indeed the moment he'd been longing for.

'You ought to be celebrating passing all those exams. How about, how about coming to the Odeon with me tonight?' He held his breath, hardly daring to look at her.

Lynda thought for a second about trying to sound casual, but she couldn't manage it, she'd been waiting too long for this invitation, and grabbed it before he could change his mind.

'Yes, OK, Dan, I'd like that.'

She said his name on purpose. Alone in her bedroom she'd been practising what she would say when he asked her, and felt that if she used his name it would somehow make a claim on him, make him her man.

'Shall I call for you?'

What a terrible thought, Dan coming into The Black Bull, seeing where she lived.

'No! No, it's all right. I'll meet you outside. What time?'

'About seven?'

'Right. What's on?'

'The Pajama Game'. You haven't seen it, have you?'

'No.'

She'd seen it last year with Jean when it first came out, but she didn't feel guilty about telling the lie. For heaven's sake, she'd been waiting so long for this date with Dan Heywood and, she hoped, they wouldn't be watching the film much anyway.

Fortunately for Dan, his mother was attending a concert in Manchester with the Holy Trinity Church Ladies Circle that evening, so she was not aware of her eldest son's date with Lynda Collins. Geoff Heywood, whose evening was to be spent being beaten at chess by his eleven year old son, Richard, assumed that Dan was going to the cinema with his friends.

That may have been true, in that some of Dan's former school-friends were in the Odeon that evening, but Dan booked seats in the circle. His friends mostly frequented only the cheaper seats in the stalls, and he wanted to make sure they wouldn't observe him, blushing, but gently and firmly guiding Lynda to the centre of the back row. He wouldn't have known if anyone had seen him, because all of his senses, his whole being was taken over by the sensation of Lynda being close to him. As soon as the lights dimmed to darken the deep red plush seats he was aware of nothing but the warmth of her arm touching his, and the gentle sigh of her breathing.

It was during the song 'Hey There, You with the Stars in Your Eyes' that Dan put his arm round her. She turned to him and his kiss was just as warm and gentle as she had dreamed it would be. But the intensity of the feeling which that kiss stirred within their innocent bodies took both of them by surprise. They couldn't stop kissing and holding on to each other, and when the film ended and they came out into the cool air, they quickly moved away from the revealing bright lights of the foyer.

Dan walked her to the bus stop, with Lynda praying that no-one she knew would be travelling home at the same time. When he asked her to come with him to the cinema again the following week, Lynda said yes straight away. She knew it wouldn't be easy to get time to see Dan, but somehow she'd manage it without her Dad finding out. It wouldn't be quite so difficult for Dan, who wasn't usually asked to work in the evenings, but for both of them, it went without saying that their romance had to be kept secret.

All through August and September they told their parents lies about where they were spending evenings and Sunday afternoons. All they wanted to think about was the time they spent together in the cinema, or walking among the full-seeded grasses, clover and daisies in the fields and meadows which edged their way up to the gentle hills, away from the noise and blackness which had taken over the valley.

Their constant companion on these walks was Dan's nine year old black Labrador, Jess, who provided Dan with the excuse to escape on his own and meet Lynda. Jess wagged her tail and thought it was a game when they dodged into gateways or behind trees to avoid encountering anyone who might report back to their parents. Once they were in the fields the dog was happy to explore rabbit holes or snooze in the sunshine while the young couple spent time in their favourite hiding place in a hollow by the side of a stream, where ancient hawthorn bushes gave them shelter from disapproving eyes. Not that there was anything really to disapprove of. Too scared to do anything else, they obeyed the rules of the 'Doris Day Films School of Love Making', which allowed them to venture only as far as fervent kisses and hands sliding over fully dressed bodies.

John Stanworth's mother, Sheila, was the one who saw them together, one Saturday afternoon in late September. It was one of those exhilarating autumn days when the trees are threaded with bronze and gold, and people enjoy the warm scent of the fallen leaves and a last chance to feel the sun on their faces before having to bow their heads against the chill wind and rain of winter.

The four members of the Stanworth family were on their way to Old Manor Farm to take tea with the owners, Mr & Mrs Laycock, whom they were to meet for the first time. Sylvia Stanworth, John's slim, fairly pretty, older sister, had just become engaged to the Laycocks' younger son, Graham, who specialised in reliability and steady ambition, and was said to be already picked out as a possible future assistant manager at the local branch of The County Bank.

For this special occasion, Sheila Stanworth, whose diligent, straight-laced, working-class parents had bequeathed their daughter a relatively modest amount of money, but plenty of social ambition, had chosen her apparel very carefully. Her woollen, box jacketed suit, in an unusual shade of peach, was impeccably tailored and she wore a hat of gently gathered peach and cream satin which would not have been out of place at the wedding itself.

Her daughter wore a dress and jacket resplendent with blue and white daisies. Her shoulder length straight hair, like her mother's the colour of over wintered beech leaves, was flicked up at the edges, and on it balanced a straw hat with a matching daisy chain coyly nestling in its deep upturned brim. Both of these outfits had been designed and made by Sheila, whose mother had trained her as a milliner and dress-maker, thus giving her a trade which was respectable, even though not very well paid.

Sheila's husband, Ted, was a broad shouldered former policeman who had retired with a good pension after twenty five years of service, and was now, in his forties, a chauffeur without a uniform. Today he was wearing the itchy, uncomfortable, dark grey striped 'best suit' which Sheila had persuaded him to buy in the sale at a high class shop. Their son, however, having allowed his mother to bully him into accompanying his parents on this visit, had drawn the line at wearing his navy blue suit which, following the recent unexpected addition of two inches to his height, was now too tight and a little short in the sleeves.

Sheila, who congratulated herself every day on having produced such a good looking son, would have liked John to take more notice of her wishes. She could, however, be persuaded to admit that, compared to some people's sons, he was a saint. John was, like his father, usually inclined to favour a peaceful life, but today a compromise had had to satisfy his mother; John didn't have a jacket, he wore a white shirt and, after considerable negotiation, one of his father's ties.

This carefully dressed quartet was making its way, in a moderately slow, and fairly tense procession, towards the farmhouse. Sheila, who was neither as slim nor as tall as she would like to be, paused to stand on a large stone to look over a wall and survey the amount of land belonging to her daughter's future family. While admiring this vista she saw Jess racing up a nearby field in pursuit of the stick Dan had just thrown for her.

'Isn't that Daniel Heywood?' Sheila asked, clamping her hat more tightly on to her tightly permed hair, as she tilted her head to peer over the wall.

'Come on, Mum, we don't want to be late.' John took his mother by the elbow and tried to lead her away from her viewing point. He'd seen that it was Dan and that Lynda was with him.

Dan hadn't been able to resist sharing his wonderful secret with his old school-friend, John Stanworth, especially as Dan looked upon him as a source of advice about how to please young ladies. John was generous to his friend and gave him a few hints, especially about how far you could go when it came to exploring female anatomy, but he'd found it hard to hide his jealousy. He seriously fancied Lynda Collins, but he was as afraid of rejection as the next man, and when Lynda had showed no interest in him, he'd crossed her off his list of possible girlfriends. Then Dan had started going out with her, and suddenly John had been unable to ignore how desirable Lynda was, and had also realised that he could easily fall in love with her. But a mate was a mate, and it was Dan's first love, so John felt it was only fair to give him a chance.

He knew Dan was keeping his romance a secret and saw the danger of his Mother seeing Dan and Lynda together. He tried to hurry her up the path to the house, but she wasn't going to be distracted.

'He's with a girl!' Sheila shrieked.

'Mum, shush,' Sylvia said urgently, looking at the door of the farmhouse. She didn't want the Laycocks to be subjected to the full force of her mother's personality just yet, but Sheila was too fascinated to heed her daughter.

'Who is she? John, do you know?'

John Stanworth rarely told lies, not even to his Mother. He tried to pretend he hadn't heard the question, but Sheila grabbed hold of him and pointed to the couple in the distance. 'You do know her, don't you? Who is she?'

'Lynda Collins.'

'Where does she live?' One's place of residence was always among the first criteria Sheila applied in any assessment of a person's worth.

'The Black Bull on Stanley Road.'

'A public house? And on Stanley Road? Oh, dear. Does Daniel's mother know?'

John was thankful to be saved from replying by the appearance of Harry and Enid Laycock at the door of their home. Daniel and Lynda were slotted away in the gossip file of Sheila's mind to be dealt with later. For now she had to concentrate her attention on making a good impression on the Laycocks, and praying that Ted would not repeat any of the farmyard jokes which he and John had been collecting to tease Sylvia.

It was not Ted Stanworth who was of concern to their hosts; they could see that this easy-going man, with a smile crinkled face was someone who'd be comfortable at their kitchen table, but his wife had made Enid Laycock glad that she'd removed her homely apron before coming out to greet their guests. She'd taken one look at Sheila's hat and begun to wonder if she'd be able to find anything in common with her son's future mother-in-law.

Dan and Lynda hadn't seen the Stanworth family arriving at the farmhouse, but during the service at Holy Trinity Church the following morning, Dan did wonder why John, also a reluctant church-goer, was making some kind of covert signal to him. He also wondered why Mrs Stanworth kept looking sideways at him from under the deep flowing brim of her hat. After the service John hurried over to talk to Dan who was waiting by the Daimler while his mother held court among the members of the congregation she favoured.

'Dan, my Mother's seen you with Lynda.'

'Where?'

'In the fields by Manor Farm. We all went to meet the Laycocks, and my Mother spotted the two of you.'

'Oh, hell. What did she say?'

'She asked me who Lynda was. I didn't tell her much but she'll be finding out all she can, I bet.'

'Oh. And then she'll tell my Mother.'

'Yeah. Sorry. It was nice while it lasted, eh?'

'What do you mean?'

'You and Lynda.'

'I'm not going to give her up, if that's what you mean,' Dan asserted, but his hands were damp with sweat as he drove his Mother home.

His fear was to continue for a few days yet. John was right, Sheila had decided she needed to find out more about the girl in the skimpy summer dress so that she could earn Ellen Heywood's respect as a reliable informer.

Sheila had, for a year or two now, been making dresses for Ellen Heywood, who appreciated her flair and reasonable prices. Ellen was tall and had made sure that having two children had not been allowed to impair her figure. She was proud of her looks, the noble, high cheek-boned profile which she had inherited from her father, and which she knew would enable her to look regal even in old age. She had recently had her thick, gleaming black hair styled to wave gently from a side-parting and to frame her face and neck in well controlled curls and, as her fortieth birthday loomed on the horizon, she prided herself more and more on presenting a striking figure when she walked into a room. The dark blue velvet evening dress she had ordered would comply with that requirement, the colour complementing her blue-grey eyes, and on Wednesday afternoon she arrived at the Stanworths' house on Stanhope Road for a fitting.

Sheila was proud to welcome her into her home. Stanhope Road was a well-thought of area of Milfield, bordering on the genteel, and had been slightly beyond their means, but Sheila had insisted they must live there, whatever sacrifices might be required. Number 17 was a large, sandstone terraced house with an attic large enough to be a fourth bedroom. There was a long garden at the back which kept Ted Stanworth very happily occupied, and at the front was a neat garden leading to a large bay window and an impressive entrance. On the front door was a substantial, keenly polished brass knocker in the form of a lion's head which Sheila regarded as an indication of nobility. She seemed oblivious to the fact that the aggressive expression on the lion's face made any visitor to her home doubt their welcome.

It was, very definitely, her home, even though it had been paid for mostly with Ted Stanworth's salary and many hours of overtime when he was a policeman. The money Sheila's hard-working parents had managed to put aside during their economical lives had been added to Ted's much smaller inheritance to make up the deposit. Ted's father had been a miner, and his mother a weaver, and, driven by the fear of ending up in the workhouse, they had both worked every minute they could, with the result that their five children had hardly known them.

Ted Stanworth had vowed that when he married he would earn enough money to ensure that his wife didn't have to go out to work. He wanted a home where good meals were cooked and children came home from school to a clean house and a warm fire. He had achieved most of that, but several years ago Ted had started to wonder if he had chosen the right dream.

The bedroom which Sheila, knowing the advantages of earning some money for herself, had set up as her dressmaker's parlour was at the back of the house, and had heavily draped red velvet curtains to ensure privacy. One end of the room was fully occupied by a large work table, a small chair next to a Singer treadle-sewing machine, and a well-built dressmaker's dummy whose proportions were, for this visit, disguised under an elegant Edwardian cloak.

At the other end of the room there was a small round table covered with a floor length plush velvet drape topped by a white lace-edged tablecloth. Next to it stood a reproduction Louis XV gilt-wood chair which Sheila had bought for a few shillings at an auction and re-upholstered. It was on this chair that Ellen Heywood was invited to sit and take tea. Usually she refused Sheila's invitation, but during the pinning of the hem of her dress Sheila had made, oh, so casually, a remark which Ellen needed to follow up.

'You say that you saw Daniel at Old Manor Farm - with a young lady?'

'With a girl, yes. I would hesitate to call her a lady.'

'And why is that?'

'She's the daughter of a publican.'

'I see. What is her name?'

'Lynda Collins. Her parents are Ray and Doreen Collins who run The Black Bull public house on Stanley Street. Not a very nice area.'

Hearing the name Doreen Collins brought such an unpleasant memory to Ellen that she had to grip the handle of Sheila's best china cup very tightly for almost a minute. Then she raised it unsteadily to her lips and drank slowly to enable her to avoid looking Sheila Stanworth in the eye.

Sheila had observed Ellen very closely, and wished she knew what thoughts had clouded their way across her eyes, but she knew there was no chance of their being confided to her. So while Ellen sipped her tea, Sheila told her what she had been able to find out about the Collins family. She paid particularly attention to Ray Collins, whose name was known around the town because of his habit of sampling the hospitality at other pubs in Milfield; and someone had also mentioned that he seemed to have, in spirit, remained a bachelor.

Sheila was careful to temper her communication of tittle-tattle about the Collins family with expressions of Christian feeling, as befitted a zealous member of the most dogmatic ranks of the Church of England.

'I know the poor girl cannot help what her background is, but I'm afraid the way she was dressed was, shall we just say, not in good taste. I'm not one to gossip, as you know, but, I thought you ought to be told, before any - unfortunate occurrences.'

Ellen gripped the narrow arms of her chair, as she translated Sheila Stanworth's raised eyebrows and knowing look into a worrying possibility.

'I wouldn't have said anything, because Daniel is such a good boy, but at their age our sons are vulnerable when it comes to relationships with young women, particularly ones whom one would not wish them to marry.'

'Quite. Well, I must go, now. Thank you for the tea, and for your concern, Sheila.'

It was the first time Ellen had called her by her Christian name, and Sheila was thrilled at the breakthrough, but managed to pretend it was the most natural thing in the world that she and Ellen Heywood should be on first name terms.

'Not at all,' she replied, and then, daringly added, 'Ellen'.

Ellen Heywood flinched a little, she wasn't sure she had intended to increase the intimacy of her relationship with Sheila Stanworth, but then, one did sometimes need to know what was going on beyond one's immediate circle of suitable friends. And she certainly was grateful for the warning which Sheila had discreetly delivered this afternoon.

'I trust you will keep this matter to yourself.'

'Of course. I do hope Daniel will see sense.'

'He most certainly will. Goodbye, Sheila.'

Dan and his father, dog-tired but enjoying a laugh as they drove home in one of the bakery delivery vans had no idea what a hard time was awaiting them. Geoff Heywood wasn't a big man, he was a man you wouldn't notice in a crowd, except for the courteous way he stepped aside to give you precedence. His slightly balding head made him look older than his forty-three years and the only remarkable thing about him was the muscularity of his shoulders and arms, which had been well developed through many years of being a baker. He was a good baker and confectioner, and he was also a good mimic.

He was now performing a pitch perfect imitation of Alice Smith's voice, which tended to turn slightly squeaky when seeking a favour.

'Are those Cornish Pasties, Mr Heywood?'

Geoff snorted with laughter again, 'What did she think they were, 'rats en croute?' he joked, mocking his wife's efforts to educate him about French cuisine.

Ellen had, as a young lady, been taken to France, and was astute enough to foresee now the culinary revolution which was to invade England. She had, therefore, recently decided that it might expand her husband's business and his status in the business community of Milfield if he and Daniel learned at least a smattering of French culinary terms.

Dan laughed. Little Alice Smith drove him and his Dad crackers at times, but she had a real flair for decorating cakes.

'I don't know why she doesn't just ask for them outright instead of mealy-mouthing around,' Geoff complained. 'She should know I'm always glad to give her any left-over stuff.'

'She doesn't like to ask, it's her Mother who pushes her into it.'

'Yeah. Like she pushed her into getting engaged to that chap who left her standing at the altar. She's never got over it, poor lass.'

Geoff checked the time on his pocket watch. 'We're late. It'll have to be a quick wash and change, or your Mother will give us hell.'

Dan, who usually drove the van because he enjoyed driving and his father didn't, pulled into the parking area at the back of Kirkwood House. Geoff got out and hurriedly opened the doors of the large wooden garage which had been constructed to house the delivery van. When they had moved into Kirkwood House after the death of Alexander Buchanan two years ago, Ellen had insisted that no tradesman's van would sully the grounds of her father's house, even if it did belong to her husband's small but very reputable company. The more elegant garage at the far end of the driveway was reserved for Alexander Buchanan's Daimler.

Dan and Geoff were still wearing their thick brown cotton coats from the bakery but took them off as they entered the house, and dropped them in the linen basket positioned for that purpose in the scullery by the back door. As usual, on entering Geoff sniffed the warm air of the kitchen and winked at the elderly cook, Molly MacFarlane, who had come with the Buchanans when they had moved to Milfield from Edinburgh.

'Smells good enough to eat, Molly. Sorry we're late. Can you hold it for five minutes?'

'I've been told to postpone dinner for longer than that, you'll not be eating until after seven this evening apparently.'

'Why? I'm starving!' Dan protested.

'You'll have to ask your Mother, she's waiting for you in the drawing room,' replied Molly tersely. She was not best pleased at having to risk drying up the joint of beef which had already been put to roast when Ellen Heywood had swept into the kitchen on her return from Sheila Stanworth's. The cook often wished that her mistress had taken after her mother rather than her father.

Molly had been employed originally by Ellen's mother, Constance Buchanan, a gentle, beautiful, fair-haired creature who had been coveted, but not cherished by her ambitious husband. Alexander Buchanan, then a young lawyer who had suffered the humiliations of having to struggle to finance his training, had taken money into consideration when choosing a bride.

'Oh, hell, what's up now?' Geoff Heywood wondered out loud as he and his son galloped upstairs to change; they knew better than to try to set foot in Ellen Heywood's favourite room while still wearing their work clothes.

Ellen could not wait to give vent to the anger which had increased in her head like a throbbing abscess since she had closed the front door of 17 Stanhope Road. She had shut it so firmly that the lion's head had moved a little on its mounting, sending a rap of admonition echoing through the house.

'Sit,' she commanded as soon as Dan and her husband entered the room. They obeyed, glancing at each other like two small boys wondering which misdemeanour was to be brandished at them.

'Geoffrey, I regret to have to tell you that Daniel has been deceiving us.'

'Oh? What makes you think that?'

'He has been seen with a girl.'

'Oh, yes? Well, it's only to be expected at his age that he'd be interested in young ladies.'

'Geoffrey, you are not understanding the situation. Firstly, this has been kept secret from us, I can only assume by telling us lies, which is unforgivable. And secondly this 'young lady' as you describe her is not suitable company.'

'Why's that?'

'Her name is Lynda Collins. She is the daughter of a publican with a far from admirable reputation, the landlord of a slum property not far from the area known in some circles as The Clough.

In the desperate cause of defending Lynda, Dan found the courage to speak up against his mother. Knowing that he was not by nature a brave young man, he rode this rare wave of courage to its full height. 'It's not her fault where she lives.' He turned to his father for support. 'She's really nice, and I, I love her. And I want to marry her.'

Ellen's uttered a high-pitched cry of scorn. 'Out of the question!'

'Well, . . . ' Geoff Heywood was also not born with natural courage, but he did have strong feelings about what was fair and what wasn't.

'You haven't met the girl, Ellen.'

'And I'm not going to. Her mother . . . ' Ellen stopped herself, the fact that Lynda was the daughter of Doreen Collins was not something she wished to mention. 'I have heard enough about this girl to know . . . '

'Who from?' asked Dan, becoming uncharacteristically belligerent. 'Who's told you about her? I bet they don't even know her. You do Dad, she works in the Belmont Road shop.'

'Yes.'

'You have employed this girl, Geoffrey? You didn't tell me.'

'There was no need, she's just . . . . '

'Exactly! A shop girl.'

'What's wrong with that?'

'Daniel, hold your tongue. And you will not use that tone of voice in my house.'

Geoff was irritated now. It took a lot to annoy him, but ever since inheriting her father's property and money, Ellen had acquired an arrogance which went beyond even what he could tolerate. And he'd had to tolerate a lot in his married life, it was the price he'd been willing to pay to possess the woman who had been his first and only obsession, and whom fate had delivered to him against all the odds. But now, after almost twenty years of marriage, he was becoming weary of living a life which, he'd now realised, had not made him happy. He knew that it hadn't made Dan happy either. Oh, he was as easy-going as his father, and never lost his sense of humour, but Geoff had seen in his son the same need to be loved that he himself felt. And love didn't seem to have a place in Kirkwood House, except when their youngest son, Richard, was with his mother.

So Geoff Heywood, shoulder to shoulder with Dan, made his wife reveal who had told her about him and Lynda, and later that night, as he and Ellen lay in bed, Geoff tried hard to persuade his wife to wait and see how the young love affair developed.

But Ellen had made up her mind, and she certainly did not want to risk her son having to make a hasty marriage. No, she determined, he must be separated from Lynda Collins, permanently, and as quickly as possible. Ellen didn't tell her husband, but she had already thought how that might be achieved.

CHAPTER THREE

On Fridays Madge Collins spent the evening at The Black Bull. She'd spent many mornings there, too, in the last year, cooking a midday meal for her son. She always made sure there was plenty for Lynda to have warmed up when she got home, and a small portion for herself, which she liked to eat in her grand-daughter's company. Madge's cooking was as plain as her looks, but it was tasty and nourishing and Madge loved to see Lynda enjoying it, even though this evening she was eating it a bit fast.

'You're in a hurry to get to Jean Clayton's, aren't you?'

Lynda blushed, and, not wanting to repeat to her grandmother the lie she'd told her father, she said nothing. Madge had noticed the blush, and smiled to herself.

'You don't fool me, you know. I'm not that old that I can't tell when somebody's courting. You're not going to Jean's, you're meeting a lad. Who is it?'

Lynda, relieved to be pushed into confiding in her grandmother, told her about Dan, and confessed that she was going to the Odeon with him that evening.

After Lynda had gone out Madge did the washing up and then went to sit in her usual chair in the snug and have a drink and a chat with her old friends. Friday was the best night of the week for good company, she'd always found, for customers had just been paid for their week's work and so felt confident, for an hour or two at least, that they could pay their way in the world. As well as drinking a couple of glasses of stout and catching up on local gossip, Madge would also kept an eye on what was going on between Ray and Lorraine Garvey.

She'd thought at first that the only reasons Ray had employed Lorraine were a good cleavage and long dark hair which she coiled seductively over her bare shoulders; but she'd soon seen that the barmaid also knew how to charm the customers, the women as well as the men. Lorraine paid compliments, shared confidences, and told slightly risqué jokes with her dark, flirty eyes darting from one face to another, checking that they each of them thought that the attention was really meant for them alone. But now, after watching her, Madge considered Lorraine a bit too clever, a little too skilled at weighing up advantages for herself. Like the way she'd persuaded Ray to let her work on Friday nights now, pretending it was to give Lynda a chance to go out and enjoy herself.

Lynda had been grateful, but Madge was convinced that Lorraine had also worked out that Friday was when customers were most likely to feel generous. Madge watched Lorraine spotting and playing on people's weaknesses, and the customers becoming eager to buy a drink or give a tip to the barmaid who served them with a bit of flattery as well as the tipple of their choice.

Madge also didn't like the way Lorraine stood too close to Ray whenever she could, and giggled when he playfully ran his hand over the tight-skirted flesh of her bottom. It was still less than year since he had lost his wife, and Madge was ashamed that he was making his lust for another woman so obvious. She wished she'd been able to make her son a better man. She'd always hoped that he would change, but by now she had accepted that he'd never understand the need to behave differently. She didn't like it, though, and, without telling anyone, she'd recently made a will.

Madge Collins had never earned a great deal of money, but she'd always been used to living on very little and she had worked till they'd forced her to retire. She'd also managed to save a bit of the money from the life insurance which her dear, gentle, prudent and generous husband had insisted on taking out when they got married. She'd made a will so that the money she left would now be divided between her son and her two grandchildren, instead of it all going to Ray as next of kin.

Madge would have liked to leave a larger share to Lynda, but she'd seen that favouritism always led to bad feeling, and so she treated the three of them equally. Anyway, it looked now as if Lynda might have found herself a good match, if Daniel Heywood had any sense.

It was pouring with rain and Lynda had got soaked running from the bus station to the cinema. She was cold, her thin cotton raincoat was clinging damply to her slender body as she stood in the corner of one of the Odeon's impressive doorways. Instead of rain it was now tears running down her cheeks.

'I thought you loved me Dan. You said you loved me,' she sobbed.

'I do. But . . . .'

Dan couldn't say any more, men weren't allowed to cry, that had been drilled into him all his life. Even when his beloved Nana Buchanan had died when he was five, he'd had to quickly brush away the tears that had insisted on escaping down his grief-stricken, cherubic face.

'They can't do this to us, Dan.' Lynda found herself getting angry. 'I'll come home with you now and we'll tell them.'

'No, you can't!' Dan panicked at the thought of his mother's reaction.

'Why not? Are you ashamed of me or something?'

'No. No, of course not.'

'Well, come on then.' Lynda, driven by her need of Dan and his love for her, didn't let herself think, she just grabbed him by the arm and headed back to the bus station. They hardly spoke to each other on the journey to Wellington Road, fear silenced them both. Lynda was already wondering if she was getting them into more trouble, but she didn't know what else she could do. She had to try to stop them taking Dan away from her.

She knew she was beaten as soon as she saw Kirkwood House towering over her that night as she and Dan walked slowly up the steep driveway. She'd realised when she'd secretly come to look at it before that this was a world different from the one she knew. But now, just looking up at the huge black stones and pillars of the house, surrounded by huge old trees and perfectly ordered shrubs and flower beds made her feel small. She sensed that the power and confidence engendered by the wealth of a family who could own such a house was already overwhelming her.

Dan had no key to his home, his mother did not think it was necessary that he should have one. He didn't want to take Lynda into the house by the back door, as if she wasn't important, so he boldly lifted the heavy thistle shaped door-knocker and let it strike twice. Geoff Heywood opened the door and then felt his mouth also open, in amazement. He stared for a moment at his son's pale, frightened face, and the bedraggled young girl standing beside him, shivering in her thin, damp clothes and then instinctively opened the door wide to let them in. Following them through the hall, and still speechless with shock, he glanced fearfully upstairs where Ellen had gone a few minutes ago to say goodnight to the boy who was only person who really mattered in her life now that her father was dead.

Dan led Lynda into what Ellen insisted on grandly calling 'the drawing room' and up to the fire which blazed in the huge Victorian fireplace and glittered among the ornate and highly polished brass which surrounded it. He was relieved to see that his Mother wasn't there. His Dad finally got over his surprise and stepped forward.

'Lynda, isn't it? Pleased to meet you, again,' Geoff greeted her hesitantly and reached out for the poor girl's hand.

Lynda placed her thin, cold fingers gratefully in the warmth of Geoff Heywood's large, well-cushioned hand, and smiled shyly into his kindly face which, she thought, resembled a cheery full moon.

In the short silence which followed they heard swift footsteps descending the staircase and crossing the hall. Dan and Geoff both stiffened to attention, but Lynda almost laughed at the melodrama of expression which raced across Ellen Heywood's narrow, finely sculpted face as she entered the room and saw her standing between her husband and son. Lynda felt stronger now, but she noticed that Geoff Heywood flinched as his wife glowered at him, conveying her displeasure at his being foolish enough to allow this girl into their home.

Ellen, unusually, did not know what to say for a moment, she was so astonished that Lynda had had the effrontery to come to the house. She knew that it must have been Lynda who had insisted on coming, for it would not have been Daniel's wish to give rise to such a confrontation. And a confrontation it would be, Ellen perceived that from the glimmering of defiance which she discerned in the girl's eyes. Her mind raced as she calculated how best to defend herself against this infiltrator, and then she remembered one of the approaches her father had used to disarm opposition.

'Good evening. Miss Collins I presume,' she said, with icy politeness, and then immediately turned to her husband.

'Geoffrey,' she said reproachfully, 'have you not offered our guest a cup of tea? I think Molly is still in the kitchen, and I'm sure she won't mind. And do take Miss Collins' coat with you for Molly to hang up to dry.'

Lynda quickly removed her raincoat, and as she did so became acutely aware that it was cheap, shabby and slightly grubby. Geoff saw the way she looked at it, and taking it from her, scuttled away to the kitchen, bewildered by Ellen's seemingly welcoming reaction, and wondering what she was up to.

His wife's humiliation of this unsuitable match was perfectly paced and extremely well-calculated. Ellen, very much mistress of the house, gestured towards the sofa facing the fire.

'Do sit down.'

She watched Lynda perch hesitantly on the edge of the Chesterfield and look up beseechingly at her son. Dan sat down next to her and Lynda reached out her hand and grabbed hold of his. Ellen gave a tight little smile, and Dan made the mistake of beginning to hope.

Certain that she had full control of this encounter, Ellen Heywood leaned back in the chair which had been her father's, and began the interrogation.

'So, we meet you at last, Miss Collins.'

Dan leaned forward to correct his Mother. 'Lynda.'

Ellen ignored him.

'I had heard that Daniel had been seen with a . . .' the pause loaded the description with doubt, 'a young lady, but he hadn't told us about you? Why was that, Daniel?'

Dan could think of no honourable reply and was grateful to see his father re-enter the room.

'Molly will be straight in with the tea, and scones. She's our cook', he explained to Lynda, 'been with us for years. She likes to make her own scones – won't have mine!' he laughed.

'I made scones in at school once, they were awful. Don't know what I did wrong.'

Encouraged by Geoff's smile, Lynda fought off her nervousness with chatter. 'And my meringues didn't work out either, everybody else's were fluffy and crispy but mine just went all chewy and horrible.' Gaining bravado, she tried a mischievous grin, 'I reckon Mrs. Watkins, the domestic science teacher, a right old witch, put a curse on the stuff I made. She hated me.'

'Did she?' Ellen sounded dangerously intrigued.

'Yeah. Well, no, I don't mean . . . .'

Geoff sought to come to Lynda's rescue. 'Do you not like cooking?'

'No.'

'Neither did I. Baking I mean, when I first started.'

Ellen put a stop to this cosy chat.

'You left school this summer and are now employed by my husband, are you not?'

'Yeah.' Lynda didn't know why this woman was asking questions she already knew the answer to.

'Do you like working in a shop?'

'It's all right, but I'd rather still be at school doing my A levels.'

'Oh, dear. Perhaps Mr Heywood shouldn't have given you a job and taken you away from that opportunity.'

Lynda glanced apologetically at Geoff Heywood. 'It wasn't his fault. It was my Dad. He thinks I should be out earning money when I'm not working for him.'

Ellen's eyes narrowed with intent. 'Working for him?'

'In the pub.'

'Oh, you live in a pub.'

Geoff was beginning to get irritated by Ellen asking this poor girl for information which she already had.

'You know, Ellen. 'The Black Bull'.'

'Oh, yes, in Stanley Street, very close to that awful area, The Clough, isn't it?'

Lynda felt the need to correct her and snapped. 'Not that close.'

The silence which followed what was obviously perceived as an impertinent tone, was broken by the arrival of Molly with the tea tray. She was not in the best of tempers; when Geoff had been dispatched with the order, she'd been dozing off listening to the radio in the cosy sitting room Ellen's late Mother had set up for her next to the kitchen.

'Do you want me to pour, Madam?'

Ellen nodded but to her annoyance Geoff quickly stood up. 'No, it's all right, Molly, I'll see to it.'

'I'll say goodnight, then,' she said, closing the door slowly so that she could take a good look at the young girl Dan had dared to bring home.

Lynda, still shivering a little through cold and apprehension, made her cup rattle in its saucer. Her hand still shaking a little, she transported two overbalancing heaped spoonfuls of sugar to her cup of tea, and watched sugar scatter across the finely embroidered tray-cloth. Then she placed the damp spoon in the sugar bowl, next to the dry one already there, thus giving Ellen the opportunity to correct her mistake by pointedly removing it. In one of the many silences among the stilted conversation Lynda loudly slurped her tea and saw out of the corner of her eye Ellen's slightly disgusted expression, and Dan's squirming embarrassment.

Lynda, having never been properly taught good manners, spoke with her mouth full, even spitting out crumbs as she nervously endeavoured to answer Ellen's carefully chosen, but seemingly innocent questions about her family, and their way of life. Both Dan and his father, unwilling and unhappy spectators, could only watch and despise their helplessness.

Ellen, beginning to enjoy herself in a way, now devised the final moment of this little drama; she would, she decided, end this confrontation with what would seem at first to be a compliment, and she would follow it with a sentence of death to the relationship. She looked pointedly at the French ormolu clock which reigned over the mantelpiece. 'Well, I think it's time you drove this young woman home now, Geoffrey.'

'I'll drive,' Dan offered eagerly.

'No. Your father will drive, you will stay here. Geoffrey bring Miss Collins her coat.'

Dan and Lynda stood up and endured another tense silence until Ellen, surveying Lynda's dress with its tight fitting bodice and slightly provocative neckline, smiled as if about to pay her a compliment.

'Your dress, is that the modern fashion? The neckline is . . . '

Lynda, in a last desperate attempt to make an impression, fell into the trap.

'A bit Jayne Mansfield? Yeah. Dan likes film stars like her, so I . . . '

She stopped as she saw the expression of distaste on Ellen's face and heard Dan's sharp intake of breath.

'I see,' Ellen said coldly, her voice heavy with disapproval as she turned to glare in disgust at her son.

Geoff walked back into the room, and saw that their visitor was close to tears.

Gentleman that he was, Geoff Heywood helped Lynda into the coat as if it were the finest mink, and was holding the door open for her when Ellen delivered her coup de grâce.

'By the way, I don't know if Daniel has told you, but we plan to send him to London soon for some training. I have connections there. Cousin Charles,' she added for the benefit of the two men who were dumbstruck with the shock of the announcement and the realisation, as they saw Ellen's triumphant smile, that it was a fait accompli which she was presenting to them all.

The tenants of the humble terraced houses and the pungent tramps hanging around outside the doss house on Stanley Road, stared in awe at the Daimler which drove up to the doorway of The Black Bull. Such a vehicle had never been seen in this part of town, and to tell the truth Geoff was worried about leaving it unattended for even a few minutes. But he would not just dump Lynda in the street, not after the way she had been treated by his wife. He had seen her brush away silent tears on the journey from Kirkwood House. She looked as if she'd had all her youthful strength and spirit sucked out of her by the trial she'd undergone in that drawing room whose finery she had gazed upon with both wonder and misery.

He gallantly opened the car door for her and began to escort her into the pub. She tried to stop him as they reached the entrance.

'You don't need to see me in, Mr Heywood,' she whispered. 'Please.'

They could already hear raucous, ale-fuelled laughter coming from inside, and then came one of Lorraine's high-pitched squeals. But Geoff insisted on doing her the courtesy of escorting her in, and soon wished he hadn't.

Ray Collins had, as usual, been drinking as though the beer cost nothing, and was consequently free of any self-restraint. As soon as he saw Geoff Heywood and his daughter together, Ray's mind filled with sordid speculation and insulting questions. Hearing their brief explanation of why Lynda had been brought home, he played to the audience of customers propping up the bar.

'So your lad took our Lynda home to meet you, did he?'

'Yes.'

'Sounds serious. I hope he's been behaving himself.'

'Dad, shut up!'

'When's the wedding?'

'I'm afraid there isn't going to be a wedding, Mr Collins, and now if you'll excuse me, I'll say goodnight.'

'Hold on a minute.' Ray, who had come round from behind the bar, placed himself between Geoff Heywood and the way out. Madge, hearing all this from her seat in the snug, hurried into the bar and placed a hand on her son's arm, moving him back a little.

Ray's voice was getting louder. 'Is your son not going to marry my daughter?'

'No.'

'Why not? Is she not good enough?'

Ray's belligerent manner made Geoff begin to stammer a little now. 'They're too young.'

'Not too young to get up to a bit of 'How's your father!' Ray turned to leer round the onlookers who roared with laughter. Geoff, upset that Lynda was being put through even more torment, looked at her with eyes full of pity, raised his hat and hurried back to the safety of the car, which he blessed for starting first time.

Madge immediately put her arm round Lynda's shoulders and guided her into the privacy of the living room, where her grand-daughter sobbed and told her every detail of the worst evening of her young life.

'I love him, Grandma, and he loves me. But his Mother – she looked at me like I was something the cat dragged in.'

'Take no notice of her. You're good enough to marry anybody.'

'They're sending him away. I won't see him again.'

'Of course you will, they can't send him away for ever. But, . . . ' Madge paused. She could see that Lynda couldn't take much more, but decided to say what she thought, in the hope that it might save her poor child from cherishing too many hopes. Harsh experience had taught Madge Collins that in this life, if you wanted something, or someone, you were more than likely going to be disappointed.

'Look Lynda, love, I know you think he's the only one for you. But he might not be. Give it time love, and wait for the right man to come along. It could be Dan Heywood, but it could be somebody else altogether. You just have to wait and see.'

Sheila Stanworth didn't wait very long to find out if her revelation had been of service to Ellen Heywood. As soon as the dress she was making was ready she went to Kirkwood House; she managed to push her way past the maid in order to hand over the dress personally, taking Ellen by surprise with her sudden entry into the drawing room.

Sheila made bright, very polite conversation and was careful not to mention the bill, which she had tucked discreetly in the pocket on the front of the bag containing the dress. She took the trouble, but only for her wealthiest clients, to deliver the finished garment in a bag she had made herself from off-cuts of material. Ellen soon became irritated by Sheila's oblique enquiries and, to get rid of her, volunteered the information about Dan's forthcoming educational stay in London.

'Oh, very good, what a marvellous opportunity for him,' was Sheila's response. Then she could not resist adding, 'I can imagine a certain young lady being very upset, though.'

'There is no 'young lady' in the sense I think you mean. That was a misunderstanding, I believe.'

'Oh. Well, I'm glad to hear it. They're all too young to think of romance, anyway, aren't they? That's what I've told our John, he needs to make his way in the world before he even thinks of getting involved with anyone.'

Ellen nodded politely, and waited for her to leave.

Dan arrived in London less than two weeks after his mother had shocked him with the announcement of his fate. He didn't see Lynda before he left, his mother made it clear that, if he disobeyed her in that, she would insist that the unsuitable girl be dismissed from her job at his father's shop.

Dan hated not even being allowed to say goodbye to Lynda, but promised himself that he would write to her once he got settled in London. He did say goodbye to his friend John Stanworth, though, and told him what had happened.

John was angry with his mother for causing his best mate such pain, but he was also secretly grateful to her for, unwittingly, giving him a chance to win Lynda Collins for himself.

CHAPTER FOUR

Jean Clayton always dreaded Christmas. It was the second Saturday in December, and she was standing, in the freezing cold, with her little sister outside Mason's toy shop in the centre of Milfield. Marilyn had her nose pressed against the window and her breath was making little clouds on the glass. There were two doll's houses on display; the smaller and cheaper one had a roof covered with red, tile-patterned paper, and its front was open to reveal rooms set out with neat, simple miniature furniture. There was a living room with a table and chairs and a green three-piece suite, a kitchen with tiny pots and pans, two bedrooms, one with a double bed, and one with two single beds, and a bathroom. Jean envied those dolls with their smart house and new furniture.

Next to a huge dappled grey rocking horse stood the other doll's house, which was a three-storey mansion fit for the Queen to live in. Among other elegant furnishings it contained a velvet sofa and a chaise longue and there were even tiny, battery powered electric light bulbs.

'I want that one,' Marilyn shouted, pointing excitedly.

'Yeah, but . . . .'

This was the worst part of Christmas for Jean. What could she say to a child who had as much chance of receiving a present like that as Jean had of going to Hollywood. Jean also gazed at the beautiful doll's house which had enough rooms for each of the dolls to have its own bedroom. Just imagine, she thought, a bedroom all to yourself, somewhere you could get undressed without being watched. Lynda had her own bedroom at The Black Bull and Jean envied her that. She loved going round to sit in Lynda's room and talk, just the two of them, and try out the bits of make-up they bought at Woolworth's. She'd seen Lynda a bit more often since Dan Heywood had been sent off to London, and they'd arranged to meet this afternoon outside the toy shop to take Marilyn to the Santa's Grotto which Mr Mason set up every year.

'Will Father Christmas bring me the big doll's house?' Marilyn asked.

Jean felt like crying, but instead muttered, 'I don't know. He might not be able to.'

Marilyn looked up at her with eyes like a Basset Hound's, and Jean could see tears welling up, ready to accompany the high pitched whimper which was already making its way out from Marilyn's down-turned mouth. Lynda arrived just in time to save Jean further torment by saying, 'He's promised that house to one of his best fairies.'

Marilyn turned round in complete belief, as she heard Lynda's voice, and beamed as Lynda handed her a small white paper bag. As Marilyn pushed her fingers into the bag to choose the first jelly baby to have its head bitten off, Jean and Lynda looked at each other in total understanding of what they would have to handle in the next half hour. Jean had again tried to tell Lynda that Marilyn was now too old for this seasonal visit to Mason's toyshop, but Lynda loved Christmas, and this was a magical part of it. So, having no younger siblings of her own, she'd insisted for the past three years that she and Jean should take Marilyn to see Father Christmas. She'd managed to get a couple of hours off work that afternoon so she could give the little girl this treat.

Mason's was a shop which most of the people from their neighbourhood didn't dare to enter, knowing that their lack of money would be so obvious that they might be asked to leave by some haughty member of staff. Lynda, however, had been blessed with her grandmother's audacious courage and so, with Marilyn clutching her hand, she waltzed in through the imposing, festively garlanded doorway. Jean followed, walking quickly through the shop, hoping they'd get into the silver spangled grotto at the far end before they were spotted, but Lynda strolled along as if her pockets were bulging with ten bob notes. She encouraged Marilyn to pause at all the displays of large expensive toys, and didn't pull her away when she reached out, with hands sticky with sugar from the jelly babies, to touch some of the large furry teddy bears and rabbits.

Angela Mason was getting a bit too big, not to mention too old, for the fairy outfit with sequined wings and droopy chiffon skirt which her father had, several years ago, considered a good investment. She was poised at the entrance to the grotto holding a wand in one hand and a silver basket in the other. As the three misfits approached, she taxed her mind with the question of whether she should offer them the silver basket, but the decision was taken from her as Lynda propelled Marilyn into the grotto and swiftly dropped the required coins into the basket.

When they left the shop Jean, watching Marilyn happily dancing along the main street with the lollipop and small present which Father Christmas had given her, again became despondent as she remembered what her little sister had said to Santa.

'It's not fair, I shouldn't have taken her.'

'Yes, you should. She still believes in Father Christmas, Jean. It's magic, lying in bed thinking you can hear the sleigh bells. Let her enjoy it while she can.'

'But she'll only be disappointed. She asked him for a doll's house, Lynda! She'll be lucky to get a second hand doll, never mind a doll's house.'

'What are you getting her?'

'I don't know. I was waiting to see if I'd get a bonus, but I've got a cut in pay instead.'

'How's that?'

'They've moved me to the packing section, and it's less money.'

'I thought they were training you as a machinist.'

'I'm not fast enough.'

'Oh. They're a lousy firm to work for, Marsden's. You want to go somewhere else.'

'Yeah. But where?'

'How about Heywood's? The money's not exactly top wages but you get a share of what's left over every day. Mrs Fielding was saying we could do with somebody else to help cope with the Christmas stuff. Let's go and ask her now?'

'Can we? Oh, where's Marilyn?'

'She's just gone into Woolworth's. You go and get her, I'll wait here.'

Lynda had seen Dennis Clayton approaching, shouting and laughing with the noisy mates who'd been to the football match with him. Dennis was a tall, well-built twenty-four year old, with brown hair so naturally greasy that he didn't need to use much Brylcreem to slick it back in the DA style that was still fashionable among some of the men in Milfield. Neither Jean nor Lynda liked the style; Jean because she'd found out that DA stood for duck's arse, and Lynda because she preferred soft, well-washed hair like Dan Heywood's.

Lynda didn't like Dennis Clayton much either, he had a way of looking at you with a twisted smile and eyes narrowed so you couldn't tell what he was thinking, but knew it wasn't anything you'd like. He made her feel uncomfortable, the way he looked her up and down when she went round to the Claytons' house. Jean had noticed Dennis's unwanted attention and had warned Lynda never to let him get her on her own. Lynda had decided she was willing to take a risk with Dennis today though.

'Dennis! Hiya!' she called and flaunted up to him, smiling as if he were the man of her dreams. There were appreciative looks from the other men as she walked past them. She recognised Mick Dawson, a burly foundry worker with thick red lips and crooked teeth. He sometimes included The Black Bull on his rowdy pub crawls, and for a moment Lynda felt a touch of fear.

'Hey up, Dennis,' shouted Mick, 'your girlfriend's here.' Leering at Lynda and winking at his comrades, he added, 'He likes 'em young.'

Lynda felt like slapping his stupid face but, remembering why she was doing this, she controlled her anger and continued to smile. Dennis, enjoying the attention, grinned at them and slung his arm across Lynda's shoulders. She forced herself not to recoil from this clumsy embrace and the beer fumes he breathed into her face as he spoke.

'Hello, Lynda, love. What brings you here?'

'Me and Jean have just taken your Marilyn to see Father Christmas. Dennis, she's asked him for a doll's house. Can you make her one?'

'Can I hell!'

'Oh, go on, Dennis. You're really good with your hands.'

There were great bellows of laughter and suggestive nudging at this, just as she'd known there would be. Lynda had learned enough about male humour from working behind the bar to know exactly how to play to this crowd. She also knew from Jean that Dennis had been good at woodwork when he was at school.

'Please, Dennis, for Marilyn. She's set her heart on a doll's house. Oh, go on, Dennis.'

The gang joined in, taking up her words like a chant from the football terraces.

'Go on, Dennis. Go on, Dennis. Go on, Dennis. You bloody mean sod!'

John Stanworth, also on his way home from the match, heard this raucous jeering and saw Lynda surrounded by the men. Instinctively he headed across the street to rescue her, in spite of wondering what he would be able to do against such a crowd. He was lucky; before he reached them, Dennis Clayton had given in.

'All right, all right. I'll make her a bloody doll's house.'

Lynda, playing out the drama as she knew she had to, flung her arms round Dennis's neck and gave him a big kiss – prompting whistles and lustful rumblings from the rest of the pack. Then she wriggled out of his arms, away from his clammy hands and the stink of his sweat and moved away as fast as she could. Dennis was so focused on lapping up the lecherous speculation and approbation from his peers that she'd gone before he'd realised it.

John, disturbed by strong feelings of male jealousy as he saw Lynda kiss Dennis Clayton, caught hold of her arm as she hurriedly crossed the road.

'Lynda! Are you all right?'

'Oh. Hiya, John. Yes, I'm OK.'

She saw Jean coming out of Woolworth's with Marilyn, and waved to attract their attention, but didn't move away from John Stanworth. There was something she needed to know from him.

'How are you, John? Been to the match?'

He nodded, trying to think how he could take advantage of this chance meeting.

'Have you heard from Dan?' Lynda asked, trying not to sound anxious. John hesitated, but decided he had to tell her.

'I saw him last night. He's just got back from London. Didn't you know?'

'No.'

'Oh. Well, I expect he'll be in touch soon,' he said trying to sound more confident than he felt about that.

John had asked Dan about Lynda, but Dan, unusually for him, had been evasive. John was hoping that the love affair between his friend and Lynda was all over, but he also didn't want her to be hurt, and so began gently preparing the ground for the break-up which Dan had hinted at.

'He seems to have had a great time in London.' John continued, deliberately casual, pretending he didn't know how important Dan was to Lynda. 'He's been doing all right, and he's met some people who are big film fans, like he is.'

'Yeah, I know.'

That was what was worrying Lynda. In his last letter, written several weeks ago, Dan had told her all about these new friends and the films he'd seen, and about going to the theatre in the West End, a world Lynda couldn't even imagine. She'd written back but hadn't had a letter or anything from him since then.

'Hello, John.' Jean, when she'd seen whom Lynda was talking to, had hurried up the street, ignoring Marilyn's protests at being dragged along at such a pace. John nodded and smiled at Jean, but looked at Lynda as he asked, 'Are you going to the dance at the Carlton next Saturday?'

'Yes,' Jean replied eagerly. 'We are, aren't we Lynda?'

Lynda saw the hope in her friend's eyes, and knew she couldn't disappoint her. And she had a reason to go herself now that Dan was back in Milfield.

'If I can get the night off, yes.' Then, carefully matching John Stanworth's casual tone, she asked, 'Are you and Dan going?'

'I am. I don't know about Dan.'

Lynda didn't listen to his doubt, she was pretty sure Dan Heywood would be at that dance if he knew she'd be there. And she saw the way Jean was gazing up at John.

'We'll see you there, then. Tell Dan that me and Jean are going, will you?'

'Yeah, O.K.'

'Come on, Jean, we've got to get to Belmont Road before Mrs Fielding goes home.'

Christmas came early for Jean Clayton that year. She got the job at Heywood's, and the following Saturday she was at the Carlton ballroom dancing with John Stanworth. Ray Collins had said 'no' at first when Lynda had announced she wanted to go out dancing the next Saturday, but Lynda had decided to stand up for her rights. Madge had had a quiet word with her about Lorraine's tactics and Lynda was annoyed that she hadn't realised earlier how much she was being manipulated.

She knew there was no question of her being absent from the pub over Christmas, their most profitable time, but she wasn't going to let them take all her Saturday nights away from her. Terry had already been allowed to refuse to work on Christmas Eve, and in the end Lorraine, who was learning not to push Lynda too far, persuaded Ray that it was in their best interests to let his daughter have that Saturday night off. Lorraine wanted time to enjoy all the sociability of Christmas, and for that she needed Lynda behind the bar doing most of the work.

The Carlton Ballroom was Harry Benson's paradise, his little kingdom where the former ballroom dancing champion ruled as supreme showman and bandleader, and made a bit of money. It wasn't a very large ballroom, and being up a side-street rather than in the centre of Milfield, it wasn't in the best position, but it was, in the opinion of its proprietor, classy.

Along the sides of the beautifully polished dance floor there were red plush tip-up seats which Harry had bought for a knock-down price from a music hall which had closed. There was a small bar in one corner, where Harry's wife, Betty, supervised the sale of fizzy drinks, beer and Babycham. In contrast to her husband, who was tall, with square shoulders and perfectly poised arms, and a face which he liked to think suggested noble Roman ancestry, Betty Benson, a woman devoted to sequins, was now slightly plump and petite, but with height added by her carefully arranged, unnaturally platinum blonde hair and dangerously high-heeled shoes.

At the far end of the ballroom was the stage, heavily draped with curtains of deep crimson velvet on which Betty had painstakingly sewn silver satin stars. The stage was just large enough to accommodate the Harry Benson Band: a piano, double bass, saxophone, drums, and clarinet played by Harry himself, when he wasn't conducting, singing or dancing centre floor with his wife. In their younger days he and Betty had won medals for their quickstep and fox-trot but, having realised that their talent was less than they'd hoped it would be, they had settled for giving dancing lessons and running their own ballroom.

At nine o'clock the band were taking a break, and Harry was trying to ignore the fact that more of the younger customers had got up to dance since he had started playing rock and roll records. John Stanworth was dancing with Jean, but watching Lynda who was sitting very still and staring at the door, willing Dan Heywood to walk through it. She'd used some of her savings to buy a special dress. It was a 'Jane Russell special' in red satin with a low neckline and a straight skirt which flicked out into a deep frill just below the knee; it made her look glamorous, and would, she was sure, make Dan fall in love with her all over again.

It had made John Stanworth fall in love with her; it had made him catch his breath when he arrived at the Carlton that night and saw her standing at the bar, buying a lemonade from Alice Smith. Alice helped out at the Carlton on Saturday nights for a bit of extra spending money, and the chance of meeting someone who would mend her broken heart.

Lynda had noticed John arriving, and his reaction to her. She'd been flattered, but it was Dan she was looking for and John had seen she was disappointed that he had arrived alone. Soon, he realised, he was going to have to tell her why Dan Heywood wasn't going to come to the dance. But not yet; he didn't want her to go home, not before he'd had the chance to hold her in his arms. He'd been thinking about nothing else all week, but he knew he'd have to play it cool, just be friendly, so it was Jean he asked to dance first. He liked Jean, and he felt sorry for her, so he was happy to dance with her for a third time before escorting her back to her seat next to Lynda.

'Can I buy you ladies a drink?'

'Oh, thanks. I'll have an orange juice, please.' Jean smiled adoringly at him, thrilled that he was signalling that he'd sit with them.

'What about you, Lynda?'

'No, I'm O.K. thanks,' she said, her gaze drifting once more toward the entrance.

'Did Dan say what time he'd be getting here?' she asked.

John had been dreading this moment. 'Dan's not coming,' he answered quietly. Then, hating himself, but doing it anyway, he forced her to start facing the truth about her relationship with Dan Heywood by adding, 'Didn't you know?'

For once Lynda spoke without her pride protecting her, not caring if she sounded upset. 'No. I thought he'd be here.'

John hastened to soften the blow, but not too much, he wanted her to realise that Dan wasn't for her. 'His mother had other plans for him.'

'Oh, I see. Yes, she would have.' Lynda's tone, like her eyes, had hardened.

John leaned close to her. 'Let me get you a drink.'

'O.K.' she sighed. 'I'll have another lemonade.'

Jean watched John walking towards the bar, and excitedly grabbed Lynda's arm.

'Isn't he fabulous? He's danced with me three times now. Do you think he likes me, Lynda?'

'Of course he does, why wouldn't he?'

'Have you seen all the other girls looking at us? They're dead jealous. Everybody wants to go out with him.'

'I don't.'

'Well, you've got Dan.'

'Yeah.'

'I hope John asks me for the last waltz. You won't mind, will you, if I let him walk me home. You'll be all right, won't you?'

'Yeah. I'm going home early anyway. In fact I'm going now. Drink that lemonade for me, will you?'

On Christmas Eve The Black Bull looked better than it had for years; all the customers said so, and even Madge had to admit that Lorraine had 'trimmed up' well for Christmas. There were red and gold paper garlands and bells strung along the walls and twisted green and white crepe paper ribbons stretched corner to corner across the ceilings.

Hanging decorations was just the kind of job Lorraine liked doing, no heavy lifting or getting your hands dirty, just climbing up steps, and having to think up saucy ways of refusing offers from male customers keen to hold the ladder steady and look up her skirt. She'd thrown out the box of old decorations and Lynda had quickly rescued them. She'd taken out one or two items which had been her Mother's favourites, and then passed the rest on to Jean, who was delighted to be able to make the Claytons' cold, dingy living room look as if Christmas really might happen.

Lorraine had spent a lot of money on the new decorations and Ray, after a few grumbles, had accepted her argument that it would pull in the customers. And she was proved right, the place was packed out on Christmas Eve and Ray and Lynda were run off their feet pulling pints and serving more whisky than they sold the rest of the year.

Madge, who'd been standing at the sink washing glasses so long her legs ached, looked round at Lynda. 'Where's Lorraine?'

'Gone to collect some glasses. We were running short.'

'That was ages ago.'

Lorraine, with a tinsel crown in her hair, had been having a lovely time, spending most of the evening twirling around like a flirtatious fairy. Madge wiped her hands on her apron and looked round for the missing barmaid.

'There she is, heading for t' piano room. Playing Lady Bountiful with them mince pies you got from Heywood's. By hell, she knows how to avoid hard work, does that one.'

Ray knew that was true, but he could only think about the night out together which he and Lorraine were secretly planning for Boxing Day, and so defended her. 'She's keeping the customers happy.

'Well you'd better get her over here soon. It's nine o'clock and me and Lynda are taking a break. We've been stuck behind this bar since six.'

So the next time Lorraine appeared, Ray called her over, and she reluctantly took her place behind the bar. She didn't want to antagonise Ray's mother, and she especially wanted to keep Lynda on side to cover the rest of Christmas. So it was Lorraine who served John Stanworth with a pint of bitter and a flutter of her eyelashes when he walked into the Black Bull.

'Having a good Christmas, John?'

'Yeah. Is Lynda in?'

'We've just sent her and her Grandma for a break. Will I do instead?' teased Lorraine, licking her 'Sorrento Scarlet' lips.

'Where are they?'

'I think they went into the piano room.'

Watching him walk away with his pint, Lorraine thought she wouldn't mind a turn under the mistletoe with that good-looking young man.'

John smiled as he was enveloped in the warmth and the sound of happy people belting out Christmas songs to the enthusiastic piano accompaniment played by Dorothy Chadwick, who was the right side of at least half a bottle of sherry. There was standing room only, and John could see Lynda in the centre of the crowd, her eyes shining as she led the singing of 'The Christmas Alphabet'. They'd just got to the line about everyone getting kissed under the mistletoe when John managed to catch Lynda's attention. He slowly raised his glass to her, and no-one could misunderstand the look in his eyes. Held captive for a moment in the spotlight of his admiration, Lynda hesitated, but then smiled at him. John made up his mind in that moment that he was going to kiss her before he left that night.

He'd been to The Black Bull twice since Lynda had, as he thought of it, run out on him at the Carlton Ballroom. He'd left soon afterwards, unaware of the distress that caused Jean Clayton. He'd gone on a pub crawl with some other lads, drowning his disappointment and getting into big trouble with his mother for coming home in a staggering drunken state.

He'd been careful not to make it too obvious why he'd suddenly started coming to have a drink in The Black Bull. The first time he'd turned up with a couple of mates, but the second time he'd come alone. He'd chatted not only to Lynda, but also to Ray, and to Madge, who liked the easy way he talked to them. John Stanworth had seen enough of his mother's snobbish behaviour to know that he preferred to follow his father's example and 'be all right with everybody'.

Lynda had been surprised, and unexpectedly pleased, by the way he'd walked into the pub and not made her feel embarrassed about living there. She felt hurt that Dan had never come to find her at The Black Bull, that he'd never tried to see her since his return to Milfield, not even at the shop. She guessed that Mrs Heywood was the cause of his staying away from her, but she still thought that he should have defied his mother and come to see her.

John stood tall, and hopeful, as Lynda fought her way through to the doorway where he stood waiting for her. 'Merry Christmas, Lynda.'

'Merry Christmas, John,' she responded, looking up at him a little shyly.

She had become less sure of herself with John Stanworth in the last week or so; she'd enjoyed talking and laughing with him, and had been a little taken aback, in view of his reputation as a girl-chaser, that he hadn't made a pass at her.

It wasn't that he wasn't interested, she could see that from the way he looked at her, and admired every movement of her body as she worked behind the bar or went round collecting empty glasses. It flustered her, made her blush, and that worried her. Why could he make her feel that way when she was still in love with Dan Heywood? At first her conversations with John were all about Dan, but soon she realised that there was nothing more to say, and that John couldn't defend his friend's neglect of her.

'Can we have a drink and a chat,' he requested, 'if we can find somewhere to sit?'

She was already moving towards the bar where customers were good-naturedly elbowing each other aside as they tried to get served.

'Sorry, I can't. I've got to go back behind the bar, we're short of staff.' As she took her place behind the pumps, she added in a loud voice, 'My Dad gave our Terry the night off. Didn't you, Dad?'

'Well, I never expected it to be as busy as this.' Ray retorted defensively.

'Can I help, Mr Collins?' John asked. 'I've no experience of pulling pints but I can fetch bottles and I don't mind washing glasses.'

Ray beamed at him, 'Thanks, lad, get in here. I'll pay you.'

John didn't refuse the money Ray offered him at the end of the evening, but he would have gladly done the work for nothing, just to be close to Lynda. She was impressed with how quickly he learned the prices, and amazed that he was willing to spend half the time helping Madge wash glasses. Madge and he exchanged banter while they worked, and Lynda was delighted to hear her grandmother roaring with laughter. As he was leaving Madge told him he was welcome any time, and prompted Lynda to see him out through the front entrance. John smiled his thanks at Madge, who tactfully quickly disappeared into the living room where Lorraine was watching Ray counting up the night's takings.

Lorraine had hung a huge bunch of mistletoe in the doorway and as Lynda began to walk past it John put his hands on her shoulders and turned her towards him. Glancing up at the mistletoe as if for permission, he kissed her. He'd intended it to be a gentle, romantic kiss, but he'd been waiting so long to hold her in his arms that he lost control and fastened her to him in a passionate embrace. When he let her go, she was too stunned and breathless to speak at first but then, her lip trembling, she whispered.

'I'm Dan's girl.'

'Are you?' he challenged, giving her a long steady look before striding out into the cobbled street with a broad grin lighting up his face. He had kissed Lynda Collins and had felt her lose her resistance and instinctively respond to him. He was in with a chance!

Holy Trinity Church was a cold place to be that Christmas morning. Lynda thought somebody should have told them to light more candles, then perhaps she wouldn't have had to shiver so much. She had to clench her teeth together to stop them chattering, particularly during the responses that all the congregation knew except her. It wasn't just the cold air that was making her shudder, though, it was the frosty looks she'd been getting ever since she'd walked in and sat down in a row fairly near the front, on the opposite side of the aisle from the Heywood family's pew. She just didn't belong there, she could see that, she hadn't got a smart, warm winter coat and she certainly hadn't got a hat. Round her neck she'd wrapped the thick red woollen scarf her mother had knitted for her, and she reckoned it was the only thing stopping her from freezing to death.

The organist began to play the final carol 'Hark the Herald Angels Sing' and Lynda stood up once more, rejoicing that this marked the end of the service and singing at the top of her strong soprano voice. No-one looked round this time, but when she'd begun to sing the first Christmas Carol many heads had turned to find out who the new voice in the congregation belonged to. There had been a few smiles and nods of approval but one group of women had followed Ellen Heywood's example and raised their eyebrows before pointedly turning away from her throughout the rest of the service.

When Lynda had first arrived at the church door she had wondered for a minute if she'd be allowed in. She'd waited out of sight until she'd seen the Heywood family arrive, and had followed them through the churchyard. They were greeted by a group of their friends standing by the entrance, and all of them had observed Ellen's look of horror when Lynda had loudly said hello to her, and to her eldest son, of course. Ellen had not spoken to her, but had swiftly led her family to their pew, leaving the word to spread among a certain section of the congregation that, as far as Ellen Heywood was concerned, Lynda was someone to be shunned.

To give him credit, Dan had managed to whisper hello, but it had been obvious straight away that he couldn't cope with Lynda being there. She hoped it was just the shock that had prevented him from giving her a smile, and she'd watched and waited for him to turn and acknowledge her during the service, but he'd simply either bowed his head or focused all his attention on the vicar.

Lynda was determined to give him a second chance, though; she'd decided she'd stand and wait for him outside the church, and speak to him again, even if it meant running the risk of being rebuffed and humiliated. But now she wished that John Stanworth wasn't there to see what was happening. She'd noticed that he was sitting a few rows behind her with his father and sister, and of course, his mother. You couldn't miss Sheila Stanworth among the congregation; she was wearing a striking green and burgundy felt hat for which some poor pheasants had sacrificed their tail feathers. This eye-catching creation was very freely adapted from a design in the Vogue magazine she'd read at the hairdresser's, and it appeared to be a representation of the shock the birds must have felt when brought down in full flight.

John hadn't bothered to protest against accompanying his family on their traditional Christmas morning visit to the church. He'd thought about trying to get out of it, because what he really wanted to do was to lie in bed all morning thinking about kissing Lynda under the mistletoe, but he also believed in upholding family traditions, and this was one of them. Today his devotion to duty had been rewarded beyond measure, for the girl he loved was here. He would have been even more overjoyed had he known that he was part of the reason she had ventured into the church.

Lynda had come primarily to see Dan Heywood, of course. She had guessed that he and his family would not fail to attend Holy Trinity Church on Christmas morning, and that it would be perhaps her only opportunity to see him and speak to him. She had to know if she still had a chance with Dan, and if he still cared for her but, since last night, she was aware that she also needed to find out if she was still in love with him. The answer to the first of those questions came as soon as Dan stepped out of the church and found her facing him. 'Hello, Dan,' she said again. He looked at her, but his eyes were so empty of life and hope that it made her want to cry.

John had warned her, he had tried to explain that Ellen Heywood had somehow obtained complete domination over her son. It wasn't just that Dan was financially dependent on his Mother, there was a need of her approval which reached down into primitive depths of his soul. John hadn't explained it like that, of course, he had no gift of such insight, or the words to express it. He did understand it a little, though, from his own experience, while at the same time knowing that his Mother, thank God, did not have the same hold over him.

Ellen Heywood, exchanging Christmas goodwill with her friends and acolytes, hardly bothered to look at the young couple. She was absolutely certain that, after several prolonged and intense conversations, she had made Daniel accept that his destiny could not in any way include Lynda Collins, with her cheap make-up and vulgar taste in clothes. Geoff Heywood watched them, though, and grieved for his son's loss as Dan, unable to find any words, and ashamed of his weakness, simply shook his head as he turned away from the girl he loved. He went to sit, head bowed, behind the wheel of the Daimler, hoping it wouldn't be too long before he'd be required to drive his Mother home.

Lynda knew it was all over. She felt tears in her eyes, but there was no way she was going to cry in front of the huddle of holier-than-thou women watching, fascinated, from the shelter of the porch. She could see John's mother, Sheila Stanworth, standing on the outside of the group, still trying to edge closer to Ellen Heywood. Sheila, too, had followed Ellen's lead and Lynda had noticed her give a little self-righteous smile as she'd observed Dan hurrying to the car. In his first letter to her from London Dan had told Lynda who had betrayed them to Ellen Heywood. Lynda knew she wouldn't ever forgive Sheila Stanworth for that.

She looked at her watch, she'd have to run to get back to the pub before opening time. She hurried away from the church, but before she got to the gate she heard someone call her name. She turned to find John Stanworth standing in front of her, those dark eyes looking into hers and taking her breath away. He didn't speak; he didn't have to, Lynda knew what his question was. She glanced once more at the hunched figure in the Daimler, and then looked up at the man who had made her experience an excitement she had never felt before. She smiled at him, just a small, slightly melancholy smile but it was enough to make John Stanworth walk back towards the church a happy, hopeful young man.

His mother, who had seen him hurry after Lynda, was waiting for him, as startled as the pheasants shot out of the sky.

'Who was that girl?' she asked, hoping her feigned ignorance would elicit some innocent explanation of why her son had chased after Lynda Collins.

John, knowing very well how false that question was, replied sharply, 'Didn't you recognise her? That was Lynda Collins.' He smiled to himself at the irony of the situation as he added, 'She used to be Dan Heywood's girlfriend.'

'Oh.'

Sheila, afraid to have her dreadful suspicion confirmed, struggled to decide what to say next. 'And you know her.'

He smiled broadly. 'Yes.'

'Not your sort, though, John, I don't think,' his mother asserted, in the tone that usually put an end to any argument in the Stanworth household.

'You're wrong there, Mother,' John said firmly - ruining Sheila Stanworth's Christmas.

CHAPTER FIVE

The smoke eased its way in a leisurely fashion under the door of Lynda's bedroom. Boxing Day had been even busier than Christmas Day and she'd cursed her Dad and Lorraine for taking the night off to go for a tour of their favourite pubs.

Lynda had been exhausted as she'd crawled into bed, leaving Terry to put the takings in the secret hiding place behind the old meat slab in the cellar. She was sleeping heavily, and dreaming about John Stanworth so she didn't wake up until the beer bottles started exploding in the bar. She opened the door and, choking on the fumes, staggered across the landing and into her brother's room.

'Terry! Terry, wake up, there's a fire!'

He snorted and turned over, his brain still numbed by the half bottle of whisky he'd treated himself to as a nightcap. Lynda took hold of his shoulder and shook him, but he still didn't respond so she threw back the bedclothes and started to drag him out of bed.

He swung his arm at her. 'What the hell are you doing?' he grunted, and then woke up as his lungs filled with smoke. 'Bloody hell! Let's get out of here.'

He leapt out of bed, and struggled into his trousers as he ran on to the landing.

'Come on. We'll jump out of your bedroom window on to the lavatory roof.'

She started to follow him, but then stopped. 'What about Dad?'

'He's round at Lorraine's. Come on!'

Lynda hesitated, glancing across at the door of her Dad's bedroom. It was still ajar, as it had been when she went to bed. Terry was wide-awake now, and terrified.

'Come on, you silly bitch,' he yelled, grabbing her by the arm and dragging her back into her bedroom. He pushed hard at the rotten sash window frame but it refused to open more than a few inches.

'Bloody hell!' he screamed.

'You have to get right underneath it, it'll open if you shove hard enough.' Lynda suddenly found herself calmer, from somewhere came a certainty that they would escape. She looked round the room and her gaze rested on the fireplace. Her money was on the shelf in the chimney. There was a grating sound and a thud as Terry got the window open.

'Come on! What the hell are you doing?'

She reached up and grabbed the tin box. On her way to the window she pulled her eiderdown off the bed and bundled it out of the window to have something a bit softer than a stone roof to land on.

She wrapped the comfort of the pink eiderdown round her shivering body as she stood in the street and watched The Black Bull burn. Terry had run to the phone box at the bottom of the hill and called the fire-brigade but by the time they got the fire under control all the downstairs had either burned or become invisible in the shroud of smoke. It wasn't until an hour later that they found the body of Ray Collins.

Two policemen drove Lynda and Terry round to Madge Collins's little terraced house on Tate Street, and stayed until Lynda had broken the news to her grandmother. When they'd gone the three members of the Collins family sat for several minutes, motionless as if frozen by the silence. Then Madge spoke, very quietly but in a voice heavy with anger.

'Why didn't you wake him up?'

'We didn't think he was there, Grandma,' Terry protested. 'He told me he was going to sleep round at Lorraine's.'

'You should have checked. Did you not even look in his bloody bedroom?'

'No.' Terry looked at Lynda, who sat there, wide-eyed, remembering the bedroom door which hadn't been closed. Another tense silence, heads bowed, and then Lynda and Terry heard a high pitched moan and looked up to see Madge, her lips pressed tight shut but her body swaying backwards and forwards as she sat in the shabby armchair by the fire which had turned to cold ashes hours ago. Then, she began to cry out, quietly at first then louder and louder till the words seemed to take hold of her body and rock it harder.

'My lad! My lad. My little boy. My little boy. My little baby. First my husband, then my little lad. Who's next, eh? I hope to God it's me!'

Then she gave way to her grief, and Lynda sat on the arm of her grandmother's chair and held her as they wept together, with Terry trying to hold back his tears and be a man, but having to turn his head away and rub his eyes with his fists.

There was a pretty good turn out at the funeral, everybody said so. The landlady at the Britannia Inn across from St Matthew's Church provided ham sandwiches and Silverskin pickled onions for the dead man's customers and the representative from the brewery, who became evasive when Nathan Oldfield shepherded him into a discreet corner and asked whether The Black Bull would now be closed down. Nathan was disappointed with the man's answer and moved over to buttonhole Terry. Nathan had been to so many funerals he'd started disregarding most of the niceties of funereal conversation. Instead he bluntly, but in a suitably subdued tone, of course, presented the questions other people wouldn't like to ask, but they'd want to know the answers to them in the bar later. Nathan wouldn't have to buy his Guinness that night.

'Will you become landlord now?' he asked Terry.

'No, I don't think so.'

'Ask that bloke from the brewery now, before somebody else puts their bid in.'

'No.'

'Oh, I'm sorry, not the time is it. But don't leave it too long, there's one or two I can think of who'd fancy their chances of running the Bull.'

'They can have it, I don't want it. I've got other plans.'

'Oh, sticking to being a mechanic, are you? Well, it's all right, but there's not that much money in it.'

'There is if you've got your own garage.'

'Oh, like your uncle in Australia, you mean?'

'Yeah.' A loud moan made him look towards the far side of the room. 'Excuse me, Nathan, my Grandma's looking upset.'

Nathan turned round, as almost everyone else had, to find out what Lorraine Garvey was saying to Madge Collins.

Lorraine was sobbing, and having drunk several glasses of vodka and orange in memory of her lover, was talking more loudly than she should have been. Madge was wide-eyed and breathing in short uneven gasps as she was forced to listen, in front of everyone, to Lorraine's wailing. Madge wanted to hit the silly woman who couldn't seem to realise that she didn't want to hear how comfortable Lorraine's double bed was, or how her elderly mother didn't mind turning a deaf ear on the nights Ray came round.

'Oh, it's all my fault!' Lorraine wailed. 'If only we'd gone back to my place, like he wanted to. I'd set my heart on staying at the Vernon Hotel, a bit of a treat, like. He said it'd be a waste of money, and I . . . ,' She paused and held her crumpled, tear-soaked handkerchief to her mouth for a moment before blurting out her guilt.

'I called him a tight bastard, and stormed off home. If I'd let him come home with me, he wouldn't have been at the Bull, and . . . .Oh, I'm so sorry, Mrs Collins.'

'So am I,' snapped Madge, 'but it won't change things. I'm going home now. Terry, will you settle up for the sandwiches?'

'The brewery bloke said they're paying,' Terry whispered as he helped her into the thick winter coat which suddenly felt too big and heavy for this seventy-two year old whose whole being had been drained of its strength by her son's death.

'Oh, right. Come on then, Lynda, we're off.'

'No, wait!' Lorraine saw Madge's look of exasperation at hearing her cry out again, and added quickly. 'I need to have a word with Lynda, Mrs Collins, if you don't mind.'

'Catch us up, then, Lynda, will you?'

'Yeah, I won't be long,' Lynda reassured her, as she wondered what other embarrassing revelations Lorraine was about to pour forth.

She walked deliberately away from the crowd of mourners who were still hovering round with ears and eyes at full alert, and put on her coat. She hurried out into the street, making Lorraine trot after her across the road to the thick stone pillars which formed the entrance to the churchyard. The gateway offered not only some shelter from the north wind which had made them shiver at the graveside, but also some privacy. She'd no idea what the barmaid thought she had to say to her, but she did know, like Lorraine, what it was to feel guilty.

'What is it, Lorraine?'

'I feel terrible. It's my fault he died.'

'No, it's not.'

Lorraine wasn't listening, she was taking a bundle of letters from her handbag.

'I can't have this on my conscience as well. Please forgive me.' She handed the letters to Lynda.

'What's this?'

'They're your letters, the ones that Dan Heywood sent you. I hid them from you. I told your Dad. We both agreed it would be better if it was finished between you and Dan.'

For a minute Lynda could hardly breathe. 'Better? Better for who?' she demanded.

Lorraine started sobbing again. 'I know. I know it was selfish. We wanted you to stay at the pub and . . . . .'

'Give you an easy time! You lazy, selfish bitch! I thought Dan had stopped writing. I thought he'd given up on me. I thought I'd lost him, and now, thanks to you, I have!'

Lorraine was calmer now, and ready to stop giving herself a hard time.

'Yes, but . . . . These things turn out for the best in the end. You'll meet somebody else. There's John Stanworth, for a start. You might even want to thank me, in the end.'

'Thank you? I don't even want to bloody set eyes on you again!' Lynda felt like hitting her, but there was such misery in Lorraine's eyes that she just shook her head and walked away.

Later, Lynda was glad she hadn't hit out at Lorraine because, though she hated to admit it, Lorraine, in a way, might have been right. When she read Dan's letters later, and secretly, in the small back bedroom of her grandmother's house, she was disappointed. The letters weren't full of the love and longing that she had expressed in her letters to him; instead they contained mostly stories of meeting people she wouldn't know how to mix with, and suggestions of books she should read.

'When the hell have I got time to read books?' she muttered to herself as she turned the pages. 'And where would I get the money to buy the smart clothes London women wear?'

The worst thing about the letters, though, was the lack of passion. Lynda had wanted Dan to tell her how beautiful and desirable she was, and how he couldn't live without her. A few days after the funeral he sent her a condolences card, but he hadn't written anything in it, no hope that he might see her again.

John Stanworth hadn't sent a card, he'd come round to Madge's house as soon as he'd heard, asking if there was anything to do to help. And as it happened, there was, because Lynda had nothing to wear, everything she possessed had been damaged by either the smoke or the water from the firemen's hoses. John's sister, Sylvia, had put on a bit of weight and had clothes which were now too tight for her, but which would fit Lynda. It didn't take John long to persuade her to hand them over, especially as she planned to buy new clothes when she got married. Many of the clothes had been made by Sheila Stanworth, who didn't like the idea of Lynda Collins wearing them but knew when Christian charity had to come first.

Lynda was grateful for these gifts, and surprised at what a difference wearing Sylvia's clothes made to her. She felt more grown up, and more confident, especially in the navy two piece suit that she wore for her interview with Duncan Wilson a couple of weeks after the funeral. Duncan's mother, Freda, had come to the funeral to see Madge, and to offer help. She'd never forgotten that Madge had lent her and her late husband some money when they were desperate. It hadn't been a lot, Madge had had little enough herself, but it had saved them and their child from going hungry.

Freda was in her late fifties now, and was ready to think about one day retiring from running her café on Hudson Street. She needed someone to train as manageress and she reckoned Lynda would do nicely, and return a favour at the same time. Her son, Duncan, a lazy young man with receding hair and an inability to resist cakes, wasn't keen on the idea, but Freda still held the purse-strings so he had to go along with it.

He was impressed when Lynda turned up in a smart navy suit, and she had no problem doing the mental arithmetic test he'd devised for her. It had taken him a while to work out the sums himself, as his mother had noticed.

'You're working at Heywood's at the moment. Why do you want to leave?'

'I don't particularly, but this sounds like a better job.'

'It won't be much more money,' he stated bluntly; then, thinking of the argument he'd had with his mother over this matter, he added, 'not at first, anyway.'

'I understand.'

Lynda had kept a smile on her face, but formed the opinion that here was another tight-fisted man who liked the power of money. He also liked looking at her legs, she'd noticed, and she wanted this job, so she crossed her legs, allowing her skirt to ride up and give him a better view. She told Jean later, on their way home from the shop, that she reckoned it was her legs that had finally got her the job.

'That's disgusting.'

'What, him, or me?'

She noticed that Jean didn't answer that question directly.

Instead she commented, 'He doesn't sound a very nice bloke to work for.'

Lynda agreed with her but didn't say so. She knew, but couldn't say, that Freda's offer of a job couldn't have come at a better time.

Instead she reassured her friend. 'He's more pathetic than bad. And anyway, I'll be working for his Mother, not him.'

'When are you giving your notice in?'

'Tomorrow.'

'Mrs Fielding won't be happy.'

'She'll understand. It's a better job, better prospects.'

'Yeah, lucky you, eh? See you,' Jean said sharply and began to walk away. They'd reached the corner of the street where their route home divided but Lynda grabbed hold of her arm.

'Hang on a minute! What's all this sour face, and 'lucky you' business?'

'Well, you are lucky, aren't you? New clothes, new job – new boyfriend.'

'I've only been out with him twice.'

'Yeah, but he's keen, isn't he?'

Lynda felt her cheeks burning as she remembered the way John Stanworth kissed her. She couldn't deny that he was serious about her. It was true that they'd only been out on a date twice, but he'd been round at her grandmother's almost every day since the funeral. He got on well with Madge, and had even managed to make her laugh a couple of times, but it was Lynda he wanted to see.

'Yes, he's keen,' she admitted, 'but it's early days yet.'

'No, you've got him. I can tell.'

'And you're jealous, I can tell that.'

'I love him, Lynda, and you knew I loved him before you started going out with him.'

Lynda was nothing if not honest. 'Yeah, O.K. I knew you loved him, and I'm sorry. But it's not my fault he wants me and not you.'

'But do you love him?'

'I don't know. I'm all mixed up about everything at the moment. But I didn't take him off you, he hadn't even asked you out.'

'He might have done, if you hadn't . . . .'

'Hadn't what? I didn't chase after him, he came looking for me.'

'You didn't have to go with him. You could have given me a chance. You were supposed to be my friend, Lynda, my best friend.'

'I am!'

'Not if you're John Stanworth's girlfriend, you're not!'

Jean ran away then, tears running down her face as she headed back to the miserable home she was so desperate to move out of. She loved John Stanworth, there was no doubt about that, but she also loved the idea of getting married. She knew it was her only chance to escape from that demanding and ungrateful household. Jean had been out with boys, but always in twosomes, and it had always turned out to be Lynda that her 'date' was really interested in.

Lynda's cheeks were moistened by tears, too, as she watched Jean running away, but she was feeling angry as well as hurt. Jean had no right to be mad with her like that, she fumed, she couldn't help it if John Stanworth wanted her for his girlfriend. She thought the world of Jean. She'd do anything to help her, Jean ought to know that, and Lynda had helped her friend more than she knew, more than Lynda could tell her. Jean was right that Lynda had been lucky to get the job at Freda's café, but what Jean didn't know was that, if Lynda hadn't got the job, Jean would have been out of work by the end of the month.

Geoff Heywood had had to inform Annie Fielding that, after the Christmas trade had died away, she would have to lose one of her shop assistants. Lynda had overheard the conversation, and when Geoff Heywood had seen her later his shamefaced look had told her she was still an embarrassment to him. After he had left, she'd managed to have a quick word with Annie while Jean was busy serving in the shop.

'I'm sorry,' Annie had whispered, 'but one of you has to go.'

'And it'll be me.'

'No. It's not you I'm letting go.'

'Yes, it is, Mrs Fielding. Jean loves this job and . . . .' She stopped herself from saying that Jean needed the job more than she did, she could see that Annie was aware of what she was thinking.

She squared her shoulders and tilted her chin, as she always did when she was about to battle her way through a situation. 'I'm ready for a change, anyway. And don't worry, I'll get another job. But don't say anything to Jean.'

It was this last remark that confirmed to Annie that she had guessed rightly why Lynda had made her decision to leave, and Annie had difficulty stopping herself from giving the girl a hug. Annie was aware, almost as much as Lynda, how important this job was for Jean and her younger brother and sister. Annie had discreetly made sure that there were always some broken cakes and pasties for Jean to take home at the end of the day. She had done as Lynda had requested and not let Jean know what was going on, but she was greatly relieved when Lynda announced that she'd found another job.

There was more good news that week. Terry wondered what was going on when he arrived at his grandmother's for Sunday dinner and found she'd bought a leg of lamb. Terry had been living at his friend Alan's house since the fire, as there wasn't any room in the small back-to-back his grandmother had moved into when she retired, but he went to Tate Street for all his meals.

'Bloody hell, roast lamb!' he exclaimed as the three of them quickly sat down to eat the best meal they'd had since Christmas Dinner. 'Have you had a win on the Pools or summat?'

Madge's main pleasure in life was her betting. She filled in a Littlewood's football coupon with the family's dates of birth and her other lucky numbers every week without fail, and once had won a dividend of twenty pounds - not a lot of money to some people, but enough to make a difference to the Collins family. She also placed bets on horses, and won sometimes, but didn't always tell her family about that.

'No such luck.' Madge smiled first at Terry and then at Lynda, and then made them finish the meal and carry their empty plates into the scullery before she sat by the fire in what had been her husband's armchair, and told them her news.

'The insurance money has come through.'

'What insurance?'

'The contents insurance.'

'My Dad didn't pay it,' Lynda said, remembering how she'd tried to persuade her Dad to renew the insurance but he, with Terry backing him up as usual, had decided they didn't need it.

'I paid it. Your Dad didn't know.'

Madge had also had a row with her son when Lynda had told her about the insurance, but she didn't want to remember that.

'How much is it?' Terry asked eagerly; this could be the solution to his problem.

'Enough for you to pay back that money you borrowed to buy clothes, our Terry. And you can get some decent shoes now, Lynda, you'll need them, running round serving in Freda's café all day. And you'll be able to put down a deposit to rent a place of your own, our Terry, instead of sleeping on Alan's settee.'

Terry swallowed hard, afraid to tell his secret, but knowing that he must. 'I won't need to do that, Grandma. I'm going to Australia, to uncle Len's at the end of next month.'

It was terrible, those few short weeks before Terry left them. They couldn't blame him, as Madge kept saying, 'There's more opportunity for him yonder, and it doesn't rain all the bloody time like it does here.' But Lynda was frightened. She knew that Ray's death had broken her grandmother's heart, and to lose Terry as well might kill her. She hated Terry for doing this to them, and she hated her Dad for conniving with him, secretly putting money aside to enable his son to emigrate.

Terry always had been able to get whatever he wanted from his Dad and now he'd persuaded Madge to give him most of the insurance money. He'd promised he'd send the money back from Australia as soon as he could, but neither Madge nor Lynda believed that would ever happen. Lynda tried not to let her grandmother see how hurt she was at this blatant show of favouritism, but Madge, sharp as ever, saw what she was feeling.

'Don't worry, lass, I haven't forgotten you. I'll not see you short of money when you need it.'

'I'm all right, Grandma, I've still got my savings, remember.'

'Oh, aye, your little tin box.'

'Yeah.' Lynda, her eyes filling with tears again as she looked at her grandmother's face, its wrinkles etched deeper by her grief, and her body which had bowed under the burden of her grief and would never straighten with pride again.

'I feel terrible, Grandma, that I didn't look in Dad's room, but I remembered to get my money. I did love him, you know. Only . . .'

'Hush, child. What's done is done. You mustn't blame yourself. You've got a life ahead of you, and it's short enough is life; don't waste it worrying about the past. Think about that young man of yours instead.'

Lynda blushed at the knowing smile her grandmother gave her. Any thought of John Stanworth made her pulse race these days, but her experience with Dan Heywood made her reluctant to set herself up for another humiliation.

'He's not my young man. We've only been going out a couple of months. And his mother doesn't want him to have anything to do with me. She wants to keep her precious son all to herself.'

'Then she's a fool, she'll drive him away in the end if she carries on like that. You keep your children best by letting them go.'

'She's just like Mrs Heywood. She'll never let John go – not to the likes of me, anyway.'

'Then you'll have to fight for him, if you want him, our Lynda. Don't you let yourself get beat this time. Sheila Stanworth will be jealous, it's only natural, but she'll have to get over it. I was jealous of your poor Mother at first, knowing she was taking my son off me. But in the end I was glad, because she loved him and she looked after him.'

'I wish she'd looked after herself more, then she might still be here.' Lynda said bitterly.

The day after her father's death Lynda had suddenly realised she was now an orphan, and since then she'd been missing her mother even more than before. And, although she didn't like to think about it, she knew it might not be long before she lost her grandmother, too.

Madge silently acknowledged the truth of what Lynda had said about her mother, even though her grief pushed aside any thoughts of her son's imperfections. Madge had also been thinking about Doreen lately, and the life she'd had with Ray.

'She was a good woman, your Mother. She was willing to share my son with me – though I think it got on her nerves sometimes, that he'd take more notice of me than he would of her.'

'She never said.'

Madge laughed ruefully, 'She never said a lot of things, didn't your Mother. It's not good to keep things bottled up too much. Say what you think, and be done with it, that's always been my motto.'

Saying what you thought had never been the way in the Stanworth household. Sheila Stanworth placed so many subjects off limits that safe topics of conversation were hard to come by. Sex, of course, was completely out of the question, politics was limited to Sheila's occasional affirmation of her support for the Tory Party, and money, the supply of which was never going to match Sheila's needs, was only discussed in front of the children when absolutely necessary. Most of the time the distribution of Ted Stanworth's income was decided upon in the twin-bedded marital bedroom, usually just as Ted, having long ago abandoned hope of maintaining any conjugal rights, was desperately seeking the solace of sleep.

Sylvia's forthcoming wedding had meant that there had been more conversation than usual in the last few months, mostly between Sylvia and her mother. The two men in the family were sometimes consulted, on the understanding that their views would invariably be found to be fairly useless. If possible, Ted and John would find some excuse to go out when the minutiae of nuptial arrangements began to threaten their sanity, but these retreats were often frowned upon by Sheila, especially if she suspected that the fugitives would be heading for a local hostelry.

Ted Stanworth often wished he had a dog to facilitate his absenting himself at times of domestic trauma. Indeed he had once even suggested the idea, but Sheila had insisted that the only dog she would accommodate would be a professionally groomed miniature poodle. Ted had made more than his share of compromises in his life, particularly since his marriage, but he was man enough to turn down flat the prospect of walking through the streets of Milfield attached to the lead of a poodle with a daft hairdo.

One evening in March the Stanworths were gathered round the table in what Sheila insisted on calling the dining room rather than the living room, in spite of the fact that it was the room they lived in as well as having their meals there, and the conversation centred once more on the wedding guests. One of Sylvia's friends, Joanna, had written to say she couldn't come now as she would be in the South of France that weekend. Both Sylvia and her mother were disappointed as Joanna had become something of a celebrity in Milfield terms, having gone to London to pursue a career as a model and been featured not only in mail order catalogues but also in 'Woman' magazine.

Sheila was very impressed by such stardom. 'It's very disappointing that she can't come, but you can't turn down the chance of going to the South of France, can you? And being invited by a magazine photographer as well.'

'Yes. Lucky girl,' Sylvia commented dryly, having a shrewd idea what Joanna's relationship with the photographer might be.

John who had, for once, been listening with interest to this wedding talk, asked eagerly, 'So there's a spare place then. Can I invite somebody?'

'Depends who it is,' Sheila replied swiftly, 'You could invite Daniel Heywood.'

Sheila had invited Ellen and Geoffrey Heywood to the wedding and had been delighted that her invitation had been accepted. The Laycocks, after Sheila's less than subtle hints, had eventually realised that they needed to offer to pay for at least half the wedding reception if they wanted any of their friends to be there. There was a limit to their generosity, however, and inviting the Heywoods' elder son, as well as everyone else Sheila had pushed on to the guest list, was where Harry Heywood had drawn the line.

This had embarrassed and annoyed Sheila, who had also thought that being able to invite an eligible bachelor like Daniel Heywood would impress some of the guests. Ellen Heywood had not been concerned about the omission, as Dan would, in any case, be needed at home to take charge of his younger brother if his parents were to bestow the honour of their presence at this wedding.

'Yes,' she reiterated, 'you could invite Daniel. After all, he is your best friend.'

John flinched at that. He and Dan had been avoiding seeing each other since he'd started going out with Lynda; Dan because he couldn't bear the thought of another man with Lynda, and John because he didn't want to risk her seeing Dan and finding out she was still in love with him.

'It's not Dan I want to invite, it's Lynda.'

'Well, as I've said before, John, I'm not sure Lynda Collins is the kind of girl you should be going out with.'

'But I am sure. And I want you to invite her to our Sylvia's wedding.'

'Well, I won't, and that's final.'

'Why not?'

Sheila Stanworth was startled, and, to be honest, a little apprehensive, when she saw the mutinous look in her son's eyes. She was worried; she'd hoped that he would lose interest in Lynda Collins after a couple of weeks, as he did with most of the girls he went out with, but now, after three months, he seemed more keen on her than ever. Sheila knew that she'd have to be careful if she were not to antagonise him, and drive him to become more committed by having to defend his girlfriend. She'd seen that happen to other parents, whose disapproval had led their sons or daughters to leave home, or even run off to Gretna Green.

'She won't know anyone there.'

'She'll know me.'

'Yes, but you'll be busy escorting Helen.'

Helen Dalton was one of Sylvia's two bridesmaids, the other being Graham's ten year old sister, Jane. Sheila had often thought that Helen Dalton, beautiful, and from a very respectable family, might make a good match for John - one day. Her son wasn't ready for marriage yet, though, and Sheila didn't want even to think about losing him to another woman, it was hard enough having her daughter preparing to leave home.

John had previously quite fancied having Helen Dalton on his arm; some of his mates had been really impressed when he'd mentioned casually that he'd be escorting her at his sister's wedding. He had no interest in her now, though, Lynda was the girl he wanted, and he didn't want to wait much longer. It was driving him insane, his need of her, but he didn't get angry with her for pushing him away whenever he showed signs of losing control – he didn't dare. One reason was that he wasn't sure how she felt about him, the other was that he was scared he wouldn't be the most skilled of lovers. He'd read a little booklet one of his friends had inherited from an older brother, and he'd skimmed through a couple of dirty books but, despite his reputation for success with girls, he hadn't actually 'gone all the way' with any of them. He knew that the chemistry between him and Lynda was more powerful than he'd ever experienced, and all he could think about was touching her, caressing her and feeling her respond to him.

Every time they managed to find a place where they could be alone, and gradually become more daring, Lynda became more enthralled by John Stanworth. His need of her made her feel powerful and gave her a level of confidence she had never felt before. This confidence gave her energy and the capability to succeed. She was making a reputation for herself at Freda's café, she was well organised and good at dealing quickly with orders. She was also really well-known for her ability to entertain the customers, male and female, and especially for her witty backchat to the men who congregated there at noon for some home-cooking, and a brief respite from their hard graft at the brewery or the engineering works.

Lynda's wage was still about the same as it had been at Heywood's but Freda, who could see that Lynda would soon be capable of running the place, had dropped a hint that it would improve, and in the meantime the tips she received amounted to quite a few shillings each week.

Madge was proud and delighted that Lynda was making progress in the world of work, but no-one was more pleased than Terry. He never thought to say anything about it, though, until they were standing on Platform 2 of Milfield railway station, waiting for the steam train that would take him on the first stage of his journey to Australia.

Madge had said goodbye to him in her living room, taking off her overall for once, and clutching him to her bosom with all the strength she possessed. She'd looked him steadily in the eye as she'd said, 'Ta-ra, lad. Take care, eh?' before almost pushing him out of the door. No-one would ever know that after closing the door she'd sat down and sobbed until her whole body ached with her grieving.

Terry was a bit disappointed at the lack of emotion his grandmother had shown.

'You'd think there might have been a tear or two,' he complained.

'She didn't want you to see her upset. She'd want you to remember her with a smile on her face.'

'She didn't say much either.'

'What could she say? See you soon?'

Terry was silent, biting his lip and looking away. He and his sister both knew that his grandmother would never see him again, and it was possible that Lynda wouldn't either.

They were standing close together to protect each other from the wind which always sneaked around in the station and felt cold, in spite of the fact that only a short distance away the railway track was glinting in the April sunshine. They didn't take shelter in the waiting room because there were other people in there, and they didn't want anyone listening to what they had to say, even though it was, in the end, very little.

'You'll take, care of Grandma, won't you?'

'Of course I will.' Lynda hoped she didn't sound angry with him, but she certainly felt it. It wasn't fair of him to leave her with that responsibility, it wasn't fair of him to leave her on her own to cope with everything. And even though he was lazy and selfish, she'd miss him, for at that moment, looking at her brother's daft face for perhaps the last time, she realised she loved him.

'You'll get wed, soon, I expect.' Terry was, for once, using his imagination and realising that Lynda might soon be on her own completely, and he didn't want that.

'Will I?'

'Yeah. Aren't you going to marry John Stanworth?'

'He hasn't asked me.'

'He will.'

'His Mother won't let him.'

'She will if you make her.'

'How can I do that?'

'Tell her she's about to become a grandma.'

'Don't be stupid. I'm not going to risk getting pregnant. I've seen what happens
to girls with a bun in the oven and no husband.'

'You don't have to get in the family way. Just make sure she knows you will if she doesn't let him marry you. She won't want showing up in front of all them church friends of hers.'

'Give over, our Terry. I'm not doing owt like that.'

'Where's the harm? John Stanworth wants to marry you, believe me. I've seen the way he looks at you.'

Lynda was glad that the train arrived and ended the conversation. It rumbled into the station and the squealing of its wheels and loud hissing of the steam made it difficult to hold much more of a conversation. Terry thrust his two heavy suitcases into a carriage, hugged his sister hard and found he couldn't speak, so he let go of her suddenly and leapt into the carriage. She watched him heave the cases onto the luggage rack above the bench seat. He fussed over the task, giving himself time to get over the sudden unmanly feelings which had come at him from left field. When he turned and leaned out of the open window to take her hand Lynda was surprised to see he was blinking back tears.

His voice was gruff as he said, 'Look after yourself, our kid. I'll write to you as soon as I get there. And you write straight back.'

'Yeah, I will. I promise.'

Looking down at the sister who had grown almost as tall as himself, but who was still his little sister, Terry could suddenly hardly cope with his guilt.

'I'm sorry, Lynda,' were the last words he said as the thundering locomotive belched out soot and smoke and carried him out of her life.

Sylvia Stanworth's wedding was one of the greatest achievements of her mother's life. Sheila had made her daughter a satin and lace wedding dress from a Vogue pattern; it was designed to accommodate young brides who, the fashion editor was aware, would always have difficulty achieving the waif-like physique of the models featured recently in the magazine. Sylvia knew she wasn't Hollywood starlet material, but made the best of her average prettiness by always making sure she looked neat and polished. She'd bought a very pretty bridal tiara and her hair curled out delicately from under the long, lace trimmed veil which made her look tall and elegant.

Sheila had never felt so proud and so sure, for once, that she was not a disappointment to her parents. She could imagine them looking down from heaven, admiring the flowers, the dresses, the smiling guests and the happy couple, and congratulating her on having achieved success. Sheila had been trained never to cry, but a few tears did insist on trying to ruin her make-up and had to be dabbed away with her lacy handkerchief.

Ted Stanworth felt emotional, too, and very much aware that he was losing his beautiful daughter. Sylvia had always been closer to her mother, but he remembered how as a child she used to put her little hand in his, and how she'd dance before him to show off her pretty dresses. Sylvia was fond of her Dad, and grateful to him for being, like her Graham, a man who understood his duty to provide for his family, but since her teens the two of them had never found much to talk about together.

One person who did talk to Ted was Graham Laycock, and the two men shared a secret that would not be discussed with their wives until it was absolutely necessary. The County Bank had indicated to Graham that, to achieve the promotion they knew he deserved, he would be transferred to another branch, as soon as an opportunity arose. That would mean moving to another town, possibly a considerable distance from Milfield.

Ted knew what effect this would have on Sheila, and was trying not to think about it as he walked out of the church with Enid Laycock on his arm. He liked Enid, she was a comely, warm-hearted woman - home-loving in a way which expressed itself, not in highly polished furniture and china displayed in a cabinet, but in the scent of pies and cakes which always welcomed you into her kitchen. He'd enjoyed his visits to the farm and the home life he found there had caused him to do a lot of uncomfortable thinking over the past few months. Today those thoughts were threatening to spoil his enjoyment of his daughter's wedding day, so he pushed them aside as he smiled for the photographer, but he knew they'd be back before long.

John Stanworth didn't notice that his Dad had anything on his mind, he was having a great time, posing for the photographs, and smirking at the admiring looks he'd been getting all day, especially from Helen Dalton. In spite of, at first, considering him too young and certainly too unsophisticated for her, she'd been quite surprised at how attractive, charming and well-mannered, her friend's brother proved to be. John found that his smart new suit gave him extra confidence, and he'd been able to cope pretty well with his duties as an usher. So by the time he had to take his place outside the church for the photographs he was beaming with success. He was so caught up with himself that it was quite a while before he noticed Lynda standing to one side of the church gate.

John had made the mistake of telling her about there being room for another guest at the wedding and his mother and sister's refusal to invite her. Her response had come quick and sharp.

'I wouldn't want to go anyway, but I'm disappointed you didn't stand up for me.'

'I did. I told them that if you weren't going, then neither was I. But . . . .'

'But you had to give in in the end.'

'Yeah. I'm sorry, Lynda, I really am.'

She saw the misery in his eyes and relented. 'It's OK.'

'Will you come to the church? They can't stop you doing that.'

'What, and feel even more out of it? No thanks.'

But there she was, standing next to her grandma in among a small group of women who were on their way to spend an afternoon shopping but, having heard the church bells, had decided to stop and treat themselves to the spectacle of a wedding. Two of these women, Doris and Eileen, had worked with Madge Collins at Victoria Mill and made a great fuss of her. They'd called to offer her their sympathy after the fire at the pub but hadn't seen her since, and were shocked at how she'd aged. Fortunately they didn't ask about Terry, but concentrated on complimenting Madge on the beautiful grand-daughter standing beside her.

Lynda hadn't wanted to go to the wedding but when her grandmother had said she'd like to see it, there had been no way she could refuse. Madge hadn't been out of the house all week, still unable to face talking to anyone about Terry, so Lynda was glad of anything that would lift her out of her sorrow.

In Madge's opinion Lynda should have been invited to this wedding, and she wanted to look them in the eye, these people who seemed to think her grand-daughter wasn't good enough for their son. Lynda had been careful not to wear one of Sylvia's hand-me-downs, but had chosen a pale blue dress she'd bought with some of the insurance money. Madge had insisted that they dressed smartly for their outing,

'We'll show the beggars we're as good as they are,' she'd said defiantly as she'd rammed her battered best hat over her grey hair which Lynda had endeavoured to curl with 'a home perm'. She'd linked arms with Lynda and had marched proudly through the streets to the church, and was now still hanging on to her as the bridal party emerged from the church.

'Ooh, doesn't she look lovely,' Doris cooed as Sylvia posed with her new husband in the church doorway.

'That dress will have cost a bob or two,' commented Eileen.

'No, her mother made it,' Lynda felt bound to explain.

'Perhaps she'll make yours as well, Lynda,' Madge said, winking at her.

Eileen picked up on the remark, her curiosity being one of her strong points. 'Oh, are you getting married?' she asked. 'Who to?'

'Wait and see,' said Madge, and turned as she heard a sharp intake of breath behind her. Jean Clayton was standing there, eyes wide and looking questioningly at Lynda.

'Hello, Jean, long time no see,' said Madge. 'I thought you'd be at work today. You are still at Heywood's, aren't you?'

'Yes,' Jean replied, looking at Lynda. Jean had found out from Annie Fielding that she had reason to be grateful to Lynda, and slowly she and Lynda had rebuilt their friendship.

'Hey up, have you seen the bride's mother?' Eileen cried out, 'Look's like there's some poor ostrich somewhere with a bare backside.'

Sheila Stanworth had indeed surpassed herself in the array of ostrich feathers which swept across the front of her hat and so far down in front of her eyes that she had to squint through them to see what was happening.

In fact she missed some things, like the look on the face of Lynda Collins when she saw John smiling into Helen Dalton's eyes, and leaning close enough to kiss her. Sylvia saw her reaction, though, and felt sorry for the girl who had so little on a day when she had so much.

Jean also observed how John was behaving and, although she still loved him more than anyone, she had made herself come to terms with the fact that it was Lynda he had chosen.

She whispered angrily to Lynda, 'What's he playing at?'

Jean was determined that if she couldn't have John Stanworth, then it should be her best friend who got him, not some stuck up, wealthy young woman who didn't need him.

'I don't know,' Lynda said, almost choking with the fear that Helen Dalton might take her man away from her. In that moment Lynda realised that she loved John Stanworth, and wanted to be his wife.

Madge, too, had noticed what was going on and, as usual. wasn't slow to comment.

'Looks like there's somebody else after your young man, Lynda,' she pointed out quietly.

'She's not having him, nobody is. He's mine, Grandma.'

'I'm glad to hear it. But take my advice, love, and don't make him wait too long. For my sake as well as yours. There's only one thing that can make me happy now. And that's to see you wed to a good man.'

It was at that moment that John saw Lynda, and realised that she must have seen Helen Dalton clinging to him. He broke away from the family group, shaking off his mother's hand as she tried to hold him back.

'Lynda!' he called.

She heard him but turned her back, pretending she was talking to the women around her. They stood aside as he came to stand beside the young girl. He put his arm round her shoulder and pulled her close, ignoring the people staring and Doris and Eileen nudging each other.

'I'm glad you've come, Lynda.'

'Even though I wasn't invited.'

'You should have been. You're my girl.'

'Am I? It didn't look like it a minute ago.'

'What do you mean?'

'Her.' Lynda snapped, nodding towards Helen, who was looking across at the escort who'd suddenly left her standing there on her own.

'I was just . . . .'

'I saw what you were doing. And it's OK. I can see she's high class as well as good-looking, and your mother obviously approves of her.'

Lynda was scared; but driven by her jealousy and her longing to make her grandmother happy before it was too late, she carried on, throwing down the challenge, shouting it loud and clear.

'If I'm not good enough for you, John Stanworth, just say so! If you want to finish with me, then do it, now.'

He was scared, too. No, more than that, he was suddenly terrified of losing her. He spoke urgently, and loudly, not caring that everyone around would hear him.

'I don't want to finish with you, Lynda. I want to marry you.'

CHAPTER SIX

They were standing outside the Peacock Hotel, watching Graham Laycock's car disappearing round the corner when John told his parents. Graham's older brother, Sam, had taken his duties as best man very seriously, determined to cause his strait-laced younger brother as much embarrassment as possible. He'd made sure that plenty of signs alluding to the bridegroom's honeymoon obligations were attached to the car, as well as balloons and tin cans.

Sheila was standing on tiptoe, waving her handkerchief, and, as usual, finding something to worry about.

'I don't know how Graham is going to get his car cleaned up before they get to the hotel.'

'Don't worry, love, he'll have it organised', Ted reassured her.

'I hope so. I don't know what kind of impression they'll make if he doesn't. Right, we'd better say goodbye to everybody now. Shall we call a taxi? I'm ready for home, aren't you?'

'Well, Geoff Heywood has asked me to stay and have a drink with him.'

'Oh.'

'We haven't seen each other for a while. You don't mind, do you?'

If it had been anyone other than Ellen Heywood's husband Sheila would almost certainly have vetoed Ted's plan, but she liked to boast about her husband's friendship with Geoff Heywood, which had begun when they were at school. Also Geoff had, at Alexander Buchanan's insistence, become a freemason, an organisation Sheila was hoping her husband might one day be invited to join.

'I'd have preferred you to take me home, but if Geoff's invited you, John can take me instead.'

'I'm off out as well, Mum, with Graham's Dad and Sam.'

'I see. You're leaving me on my own then.'

Ted winked at his son and played his ace card. 'Mrs Heywood said that Dan will take you home when he and Richard come to collect her.'

'Oh. Well, I suppose . . .'

Ted smiled to himself, he had known that the idea of going home in the Daimler would appeal to his wife. 'Perhaps Ellen will ask you in for a sherry.'

'Yes.' Sheila glowed with the possibility for a moment. 'You won't be late home, though will you, Ted? I don't want to be on my own tonight. Oh, it's terrible that it's all over. I wanted this day to go on for ever.'

John, who'd had a few drinks at the reception to give him the courage to break the news, thought, quite wrongly, that this was the right moment.

'Never mind, Mum. You'll have another wedding to look forward to soon.'

'Will I? Who's getting married?'

'Me and Lynda.'

'Over my dead body!' Sheila exclaimed, loudly enough to make heads turn.

'Dan's here, Ellen's already in the car. They're waiting for you,' Ted announced, thanking God that he and Geoff had worked out the best time for Dan to arrive.

They only stayed at the Peacock for one drink. It wasn't, Harry and Sam Laycock declared, a place where a man could feel comfortable and anyway it was too pricey for serious drinking, so they all walked to the Red Lion in the town centre. Ted, whose wallet was feeling a bit thin after he had paid for all the drinks at the reception, was relieved when Geoff insisted on paying now, and took their order. They all stood at the bar for a while, chatting with the landlord and some of his regular customers, explaining the reason for their suits and ties and exchanging a lot of banter about the pitfalls of marriage. Then they settled themselves at a table in a quiet corner.

'Did I hear you order only half a pint of bitter, John? What's up, are you not feeling well?' Harry Laycock teased, his voice booming as it always did when he'd had a few drinks.

'No, I'm OK, but I've got to go somewhere.'

'Oh, aye?' Harry laughed. 'Meeting your girlfriend, are you? That's the only thing I can see tempting your lad away from a night at the pub, eh Ted?'

Ted was silent, he didn't want to think about what John had told his mother and the amount of upset it would cause.

'Yeah, he's blushing,' Sam Laycock joined in. 'Lynda Collins, isn't it?'

John nodded.

'I thought she might have been at the wedding,' Harry stated mischievously, knowing he was stirring up trouble.

'We'd have liked her to be there, but, like we all said, you can't invite everybody, can you?' Ted responded, slightly embarrassed.

'No wedding bells for you, yet then, Johnny boy? Like our Sam.'

'Shut up, Dad,' interrupted Sam, who wasn't keen to talk about matrimony. It was something he'd decided to avoid for a while after a neighbour's daughter, who had been his childhood sweetheart, had told him she'd found someone else.

John looked at his Dad, and decided that making his plan to marry Lynda public knowledge would help to discourage his family from trying to make him change his mind.

'No, Mr Laycock, I am getting married. Soon,' he added and watched his father's face become even more furrowed with anxiety.

'Who's the lucky girl?' asked Geoff Heywood, picking up on the conversation as he returned from the bar with their order.

'Lynda Collins,' Harry told him. 'You know her, don't you, Geoff?'

Geoff turned pale and his hands shook a little as he quickly and unsteadily put the tray on the table. He glanced at Ted, in whom he had confided his horror at the way his wife had treated the young girl.

'Yes, she used to work for me.'

'And before that, she used to pull pints at her Dad's pub, didn't she? You're a lucky lad, getting her,' Harry sighed, thrusting back his broad shoulders and rubbing his muscular thighs with his large, work and weather-beaten hands.

His eyes enlarged with unashamed lust as he declared, 'If I were twenty years younger, I'd have given you a bit of competition for that young filly.'

John glowered into his beer, he couldn't bear any man to even think about Lynda; she was his, or soon would be. He drained his glass swiftly. 'Thanks for the drink, Mr Heywood.' He nodded towards the rest of his companions. 'Goodnight. Talk to you later, Dad.'

'Can't wait to see her, eh?' Harry shouted after him, and grinned at the others. 'And who can blame him?'

About an hour, and several pints, later the Laycocks set off to visit a couple more of their favourite haunts, leaving Ted and Geoff to enjoy another pint and try to make sense of what their lives had become.

'They rush into marriage too soon, these days, don't they, Ted?'

'I can't say anything, I was married myself at his age. You were a bit older, weren't you, when you married Ellen?'

'Yeah, but certainly no wiser. It's always the same, a man sees a woman he wants, and goes after her. Can't wait to get her in his bed.'

'And then they can't wait to kick you out,' Ted Stanworth added bitterly, and then looked away, cursing himself for having let the drink betray a shameful secret.

Geoff saw his friend's discomfort, and placed a reassuring hand on his arm. 'We've neither of us been lucky that way. Ted. We'll have to take a leaf out of Henry Morton's book – I assume he's still carrying on with his lady friend at the hotel in Lytham.'

'Looks like it. He had a big smile on his face when I drove him back from there last week. He'll have to watch it, though, if you hear him talking about it at the Freemasons so do other people.'

'I hope his wife doesn't find out, she's a nice woman is Emily Morton. Still, at least their kids have left home. I don't think it's right if you've still got children living at home.'

'I won't have any kids at home soon.'

'Oh, well,' Geoff laughed, 'then you'll soon have your freedom – all you've got to do is find a lady friend.'

'I think I already have.'

Geoff almost choked on his beer. 'You what?'

Ted was usually a very private man, but today, with all the thoughts which had been swirling round in his head, he needed to confide in someone. 'Her name's Rose. She's got a café in Blackpool, near the boarding house I stay in when I take Morton over there.'

'Bloody hell, Ted. I never thought you were the sort to . . . . '

'Neither did I. Don't worry, nothing's happened between us, but I won't say I haven't thought about it.'

'You wouldn't leave Sheila.'

Ted sighed. 'No, I couldn't do that to her, but, hell, Geoff, you wonder what your life has been sometimes, don't you?'

'Yes. We both married in haste, that's our trouble.'

'Yeah, and it looks like our John's about to do the same. But it'll be different for him. If Sheila will let him, I reckon that he'll stand a good chance of being happy with a lovely girl like Lynda Collins.'

'Yes, and that's the chance I wish our Daniel hadn't missed.'

'Oh, I'm sorry, I forgot.'

'It's not your fault. It's Ellen, thinking she knows what's right for people. She means well, but . . . . '

Geoff paused to drain his glass and to reflect. 'I thought it'd be different when her Dad died, you know, Mr Number One. I thought she'd have more time for . . , but it's all our Richard now. And I'm afraid she might ruin him, just like her father ruined her.'

He looked at his empty glass. 'I think we deserve another one, don't you?'

Madge Collins had never danced around any man, not even her husband, but she was almost dancing round John Stanworth that evening. He was going to be Lynda's husband, he'd asked her to marry him in front of everybody at the church gate that afternoon. Suddenly Madge was filled with hope for the future; she'd belong to a family again, Lynda and John and their children. She prayed she'd live long enough to see them have children.

In her opinion, the sooner this wedding took place the better, before anybody could change their mind, or have it changed for them. She didn't want Lynda to be let down like she'd been over the Heywood's son, and if it meant rushing things a bit, well, what did that matter? She'd seen plenty of quick marriages before the war, and during it, when men and women had realised how short life could be and taken their pleasures while they could.

She hadn't got the money for a big wedding with a sit-down meal at the Peacock, but she'd not given Terry all the insurance money, and every week for years she'd been saving what bit she could towards the day her grand-daughter would marry. This evening Madge Collins had that glint in her eye that even the mill-owners used to worry about; when she got that determination of hers fired up like this, nothing would stop her.

Over the past few months Lynda had felt like crying as she'd seen her grandmother become a little old lady whom life had at last defeated. Now she watched with joy and wonder as she saw her Grandma squaring her shoulders and tilting her head in the old proud way, and her whole being suddenly filled with energy and spirit. And it was all thanks to John Stanworth falling in love with her grand-daughter.

Madge had never seen any point in being anything but direct. 'So when's it to be, this wedding?' she asked the two young people holding hands as they sat on the shabby settee in her living room.

'Grandma!' Lynda exclaimed. Ever since they'd returned home after watching Sylvia Stanworth come out of the church, Madge had talked about John Stanworth's proposal and plans for the wedding. Lynda had had difficulty stopping her announcing to all the neighbours that her grand-daughter was engaged. Lynda didn't want to tempt fate; John had spoken in the heat of the moment, amid all the excitement of his sister's wedding day. She wanted to wait until she'd seen him on his own, until she knew that he'd meant what he said. Now her Grandma was getting carried away again, pushing John into commitments that he might not want to make.

'I don't know, Mrs Collins. I haven't really thought . . . .'

'Well, get thinking, now!' Madge demanded, her usually deep voice almost shrill with excitement. 'I can't afford a big 'do' like your Sylvia's wedding, but I'll give our Lynda a good send-off. It'll take a bit of organising, you'll have to book the church and have the banns read.'

'I'm not getting married in a church,' Lynda interjected vehemently.

'Of course you are.'

'No, I mean it, Grandma. I'd rather get married at the registry office.'

'What, and have folk thinking you're getting wed because you've a bun in the oven?'

John, whose thoughts since he'd proposed had focused mainly on the prospect of his wedding night, looked away, his face matching the coals smouldering in the fireplace.

Lynda spoke out clearly. 'I don't care what people think. And it wouldn't cost anywhere near as much as a church wedding.'

'She's right there, Mrs Collins,' John said, vividly recollecting all the fees and expenses which had mounted up for his sister's wedding and made his Dad furrow his brow with deep anxiety. Madge knew they had a point, and a registry office might be available sooner than a church.

'Well, we'll see. I suppose a lot of the churches will already be booked up this summer.'

'This summer?' John felt as shocked as he sounded.

'We can't get married so soon, Grandma. There's no hurry.'

'There might not be for you, but there is for me. I don't know how long I've got. And it's no good you pulling a face. There's no getting away from the fact that I'm seventy-three next birthday. Lynda, love, please don't argue with me about this. I want to see you wed before I go.'

Lynda caught her breath as she saw the look in her grandmother's eyes. Never before in her life had she seen Madge Collins pleading.

'OK, Grandma. If it's all right with John.'

'Of course it is. How about June, or July?' he suggested, feeling intoxicated now, not with the beer he'd drunk, but with the thought of having Lynda as his wife.

'Before the football season starts?' Lynda joked.

John laughed, but didn't take the opportunity to change the subject. He understood Madge's need, and his own, and he realised that if he was going to have Lynda, this was the way it would have to be. He'd have to be as assertive as Madge, or risk letting his mother wear him down. She'd made his life hell at home ever since he'd been seeing Lynda, but he wasn't going to let her stop him, not this time. He'd promised to marry Lynda Collins and, although not yet twenty-one, John Stanworth was already a man with a reputation for keeping his word.

'June or July, whenever they can fit you in at the registry office. I'll leave you to talk it over between you.'

'Where are you going?' asked Lynda.

'To the pub.'

'The pub? Do you mean the Britannia?' Lynda was surprised and delighted; her grandmother hadn't been to a pub since Ray's funeral.

Madge knew what was going through the young girl's mind. 'It's as good as anywhere.'

Suddenly she looked vulnerable again as she pulled on her coat.

'We'll come with you,' Lynda offered.

'No, you won't. I'd rather go on my own.'

Madge was thinking faster than she had for a while. She'd never let them be alone in her house before, but things were different now they were engaged. It was time for them to be together, and for them to give into temptation, if that's what it would take to prevent Sheila Stanworth putting a stop to this wedding.

'Can I tell my friends the news?' she asked as she opened the door.

'No, not yet, eh?' Lynda wasn't sure about all this, it was all happening a bit fast for her.

'Why not?' John contradicted her, 'I've been telling people. You tell whoever you like, Mrs Collins. Nice to have a bit of good news to spread around.'

Madge's smile was as radiant as if she were a young bride herself, 'It certainly is. Goodnight, you two.'

As soon as the door closed John took Lynda in his arms and began kissing her as if he would never stop, and she was happy to let him. She clung to him as his hands touched every part of her body, and she let him undo her blouse, but when he unfastened his trousers she pulled away.

'No, John, we can't.'

'Yes, we can. We're getting married, Lynda.'

'We don't know when yet.'

'Oh, come on,' he begged, kissing the softness of her bare breasts, 'I can't wait any longer, Lynda. I love you, and you love me. It can't be wrong to . . .'

She pushed him away, more firmly this time, and began to fasten her blouse.

He was angry now. 'Do you love me, or not?'

'Of course I do, but I've seen what happens when girls let their boyfriend, you know. Either the lad leaves them because they've had what they wanted, or they end up getting pregnant and having to get married. I don't want a baby for a long time yet, I want a life, I want to go places. And I certainly don't want everybody saying you only married me because you had to.'

'Who's going to say that?'

'Your Mother for a start!'

'Oh, to hell with my Mother!'

He went quiet then, he couldn't believe he'd said that. He looked down at the fabric and flesh sticking out of his open trousers, shoved his shirt back into them and fastened his belt again.

'John,' she asked, almost in a whisper, 'do you still love me?'

He looked up and saw that there were tears in her eyes. 'Yeah, of course I still love you. And let's get married as soon as we can.'

'We haven't asked your Mum and Dad yet. Your Mum won't like it.'

'No, I don't suppose she will, but I'm not going to let her stop me.'

'If we tell her how we feel, John, she might come round to the idea.'

'She'll have to, because we're getting married, whether she likes it or not.'

Going home in the Daimler Sheila Stanworth hadn't dared to talk about what was on her mind. Normally she'd have been delighted to reveal that she and Ellen Heywood had now even more in common, but both having sons foolish enough to fall for the all too obvious charms of Lynda Collins was not something to boast about. By the time he got home Geoff Heywood had decided that he wasn't going to mention it either, so the talk about Lynda Collins and John Stanworth getting married didn't reach the Heywood household. In the end it was Jean Clayton who broke the news to Dan.

It was early morning and Mrs Fielding was busy setting out the pasties and pies in the shop window, ready to tempt those who'd set off for work that Monday morning without their sandwiches. They sold more on Monday mornings than the rest of the week because, Annie assumed, there wasn't much food left in their homes after the weekend, and many would have got up late having been in the pub the night before. So it was Jean who took delivery of the loaves and bread rolls, and who made Dan a cup of tea – a small courtesy Doris extended to whoever made the early morning delivery.

Jean had said nothing at home about what she'd witnessed outside the church, and, of course, no-one had bothered to notice that she was miserable; but she had to talk to someone, and preferably someone who would agree with her that it might not happen. So, as soon as Dan had settled himself on the small wooden bench where she and Mrs Fielding sat to have their dinner and tea breaks, Jean handed him a mug of strong, sweet tea and asked, 'Have you heard about Lynda and John?'

'What?'

'They're getting married.'

His whole body went rigid. 'No.'

Jean felt so sorry for Dan, she knew his heart was feeling like a stone falling into deep, icy cold water. That was how she had felt when she'd heard John propose to Lynda. She waited quietly while Dan bowed his head and absorbed the shock. It had been harder for her, she'd had to smile and join in the chorus of congratulations. It was only on the way home that she'd been able to sit on a bench in the park and weep.

'When?' Dan asked, and then, realising he was trembling, took a drink from the steaming mug of tea to steady himself.

'I don't know yet, but her Grandma wants it to be this summer. Lynda's asked me to be her bridesmaid.'

Dan saw that Jean was as numb and unhappy as he was, and remembered that Lynda had once told him that Jean was in love with John Stanworth.

'Did you say you would?'

'What else could I say?'

Dan, sharing the same pain, knew exactly what it felt like for Jean, imagining someone else marrying the one you loved. It would be torment for her to be Lynda's bridesmaid. Then it occurred to him that he might also have to endure that terrible irony, 'I hope John doesn't ask me to be his best man.'

He had to force himself to concentrate as he drove back to the bakery, but, like Jean, he had to talk to someone, and the only person who would understand was his Dad. Geoff was loading a heavy metal tray with tins full of white dough ready for the oven. Dan looked round to check that none of the other staff were around, and then released the anger that had blurred his vision on the drive back from Belmont Road.

'Lynda Collins is getting married, Dad!'

Geoff paused, rested his hands on the tins he'd just placed on the tray, and slowly turned to face his son.

'Yes. To John Stanworth.'

'You knew?'

'Yes, his Dad told me. I'm sorry, son.'

'So am I! It could have been me, Dad. She would have been marrying me if my Mother hadn't stuck her oar in!'

'She was only doing what she thought was best for you.'

'What was best for me was Lynda! I love her, Dad. I told you.'

Geoff absent-mindedly wiped his floury hands on his overall as he tried to find something to say which would take away the pain in his beloved son's eyes.

'I did try, you know, to get your Mother to change her mind. But she's a difficult woman to deal with sometimes.'

'All the time, you mean! But it's not your fault, Dad, I should have stood up to her, instead of letting her pack me off to London. I shouldn't have been such a bloody coward.'

'You're not a coward.'

'I bloody am!'

'You take after me, then.'

Dan saw that his father had grown pale and that he was catching his breath as he spoke, and anxiously sought immediately to reassure him. 'You're not a coward, Dad.'

'I'm certainly not brave, I'm not made that way.' Geoff paused, leaning against a metal trolley stacked with oven trays. He stared at the wall as he tried to deal with a painful memory. 'Your uncle Danny knew that.'

'My uncle Danny?'

'My brother, the one you're named after. I've shown you his photograph.'

Dan recalled the faded black and white image of a tall young man in army uniform, with a confident grin and eyes that let you know he was on your side.

'He was killed in the war you said.'

'Yes. One of us had the chance of staying here to look after the bread supplies. We tossed a coin, his lucky penny, and he went to France, and . . ..'

'Yeah, it was rotten luck.'

Geoff bit his lip and blinked hard as he looked at his son. 'What I haven't told you was that when they sent his belongings home that penny was among them. It was the same on both sides. He knew I wouldn't be able to cope, you see. He knew that from when we'd played as kids, I was always the one who got scared.'

Geoff wiped a tear from his cheek with his clenched fist. 'I don't know why I'm telling you this now, except to stop you giving yourself a hard time over not being brave. If it's true, and I'm not sure it is, you've got it off me, so it's not your fault. Now I'd better get these loaves in the oven or we'll be losing even more trade to Bancroft's.

He lifted the heavy tray laden with loaf tins, took a couple of steps, and then put it down hastily at an angle, almost sending the tins sliding on to the floor. Dan leapt to grab hold of the tray and was shocked to see his father's ashen face.

'Sit down, Dad! What's the matter?'

'Nothing. I'll be OK in a minute. Bit of heartburn, my own fault for having two Cornish pasties instead of one. Get this batch in the oven for me, will you?'

'Yeah, but . . ..'

'But nothing. Don't look like that. I'm all right. But don't say anything to your Mother or I'll have a row about how much I eat again.'

Dan, as usual, did as he was told, but from then on he made sure, whenever possible, that he was there when there was any heavy lifting to be done.

There was a war going on at Stanhope Avenue, a very quiet war because there were often days when the combatants weren't speaking to each other. Ted and John were taking every opportunity to get out of the house and escape from Sheila's frosty silence and various other manifestations of her displeasure.

For the last two weeks she'd been banging their meals down in front of them, not so hard as to crack the plates but with enough force to let them know that she took no pleasure in feeding the two men who shared her home. Their favourite meals had been noticeably off the menu and she hadn't baked so much as a scone since the wedding. Ted Stanworth was as much out of favour as his son was, and all because he'd ventured to suggest that it might not be the end of the world if John married Lynda Collins. Ted was a worried man, he didn't want his wife's heart to be broken, but he wanted his son to be happy.

Before they had set off for their honeymoon, Graham and Sylvia had arranged that they would each have tea with their respective parents the day after they got back. Sheila was preparing for the return of her daughter and ally with a pleasure which expressed itself in a piece of home cooked ham and a chocolate cake. John and Ted were looking forward to these treats, but were not enjoying Sheila's anticipation that 'Sylvia would make them see sense'.

And so, on Sunday afternoon, they set off for a walk over Bailey Moor to visit Frank Hartley, whose wife had contacted them to say he was very ill and would appreciate a bit of company. Frank had been Ted's sergeant and had helped him a lot when he'd first joined the police force, so although Sheila didn't give her blessing to their outing, she accepted it with merely a shrug, and a 'Don't be late for your tea.'

It was wonderful to stride out over the coarse grass of the moor, to see the sunshine brightening the usually sombre, but today wind-ruffled waters of the reservoir, and, above all, to breathe fresh, invigorating air instead of an atmosphere heavy with conflict and condemnation. At home, needing to avoid being overheard by Sheila, they'd only been able to hold brief, whispered conversations about the problem which was threatening to break up the family. Ted didn't want to spoil the walk but he knew this might be his only chance to talk to his son before things got any worse. John had already threatened to leave home, and Ted knew that Sheila didn't want that, it would be too much to bear, especially after Sylvia getting married.

'I used to come up here when I was a lad,' he began.

'I know, you used to swim in the reservoir.'

'Yeah. Bloody dangerous. A stupid thing to do.' He paused and looked at his son. 'But we all do stupid things sometimes.'

John, grim-faced, challenged his Dad.

'Do you think I was stupid, asking Lynda to marry me?'

'No. I'd probably have done the same at your age. In fact I did, I was only just twenty-one when I married your Mother.'

'And do you regret it?'

Ted sucked in a deep breath between his teeth; and walked on. He hadn't expected a question as tough as that, but he was determined to be honest with his son.

'Yes, sometimes I do. Don't get me wrong, John, your Mother has given me a lot of what I yearned for. I've told you the sort of family I was brought up in, me and my brothers and sisters in a scruffy little house, parents out at work all the time. I wanted a clean home where I'd be looked after, and where good meals would be put on the table. Sheila's given me all that.'

'But . . .?'

John halted, turning to face his father, but Ted looked away. He believed in loyalty and he wouldn't criticise his wife, but he felt he had to let his son know what was at stake, and perhaps to help him be understanding in case, one day in the future, his Dad might find the courage to grab the chance of what was still a hopeless dream.

'I like Lynda and, for God's sake don't tell your Mother, but I think she might make you a good wife.' He hesitated, not wanting to be explicit, but wanting his son to understand what he was saying. 'I don't know if she'll learn to be a good cook and housekeeper, but, a man wants more than a good home. He wants a woman who can, and wants to, make him happy - in every way.'

He gave his son a quick, sideways glance, and then paused for a moment to stand and look at him steadily.

'Do you understand, John?'

'Yeah. I think I do.'

'Good. Now we'd better get a move on, or we'll not get back in time for tea, and I'm looking forward to that cake.'

Actually, Sheila was glad they'd gone out. It meant she had her daughter all to herself when Sylvia arrived at two o'clock. She'd lit the fire in the front room, as an indication that Sylvia's homecoming was a special occasion. Also, instead of being held back for tea-time, the chocolate cake was cut into and was received with a gratifying enthusiasm by Sylvia, who then curled up on the sofa, with the slice of cake and a cup of tea, ready to enjoy a chat with her mother. They'd always been able to talk to each other; Sheila had been an only child, and Sylvia had become the sister she'd never had, as well as a daughter.

Sylvia had always confided in her mother, told her everything, but today she had realised that from now on things would be slightly different. She was a married woman now and there were conversations she would keep for her husband. Sheila soon became aware of this, and wasn't altogether unhappy about it. She did not, for example, want to know anything about the goings-on in the marital bed, the physical side of marriage was one thing she would never talk about. She had merely asked, 'How was the honeymoon?' and been more than satisfied, in fact, even a little shocked at the wide, slightly roguish smile on her daughter's face as she'd replied, 'Wonderful.'

Sylvia had then wanted to tell her mother about her experiences in London; it had been quite an achievement, persuading Graham to splash out on their honeymoon, with three days in the capital followed by a weekend in Stratford-upon-Avon on the way home. Graham Laycock was a true bank man, he loved saving and investing with caution. He had already invested in a home of his own, with the help of a fixed rate mortgage at the favourable rate granted by the County Bank to its approved employees. Sheila listened carefully and appreciatively to her daughter's detailed descriptions of hotels and new experiences, and was already looking forward to impressing her friends and acquaintances with her own selective re-telling. But she was pleased when Sylvia had finished, for she was desperate to announce to her daughter the terrible news about her brother.

Sylvia was shocked to see her Mother begin to cry as she told her what a threat was being presented to her family. Sylvia had met Lynda Collins only a couple of times, but had not been impressed with her lack of taste in clothes, her rather loud voice, and her broad Lancashire accent. Sylvia had worked very hard to rid herself of the accent she had acquired in the schoolyard, and Sheila had even found the money for a few elocution lessons. Sylvia didn't particularly dislike Lynda, and she felt a little sorry for her, but she didn't see her as the kind of sister-in-law she would want to introduce to Graham's colleagues at the bank.

'It's just infatuation, Mum, he'll get over it.'

'He seems very determined. And so does she, of course. And that grandmother of hers seems to have a lot to say about it.'

'He won't marry without your consent, will he?'

'The way he's talking, nothing and nobody will stop him.'

'He's crazy. He's only known her a few months. And they've no money for a house or anything.'

'That's what I told John. But, your Father, I couldn't believe I was hearing it, your Father said that perhaps they could live here.'

'He didn't!'

'He did, you know. He said we had a big enough spare room now that you've left home.'

'My room?'

'Oh, don't worry, I told him straight, I'm not having Lynda Collins in my house. So he's said nothing about it since. But I can't cope with him arguing with me as well as our John. You should have heard how your brother's been talking to me. I never thought I'd hear him speak to me like that. It's her influence, of course. Oh, Sylvia, how are we going to stop them getting married?'

They were still discussing ways to do this, and Sheila was in tears again, when there was a loud knock at the front door. Sylvia went to open it and was so taken aback to see Lynda standing there that the girl had pushed past her and into the house before Sylvia had realised what was happening.

'Where's you Mother?'

'In the front room, but . . .'

Lynda was in one of her 'no-stopping' moods. She had to do this, now or never. She knew she'd little chance of changing Sheila Stanworth's opinion, but this wedding had to happen, for her Grandma's sake. Madge Collins had become obsessed with getting her grand-daughter married, and soon.

'I don't want you left on your own, when I go,' Madge had been saying over and over again, until Lynda, too, had become afraid that she would soon be alone in the world. And she knew that her Grandma was right, if they didn't get on with it the Stanworths would, little by little, convince John, first that they should wait, and then, eventually, that he should choose a better wife.

As soon as Lynda entered the room Sheila quickly put away her handkerchief and Sylvia immediately went to stand, in front of the candelabra, shoulder to shoulder with her mother against the intruder.

'What do you mean by coming barging into my Mother's house like this?'

For a moment, with Sylvia glaring at her as well as John's mother, Lynda lost her nerve, and couldn't speak. She felt small again, just as she had when she'd walked into Ellen Heywood's drawing room. She'd lost the man she loved then, but she'd made up her mind that she wasn't going to lose this time, so she took a deep breath and came straight to the point.

'I know you don't like me, Mrs Stanworth, but that doesn't matter.'

'Oh, doesn't it!'

'I want to marry John, and he . . .'

'You can stop right there.' Sheila Stanworth wasn't going to allow Lynda Collins to finish her sentence, any more than she was going to allow her to marry her son.

'You might think it doesn't matter what I, and my husband, think of your idea of marrying my son, but I can sure you it is of the utmost importance.'

Lynda had to stop herself smiling at the 'and my husband' – she knew from John that Ted Stanworth's opinion was in the habit of being over-ruled in the Stanworth household. Sheila Stanworth was a woman used to getting her own way but now, sensing the strength of feeling which had propelled Lynda Collins into her front parlour, she felt a tremor of uncertainty.

Lynda took a deep breath. 'Look, I know you don't think I'm good enough for him, but I love John and he loves me, and nothing's going to stop us getting wed. That's what I've come to tell you. My Grandma's been to town with me and we've booked the Red Lion for the reception, so it'll be July, at the registry office.'

'The registry office!' gasped Sheila Stanworth. 'My son is not getting married in a registry office. People will think . . . .'

'What? That we're having to get wed? Well, . . . the way John feels, it could easily come to that if you carry on trying to stop us getting married.'

She hadn't meant to say that, but since Terry had made the suggestion it had lodged, unwelcome, in her head. Lynda could feel her face burning with shame, but what she'd said was true, because she no longer dared be alone with John.

On hearing what, to her ears, amounted to a threat Sheila turned to Sylvia, clutching her arm for support. Her daughter, drawing on her status as Mrs Graham Laycock, tried to take command of the situation.

'Is that the kind of girl you are, Lynda?'

'No, I . . . .'

'You didn't mean what you said, then.'

'Oh, yes she did!' Sheila Stanworth spat out the words as if her tongue were coated with venom. 'She's determined to take my son from me, and if that's the only way to get him, then that's what she'll do!'

Lynda knew she'd said what she shouldn't have, but she wasn't going to take it back now, not with these two snooty women looking down on her. It felt like being in school again, and she'd learned to brazen it out in such situations, so she looked them straight in the eye, mutinous and unrepentant.

Sylvia, thinking about her recent, and actually surprisingly enjoyable experience of male passion, could well believe that what Lynda had claimed was true. However, she decided that, as a newly qualified 'woman of the world', she should adopt the stance, and tone, of a lady whose mission it was to bring reason and education to the less fortunate.

'I don't think you have thought about the practicalities of all this, Lynda. For example, where would you and John live?'

Lynda flinched, this was the question that she and John had been arguing about. He was earning steady money as an electrician, but he'd not managed to save much yet, and even with Lynda's wages added in, it would be impossible for them to pay rent for a decent house, buy furniture etc. and keep themselves. Neither of them wanted to start their married life living in a slum, and there wasn't room in Madge's house. John had concluded that the only solution was for them to live with his parents. This suggestion had led to their first blazing row; Lynda had told him, in language strong enough to shock him, that to her living with the Stanworths would be hell in Technicolor.

She certainly wasn't going to put it forward as an answer to Sylvia's question.

'We'll find something,' she said glaring at them like a stubborn child.

'I think you should go home and think about this' suggested Sylvia, modelling her calm manner and a tone of voice on Audrey Hepburn in 'The Nun's Story'.

'I have thought about it. Me and John have done nothing but think about it, for months. Can't you understand? We love each other, we want to be together. And whatever you say, whatever you do, won't change our minds. Like I said, the wedding's in July.'

'Well, we won't be there,' declared Sheila.

Lynda suddenly felt exhausted and demoralised. She had tears in her eyes; she tried to convince herself they were only tears of anger, but the truth was that she was being beaten down by their complete rejection of her. With a final effort she found the strength to hold on to her pride, but only at the cost of abandoning her resolve not to lose her temper.

'See if I care! Me and John are getting married, and that's it!' she yelled at them. 'And you can please your bloody selves whether you come to the wedding or not!'

The lion shuddered as she left.

Tea went very well. There were chips as well as bread and butter and tomatoes with the ham because Sylvia loved chips. Ted and John were happy to do nothing but eat and nod in wonder as Sylvia told them all about London. Sheila and her daughter had agreed that nothing would be said about the visit they had so unwillingly received earlier, they didn't want to spoil the meal, but during the tinned sliced peaches and Carnation milk a silence developed.

Ted was worried about the row that was to come. He was convinced that Sheila would have already told Sylvia the news about her brother and Lynda Collins, she wouldn't have been able to stop herself. The question was, would they get to the chocolate cake before all hell broke loose.

'How does Graham feel about going back to work tomorrow?' he asked, keen to keep a reasonable conversation going long enough to get the cake sliced up.

'Oh, he's quite happy.'

Sheila stood up and collected the rosebud trimmed dessert dishes. 'And he's a married man now, with responsibilities. He'll value his job even more now. Would you all like chocolate cake?'

She paused to receive the required expressions of gratitude and anticipation before going into the kitchen to get the cake.

'How are things at your place?' Sylvia asked her brother.

'All right. Mr Earnshaw's very pleased with me, sent me to one of our big customer's on my own last week. Think I might be in for a pay rise soon.'

'You'll need it if you're . . . .'

'Oh, still saving up for a motorbike, are you?' Sylvia interrupted to stop her Dad completing what she knew he'd been about to say. Sylvia wanted more time to think about her strongest opposing tactics before the subject they were all avoiding landed itself among them. Sheila, however, had decided that now, while her ally, Sylvia, was lined up beside her, was the time the matter was to be settled once and for all.

'We had a visitor this afternoon,' she announced as she poured the fresh pot of tea.

'Oh, who was that, then?' Ted enquired, helping himself to another slice of chocolate cake.

'Lynda Collins.'

Ted and John looked at each other. For a moment John stopped chewing the piece of cake in his mouth, but then swallowed and asked boldly? 'And you didn't ask her to stay to tea?'

'I certainly did not.'

'You should have done.'

Ted thought for a moment his wife was about to strike out at her son, and cut in.

'Had she come to see John?'

'She had come to inform us that she, and her grandmother, had arranged a wedding, with a reception in the Red Lion, of all places. This wedding, apparently, is to take place in July at the registry office. And the bridegroom is, she claims, to be our son, who, however, does not seem to me to have been involved in the arrangement.'

'What are you talking like that for, Mother? Of course I've been involved. I told them about the wedding last week, Sylvia. And they knew well before that that I'd asked Lynda to marry me.'

'It all sounds a bit hasty,' Sylvia said in the reasonable tone she'd decided suited her role as the 'voice of good sense' and the wife of a future assistant bank manager.

'That's what we said,' Sheila agreed. 'John knows very well that we're completely against the idea, aren't we, Ted?'

'I wouldn't say that. If they're in love . . .'

'In love!' Sheila mocked.

'Aye, love, if you can remember what that is.'

'Dad!' Sylvia had never heard that bitter tone in her father's voice before.

Sheila's voice was shrill now. 'Lynda Collins is not suitable!'

'She suits me!' John shouted.

'Well, I'm your Mother, and I don't think she's good enough.'

'Well, you're wrong. She's wonderful. And she loves me. And I'm going to marry her, whether you like it or not!'

Sheila was angry now, too angry to be prudent, too used to winning. 'If you marry that girl I shall never speak to you again, John. I'll have finished with you. You will no longer be my son.'

Ted was horrified. 'Sheila!'

'It's no use you looking at me like that, Ted, I've made my mind up. You have to choose, John. It's Lynda Collins or me.'

There was a silence, then the sound of John's chair being pushed away from the table as he stood up. He didn't look up because he knew there were tears in his eyes.

He turned and left the house which had suddenly stopped being his home.

CHAPTER SEVEN

Dan felt sick as he sat on the edge of his bed, winding his best silk tie slowly round his clenched fist. He didn't know how he was going to do this, stand beside John Stanworth as his best man and help him marry Lynda Collins. Dan had been having nightmares in which he'd knocked John aside and shouted that he was the man who was marrying Lynda, and that nobody was going to stop him.

If only he'd had the courage to defy his mother as John had defied Sheila Stanworth and insist he was marrying Lynda whether she liked it or not. He knew she was refusing to come to the wedding, but John had told Dan that 'she could please her bloody self'. It was obvious to Dan that John was hoping she'd change her mind. If she didn't, his friend would need his support more than ever, and Dan didn't let his friends down. But it was a helluva thing to ask.

He stood up and his hands shook as he put on the tie and then lifted the jacket of his best dark suit from its hanger. As he slowly put it on he felt the small box he'd placed in the pocket the night before, afraid he'd forget it. He opened it, stared again at the small gold ring and cursed John for not having the imagination to perceive that he was still in love with Lynda Collins.

There was gentle knock at the door and Geoff Heywood walked in, feeling like a badly wrapped package as he bulged out of his waistcoat and tight-collared white shirt.

'You look smart. Your Mother was right, though, I should have got a new suit. Are you ready, lad?'

'Yeah.' Dan looked into his father's eyes and saw that he understand how hard this was for his son.

'I'll drop you off at the registry office, and then pick up John and his parents.'

'John and his Dad. His mother's not going.'

'I thought she'd changed her mind. They're going to live at the Stanworths' after the wedding, aren't they?'

'Yes. But only because John's Dad put his foot down, and said it was his house as well as hers, and he won't see his son homeless even if she will.'

'Ooh. He's a braver man than me, Ted Heywood.'

'No, Dad. It's his house, that's all. It doesn't belong to a ghost like this bloody place. Come on.'

They left the house quickly, with Ellen watching from behind the curtain in the drawing room. Ellen had been invited to the wedding by Ted Stanworth who considered it only right as she had agreed, after some persuasion from Geoff, to allow the use of the Daimler as the groom's wedding car. Ellen, declaring her support of Sheila Stanworth's disapproval of this marriage, had declined the invitation. Ellen did not, in any case, wish to see the pain, and accusation, which she knew would be in her son's eyes on this wedding day which he still felt should have been his. But Geoff would be there to witness it, and would share his son's sorrow.

There was more anger than sorrow in the air at the Stanworths' home. Ted had spent over an hour in the bedroom trying to persuade his wife to change her mind and go to her son's wedding.

'Sheila, you can't do this. You can't spoil his day.'

'He doesn't want me there.'

'Of course he does. Come down and talk to him.'

'What, after he's ignored me all morning?'

'It'll never be right between you if you don't go to his wedding. He'll never forgive you. You know how proud and stubborn he is.'

'Don't I just!'

There was a silence as Ted hunted desperately for words which would persuade his wife to go with them. John's shout startled them both.

'Dad! The car's here!'

Ted saw the panic in Sheila's eyes.

'At least come down and see him off.'

She followed him slowly down the stairs and into the hall where John was already standing by the open front door. He saw his mother following his Dad and for a moment thought that she had relented, but then realised she was still wearing her plain dress and no hat. He blinked back a tear and hurried out of the house, not realising that, had he asked her once more to come to his wedding, his mother would have run back up the stairs and hurriedly changed into the new dress which was hanging in the wardrobe ready for the occasion.

There were no brand new dresses in the shabby terraced house on Tate Street. Lynda and her Grandma had decided they were not a priority, not when Lynda was desperate that she and John should spend as little of their married life as possible living under the same roof as Sheila Stanworth. It hadn't been easy to stick by the decision not to spend money on what should be the most beautiful day of her life, and Lynda had been tempted to take a portion of her secret savings and buy herself a new wedding dress, but her Grandma had advised her against it.

Madge, who had seen too many women suffer from their lack of financial independence, had even persuaded Lynda not to tell John about those savings in a post office account, her mother's small legacy plus what she had added to it. Madge believed that every woman should have some money put away secretly, as 'mad money' - just in case the day came when she had to be able to walk away. Lynda, having shrewdly observed a lot of marriages where the woman seemed to have no rights, could see the sense in having such 'mad money' - just in case.

So Lynda's ivory satin wedding dress had been purchased from a Mrs Talbot who supplemented her widow's pension by discreetly trading in second-hand bridal gowns. Lynda had taken care to choose a fitted dress that would leave no-one in any doubt that she was not marrying because she was pregnant. Mrs Talbot had also sold them a pale blue, full skirted taffeta bridesmaid's dress for Jean Clayton, who had cried when she saw herself in the mirror, looking more beautiful than she had ever thought possible. She was trying not to cry again now as Lynda finished doing her make-up, adding a touch of rouge to her pale face and patting another layer of powder on her persistently shiny nose. Jean had cut John Stanworth out of her dreams, and had avoided seeing him, but today she was afraid she might lose control of her emotions.

Lynda wasn't nervous, she'd made up her mind she was going to enjoy her wedding day, even though it had been hard work trying to pretend that she was having the wedding she wanted, and not the big white wedding with champagne reception that she'd once dreamed of. Lynda didn't care about Sheila Stanworth not coming, though she knew John did. She'd even stopped worrying about what it was all costing, especially after Freda Wilson and Geoff Heywood had contributed the wedding cake and most of the catering as a wedding present. But she was upset that Terry wouldn't be there to give her away.

It was a constant sadness to Madge Collins that her grandson was on the other side of the world and that she would probably never see him again. For a short while she had hoped that he might come home for his sister's wedding, but she'd quickly realised that it just wasn't possible. He'd sent a bit of money as a wedding present but wasn't earning anywhere near the kind of wages that would enable him to travel back to England, even if he'd wanted to.

Henry Morton's Bentley had been given an extra polish by Ted Stanworth and trimmed with broad white ribbons and roses by Emily, Henry's wife. It caused everyone to come out of their houses and gawp as it edged its way along the narrow stretch of cobbles between the mucky, fag-end filled gutters of Tate Street. It had been Emily's idea to lend the car, and persuade her husband, who hated driving, to act as chauffeur. Emily felt sorry for Lynda and Madge Collins, and she was very fond of Ted Stanworth, who was not only their chauffeur but also the invaluable handyman who kept their house and Emily's beloved garden in tip-top order. Emily knew that Henry, out of principle, did not pay Ted enough for what he did, and this was her way of making some recompense for that.

Madge, watching from her doorway, saw the car approaching and called out to the two girls who were still fussing over details. Madge, wearing the new dress Lynda had insisted on buying for her, and a soft powder-blue velvet hat borrowed from a friend, beamed at the neighbours who were already cheering and waving, ready to watch her and her granddaughter set off for the wedding.

'Good afternoon, Madge,' Henry Morton greeted the old woman who had once worked for his father. He smiled benevolently as he walked round the car and opened the front passenger door for her.

'Hello, Henry. Thanks for this. Come on, Lynda, love,' Madge called into the house.

She didn't want to get into the car yet. She waited until she'd watched her beautiful grandchild step out into the sunshine to be greeted by a sigh of admiration which swept along the whole street.. Lynda and Jean smiled and waved excitedly at the neighbours as Henry, enjoying playing the gentleman, opened the doors and helped them into the Bentley which quite a few workers on that street had helped to pay for.

Graham and Sylvia, in their 'Sunday best' clothes enhanced by white carnations, had decided to wait outside the imposing, soot-darkened sandstone, civic building which was part of Milfield's inheritance from the time when it had been one of the cotton capitals of Lancashire. Inside were offices and small reception rooms encumbered by heavy mahogany furniture, and at the far end of the entrance hall was the gloomy oak–panelled registry office. The couple stood by the iron railings round the small square of dusty garden opposite the registry office, away from the other guests - a small number of John and Lynda's school-friends and workmates, and the long-time friends of the Collins family. Graham and Sylvia were having a private, and worried, conversation.

'I hope she'll have changed her mind.'

Graham took off his glasses, and, with a determined expression on his face, began to polish them with a small square of special cloth. 'She will.'

'You don't know my Mother.'

'Oh, I think I do,' he asserted as he replaced his glasses in their rightful position. Graham Laycock was an astute young man, it hadn't taken him long to get the measure of his mother-in-law. 'Like you said, she's made that new dress, and bought a hat and gloves.'

'Yes, but it might be, like she said, just her new summer outfit. Oh, we don't want her falling out with John for good.'

'No, we don't.'

Graham had recently told his wife about the Bank's plans for him. Sylvia quite liked the idea of their moving away to further her husband's career, but she knew her mother wouldn't. Sylvia had been appalled at the idea of her bedroom being taken over by John and Lynda, but her innate common sense, which had always helped her to look after her interests, had made her realise quickly that having her brother remain at home might ease her way out of Milfield.

She and Graham hurried back across the road as the Daimler drew up outside the registry office. Sylvia caught her father's eye as he stepped out of the car and opened the rear door as an extra courtesy to the bridegroom. Tight-lipped, he shook his head.

'John!' Sylvia ran forward to surprise her brother with a kiss on the cheek. He shook himself free as she squeezed his arm, but she wasn't offended; she could see he needed to keep away from any family feeling if he were to survive the hurt being inflicted upon him by his mother's absence. It took a lot to make Graham Laycock angry, but he was angry when he saw his proud young brother-in-law struggling to smile at the well-wishers who greeted him.

' You go inside, Sylvia. I won't be long.'

'Graham? Where are you going?'

'To get your Mother.'

A respectable twenty minutes later the small crowd waiting outside the registry office cheered as Lynda, Madge and Jean arrived in the Bentley. Lynda waved and curtsied to them and she and Jean were about to walk up the steps when a small voice called out, 'Wait a minute!' and Alice Smith hurried up to them.

'Mrs Collins, your friend George Carter can't come,' Alice, who always loved a drama, announced in a stage whisper.

'What?' Madge and Lynda's smiles faded away.

'His wife asked me to tell you, and say she's very sorry. He's had a heart attack, she's with him at the hospital now.'

'Oh, no!'

'She said you'd asked him to give Lynda away. Is that right?'

'Yes.'

'Apparently, he got so het up about the wedding that . . . .'

'Oh, no. Poor George.'

'What will you do about . . . .?'

Lynda looked round the group of guests and called to Kathleen Kelly. Kath, a pretty, capable young woman in her thirties, had known Lynda since she was born – literally as Kath had been the trainee midwife who had assisted at her birth. Kath had become Lynda's mother's closest friend, and her husband, Bernard, had sometimes played the piano at the Black Bull on Saturday nights. Bernard had been Lynda's first choice to give her away but he had been going back to Galway for his mother's seventieth birthday.

'Kath, is Bernie back from Ireland yet?'

'No, love, like I said, he's hoping to be here later this afternoon. Anything I can do?'

'No. Thanks, love.'

Madge hesitated, but there was no other answer. 'Lynda I'm your next of kin. I'll have to do it.'

'Oh, no,' Alice Smith clasped her hands to her small bosom in horror, 'That won't look right. It should be a man. What a shame your Terry . . . .'

'Yes, I know.' Madge snapped at the tactless little woman.

Geoff, who'd been asked to let the groom and best man know when the bride arrived, saw Madge looking agitated. 'What's up?'

Alice answered eagerly, 'There's nobody to give Lynda away. Madge says she's going to do it, but it really should be a man, shouldn't it?'

Geoff instinctively offered to help. 'I'll do it. If you'd like me to, Lynda, Mrs Collins?'

Madge hesitated, but Geoff Heywood, standing there in his best suit, had always been a good man. And this was a wedding, and she wanted it to be right and proper. Madge made the decision. 'Yes. Thank you. That's all right with you, isn't it, Lynda?'

It wasn't, but Lynda saw her Grandma needed help and there was, in any case, no time to think or argue. The registrar had been reluctant to fit another wedding ceremony into his busy summer schedule and 11.45 that day had been a compromise hard won by a persistent Madge and Lynda.

'O.K. Come on, we'd better get inside,' Lynda urged, 'it's nearly time.'

It was seventeen minutes past eleven by Graham Laycock's watch as he rapped loudly at the door of 17 Stanhope Avenue. Sheila didn't want to answer the door, she didn't want anyone to see she'd been crying, but the caller was obviously not going to go away.

'Graham? What are you doing here? You should be at the wedding.'

'So should you,' Graham retorted, marching into the house past Sheila who was too stunned to reply. She admired her son-in-law and was aware that, although he presented a calm, mild-mannered persona he was a man who knew what was right. What she didn't fully realise was that nothing and no-one could move him once he had made a carefully considered and, to him, rational decision. He had made such a decision today. Standing in the hallway, he spoke slowly and formally, as if reprimanding a wayward but valued bank customer.

'I have come to take you to your son's wedding.'

'No. I have no wish to see him marry that awful girl.'

'You cannot win, Sheila. You cannot prevent this marriage, it is taking place,' he looked at his watch again, 'very soon. I have always thought you a sensible woman, Sheila, and I have great respect for you, but you will lose my good opinion for ever if you do not come with me now.'

'John doesn't want me there.'

'You know that's not true. But what you don't seem to realise is that you could lose him for ever, if you do not go to his wedding. Believe me, Sheila, I know about such situations. I have friends who are solicitors who have seen families torn apart, and people dying without forgiveness, and all because of too much pride, and too little willingness to compromise. I always thought you valued your family, that it was the centre of your world.'

'It is.'

'Then why are you about to destroy it?' His tone was even firmer now, his eyes forbade any argument. 'Come with me, now.'

Sheila Stanworth uttered a sigh which sounded like exasperation, but was in fact relief. She looked with gratitude at this man who was forcing her to change her mind, and simpered.

'I can't go like this. Oh, what shall I wear?'

Graham Laycock, thinking of the outfit Sylvia had described as 'lying in wait, ready to spring out on the world' in Sheila's wardrobe, found it very difficult not to smile. 'I'm sure you'll find something suitable.'

The room used for wedding ceremonies at the registry office was cold and funereal in atmosphere. Its oak panelled walls and thickly carved, ugly furniture offered no sense of welcome, and certainly no comfort. The dark brocade curtains were so heavily draped that they seemed designed to defend the room against any sunshine which might attempt to infiltrate the proceedings.

Lynda felt all the excitement crushed out of her as soon as she entered and saw the short rows of people perched awkwardly on the straight-backed wooden chairs. There were only twenty or so friends and family members there, and because most of them knew about Sheila's opposition to the marriage there seemed to Lynda to be an air of uncertainty in the place.

Then John turned to look at her, and the amazement and joy on his face made her smile and look even more beautiful. Geoff Heywood held out his arm, Jean bent down and fussed over the arrangement of the small satin train and the slightly limp veil which Mrs Talbot had not quite managed to restore to its earlier glory, and the bride commenced her walk down the aisle.

It was only a few yards, hardly what you could call a procession, Lynda thought to herself, regretting now that she had refused to be married in a church. It was all so unromantic: no proud organ music, no choir singing joyously, just the disinterested voice of the registrar who shuffled papers, and made it obvious that to him this was just another boring task to be carried out. Until he came to the demand that anyone who objected to this marriage should step forward.

The guests, as usual at this moment, held their breath and in that silence the heavy oak door was thrust open and Sheila Stanworth made her entrance. She paused, enjoying seeing everyone staring at her, obviously open-mouthed in admiration of her gold lacquered straw hat and lilac and gold dress and jacket. Graham Laycock only saw horror and apprehension in the faces turned towards them, and quickly propelled Sheila forward towards the seats he knew Sylvia had reserved for them.

Before she sat down, Sheila looked at her son and smiled as if nothing had ever been amiss. She was gratified to see his relief, and joy. Lynda saw it, too, and sought to share a little of this implicit approval from her future mother-in-law, but received only a condescending nod, which Sheila then repeated for the benefit of the registrar, to give him permission to proceed.

'Who gives this woman's hand in marriage?'

'I do.'

Geoff Heywood stepped forward, holding Lynda's hand, and then froze as he saw the expression in his son's eyes. Geoff cursed himself for not realising that what he'd volunteered to do, was to give the woman his son was still in love with, to the wrong man.

In the gaudily decorated upstairs room of the Red Lion he took Daniel into a quiet corner and apologised.

'It's all right, Dad. It's not your fault. We both know who . . . .'

'Yes, but . . . .'

'Don't worry, Dad. I'll get over it,' Dan said, knowing he was lying.

'You'll meet someone else.'

'Yes, plenty of pretty girls in London. I'll be away from here soon.' Dan had already left his suitcase at the station and was booked on the train back to London later that afternoon. He wanted to get away from this painful occasion as soon as possible.

The staff at the Red Lion had assumed that, although this was a buffet reception, there would still be a requirement for a 'top table' for the happy couple and the most important guests. The wedding, however, had caused so many arguments that many of the details about arrangements had not been fully discussed, and so there was a lot of awkward shuffling as 'the V.I.Ps', or at least the ones who didn't want to sit next to Sheila Stanworth, took their seats at the top table.

Sheila who, in spite of her declaration that she would not be at the wedding, had assumed the role of director of the formalities, and had insisted that there should be speeches. And so, when everyone had helped themselves to trifle or Geoff Heywood's famous chocolate cake, Ted stood up, and was ignored until Sheila tapped briskly on a glass with her spoon. He cleared his throat, clutched at the sweaty piece of paper and tried to speak slowly.

'First of all I'd like to thank you all for coming, and to thank everyone who has contributed to this wonderful celebration. On the catering front that includes Freda Wilson and Geoff Heywood – and,' he peered at the hastily scribbled insertion in the speech, 'of course Geoff made an extra contribution at the registry office.'

Having had to go off-script to include Geoff's last minute starring role, Ted lost his nerve and his place on the scrumpled piece of paper he was relying on. 'Anyway, thank you for a lovely spread.'

A heavy sigh from Sheila told him he wasn't doing a great job, and he hurried on to the final part of his 'as short as possible' speech.

'My son John, sorry, our son, John, is a very lucky man to have found himself such a beautiful bride.' Without looking, he knew that his wife would be studying the remains of the chocolate cake and cream on her plate, and was relieved when there were shouts of applause from a section of the guests, led by Kathleen Kelly.

'And I'd like you to join me in wishing them every happiness in the future.' He raised his glass, 'The bride and groom. John and Lynda.'

John stood up to acknowledge the applause and cheers, and forgot every word of the speech he had prepared with such difficulty, and also forgot a copy was in his pocket.

'Thank you. Thank you, Dad, and thanks for coming, everybody. I've never made a speech before, so I hope you don't mind if I keep this short and sweet. Like I said, thank you.'

'Presents.' Lynda whispered.

'Yeah. Thank you for all your presents. We hope we'll have a house to put them in one day. We're going to save up hard for furniture, table and chairs and that . . .'

'And a bed!' shouted one of his workmates, who had drunk enough to let his mind revert to his usual main preoccupation. Sheila began to examine and trace with her finger the fine threads of the white linen tablecloth. John, looking embarrassed and proud at the same time, turned to adore his bride.

'And I'll finish now, but first I want to say the biggest thank you, to my beautiful wife for, having me.' He sat down but Lynda whispered to him again and half standing he added. 'And thank you to our lovely bridesmaid, Jean.'

Jean smiled shyly and tried to believe that at least some of the applause was for her.

Dan had not wanted to make a speech but knew that as best man it was his duty. He began by making a fuss of Jean Clayton, who he knew was in as much pain as he was.

'I'd also like to say a few words about Jean. Lynda chose her as her bridesmaid not just because she knew she'd look lovely, but also because Jean is her best friend. And that is why John chose me as his best man, because I was, am, his best friend.

We've been friends since we were at junior school together and he thumped a bully for picking on me and calling me a softie. He's looked after me ever since, and shown me how to be 'one of the lads' climbing trees and pinching apples, and doing all sorts of other things that lads don't want their mothers to know about.'

He shyly acknowledged the laughter, and then took a deep breath as he turned towards the bride and groom, and looked steadily at Lynda.

'I'm ashamed to admit that that bully was right about me, I am a softie, I've been a coward, not found the courage to stand up for myself, for what I wanted, even when my future happiness was at stake.' He paused for a moment as his eyes met Lynda's and were filled with the regret he knew would never leave him. Then he became aware of the silence in his audience and steadied his voice.

'So, John knows I'm a coward. But the important thing is, John knows not only that, he knows all my faults, and he still likes me and wants me to be his friend. That's worth a lot, somebody knowing your faults and weaknesses, and still sticking with you.'

Dan paused to take a deep breath, he was realising as he said these words that they really were true and that, although he hated John for taking Lynda, that didn't stop him loving him.

'I don't know why John decided to be my friend and look after me that day at school and ever since, but I'm very glad he did. We've had our differences, and hurt each other sometimes, but I hope that, come what may, he will always be my friend. Because I know I will always be his, and I'll always be proud to be his friend, like I'm proud to be his best man today.'

There was another silence, followed by a slow ripple of applause. John walked over to Dan and shook his hand. 'Thanks, mate, thanks a lot.'

'I have to go now, John. Got a train to catch.' Not daring to pause and wave to anyone Dan fled out of the room, out into the street, and into a dark alleyway where he could hide for a moment or two and shed his tears.

Jean had felt every word of Dan's speech, but she worked very hard at looking happy all through the reception. She concentrated on pleasures such as the plentiful food and the compliments about her dress. And in the end she found herself enjoying the party. Everyone did – even Sheila Stanworth who, with her son-in-law keeping an eye on her, was gracious to all the guests who dared approach her. She almost joined in the singing when Bernie, who arrived just in time to drink a swift pint of beer before starting to play well-loved songs.

Lynda was having such a good time she was almost reluctant to leave to catch the three o'clock train to Blackpool. As she and John were about to go, Kath took hold of her arm and gave a little wave to Bernie who started to play 'You Must Have Been a Beautiful Baby'. All the guests began to sing joyously and Kath pulled Lynda close to her.

'You'll remember this, darlin'. Your mother singing her heart out on a Saturday night at the pub.'

'Yeah, it was one of her favourites.'

'That's because she was very proud of her beautiful daughter. She would have been so proud today. And she would have wanted you to be happy. So you make sure you have a happy life, Lynda. Promise.'

'I promise,' Lynda said, with tears in her eyes.

The only reason they could have their three night honeymoon in Blackpool was that Madge Collins had paid for it. She and Alfred hadn't been able to afford a honeymoon of any kind and it had always been a regret. Madge had raided her savings for her granddaughter and her bridegroom and she had done them proud. The boarding house her friend had recommended was small but smartly painted in white and Wedgewood Blue. And the landlady had a broad smile and an equally broad mind. She fluttered her eyelashes at John as she took his hand, and then winked at Lynda.

'Mrs Simpson. Not that one. Haven't got the Prince, or the jewellery either. But I have got a divorce. Don't mind, do you?'

Lynda smiled at her. 'Not if you don't'.

'Do I hell! I had a party when the decree nisi came through.' She rested her hand on Lynda's shoulder, 'Not something to think about on your honeymoon, though – give yourselves a couple of weeks, or at least a couple of nights! Mind you, one night was enough for me – should have done a runner straight away!'

Lynda liked this woman. There'd be no embarrassment here. As if reading minds was another of her attributes Mary Simpson continued,

'You're in the best room, over the lounge, but don't worry, we'll have the tele turned up loud.

Their bedroom had a bay window with a view of the sea. John stood behind his wife and clasped his arms around her as she stood gazing at the sunlight on the waves. She turned and kissed him and then led him towards the bed.

'What are you doing?'

'There's no rule says we have to wait till tonight, John, is there?'

The next morning Lynda slid out of bed at six o'clock, paused to look at John and tried to recognise this man who was now truly her husband. He looked different somehow, no longer the John whose image had filled her imagination whenever they had been apart, but something of a stranger. She shook her head and told herself not to be so stupid because they were closer now than ever. Or should be.

She slipped on the dress and cardigan she'd placed on the chair the night before and then quietly let herself out of the house. Taking in a deep breath of cool sea air she ran across the road and down on to the silent beach. The sea was calmly and forcefully pushing its way back towards the sea-wall, but there was still a broad, unblemished stretch of smooth sand glinting in the early morning sun. Lynda took off her sandals, thrilled at the touch of the sand under her feet, and ran towards a shallow oval of sea-water waiting to be reclaimed by the tide. She hitched her dress up into her pants and splashed through the water. Then she paddled along the edge of the sea itself, feeling the tugging of the waves and breathing in freedom as she gazed at the horizon and let herself be held in a thought-free stillness.

Later, when a dog barked at the joy of skittering across the sand, Lynda looked round and reluctantly turned to walk back towards the promenade. Glancing back at the sea, she thought for a moment of some of the dreams she'd been holding on to, and calmly let them go. Life with John Stanworth wouldn't be like in the films, she realised that now, but it would be good. They'd have lots fun and lots of loving, and a home of their own – soon.

CHAPTER EIGHT

Coming back to Milfield after their honeymoon, Lynda was dreading moving into the Stanworths' house, but she'd had to realise that they didn't have a choice. Sheila's house was, of necessity, where they were going to live, but it was never going to be Lynda's home.

'I've ironed your shirt ready for tomorrow, John.' That was Sheila, straight into the practicalities as soon as they walked through the door, and not even looking at Lynda.

'Oh. Thanks, Mum.'

'Nice to see you.' Lynda tried to stop herself sounding sardonic; she'd promised John she would try very hard to get on with his Mother.

'Aren't you going to ask them if they've had a good time?'

Lynda winked at Ted. 'Of course we had a good time. We were on our honeymoon.'

Sheila looked as if she was going to be sick. John, bright red, picked up their suitcase again. 'I'll take this up out of the way.'

'As you know, Sylvia said you could have her room. So I've moved the rest of her things into the little bedroom.'

Years ago Ted and Sheila had made the attic into a bedroom for their daughter, but it wasn't very large. 'It'll be a bit of a tight squeeze for you, Sylvia's is only a three-quarter bed.'

Sheila glared at her husband who had wanted to buy the couple a double bed as a wedding present. 'Beggars can't be choosers.'

Ted frowned and headed for the kitchen. 'You'll be ready for a cup of tea.'

Lynda took hold of his arm and gave him a peck on the cheek. 'Sit down, Dad, I'll make it.'

Sheila immediately pushed past her to defend her territory. 'You stay where you are. I'll make the tea.'

Sheila went to bed early that night, complaining of a headache, and making sure Ted would be the one to lock the front and back doors. John and Lynda stayed up to have a chat to Ted, and to tell him the jokes they'd remembered from the comedian at The North Pier show. Then they went to bed, leaving Ted sitting by the final glow of the fire, and trying to remember what it was like to be young and happily married.

The bed inevitably creaked a bit under the weight of the loving couple. 'Your Dad was right', Lynda whispered, 'it is a bit of a squeeze. But I don't mind,' she giggled, snuggling her body as close to John's as she could. He kissed her, and wished that his Mother wasn't in the bedroom below theirs.

Duncan Wilson called in at the café on his way to work because he knew his mother would be there, and he wanted to show her he was capable of taking charge of the café, and Lynda. Freda had reduced the time she spent at the café, but she still liked to work there on Tuesday mornings, even though she knew Lynda didn't need her help. It didn't suit her to retire just yet, she told everyone, she preferred to be in the land of the living.

When Geoff Heywood arrived with the bread Freda was in the back kitchen and Duncan was needlessly re-arranging the salt and pepper pots, and bottles of Heinz Tomato Ketchup and HP sauce on the slightly rickety shelf at the side of the counter. He was also appreciating the extra view of Lynda's legs as she bent over to give an extra polish to the tops of the tables.

'Morning, Duncan, Lynda. A dozen extra finger rolls wasn't it?'

'Who ordered those?'

'I did. Your Mother said I could. Thanks, Mr Heywood. How are you doing?'

'Very well. All these people following your lead and having a summer wedding makes for good business.'

Duncan grunted. 'Summer doesn't do us much good here. I think we should start closing early, you don't get many customers in the afternoons.'

'We would if we got a freezer and started selling ice-cream like I said, and put some tables outside.'

'Huh! These young girls are good at spending other people's money, aren't they Mr Heywood?'

'Sounds like money well spent to me. If it was my café, I'd do what Lynda suggested, and pay her a bonus for her ideas.'

Lynda held out her hand. 'Yes, please, Mr Wilson!'

'You're lucky I'm still employing you, never mind paying you extra. If I had my way I'd get rid of this place.'

'Would you now?' Freda Wilson had walked in just in time to hear her son's peevish remark. 'You'll have to wait a bit for a chance to do that. We old people are awkward beggars, we live too long, Geoff, that's the trouble.'

'You carry on being awkward, Freda. And I'll carry on selling cakes! See you later!'

Duncan, his face a little red from the effort which quick thinking always cost him, opened the door and followed Geoff Heywood as he left.

'I'll see you later in the week, Mother. Mr Heywood, could I have a word?'

Freda watched him hurry away and sighed. 'I wonder what that'll be about. Best not to know, perhaps. I'll put this bread away, Lynda, while you nip over to the market and get the salad stuff you need. You're doing really well with those new sandwich ideas. Did you order the extra finger rolls for them?'

'Yes, Mrs Wilson, they're here. I won't be long. Can I help you with the cottage pies when I get back? You said you'd show me how you make them.'

'Yes, I will. I'll just fry the onions and let you do the rest.'

Lynda loved working at the café, and was resisting Sheila's attempts to push her into getting a better paid but mindless assembly-line job at a local factory. She loved being with the customers, and also envisaged that one day she could be allowed to manage the café on her own, with the appropriate increase in her wages. Freda was already quietly training her for the job, sending her to buy from suppliers and now letting her learn her recipes.

Lynda was very fond of Freda, who was a good friend to her Grandma. Freda had started inviting Madge to have lunch with her at the café on Tuesdays before taking her along to the beetle drive at St Mary's church hall. Madge arrived towards the end of the lunch-time rush, and Freda always made sure there were two portions of the hot dish of the day set aside for them.

'That were grand,' Madge sighed as she put down her knife and fork.

'Your Lynda made it.'

'Did she? Hey, our Lynda, that cottage pie was lovely.'

'Thanks, Grandma. Mrs Wilson showed me how she makes it this morning.'

'You'll do well if you can learn to cook like Freda, everyone knows her stuff's special.'

'I know, I'm hoping you'll teach me some more of your recipes, Mrs Wilson.'

'It'll be a pleasure. She's a quick learner, Madge.'

'I know, but you've got to have somebody good to learn from. I can cook well enough to eat, and so could Lynda's Mother, but we were neither of us the best cooks in the world.'

'Does John's Mother let you cook?' Freda enquired

'In her kitchen – no chance! I'm only allowed to skivvy, you know, peel potatoes and wash up, and woe betide me if I put something away in the wrong place.'

'She likes being Queen Bee too much, does Sheila Stanworth,' grumbled Madge as she watched her grand-daughter clearing the tables. 'She's got some good recipes, but she won't teach them to our Lynda.'

'Well, I'll teach her all of mine. I haven't got a daughter, so it'd be nice to have some other woman to pass them on to.'

'That'd be marvellous training for our Lynda. People always need feeding.'

'That's what I try to tell Duncan about this café, but he's not interested. He wants me to sell it and give him the money to put into this holiday camp his friend's setting up.'

Lynda put down the pile of plates she was carrying. 'Oh, you're not going to sell the café, are you, Mrs Wilson?'

'No, but I'll need somebody to run it for me soon. That's why I want to teach you.'

Madge clapped her hands with pleasure. 'Ooh! That'd be marvellous, Freda. What do you think, Lynda?'

'I'd love to.'

Freda smiled. 'Have you thought about going to night school to study book-keeping? Then you could learn about the money side of running a business as well.'

'That's a good idea. She's got the brains for it. How much does it cost to go?'

'Not a lot. I can lend you the money if you like, Lynda.'

'Yes, please. Thank you very much, Mrs Wilson.'

'I can't guarantee you'll get to run the café after I've gone, though, love. Our Duncan will do what he wants then, but don't worry, I'm not going anywhere yet, God willing. Now, what shall we have for afters, Madge, a nice cream cake?'

There was a knock at the door as Lynda was sweeping the floor after she'd closed the café for the afternoon. She looked up to see the cheery face of Kath Kelly and hurried to open the door.

'How are you, Kath?'

'Fine. How are you, Mrs Stanworth?'

Lynda blushed with pleasure at the 'Mrs'. 'All right, thanks.'

'And how's married life? Enjoying sharing a bed at last?' Kath was a vivacious Irish woman from a large, irreverent family and no topic was out of bounds as far as she was concerned.

'Yes, but . . .'

'You wish you weren't living in his Mother's house. I expect Sheila's got a list of rules for you.'

Lynda recognised that Kath was what she desperately needed, a broadminded friend she could confide in, and seized the chance to talk to Kath woman to woman.

'She seems to make up a new rule every day. I can't seem to do anything right. Yesterday she played hell with me for hanging my stockings up to dry overnight in the bathroom. And she took my knickers - sorry, 'undergarments' - off the washing line because the neighbours might see them.'

Kath laughed out loud. 'Oh, my goodness, the shame of it! And I expect you get a dirty look if she's heard the bedsprings creaking the night before.'

'Worse than that, she made Ted have a word with us, letting us know that they can hear everything that goes on in our bedroom. I don't know who was the most embarrassed, poor Ted or me and John. Honest, Kath, she's trying to put an end to us being married.'

'Well, she won't succeed. John's crazy about you.'

'He used to be. But now he makes love like he's frightened his Mother might walk in and see us. We're desperate to move out and be on our own.'

'Well, I can't help with the moving out bit, but I can offer you and John a bit of time on your own on a roomy sofa that doesn't creak. I've come to ask a favour, would you babysit for me and Bernard on Saturday night?'

'Oh, yes. John's Dad's going to be away this weekend, it'd be murder staying in with just Sheila and we can't afford to go out.

'It's a silver wedding party for some old friends of ours. We might be late, you know what it's like when they get Bernard playing the piano for a sing-song. Our Kevin's staying round at his friend's, so it'll just be Jenny and she never wakes up once she's had a story and gone to sleep.

'It'll be a treat for us, especially with a television to watch as well.'

'Is there no tele at the Stanworths' house?'

'No, Ted's trying to persuade Sheila they should get one but she listens to Ellen Heywood who thinks television stops you reading books and having good conversation.'

'Well, I love my tele, and I've nothing against conversation, as you know!'

'You wouldn't like the sort we have with her. They always seem to end on the subject of what an ignorant girl I am. And I'm beginning to realise she might be right about that.'

'Now then, don't you start thinking like that, or she'll grind you down till you've no confidence to stand up to her. I've known a few people like her who like to criticise and be right all the time, and they're bloody dangerous!'

'They're no fun to live with, I know that. What time do you want us on Saturday?'

'Is seven O.K?'

'Yeah. Oh, it'll be a novelty to sit and have a cuddle on a sofa without getting dirty looks if you so much as hold hands.'

'Well, don't worry about me and Bernie, we'll make a lot of noise before we walk in on you! See you on Saturday.'

As Lynda stood at the door and waved goodbye to Kath, she spotted Jean on her way back from the market, struggling with bags full of the weekend meat and vegetables which the stall holders sold off cheaply on Tuesday afternoons to make room for fresh stock.

'Jean! Are you coming for a cuppa?'

Lynda couldn't believe it when she saw Jean glance her way and then walk off in the opposite direction, pretending she hadn't seen her.

'Jean!' she shouted louder this time and ran across to her.

'Oh, hello, Lynda. How are you?'

'I haven't seen you since the wedding. Where have you been hiding?'

'I haven't been hiding.'

Lynda ignored the sullen, defensive look on Jean's face and took a couple of her bags from her. 'Come on, let's sit down and have a natter.'

'I've got to get home with the shopping.'

'They can wait ten minutes.'

She opened the door of the café and put the bags in a corner. 'Come on, there's two cream cakes left and I can make you a cup of tea, or coffee. Or a milkshake. I got Freda to buy a machine to make milkshakes. What flavour do you want?'

'Have you got raspberry?' Jean was looking happier now. Lynda always made her feel as if she was somebody.

'Yeah. I'll make us both one and we'll take a couple of chairs out and sit in the sunshine. Mrs Wilson won't mind.'

For Jean it was like a day at the seaside, sitting in front of the café with Lynda. She even took off her cardigan and stretched out her arms to receive the blessing of the late afternoon sun. She let Lynda lead the conversation and tried not to look miserable while listening to the description of the good time in Blackpool, and how John had won a cuddly toy rabbit for his wife on the rifle range at the Pleasure Beach. Jean didn't want to talk about John, she was still mourning the loss of something she'd never had. In the end, though, she couldn't resist asking.

'What's it like then, being married?'

'It'll be better when we've got a place of our own.'

Jean's envy made her angry. 'Oh, you're never satisfied, you! You got to marry John Stanworth, didn't you? You should be saying how wonderful it is.'

'It is wonderful.'

'You don't sound very convinced. Is that all you've got to say?'

'Yes.'

Lynda looked at the girl who was supposed to be her best friend, and suddenly felt sad as she realised that her friendship with Jean now had its limits. They had moved on from being two young girls who shared all the secrets of teenage dreams. Lynda was a married woman and she couldn't talk to Jean like she could to Kath Kelly.

She tried again. 'Anyway, never mind about me, are you going out with anybody?'

'I've had offers. I went to the Carlton with Christine Pollard last Saturday, and we met these two lads but I didn't really fancy mine. He had really sweaty hands.'

Lynda laughed. 'Oh, and did he have wispy brown hair and crooked teeth?'

'Yeah. How did you know?'

'I danced with him once, don't you remember? And once was enough.'

'Oh, yeah.'

'You'll meet somebody one day.'

'Gordon Haworth asked me to dance again.'

'He's too old for you.'

'I know, but he is a gentleman.'

'His Mother runs that good dress stall in the market hall. Freda knows her and says she's desperate for him to get married and give her grandchildren.'

'I've seen her, she's a nice woman.'

'Yeah, she'd make a good mother-in-law. But it'd be Gordon you'd be marrying, and he's thirty if he's a day!'

'He's not. And talking about mothers-in-law, has Sheila Stanworth changed her mind about you, now that you and John are married?'

'No. You'd think she was royalty the way she looks down on me, but Ted told me her Dad was only a clerk at the Co-op - 'the only person the manager would trust with the takings' according to her.'

'She and Ted have done all right, though, at least they've got their own house.'

'And a mortgage. Which we're paying now, I reckon. She takes most of John's wages from him, you know. She'd take mine as well, if I'd let her. I'm saving every penny I can, well most of it. I want to rent somewhere but John says we should save up for our own place. That'll take years!'

'I'd give anything to have my own house.'

'Get yourself a rich husband, Jean. But one without a mother-in-law like Sheila attached.'

'She'll get used to you.'

'No. She's made it quite clear I'm just not good enough for her precious son, and never will be. But don't you worry, Jean, I'll show her.'

Lynda grinned at Jean and tried to look confident.

Sheila Stanworth had a set menu for every day of the week, and on Fridays it was haddock and mashed potato with parsley sauce. Lynda couldn't stand the thick floury green-speckled slime and had, several times, requested a lump of butter on her potatoes instead, but Sheila seemed incapable of dishing up the meal without the sauce. Lynda also couldn't stand the silences that lent an air of tension to so many of the mealtimes, and tonight Sheila was still sulking about John insisting on going babysitting with Lynda.

'So I'll be in on my own on Saturday night.'

'You said you were going over to Sylvia's, you could stay there till the evening,' John suggested.

'She and Graham are going out for a meal apparently. And I expect your Father will be having a nice meal out in Lytham or Blackpool. So it will be just me not having a good time.'

As usual, Lynda stepped in to defend her father-in-law. 'I expect you'll be on duty all the time, Ted, carrying Henry Morton's golf clubs round and that, as well as driving. It won't exactly be a holiday for you, will it?'

'No.'

'Well, I wish I was going to Lytham St Anne's. I've never been, you know. You should've asked Henry if I could come.'

'The wives aren't invited. It's a blokes weekend. And it's partly business.'

'I haven't been there either,' Lynda said cheekily, 'Perhaps Mr Morton would let you take me sometime. I could sit in the back with him, make him look good. Everybody'd think he had a floozy.'

'Lynda, stop it.' John urged, seeing his mother looking even more irritated.

Ted, knowing very well that Henry Morton already had what Lynda called 'a floozy', and that she was the real reason for this weekend away, felt his face redden.

Sheila was really in the mood for a moan now. 'You should have told him you were busy. He's no right to ask you to work weekends. And staying overnight as well, that's your whole weekend taken up!'

'It's my job, Sheila, it's what he pays me for.'

'He doesn't pay you enough for you to be at his beck and call at weekends as well as during the week.'

Lynda could see that Ted was feeling really uncomfortable, and waded in to support him. 'You go and enjoy a bit of sea air, Ted, we're only jealous.'

John tried to cheer up his Mother. 'You'll enjoy going shopping with Sylvia, Mum. And you said you were going to visit Uncle Freddie on Sunday.'

'There's no pleasure in that, visiting an old man in a nursing home.'

'He's always very grateful for your visits,' Ted reminded her. Sheila gave him a sharp look, not wanting him to reveal that uncle Freddie always made sure that she came back home with extra money in her purse.

Ted was keen to talk about something less risky than his weekend away, and so passed on Lynda's good news of the day.

'Did Lynda tell you she's going to do some studying, Sheila? She's going to go to night school to learn book-keeping.'

'Is she? And who's going to pay for that?'

'I've been saving up, and Mrs Wilson's offered to lend me the fees if need be.'

'Neither a borrower nor a lender be.' Sheila always had an adage handy to take the joy out of anything.

'It'll be two nights a week, after work, but she wants to do it,' John added.

Sheila was pleased at the prospect of not having Lynda cluttering up her house in the evenings, but didn't let it show. Instead she commented, 'Well, it would be a better use of your money than buying make-up and cigarettes.'

Sheila stood up and looked pointedly at the sluggish pool of parsley sauce at the side of Lynda's plate. 'Have you finished?'

'Yes.' Lynda had had enough of Sheila for one mealtime. 'I'll wash up, shall I?'

Sheila sat down again and watched Lynda collect the plates and take them into the kitchen.

'There's cake yet,' John called after her.

'I'll have mine later' she told him as she escaped into 'skivvy corner'.

When Geoff Heywood arrived back home after finishing his Saturday deliveries he found Richard in the garden laughing and shouting with a couple of school-friends. They had an air rifle and were shooting at magpies. Geoff ran towards them.

'What do you think you're doing?' he shouted.

'Target practice, Daddy.'

'Shooting at birds?'

'We got one, Mr Heywood,' James Hanford told him proudly. 'Over there, look.'

He pointed at the gleaming feathered creature lying on the ground.

'Give me that gun!'

'It's James's.'

'Well, he can go home and take his gun with him. Don't you know it's wrong to kill living creatures?'

'They're only magpies, Daddy,' Richard argued indignantly, 'you said you didn't like magpies.'

'I don't, but that doesn't mean we've a right to shoot them.'

'My father shoots grouse.' James said, looking with disdain at Geoff in his brown cotton coat daubed with flour and icing sugar.

'And so did mine.' Ellen, having heard Geoff's voice, joined them. 'It's a gentleman's sport, Geoffrey, and one which Richard may well take up one day.'

'Over my dead body.'

'Don't be overly dramatic, and do go and change out of those work clothes. What will these boys think?'

'That I have a business to run.' Geoff snapped, and, wondering yet again why he had ever thought he could be happy with Ellen Buchanan, he turned and marched into the house.

Richard, who, like his maternal grandfather, had an instinct for playing people one against the other, took advantage of his mother's irritation with Geoff.

'Could I have an air rifle for my birthday, Mummy? All our friends have them, don't they, James?'

'Yes.' James backed up his friend. 'Daddy says he'll take me up to Scotland when I'm a good enough shot. Perhaps Richard could come with us. His grandfather came from Scotland, didn't he?'

Ellen blinked for a moment. The thought of the loss of her father still caused a sharp pain in her heart.

'Indeed he did. Now, there's a rather good cake in the kitchen, would you boys like some?'

Having obediently washed their hands, the boys eagerly followed their hostess into the kitchen but hesitated when they saw that Geoff, having taken off his cotton coat, had seated himself at the kitchen table and was consoling himself with a piece of his famous chocolate cake and a cup of coffee. Never one to inflict his unhappiness on others, he stood up to welcome the boys and cut them large slices of cake while his wife poured them glasses of lemonade.

'Were they pleased with the wedding cake?' Ellen enquired of her husband. She didn't want Richard's friends to take home to their parents any impression of there being conflict in the Heywood household.

'Yes, delighted. Alice had decorated it just as they'd wanted.'

'Heywood's have an excellent reputation for wedding cakes,' Ellen explained to the boys.

'Yes, I know,' the other boy, Christopher, piped up, 'my sister has ordered her wedding cake from you, hasn't she, Mr Heywood?'

When Geoff didn't immediately remember, Ellen explained, 'Mrs Farrar will have ordered it.'

'Oh, yes.'

Geoff was aware that his business benefited from Ellen's social contacts with the mothers at Richard's school, but he would still have preferred his son to have gone to the local school, instead of the private, privileged establishment his wife and her father had insisted he attend.

'I saw Lynda Collins, this morning,' he said, aware, that mentioning the girl's name would annoy Ellen. 'She's doing very well at Freda Wilson's café. Got some good ideas.'

'Girls like her always 'have ideas'. As we well know. And it's Lynda Stanworth now.'

'Who's Lynda Stanworth?' asked Richard, turning away from his friends' banter as he caught the undertone of his parents' conversation and decided, therefore, to listen.

'No-one,' Ellen replied.

'Yet,' Geoff muttered under his breath as he stood up. Geoff Heywood was beginning to form a plan. Secretly making plans of which he knew his wife would not approve, was his way of quietly revenging himself for her habitual disdain, and her domination of their household. 'Good afternoon, gentlemen,' he said with a touch of irony as he left the kitchen.

Cora Dexter, wearing a low-cut, tight-fitting turquoise dress and enough jewellery to let everyone know she had money, was standing at the entrance of her hotel on the outskirts of Lytham St Anne's, greeting a party of golfers. The hotel had proved a good investment for Cora and her late husband, and was now still providing her with a very good life.

She looked up and gave a coquettish little wave as Henry Morton's Bentley drove slowly past on the way to its usual parking spot. A couple of the golfers smirked at each other and raised knowing eyebrows, but a sharp glance from their hostess summoned them back into the required discretion which ensured everyone's enjoyment of their weekend away.

'I'll take my case, Ted. You just take my stuff to the club house, and I'll see you tomorrow evening, about seven, eh?'

'O.K. Mr Morton.'

Ted handed over the car keys and Henry Morton gave him a small brown envelope.

'Here's the money for your bed and board, and a bit extra, so we can both have a good time, eh?'

'Thank you very much. You've got that phone number, if you need me.'

'Yes, I think so,' Henry answered absent-mindedly, as he hurried away towards the hotel entrance. Ted watched the porter approach Henry immediately to take his suitcase, and the group of golfers move aside to let him greet his hostess warmly.

Ted took the tram to Blackpool, got off at the South Pier and walked away from the promenade and up the road towards the scalloped green awning and red and white gingham tablecloths of Rose's Café. As usual there were plenty of customers both inside the café and, as it was warm and sunny, sitting at the tables outside. At this time of day it was mostly locals who gathered there for a cup of tea and a chat, mothers with toddlers seeking ice creams and babies in pushchairs, and older people who came mostly for the company, but who still were a steady source of income.

Rose Milner, a cuddly woman in her fifties, brushed aside the soft brown curls being played with by the gentle breeze, and looked up from the solicitous conversation she was having with one of her more elderly regular customers. She saw Ted approaching with his small brown suitcase and smiled but didn't wave. He smiled at her and walked round the corner to the back of the café where there were two green painted doors. One led into the rear of the café, the other, flanked by large pots of red geraniums, was the private entrance to the owner's little house. Ted stood by the geraniums, took his key out of his pocket and let himself in with a sigh of long-awaited happiness.

Ted Stanworth had seen the necessity of John and Lynda moving in with him and Sheila, but he had also seen the opportunity which their presence might provide. Ever since he had met Rose Milner two years ago, he had dreamed of packing his bags and leaving the unhappiness of his marriage and the house which wasn't the home he wanted. But Ted hadn't a heart that would let him leave his wife on her own, and when Sylvia had left to get married he had panicked, realising that before too long he would be trapped for ever in that house, on his own with the woman he was close to hating. He had no doubt that one day John and Lynda would escape from Sheila and her need to control everyone's life, but for a little while they would be there to keep her company.

He knew that now was the time to take firm steps towards his dream of sharing his life with his lovely Rose.

CHAPTER NINE

The Stanworths' Christmas tree was not very big and stood quietly in the corner of the living room. It was decorated sparsely with red and gold baubles hanging at regular intervals, five strands of gold tinsel, draped evenly across the branches. A rather dejected angel looking down from the top of the tree, which, of course, was artificial -Sheila couldn't bear the thought of pine needles persistently dropping on to the carpet. The base of the tree was wrapped in faded red crepe paper.

The dim coloured lights were switched on when visitors called, and on Christmas Day they were allowed to remain switched on from eleven o'clock in the morning until the family went to bed. In the front room the only sign of Christmas was a large red poinsettia plant in the window, and red candles in the silver-plated candelabra which Sheila had bought to add elegance to the mantelpiece.

It was Christmas Eve and Lynda had gone into Woolworth's on her way home from work because she'd heard they were selling off some of their Christmas stock. She'd bought a box of Christmas crackers and some Cadbury's chocolate Father Christmases to hang on the tree and she excitedly burst into the living room to show John her bargains.

'Look, John, chocolates for the tree. My Mum always used to get us these.'

Sheila was not impressed. 'You're not going to put those on my tree.'

'Why not?'

'They'd spoil my decoration. Anyway they're for children, and there are no children in this house.'

Never one to miss anything, Sheila saw the look which passed between John and Lynda.

'Oh, no. You're not. You can't be!'

'I'm only a month late so we don't know for sure.'

'You must try and get rid of it.'

'No, Mum, we can't do that.'

'You cannot afford to have children yet. You can't even afford your own house.'

'We'll be putting our name down for a council house. And anyway, I might not be pregnant, I've only missed one period.'

'Be quiet, we don't talk about such things in my house. We'll just have to hope it's a false alarm. And John, no son of mine is going to live in a council house and be paying rent for the rest of his life. Lynda, you can set the table. We'll use the best knives and forks as it's Christmas Eve.'

'I've bought a box of six crackers at Woolworths'.'

'I told you, Mr & Mrs Laycock said there was no need to bring anything.'

'I thought I'd put four on the table for us to have now. I'm taking the other two round to my Grandma's tomorrow.'

'When?' John asked, 'We'll be at the farm nearly all day.'

'I'm not going to the Laycocks' Christmas dinner. I know I said I would, but, I'm sorry, John, I've changed my mind, I'm going round to my Grandma's.'

Sheila didn't quite manage to stop herself looking pleased. 'I'm sure she'll be glad to have you there. We'll give your apologies to Mr and Mrs Laycock, though you should have let . . . .'

'Lynda, you should be with me on Christmas Day. I thought we'd agreed you'd see your Grandma on Boxing Day.'

'I'll be with her on Boxing Day as well. I have to, John. It's a year since . . .'

'Yeah, I know, but where do I fit in with all this? I want you to be with me at Christmas, you're my wife, Lynda.'

'I told you, I don't want my Grandma to be on her own at Christmas, or Boxing Day. Especially not this year.'

'But you said . . . .'

'I know I did, but I can't do it. I can't bear to think of her . . . .'

Sheila, trying to sound like a good Christian woman and rid herself of a small feeling of guilt, feigned innocence. 'If we hadn't been invited to the Laycocks' she could, of course, have come here.'

'No, she couldn't. I dropped several big hints about inviting her here for Christmas but you didn't want to know. You don't like my Grandma, just because she's got no money and doesn't pretend to be posh when she isn't – not like some people I could mention!'

'Lynda, shut up!'

'No, John, you shut up!'

'Hey, what's going on?' Ted asked from the doorway. 'I could hear you shouting from outside?'

'Where have you been all afternoon?' Sheila demanded. Then, spotting the extra colour in his cheeks, she leaned forward to smell his breath.

'You've been drinking!'

'Well, it is Christmas Eve. I met a couple of lads I trained, one of them is a sergeant himself now, and they wanted to buy me a pint so we called in the Red Lion. What's the row about?'

'Nothing. Just our daughter-in-law being awkward again.'

'I've decided to go to my Grandma's tomorrow.'

'And I say she should spend Christmas with me. That's only right, isn't it, Dad?'

Ted wasn't given chance to think about that, as Sheila presented the news which was her priority. 'She thinks she might be pregnant. Are you ready to be a Granddad, Ted, because I'm certainly not ready to be a Grandma.'

'Oh, hell.'

'I might not be expecting. So let's not start celebrating yet, shall we?' Lynda said but nobody heard the irony.

'Can we leave it till we know for sure, and talk about it then?' John said, desperate for the world to be less complicated for a while.

'Very well. And if Lynda wishes to spend Christmas with her grandmother instead of with us, then I think you should let her.'

Ted watched his wife, who smoothed her apron and lifted her head in a way which indicated a situation had been manipulated to her satisfaction, and enjoyed the pleasure of spoiling her victory.

'Don't worry about your Grandma, Lynda, love, she'll be with us tomorrow. I saw Graham in the Red Lion and mentioned you were bothered about Madge being on her own, and he said she was welcome to join us at his Mum and Dad's.'

Sheila objected immediately. 'Ted, what were you thinking of, putting Graham in an awkward position like that?'

'It wasn't awkward at all, he said his Mother had already asked him what Madge was doing for Christmas.'

'How will she get there?' Sheila wasn't being defeated yet.

'Graham will come and fetch John and Lynda and then go round for Madge.'

'And what about us?'

'He'll come back for us.'

'It's putting him to a lot of trouble.'

Lynda stared narrow-eyed at the mother-in-law, 'Don't worry, Sheila, my Grandma will probably not go. She's very proud, and she knows when she's not welcome.'

Ted smiled, pleased with himself.

'Oh, don't you worry, Madge is coming. I went to see her after I'd talked to Graham. She took a bit of persuading, but she's really looking forward to it now. So we'll all have a nice family Christmas together, won't we?' he said, looking at his wife, who, in the last few months had begun to sense a change in her husband's attitude towards her, and didn't like it.

On Christmas morning the sun shone through the windows of the church hall and lent sparkle to the silver paper covered stars which the Sunday school children had made for the Christmas tree in the corner of the room. There was a happy, peaceful atmosphere as the members of the congregation gathered for a festive cup of tea and a mince pie.

Ellen Heywood, as usual, wore her fur coat for this occasion and had made sure that her husband was wearing his best woollen overcoat. Alice Smith and her father, Clarence, a thin, wispy haired little man in his sixties had been the first to help themselves to the mince pies provided by the ladies of the church's unofficial catering department. When they came over to speak to Ellen, Clarence was careful to wipe away the traces of icing sugar from round his mouth, but his daughter had added another two mince pies to her plate before she followed him.

'Lovely service, wasn't it, Mrs Heywood?' said Clarence. 'Are you well?'

'Very well, thank you, Clarence.'

'All the family home for Christmas I see,' he commented, nodding towards Dan who was pretending he hadn't seen John waving at him. 'Daniel enjoying the London life, is he?'

'I think so. Although of course he's working very hard.'

'Good experience, though, he's lucky you had contacts in the hotel business.'

'Yes, a friend of my Father's.'

'Mr Buchanan's still looking after his family, then, in a way.'

'Very much so.' Ellen gave Clarence a sad smile. He had been Alistair Buchanan's tailor and, to a limited extent, confidant and she treasured any connection with her late father.

Richard, who had grown tired of standing dutifully by his mother's side and very bored with adult conversations, tugged at Ellen's sleeve. 'Can I go and get a present from under the tree now, Mummy.'

'Of course, Richard. We won't be long now, dear.'

'Growing up fast. Grammar school next year, or is he going to St. Wilfred's?'

'No, I decided against that. The Grammar school has a very good reputation.'

'And he'll be able to stay at home. Very wise, boarding school isn't for everybody.'

'No.' Ellen, who knew that her father would have wanted her to send her son away to St Wilfred's, sought to change the subject. 'Is Alice cooking your Christmas lunch?'

'We'll do it between us. Have done for the last couple of years, since . . .'

'Yes. Christmas is a time tinged with sadness for both of us, isn't it? Your losing your wife and . . .'

'And you your dear father. I still miss those little chats we used to have when he came to have his suits fitted.'

'He was taken too soon.'

'Yes, indeed. Whereas, my Ada was, I think, ready to go. She was never, what you would call an enthusiast for life, was she, your Mother, eh, Alice?'

He turned to his daughter who was just finishing the last of her mince pies and watching Daniel walking slowly towards John.

'No.' Alice agreed, and then asked the question which was first on her list.

'Glad to hear Dan is enjoying himself in London, but we miss him at the bakery. Will he be coming back for good soon?'

'I doubt it.'

'Oh, has he got a girlfriend down there then?'

Ellen did not care to admit that her son had hardly spoken to her since his return. 'Daniel is very busy. There is so much he can learn in London, culturally as well as professionally.'

'Of course.' Clarence, quick to sense Ellen's unease, gave his daughter a discreet, silencing nudge. 'He's a very lucky young man. I hope he'll not desert me and start getting his suits from Savile Row just yet. Family tradition means a lot.'

'Yes.' Ellen held out her hand to Clarence, 'Well, do have a lovely Christmas. I must go and see what gift Richard has been given.'

Dan watched his mother put her arm round her younger son's shoulders and, hoping she would wish to go home soon, turned to face John again.

'I get a room in the hotel as part of the perks.'

'You'll need it if you're working hours like that in the restaurant kitchen.'

'I like it. You know me, I've always liked cooking. And I'm working for one of the top chefs in London.'

'Are you cooking the Christmas dinner today then?'

'Yes, me and my Dad. Molly's gone to see her family in Edinburgh. What's your Mother cooking, her famous roast pork with all the trimmings and a telling off?'

John grinned at his friend as they remembered how Sheila had smelt whisky on her son's breath after a visit to Kirkwood house on Christmas morning when he and Dan had made a secret raid on the drinks cabinet.

'No, we're off to the Laycocks' place. And Lynda's Grandma's coming as well.'

'Oh, Lynda'll be pleased. What's she going to do on Boxing Day? It'll be a year since . . .'

'Yeah. Lynda wants us both to go round and see her, and we've all been invited to the Kellys' later, but my Mum wants us to stop at home. Our Sylvia and Graham are coming round for tea. I'll have to stay, even if Lynda doesn't.'

'Christmas gets complicated when you've got two families to keep happy.'

'You're not kidding.'

'Things all right at work?'

'Yeah. Not earning enough money, though.'

'I hear that Lynda's doing well at the café.' Dan had got all the news he could from Geoff, who could see he was still upset about the chance he'd missed.

'Yeah,' John replied, staring for a moment at the baby in the cardboard manger of the nativity at the far end of the hall. Sheila, walking towards them, hoped that he hadn't been confiding too much in Dan.

'Hello, Daniel. I've just been chatting to your Mother. Glad to hear that you're extremely happy in London.'

Dan was silent for a moment, realising how far from the truth that was, especially now he was back in Milfield. 'You look very well, Mrs Stanworth. And I hear you're not having to cook Christmas Dinner this year.'

'No. A big break from tradition. But I'm sure it will be very nice at the Laycocks'. We should go home now, John, I want to be ready when Graham comes to collect us.'

The Laycock family usually had their meals in the farmhouse kitchen but at Christmas they set up a dining table at one end of the large, slightly shabby, but extremely comfortable sitting room. At the other end of the room, to one side of the ancient stone fireplace with its blazingly glorious log fire, stood a very tall, wide-skirted Christmas tree which Harry dug up every year from a corner of the garden.

The tree was haphazardly festooned with baubles, angels, reindeer and Father Christmases of every size and varying degrees of dilapidation as some of them had been passed on from generation to generation and many had been made by the Laycocks' three children when very young. Tinsel and fine silver strands of lametta covered almost every branch and twinkled as they reflected the dozens of coloured lights.

Madge Collins, wearing a dark blue soft woollen dress borrowed for the occasion from Mrs Talbot's shop, had been seated next to Enid Laycock and had eaten more turkey, stuffings and vegetables than she had ever dreamed of. She laid her work-worn hand across that of Enid Laycock. 'Mrs Laycock, that was the best meal I have ever had in my life.'

'I'm very glad you've enjoyed it, but I'd be even more glad if you'd call me Enid.'

'Right. And will you call me Madge?'

'With pleasure.'

Sheila, whom the ever astute Enid had placed half way along the table, next to her daughter and as far as possible away from Lynda, observed the intimacy between the two women. She leaned forward and gave her most charming smile.

'That was an excellent meal, Enid. Thank you so much. I know very well how much hard work it takes to cook all that.'

'It was smashing, Mrs Laycock, but I wish I hadn't worn a dress with a belt!' puffed Lynda.

'Well, you'd better let it out a notch or two,' laughed Harry Laycock from his throne at the far end of the table, 'there's the Christmas pudding yet. Sam, bring it in and get me the matches, will you?'

Enid pushed back her chair, 'I've got to warm up the brandy sauce first.'

'Sit down,' commanded her eldest son as he stood up. 'me and Sylvia will see to it.'

Sylvia smiled at her mother-in-law. 'Yes, Queenie, you've done enough. I can warm up the sauce.'

'Queenie?' Sheila was taken aback at the confidence her daughter displayed in the Laycock home.

'It's the family nickname for Enid,' Harry explained, 'she's the Queen of the Kitchen, but I'm King of the Castle, of course. A man's got to be master in his own house, hasn't he, Ted?'

Ted gave a wry smile.

Sam, always happy to stir up trouble, joined in. 'I expect you're saving like mad for your own Castle, eh, John?'

John glanced across at Lynda, 'Yeah.'

'A lot of couples start off married life living with their parents,' said Graham, practising diplomacy as usual. 'Not many couples can afford their own home straight away.'

'The County Bank owns your castle,' Sam chipped in.

'We pay a mortgage,' Graham corrected him.

'Yeah, I know, but it's not bad, is it?'

'No. The Bank looks after its employees.'

Sam was starting to enjoy himself now. 'As long as they do as they're told. The Bank can order you and Sylvia to move whenever they want and wherever they want. Could be the other end of the country, and you'd still have to go.'

Graham glanced at his mother-in-law. 'Don't exaggerate, Sam.'

Sheila didn't like what she was hearing. 'But you've only just got settled in that lovely house, you've only just finished the curtains.'

Sylvia was annoyed with Sam, and tried to reassure her Mother.

'Don't worry, Mum, it could be a long time before Graham actually has to move.'

Ted looked at Graham and became worried when his son-in-law didn't confirm this.

Sylvia started to move towards the kitchen, 'Come on, Sam, let's sort out the pudding. Lynda would you like to come and get the dishes?'

'Yeah, sure.' Lynda said, pleased to be asked.

'Will you give me a hand getting some more beer up from the basement, John?' suggested Graham, keen to avoid any further questioning from his mother-in-law.

It was a little too quiet for Harry's liking after the young half of the family had left the table, so he introduced a topic that his wife had advised him to avoid.

'Henry Morton will be having a quiet Christmas, Ted.'

'Yes,' Ted replied warily, knowing Harry Laycock's tendency to grab hold of any gossip going the rounds in the Red Lion.

Enid, resigned to the task of trying to steer her husband away from tittle-tattle, said gently, 'I was so sorry to hear about his wife. She'd not been well for a long time, I understand.'

'Yes,' Sheila shook her head sorrowfully. 'She was a lovely lady. Very appreciative of all Ted did for her. She was able to keep her beautiful garden up to standard, thanks to his hard work.'

Harry ever practical, blundered in. 'You could be losing that job, I suppose, Ted?'

Sheila hadn't been aware of that possibility. 'I don't think so. Henry will still need a gardener and handyman, and a chauffeur.'

Harry was keen to contradict her. 'Not if he moves to Lytham St. Anne's, he won't,'

Sheila turned sharply to her husband.

'Moving? Has he said anything to you about that, Ted?'

'We haven't really discussed it,' he lied.

'That surprises me,' commented Harry, ignoring the warning look from his wife. 'From what I heard, he'll be putting the house on the market straight after Christmas.'

Sheila was shocked at this news. 'But why would he want to move? I know he's put a manager in charge of the factory, but his family lives in Milfield and all his friends.'

Harry's eyes twinkled mischievously as he poured himself another glass of beer. 'Not all of them. According to what I've heard, Henry hasn't been going to Lytham St. Anne's just for the golf. So it looks like there won't be many more trips to Blackpool for you, Ted.'

'No.'

Apart from Lynda and her Grandma, there was no-one visiting the graveyard next to the Methodist Chapel on Boxing Day afternoon. Madge pulled the lapels of her old black woollen coat tightly across her throat as she shivered in the cold, damp December air and watched her grand-daughter bend down to place the small bunch of Christmas roses on the grave Ray Collins shared with Alfred, his father.

'Your Mother should have been laid to rest in this churchyard as well.'

'She wanted to be where you could see the fields.'

'Husbands and wives should be together, like me and Alf will be soon.'

'No, no Grandma, don't say that.'

Lynda put her arm round her grandmother, thinking she seemed smaller and thinner every time she held her. The two women stood for a moment looking at the grave, then Madge sighed deeply and said, 'I won't see this baby of yours, you know.'

'You will. It'll need you, Grandma. Like I do.'

'I'm sorry, love, but we can't do owt about it. It's my turn next. And don't worry, it's all paid for, so much a week to that nice chap at the Co-op funeral parlour.'

'Oh, you haven't.'

'I have. You know me, I like to have everything right.' She looked round to make sure there was no-one who could see them, and took a small, bulky brown envelope out of her handbag. 'That post office account with your Mother's money in it. It is still in your name, isn't it, Lynda Collins, not Stanworth?'

'Yes.

Madge pressed the envelope into Lynda's hand, 'Keep it that way and put this money in it. There's some when the will's read, for you and Terry, but this is a bit extra, and unofficial, like.'

Lynda looked in the unsealed envelope. 'Grandma! Where did you get all this?' she gasped.

'You know I've always liked a bet on the horses.'

'Yes, but you don't win very often.'

'More often than I've told you. This is the winnings I've put away over the years. But you must promise me you'll never tell your husband about it. You haven't told him about your Mother's money, have you?'

'No.'

'I hope you'll never need it. But you never know. Now put it in your bag.'

Lynda pushed the envelope deep into her handbag. 'Thank you, Grandma. Thank you.' Lynda gave Madge a kiss on the cheek. 'But I'd rather have you than the money,' she said, brushing away a tear.

'Now don't get upset. Let's be going now.' She linked arms with her beloved grand-daughter and they walked slowly out of the moss garlanded graveyard.

'Mind you put that money somewhere safe till you can pay it in. Somewhere Sheila Stanworth won't find it.'

'Oh, that'll take some doing. I reckon she goes through our drawers when we're out. We've no secrets from Mrs Nosey Parker.'

'Except for that post office bank book.'

'Yes, she'll never get her greedy hands on that!' Lynda laughed but then bowed her head. 'I feel awful not telling John about it, but . . .'

Madge Collins was no fool. 'You're not sure about the future yet, are you?'

'No, to tell you the truth, I'm not.' Lynda confessed. 'I wish he didn't listen to his Mother so much. I thought it would be just me and him once we got married, but she puts her oar in everything, and he doesn't seem to be able to say 'no' to her. How I got him to go against her and marry me, I'll never know.'

'He's a man. And he loves you. Don't fret too much, Lynda. John's a good lad. You just need to get him away from her.'

'I'm not sure I'll ever be able to do that. Sometimes I'm not sure of anything.'

'You're young yet. Wait and see, but keep your 'mad money' a secret. If I've learned one thing in my life, it's that a woman needs her own money. Now, what time is it?'

Lynda looked at the Timex watch that had been a combined birthday and Christmas present from John. 'Oh, heck, it's ten past four, I hope we haven't missed Bernie.'

'So do I!'

'No, we're all right. There's his van.'

Lynda waved at the battered green van parked a little way from the entrance to the graveyard, and Bernie got out of it, wearing a bright green jumper with a red-nosed reindeer on the front. He took a bedraggled sprig of mistletoe out of his pocket and held out his arms. 'Hello, my darling girls. Come and give me a Christmas kiss.'

Lynda and Madge hugged him tight and kissed him on the cheek.

Madge beamed at him. 'Thanks for coming to get us, Bernie. A Kellys' party is just what we need today.'

'Well, it won't get started without you,' he declared as he opened the door of the van and Lynda and Madge squeezed themselves into the front seat.

CHAPTER TEN

By the end of 1962 Lynda Collins had truly become an orphan. That party at the Kellys' house on Bennett Street was the last party Madge Collins ever went to, but it was filled with laughter and all the old songs she loved, sung at the top of her voice. Lynda slept on the settee at Madge's house that night, and the next morning when she went upstairs to take her a cup of tea she found her Grandma had died in her sleep. She knelt by the bed and cried until there was a hammering at the door.

John stood there, furious.

'You didn't tell me you were going to stay the night at your Grandma's. You said you'd only be a couple of hours at the Kellys' and then you'd . . . .'

'My Grandma's dead. Oh, John, my Grandma's dead. I'm all on my own now,' she sobbed as he put his arms round her.

It seemed to John that he held Lynda in his arms nearly all the time for the next few days because the day after she lost her Grandma she also lost their baby. Kath Kelly was due to go home from her shift at the hospital when Lynda was brought in, so she was there to give her what comfort and care she could.

Lynda leaned her head against Kath's motherly breast and sobbed. 'God hates me, Kath.'

'Sssh! Don't say things like that. God loves you.' Kath wrapped her arms tighter around Lynda and tried to find the right words.

'I stopped going to church. It's my fault. I should have gone to church. Oh, the poor little thing. I wanted my baby, Kath. I knew it was too soon, and like she said, we couldn't afford it, but I wanted to have my baby.'

'It wasn't meant to be. I don't know why, Lynda. The doctor thinks it might have been the shock of losing your Grandma like that, but God does love you. And he'll give you a child one day. This wasn't meant to be. I know it's hard, lovely girl, but you've got me, and you've got John, and it will be all right. I promise you, one day it will be all right.'

Sheila looked after Lynda, not in a mothering, loving way like Kath, but in a practical way, seeing that there were always clean, sweet smelling sheets and pillow cases, and running upstairs with bowls of home-made soup, stewed beef with barley, and egg custards. She said very little but for a week or two all the meals she presented to the family happened to be Lynda's favourites. Then her attention was fully taken up with another death in the family, one with consequences she had dreamed of, and then immediately asked God to forgive her for those thoughts, and other consequences she had never dreamed of.

The second funeral that month was a much grander affair than the quiet laying to rest of Madge Collins. Sheila Stanworth's Uncle Freddie had always liked to spend his money having a good time, and he'd made sure the people who turned up would have a good party after his funeral. Freddie Harris had never married but had never lacked women in his life, and had spent a lot of time in London. He had plenty of money, which he claimed came from owning property in the capital and investing, or gambling as his older brother, Albert described it, in stocks and shares. There were, however, lots of rumours of black market activities but Freddie was too fast moving to be caught doing anything the police could charge him with.

When eventually his reckless living took its revenge on his health Freddie came back to Milfield, and had enough money to pay for several years in a comfortable nursing home. Sheila, his only remaining relative, had visited him all the time he was there, because she knew her parents would have expected it of their dutiful daughter. Secretly she had hoped that there would be a little of Uncle Freddie's money left for her, but it didn't seem likely in the end. It had been hard for her to observe how many bottles of whisky were consumed in his room, and how chocolates and flowers were given in return for a kiss from any pretty nurse who flattered him. Many of these nurses attended the funeral and shed tears, and told her over and over again how kind he had been to them.

Ted was not looking forward to Sheila's return from Uncle Freddie's solicitor's. She had already spoken bitterly about the way Uncle Freddie had 'thrown money away' and how he'd never had to care for anyone but himself. When she sat down at the table, clutching the copy of the will she had been given, she was pale and had tears in her eyes. Ted quietly made a cup of tea, sat down opposite her, and almost reached out to take hold of her hand.

'I'm sorry, Sheila, but you knew . . . And yet you kept going to see him, taking him home-cooking – it was very good of you. I suppose you just have to make do with knowing you did right by him. What your Mum and Dad would have wanted you to do. Like you said, it was his money and if he wanted to waste it all, there was nothing you could do about it.'

'But he didn't. He didn't waste it all. He left £100 each to John and Sylvia, even though he's only seen photos of them, apart from that one time I made them go with me.'

'Oh, that was very good of him.'

'He was good. And I said all those terrible things about him. Oh, Ted. I shall never forgive myself for all those things I've said.'

'Everybody says things in the heat of the moment. Don't be so hard on yourself.'

'He's left me a lot of money, Ted.' She began to cry again. 'And I don't deserve it.'

Ted felt a flutter of hope and excitement. 'I thought you said he'd spent it all.'

Sheila blew her nose, and then took a deep breath.

'He had. Except for what he owed my Mum and Dad. He'd worked out what it must have cost them to keep him all those years. Remember he was only eight when his mother died and his father dumped him on my parents' doorstep. Well, he reckoned that the money they spent feeding and clothing him should have been my money, and he invested it for me, and . . .'

'How much?'

She opened up the document and turned it for him to read the amount.

'You mustn't tell anyone, not even John and Lynda. I don't want them thinking they can have . . . It's not good for people to have things too easy.'

Ted sat back in his chair and watched her put away her handkerchief, and reverting back from penitent to the Sheila he knew.

'I need time to think about all this. There's a letter with the will.'

'What does it say?'

'Oh, just how he was always grateful to my Mum and Dad.' Sheila folded the documents firmly, put them in her handbag and snapped it shut.

'You will help the kids, though?'

'Yes, I'll give some to Sylvia. It will be nice for her to have her own money, and for the Laycocks to see they're not the only ones who can be generous.'

'What about John and Lynda?'

'John will have the same as Sylvia, on condition that he uses it as a deposit on a house.'

'But they'll need furniture and that as well.'

'I've been saving part of the money he's given me for bed and board, I'll give him that to buy the basics. We'll have a look round for a house for them.'

'Him and Lynda will want to choose their own, won't they?'

'What they want and what they'll get are two different things. I'm not having her choosing anything. She's got no taste and no sense. And anyway it will be John's house, not hers.'

'This house belongs to both of us.'

'Yes, but we couldn't have afforded it without my parents' money, God rest them.'

'That was only the deposit, I've been paying the mortgage.'

'Yes, I know you have. And we can finish it off now with some of Uncle Freddie's money. It will be a nice feeling, to own the house. This inheritance of mine will make a real difference to our lives, won't it, Ted?'

'Yes. Yes, it will.'

Beechwood Avenue was a row of semi-detached houses built in the 1930s. They were designed for people who had a secure income, and who wanted to move away from the smoke and grime of the cotton mills and bring up their families closer to the countryside. In fact you could see the countryside from some of the houses because the avenue ran across the top of a steep hill. Lynda, walking up the hill arm in arm with John looked across to the moorland in the distance and breathed deeply, as if sensing freedom.

There was a brisk March wind but the sun was shining on the gold and purple crocuses, and the early daffodils in the gardens, which were all neat and well tended apart from the one in front of number twenty-four.

'Your Dad's made a good start on the garden,' Lynda commented as they opened the garden gate and saw the patch of grass and weeds which had been cleared to reveal the soil and one or two plants which had survived almost a year of neglect.

'It's a helluva mess, though, like the rest of the house.'

'That's why we got it cheap.' Lynda walked over to the edge of what had once been the lawn and started tugging at the long grass.

'Yes, my Mum loves to spot a bargain, she found us a good house, I'll give her that.'

'Actually, it was me, John.'

'What?'

'It was me that found this house. I've been looking at it for months, walking past whenever I got the chance to come this way. I brought your Dad to see it, and got him to take your Mother for a walk along here so she'd 'find it'.

'Oh.'

'Don't ever tell her, though, she'd be mad as hell if she found out it was my idea.'

John shook his head. 'You're terrible you. I wish you hadn't told me. And it's not right, you and my Dad having secrets like that.'

'Everybody keeps things to themselves sometimes. Come on,' she bent down to tug at some weeds, 'let's stay out here in the sunshine a minute or two and tidy up a bit. We don't want your Dad to have done it all. This is our garden, our house.' She squeezed his arm and pulled him towards her as they looked at their future home.

'I've always dreamed of having a house with a bay window where I can have a window seat and sit and read my books.'

'You and your ideas. OK, we can give it five minutes,' he decreed, and began to pull at the dead branches of shrubs. Lynda worked along the side of the path, kneeling down to clear away the grass and weeds.

'Look at these little blue flowers I've found. What do they call them?'

'No idea. You'll have to ask my Dad. Next time you're having one of those private conversations of yours.'

'Are you jealous?'

'No, but my Mother is.'

'Yeah. She's as keen as ever to get rid of me. But not as keen as your Dad!'

'You're right there. He can't wait for us to move in here. But he doesn't want to get rid of you. You know very well he thinks you're lovely.' He gave her a hug. 'And I do.'

'I know,' she grinned as she pushed him away and moved toward the house. 'But he made sure that solicitor friend of his really got things moving, it must have been the quickest sale he ever put through.'

'I expect my Dad decided he'd had enough of my Mother moaning about you. He doesn't like arguments.'

John paused, he'd been thinking for a while that he needed to try to improve things between his wife and his Mother. 'She means well, you know, Lynda, telling you about manners and that.'

'I suppose so. I know I need to learn not to talk with my mouth full and that sort of thing, but it's the way she looks at me. It makes you feel bad when you know somebody can't stand you.'

'She'll get used to you. It'll be easier when we're not living with her.'

'You can say that again! It's really hard, John.'

I know, but it won't be for much longer, we've nearly got the house fit to move into.'

'Your Dad has, you mean. He's worked like a man possessed.'

'I think he just wants to get it finished before his birthday. Perhaps he's hoping he and my Mum will be able to go away for a holiday to celebrate.'

'Nobody's said much about his birthday. We've got to have a party for him, it is his fiftieth, after all. It should be a bit special.'

'My Mum was talking about a party with just us and Sylvia and Graham. I think she's planning a big present, though, as a surprise.'

'He needs something to cheer him up. I suppose it's getting to fifty that's bothering him. And losing his job with Henry.'

'He'll find something else. There's that supermarket the Co-op's opening, they'll need people.'

'Your Mother won't let him work there. She thinks it's terrible. Self-service! Not the done thing at all!'

'It'll be cheap, though.'

'Yeah, and the other shops in town are already worried about that. What are we getting for your Dad's birthday present?'

'I think me and Sylvia are going to share at a transistor radio for him.'

'If I had the money I'd get him a suitcase and a train ticket - that's what he needs, an escape kit to get him away from your Mother.'

'Don't talk like that.' He grabbed hold of her, kissed her and said, 'You're a trouble-maker, you!'

'I know! Have you got the key? Let's get that painting done before she comes along and tells us we're doing it wrong.'

Lynda made sure there were balloons all round the house for Ted's birthday and he had lots of cards, so the house looked quite festive as they sat round the table for his Sunday afternoon birthday tea. Sylvia, who had been learning to cook in Enid's kitchen more than she'd ever been allowed to at home, had made a chicken and mushroom pie. Sheila had boiled a piece of gammon to have with egg, lettuce and tomato salad.

Lynda had ordered a box of fancies and Geoff Heywood had called at the café that morning to deliver the cakes, but had not allowed her to pay for them. Lynda brought them home proudly, the expensive little fancy cakes from Heywood's had always been the ultimate treat for her and her Grandma.

'What have you got those for?' was Sheila's reaction when Lynda placed the box on the table. 'You knew I'd be making him a birthday cake.'

'I wanted him to have something special.'

'Oh, isn't my cake special enough then?'

Ted who was sitting in the carver chair at the head of the table, sighed and sat up very straight. 'Your cakes are excellent, you know that, Sheila, everybody tells you so.' Ted leaned forward, reached across the table and patted his daughter-in-law's hand. 'It was a very nice thought, Lynda,'

For dessert there were tinned sliced peaches and Carnation milk and then Sheila made a grand entrance with her best sponge cake filled with cream and raspberry jam. There were five candles, one for each decade, she explained, as Graham lit them and she handed Ted the knife ready for a ceremonial cutting of the cake. He got to his feet, a little shakily Lynda noticed, as she started off the singing of 'Happy Birthday to You'. The small, awkward family choir sounded a little too polite and lacking in pizzazz for her liking, so she followed it with a call for three cheers as Ted held the knife hesitantly over the cake.

'Let me take the candles off before you make a mess,' Sheila said, swooping over the cake, and then, as she saw his hand was shaking, she took the knife from him. 'Shall I do it?' she asked and began to divide up the cake and hand it round. She then sat down and awaited the required appreciation. Lynda waited till everyone had a piece of cake and then walked round to Ted at the head of the table.

'Happy Birthday, Dad,' she said, giving her father-in-law a kiss and a big hug as she handed him her present.

'Thank you very much, love.' Ted smiled at her fondly and slowly unwrapped the bottle of Sandeman's best port and the green silk cravat. 'Very posh, you'll make a gentleman out of me yet.'

'You are a gentleman in my book,' she said and gave him another kiss. 'And always will be, whatever you do.'

Sylvia, seeing that her Mother was waiting to be the grand finale, moved across to give her Dad a well-wrapped box. She watched him open the present and then explained, 'You've often said you'd like to be able to listen to the radio when you're working in the shed. John and I have shared at this, and Graham, of course.' Sylvia kissed her father on the cheek.

'Oh, this is grand, just what I wanted. Thank you, I'll spend many happy hours listening to this.' He paused, and added quietly, 'And thinking about you when I do.'

Sheila's present was a watch. 'This isn't a very expensive one, because you'll be getting another present from me. I'm going to buy you a car, Ted.'

There was a gasp from the others and an excited squeak and clapping of hands from Sylvia. 'Oh, how exciting! A car! Won't that be wonderful? You'll be able to chauffeur Mum now, and go anywhere you want.'

'You'll be able to go to Lytham St Anne's now, Mum,' John enthused. 'A car. How about that, Dad? You . . .' He paused, noticing his father was gripping the arms of his chair.

Ted tried to swallow but found his throat was dry. 'It's very kind of you, Sheila. Very generous. But I'm afraid I can't accept . . .' he pushed aside the unopened small box. 'anything. It wouldn't be right. Not this, and certainly not a car.'

Sheila couldn't keep the irritation out of her voice. 'What do you mean? Of course you can accept it. We'll both benefit. I've always wanted a car. We can have holidays, and day trips, to the countryside and to the seaside.'

'No.'

Ted's tone was suddenly very firm. 'I'm sorry. I didn't want to do this now. I wanted us to have today as a family, but . . There's no point in us getting a car, Sheila, because I won't be here to drive it. I'm leaving you, Sheila. You will have the house, and part of my police pension. Not all of it, because I need to live, too, and fortunately your uncle left you with enough . . . .'

Sheila stared open-mouthed at her husband. 'What do you mean, you're leaving me?'

John was horrified.

'You can't. You've just helped us to move into Beechwood Avenue. My Mother will be on her own if you . . ..'

132

Without thinking, Lynda gave the explanation. 'That's why he was in a hurry for us to get in the house. He thought you wouldn't move out if you knew. And we need to get out . . .'

'Did you know about this?' Sheila gasped with disbelief.

With everyone's eyes turned towards her, Lynda had no choice but to confess. 'Yeah.'

'Lynda!' John looked at his wife as if she had committed a murder.

Sheila's voice was full of bile. 'Well, I always knew you didn't like me, but plotting with my husband, behind my back, is more than I could imagine, even from a nasty little trollop like you!'

Everyone jumped in their chairs as Ted Stanworth leaped to his feet and shouted louder than he had ever dared in that house. 'Stop it, Sheila! Lynda isn't to blame for this. You are. I'm sorry if I've dropped you in it, Lynda, love, but I had to have somebody I could talk to.'

'It's all right, Ted,' whispered Lynda.

She looked down to find her hands were trembling. She clasped them tightly together and waited for Ted to explain to his son.

'I'm sorry if you think I haven't done right, son, rushing to make sure you got into your own home as quick as possible. But I was afraid, nay I knew, that your Mother, being the way she is, would never have let you move out if I was gone. I wanted you to have your own home, your own house. Something I've never had,' he continued bitterly. 'This has never been my house, has it, Sheila? It's always been yours as far as you were concerned.'

'That's rubbish. This is your home as much as mine.'

'Oh, no, it's not. A home is where you can relax, put your feet up, do what you want – be happy! I can't remember the last time I was happy, really happy in this damned house.'

Sheila leapt to her feet. 'Ted, stop it! Stop this, now! You're not going anywhere. You can't.'

'I'm sorry, Sheila. I have to. I'm fifty, and I feel a lot older. Except when . '

He paused and looked at Lynda, who gave him a little smile of understanding. This moment between them was watched by the rest of the family, and suddenly there was a silence which was like a great weight pushing everyone down into their seats. John stared first at his Mother's white face, and then at his Father standing suddenly taller than he had seen him for years, and with a dream in his eyes.

John was afraid now. 'When what, Dad?'

Ted Stanworth, looking both ashamed and defiant, turned to answer his son. 'When I'm with . . .' He faltered for a moment as he glanced round the table at the faces turned towards him. 'I'm sorry. I'm sorry to cause you all this upset, but . . . .The truth is I've met somebody. Her name is Rose.'

He paused and took a deep breath, seeming to gather strength just from speaking the name of the woman he loved.

'Rose,' he repeated. 'We love each other, and we know we make each other happy - in every way.'

'This is disgusting!' Sylvia cried out.

'You're right there, Sylvia!' Sheila shrieked, standing up and hitting her husband across the face. 'You're a disgusting, lying, ungrateful pig! I made a home for you, like you said you wanted, like you'd never had. A clean house, lovely meals on the table, a wife who stayed at home to look after you. And what do I get in return? A man who is a cheat, an adulterer who finds himself a fancy woman,' she paused for breath, and then asked slowly, 'How long has this been going on?'

Ted faced his wife without a doubt in his mind.

'Long enough for us to be sure we want to be together, for the rest of our lives. You can call me what you like, Sheila, but it won't change anything. I'd been wondering for years how I'd cope when the children had gone off to get married, and I was left here, in this house, on my own with you. You ordering me about, criticising, giving me no thanks for anything I do. And above all, no love. There's no love in this house, Sheila, not what I call love, anyway.'

'Get out!' Sheila was screaming at him now. 'Get out of my sight!'

Ted looked at her for a moment, and then went slowly upstairs to pack.

CHAPTER ELEVEN

Lynda was wrong. She'd told Ted that Sheila didn't love him, didn't need him, would be perfectly all right if he left her. She was shocked to see this woman who had always been so strong-willed, so sure of everything, suddenly become a pale, listless creature with no energy. She and John took it in turns with Sylvia to call in on her each evening, to have tea with her. At first they had to cook the meal themselves or take something with them, for Sheila had no interest in her kitchen, except to make cups of tea which, they discovered later, were topped up with whisky.

Sheila didn't leave the house, not even to go to church. She was convinced that the whole town would be talking about her, about her husband having run off with another woman. In fact nobody knew for quite a while, except Enid Laycock, who was needed to comfort Sylvia, and Freda Wilson.

'Lynda,' she asked one morning, 'Now that he's not working for Henry Morton, do you think your father-in-law would be willing to come and do some gardening for me? I'd pay a good rate.'

'No. Sorry, Freda. He won't be able to.'

'Why? Has he got another job? Or is he not so well? I haven't seen him around for a while.'

'No. Look, I know you won't go spreading it around, and people will find out anyway.'

'What?'

'Ted's not living in Milfield any more. He's moved to Blackpool.'

'Oh, with Henry Morton?'

'No, not with Henry. And not with Sheila.' Lynda looked at Freda, who soon read her expression.

'He's left his wife?'

'Yeah. On his fiftieth birthday.'

'Well, from what I've heard, nobody will blame him,' was Freda's response. 'I'm not being nosey, Lynda - well, I suppose I am really, but is there another woman involved?'

'Yes.'

'I can't say I'm surprised' Freda commented. 'Something happens to men when they reach fifty, even Duncan's father had a wandering eye for a while in his fifties. Nothing came of it, of course, he didn't have what it takes to keep one woman satisfied, never mind two. Ooh, I'm sorry, I didn't mean to make you blush, lass.'

'It's all right,' Lynda giggled. 'It's a relief to have a laugh about it instead of feeling guilty.'

'What have you got to feel guilty about?'

'They all blame me for him going. I only said what I thought when he told me he wanted to leave Sheila. I think the world of Ted, I only wanted him to be happy.'

'Don't blame yourself, love. Who is she, this lady friend of his?'

'She's called Rose. You'd like her. She owns a café as well, in Blackpool. It was when I was telling him about my ideas for this place that Ted got talking about 'Rose's café'. I started teasing him about her, and it turned out not to be a joke.'

When Freda met Geoff Heywood in Alexandra Park a week or so later she found that he, too, knew all about Ted Stanworth having left his wife. They were sitting companionably on a bench by the lake, as if it was a coincidence that they were both taking a few minutes rest there. This was, however, a meeting they had arranged, and for which Geoff had chosen the venue.

'Yes, Freda. I had heard about Ted. Harry Laycock never has been any good at keeping his mouth shut. His wife made him promise not to tell anybody, but he can't resist a good bit of gossip, especially after a few pints in The Red Lion.'

'I expect there were a few men in the pub who envied Ted.'

'Yes.'

Freda saw the pain which momentarily flickered in his eyes, and couldn't stop herself saying, 'Including you?'

Geoff looked at her, surprised by her perception and lack of discretion.

'Sorry, I'd no right to ask that? But I knew your Mother and . .'

'And you know she was against me marrying Ellen. And she was right, I suppose. But I'd been after her for years, obsessed is what they'd call it these days.' He tried to laugh. 'You think you know all about the world at that age.' He gave her a shamefaced look. 'And there were other considerations, which my Mother did understand. Ellen's father put money into my bakery business.'

'Oh. And now I'm asking you to put money into my business.'

'Yes. I've been through the books, and I'm impressed. But I want to buy the café rather than be joint owner with Duncan.'

'I see.' Freda focused her attention on the ducks placidly gliding along and casually feeding. She knew her son's limitations and his faults, but it was still hard to be made aware that Geoff Heywood had also perceived them.

'From what he's said to me, your son's interest lies more in the holiday camp business, I think, than in . . .'

'Yes, quite right. As I said, I'm doing this to give him more capital, so he can spread his wings a bit. And, of course, there's Lynda.'

'Yes. We both see that the same way. No-one needs to know I own the café, until . .'

'Until I pop me clogs! Don't look like that, Geoff, we're both old enough to know there's going to be a day when we won't be worrying about anything! Thank God!'

'No, I was thinking more, no-one will know till I kick the bucket! What do you think will be Duncan's reaction?'

'Duncan won't mind. He's been on at me to sell the café for a while now.'

'And you won't need to tell him who you sold it to?'

'No. And, like you said, nobody needs to know it's been sold. But you'll guarantee that Lynda will run it as long as she wants to?'

'Yes. That's part of my reason, as you know.'

'And mine. I promised her Grandma I'd look after the girl and this is my best way of doing it, as far as I can see.' She got to her feet, placing her handbag carefully over her arm.

Geoff stood up and held out his hand. 'We can shake hands on it, then.'

Freda Wilson's handshake was as firm as any man's. She turned to walk away, but couldn't resist a parting shot. 'Ellen won't like it.'

Geoff smiled, enjoying a moment of triumph. 'With any luck she won't find out till I'm gone.'

At the beginning of April John and Sylvia both received a letter from Ted, asking them to forgive him. Sylvia came round to Beechwood Avenue that evening with her letter and found John sitting on the shabby settee, which Lynda had inherited from Madge. They also had the armchair she used to sit in by the fire, but John had found he felt uncomfortable about using it, partly because one of its springs had broken, but mostly because it was a dead woman's chair. He'd be glad when his mother had bought the new three-piece suite she was fancying and, he hoped, passed her old one on to him and Lynda.

Lynda, proud to be the hostess in her own home, went into the kitchen to make them all a cup of tea. When she came back she found the brother and sister sitting together on the settee, comparing their letters. Sylvia was crying with anger as much as sorrow.

'It's bad enough him asking us to forgive him for what he's done, but to ask us to go and see him and meet that woman!'

'Yeah, it's a bit much, isn't it?' John said.

'Well, I never want to see him again. And, and he won't see his grandchildren either,'

Lynda almost dropped the cups of tea. 'Grandchildren! Are you . . . ?'

'Yes.' Sylvia took the cup and saucer in trembling hands, gulped back her tears and smiled. Then she cried out angrily, 'I bet he never thought of that when he went off with his fancy woman. No child of mine will want him for a Grandad!'

'He'd make a lovely Grandad,' Lynda protested.

Sylvia gave her a hard look. 'You'd better keep quiet, Lynda, you've said enough about this, which is a family matter, between me and John. Nothing to do with you.'

'Oh, I thought I was family, seeing as I married your brother.'

Lynda looked at John, hoping he would speak up and support her but he didn't seem to be listening. 'Anyway, congratulations, when is it due, the baby?'

Sylvia spoke more gently now. 'October. And it looks like it might be twins. We're going to tell Mother when we go round for tea on Saturday. You'll be there, won't you? We've got something else to tell her, which is not such good news.'

'I'm working late on Saturday, it's Freda's birthday party and I said I'd lock up for her,' Lynda reminded John.

Sylvia sighed impatiently, 'You don't have to be there, like I said, this is . . ..'

John interrupted, 'What's the bad news, Sylvia?'

'Graham is being transferred next month.'

'Oh, bloody hell! Where to?'

'Knutsford, in Cheshire,' Sylvia couldn't keep the pride out of her voice. 'A very posh area. The manager there has had a heart attack, unfortunately, so they need to put in a reliable Senior Clerk to look after things till they can find a suitable manager. And we don't know what this might lead to. As you know, the Bank has been wanting to give Graham a step up the ladder for a while. But he's having to go over there to take charge almost immediately.'

'My Mum'll be upset.'

'I know. But if the Bank says move, Graham's got no choice. I'm just glad Mum will still have you here to look after her.'

Lynda again looked at John, and this time she saw he was having similar thoughts to hers.

'Are we telling her about this?' he asked, still clutching the letter from his father.

'No. There's no point. We're finished with him.'

Sylvia slowly tore up her letter, but John hesitated. Lynda stood up and calmly took his letter from him and collected the torn one from Sylvia as if she was going to throw them both away. She put them in her pocket and, standing there looking down at Ted's two ungrateful children, she took a deep breath.

'Your Mother had a letter as well. Not from your Dad, from her Uncle Freddie, when he died. It said he'd left her the money so that she could learn to be generous and learn to live a little. He said the way her parents had brought her up, she'd never had a chance to enjoy life, to learn how to have fun. He said he hoped she'd change her ways, and stop being so miserable and judgmental. Your Dad kept hoping that, too, that she'd change.'

'Bloody hell.' John, staring at Lynda, was shocked but tempted to smile – until Sylvia spoke.

'What a horrible man, to write things like that! But how do you know the contents of Uncle Freddie's letter?'

'Ted told me. She'd hidden it in her underwear drawer, too bloody ashamed to show it to anybody I expect. Uncle Freddie told her exactly what he thought, but it made no difference. Your Dad could see she wasn't going to change. And that's why he left her.'

'Aren't you forgetting something? He'd already been carrying on with that woman for over a year before Uncle Freddie died. And you, Madam,' Sylvia almost spat out the words as she turned on Lynda, 'are a liar. My father would never, never hunt through my mother's chest of drawers, and especially not that drawer!'

Lynda had had enough of Sylvia. 'All right. I found it, and I showed it to Ted. But he was glad I did; it confirmed that he was right.'

'You despicable little . . . What do you think of your wife now, John? A fine way to return our Mother's hospitality, sneaking into her bedroom and searching through her private belongings. What were you doing, looking for something to steal?'

'No. Was I hell! But Ted had told me there was a letter, and that she wouldn't let him see it, so . . . And anyway, she used to go through our stuff when we lived there, didn't she, John?'

'Well . . . .' Suddenly John needed to get out of this room, away from all these terrible feelings. 'I'll walk you to the bus-stop, shall I, Sylvia? Graham will be wondering where you've got to.'

Sylvia, too, wanted to leave, to get back to the haven of peace which she'd found in her home with Graham, who seemed to understand the world and the people in it much more than she did.

'Yes. Will you go round to Mum's afterwards? I don't want to see her till Saturday but I don't like to think of her sitting in that house on her own all week.'

'He was round there yesterday. She made him stay the night.'

'And he can stay again tonight if she needs him to. She's our Mother, and we're going to look after her.'

'You're not. You're buggering off to Knutsford!'

'Come on, John.' Sylvia led the way out and didn't bother saying goodnight to Lynda.

Freda was past the age when she could easily throw a party at home, and too many of her friends had died recently so she hadn't really felt like organising anything. Instead she'd decided to keep the café open late that Saturday and invite friends and favourite customers to come along for free tea and cakes.

Lynda had ordered a birthday cake from Heywood's and insisted on paying for it herself this time. She'd also got some balloons and borrowed some bunting from one of the stallholders in the market hall, and the sun was shining so people were able to sit at tables outside as well as inside the café. She'd asked Freda's permission to invite Jean to come along with Annie Fielding after they'd closed the shop. She's also arranged to go to the Odeon with Jean that evening. By five o'clock it was as if there was a street party taking place round the café.

'Oh, it's just like the Coronation,' squealed Annie, clapping her hands with delight. 'We should have ordered a band to come and play so we could dance.'

'It's OK, here's Jimmy Barker, I asked him to bring his record player when he shut his music stall. Thanks ever so much, Mr Barker.'

'You're welcome, as long as me and my lad can have a piece of cake.' He nodded towards his young assistant who was staggering along behind him with a pile of records.

Freda sat at a table by the door watching the youngsters from the market stalls dancing to the latest pop records and was delighted when Peggy Haworth, who'd closed her clothing stall early, came to join her, followed by Geoff Heywood and Alice Smith who had brought her birthday cake.

'Oh, you've done a marvellous job, Alice. Thank you, love.'

'I've brought some candles, how many would you like?'

'Twenty-one, of course!' chipped in Peggy, an attractive, slightly buxom woman in her early sixties who smoked as if her life depended on it and who had an 'if you don't do it now, when are you going to do it?' approach to life. She was often an embarrassment to her shy, serious minded son, Gordon, but he loved her and coped with her antics as best he could.

Alice began to arrange the candles carefully in among the icing sugar roses as Jean, who was helping Lynda, brought over a pot of tea and cups and saucer.

'That's a beautiful cake' sighed Peggy. 'I'm hoping to be ordering a wedding cake from you and Alice one day soon, Geoff.'

'For you or your Gordon?' quipped Freda.

'Not for me, I don't want another husband, what I want is a sweet, kind girl for a daughter-in-law, somebody like Jean here.'

Jean went bright red and almost dropped the teapot.

'He won't give up, you know, Jean, he might be shy, my Gordon, but he's like me, once he decides what he wants he . . .'

Freda, never one to hold back with her opinion, made a point, 'Isn't she a bit young for him, Peggy, how old is he now, your Gordon?'

'Twenty-nine, but he's young for his age – like his Mother,' she claimed with a smirk.

Alice had been listening in with a wistful look on her face. 'All the girls look pretty these days. It was like that when I was young, a lot of competition. You have to take your chances while you can, Jean, but don't choose a lying, thieving con-man like I did, however good looking he is.'

'I won't,' said Jean, flying back to the safety of the kitchen.

She emerged just as Gordon Haworth arrived to collect his mother. Gordon, who was on his way home from his work as assistant manager of the furniture department at the Co-op, had the look of a slightly burly choir boy with a well-scrubbed face. His shoulders drooped a little as he approached and saw his mother jiving enthusiastically with Jimmy Barker. Peggy gave him a little wave and then pointed towards Jean who, with Lynda, had been ordered by Freda to close the counter and enjoy the rest of the party.

Lynda had been asked to dance by one of her admirers who wasn't discouraged by the fact she was married. This meant that Jean was sitting alone at one of the outside tables, assuming the well-practised air of wall-flowering nonchalance. She concentrated on her milk shake as she heard Peggy's loud whisper of 'Gordon, Gordon! Go on! Go on!'

Gordon, resisting being publicly chivvied by his mother, bowed his head in the attitude of despair so often inspired in him by her behaviour, and sat down next to Geoff Heywood. Geoff had decided to stay as long as he could at this party. He often preferred to eat late in the kitchen rather than share the dinner table with his wife and spoiled younger son.

'Busy day, Gordon?'

'Yes, but very satisfying. Two three piece suites and a dining table ordered.'

'Well done. You're a good salesman.'

'Oh, it's not all down to me, I've a very smart young man assisting me now.'

'But it's you people know and trust. That's worth a lot in business.'

'You should know.'

'You've almost missed the party, though. And there's a young lady over there who's missed it, too,' he nodded towards Jean, 'she's spent too much time helping out in the kitchen. It was very kind of her. Kindness should be rewarded, I always think, don't you?'

Gordon, already half way out of his chair, agreed. 'Yes, Mr Heywood. If you'll excuse me?'

'I certainly will.' Geoff smiled and poured himself another cup of tea as he watched Gordon walk purposefully over to Jean Clayton and hold out his hand. Geoff leaned back in his chair and exchanged a speculative smile with Freda as they saw Jean gratefully accept Gordon's invitation to dance.

In spite of all Graham and Sylvia's efforts to make this a celebration, there wasn't quite a party atmosphere at 17 Stanhope Road that evening. The front room was so rarely used that it always felt chilly, but Graham had turned on all three bars of the electric fire and was determinedly filling two of Sheila's best glasses with the sherry he and Sylvia had brought with them.

'Open the whisky, and help yourself, John,' he said, ignoring Sheila's raised eyebrows. 'Good thing we brought it, your bottle is nearly empty, Sheila.'

'I've needed it to help me sleep,' Sheila explained, a little defensively. 'It feels very lonely, and a bit frightening, to be in the house on my own at night. And now it looks like I shall be even more lonely soon.'

'John will still be here,' Sylvia repeated the reassurance which had been making her brother flinch a little since they'd broken the news of Graham's transfer. 'And Knutsford isn't so far away. And you'll be able to come and stay, won't she, Graham?'

'Of course,' Graham replied, with more enthusiasm than he felt, and then poured himself a quantity of whisky which surprised himself as well as his wife.

John tried to help. 'Good news about Sylvia, though, isn't it, Mother?'

'Oh, yes. I am delighted, really I am. And I'll be only too willing to come over and stay. You'll need a lot of help if they're right about it being twins.'

'Yes,' Sylvia agreed, a little nervous whenever the reality of childbirth edged into her mind.

Sheila was already making plans. 'I'd better start knitting straight away, two of everything.'

Graham found himself speaking in the firm, positive tone he was cultivating ready for his new position. 'We shall be very grateful. I'm glad you're so pleased, even though you are, of course, too young really to be a grandmother.'

Sheila produced what was, for her, a sweet smile. Graham sounding more jovial by the minute, pushed onwards. 'And what would you like to be called, Grandma or Granny?'

'I think I should prefer to be Nana, or Nan, it sounds a little younger than Granny to me. Unless your Mother . . . '

'She hasn't said anything about that yet. But I'm sure she'll be happy to be called Grandma or Granny or whatever, she's so thrilled about it. Well, here's to the future!'

Groaning inwardly, Graham, usually so good at choosing the right words, grimaced as soon as he'd proposed the toast. They all watched Sheila immediately set aside her glass and lean back in her chair. 'I'm not sure what kind of future it will be, at least as far as I am concerned.'

Graham swallowed another mouthful of whisky. 'We none of us know that, do we, really? But I'm sure there will be lots of things to look forward to.' He looked to his wife for assistance.

'Yes,' Sylvia hunted for suitably positive ideas for the deserted wife. 'You'll really enjoy coming to see our new house.'

Sheila sighed again. 'Yes, I suppose so. But it might be quite a while before you find something suitable.'

'No, it might not take too long. We're driving over there next week for the Easter weekend, to have a look round.'

'Oh, can I come with you? I've never been to Cheshire, but I believe it's lovely. It's just what I need, a little holiday, away from this house and all these memories. Oh, it would make such a difference to me,' Sheila looked pleadingly at her daughter.

Sylvia looked across at her husband, 'If that's all right with Graham.'

Graham, who couldn't see how he could get out of this one, sighed and nodded, and downed the rest of his whisky.

There was a silence while Sylvia and Graham coped with the loss of the weekend they had planned. Sheila poured herself another glass of sherry and said brightly.

'Have you heard about Henry Morton?' He's come back. Apparently his fancy woman got a bit bored with having him around full time, cramped her style I expect. Anyway he's moved in with his son and his wife. He was missing his grandchildren, too, he said.

No-one knew what to say. Graham poured himself and John another whisky. 'What are you and Lynda doing at Easter, John?'

'I don't know yet,' John lied guiltily. He and Lynda had read his Father's letter over and over and had secretly been planning to go to Blackpool to see him.

'I'd like you to do something for me,' Sheila said in a tone which expected no refusal.

'What?'

'I'd like you to go and see your Father and talk some sense into him. And tell him, it's quite all right if he wants to come home. I'm quite prepared to forgive him. And I know you don't want him to have anything to do with his grandchildren, and I quite understand that, Sylvia, but Ted has a right to know he will be becoming a Grandad. I'm sure you would agree with that, Graham?'

'Yes,' replied Graham, who, unlike John and Sylvia, had not been rendered speechless by Sheila's suggestion of a trip to Blackpool.

'So will you do that, John?'

'Yes. If that's what you want.'

'Good. Oh, and you can also tell your Father that I've ordered a television set.'

As a special treat on Easter Sunday, Rose had booked lunch for the four of them at The Embassy Hotel on the promenade at Fleetwood. John and Lynda enjoyed the tram ride from Blackpool to Fleetwood, and Ted and Rose were glad to see them relaxed and happy, with their arms round each other. When they stood in the foyer of the hotel John was worried that he wasn't dressed as smartly as the other guests and visitors at The Embassy but Rose reassured him.

'You look very handsome, and the manager is a friend of mine who'll be very upset if you don't make yourself feel at home here. Now, remember, this is on me, to thank you for all the hard work you did for me yesterday. You especially, Lynda, I can see why Freda makes a fuss of you at her café. Now, the prawn cocktail they do here is wonderful, so can I recommend that for starters? Then there's roast beef and Yorkshire pudding, and trifle or lemon meringue pie. Will that suit you, John?'

'Thank you very much, Mrs . . . ' then, as Lynda gave him a nudge, 'Rose.'

After lunch they walked back along the promenade and Rose paused at the end of a street of terraced houses. 'This is Balmoral Terrace where my Mum and Dad had a boarding house. It's a wonder we didn't all meet when you came on holiday here as a family.'

Lynda didn't want John to start thinking about his mother again. 'Can we walk on the beach?'

Rose Milner was a woman who had enough experience of life to know when to take a risk. She guessed that the reason Sheila had allowed John and Lynda to come and visit Ted, was that she was confident they could persuade him to go back to Milfield.

'You go with them, Ted. I fancy sitting on this bench and reading the paper for a while. I'll meet you at the Marine Hall in an hour, shall I? There's usually a bit of entertainment there on Sundays.' She smiled at Ted's hesitation, and nodded her reassurance. 'See you later.'

It was less than a year since Lynda had walked along the beach that morning of her honeymoon, but everything was so different now. Lynda wanted to wander away to be on her own and do some thinking, but she knew John would never manage to ask the questions which were the reason his mother had sent them to see his father. They'd been fully occupied in the café, and then were too tired to stay up and talk last night, even though Rose had gone to bed early to give them a chance for private conversation. John had shuddered at the thought of his father going upstairs to share a bed with another woman, but Lynda had hugged him and told him everything would be all right.

Ted Stanworth had changed in the last few weeks, he felt so much more relaxed and confident – confident enough to start what he knew might be a tricky conversation.

'I'm glad you've come over. I was a bit worried that you might . . .'

'Me and John had decided we were coming at Easter, even before Sheila said . . .'

'Yeah.' Ted didn't want to talk about his wife. He paused for a moment and then turned to look at them both. 'So, what do you think?' he asked.

'What about?' John replied a little sullenly.

' Rose.'

'She's very nice. Made us really welcome, hasn't she, John?'

'Yeah,' he muttered, and carried on walking, forcing his father to hurry after him a little.

'I'm sorry we were so busy yesterday, but you have to take the trade when it's there.'

'So, is that what you do now, Dad, work for her at the café? A summer job, like?'

'I help her out when she's really busy, but she's got a young girl who comes when she's needed. I've already got a bit of gardening work, and we're thinking of getting an allotment so I can supply some fruit and veg. for the café. And I get some work from the hotels, picking guests up from the station, more personal than a taxi. Rose lets me have her car and . . . .'

'Oh, does she drive? I am impressed,' Lynda commented brightly, noticing John's dismay at what sounded too much like firm plans for the future from his Dad.

'Mother's still hoping you'll let her buy you a car when you come home.'

Ted stopped and they all stood gazing out at the sea.

'John, I'm sorry, but I'm not coming home. This is my home now, with Rose.'

John's tone was bordering on the belligerent. 'What about her husband, she's Mrs Milner, isn't she?'

'She divorced him a long time ago.'

'Oh, a divorcee!'

'Don't say it like that John, it wasn't Rose's fault. Her husband was a bad 'un, went off with other women, spent all her money, and was a lazy sod.'

'Makes you look good, then, Ted,' Lynda said, trying to lighten the mood a little.

'My Mother won't want a divorce.'

'No, I know she won't. But we don't need to get divorced. I can just stay here. Rose doesn't expect me to marry her. She's happy . . . .'

'Living in sin! Bloody hell, Dad!'

'You're sure this is what you want, Ted?' Lynda asked, and held on to John's arm to try to calm him, and to give him the strength to cope with the answer she knew was coming.

Ted put his shoulders back and stood steady as a rock before them.

'I've never been more sure of anything in my life. John, I know it's hard for you, and it's putting a burden on you, having to take my place a bit. I know your Mother will need you, call upon you more than is fair.'

'She already does!' Lynda complained, trying not to mind that John scowled at her. He continued to challenge his father. 'And what about our Sylvia? You'll be a Grandad in October. You'll have to come back or you'll never see your grandchildren. Our Sylvia won't have anything to do with you, you know, if . . . .'

'She'll come round,' Lynda said, not really believing it.

'She bloody won't,' John shouted.

'I hope she will. I must admit, I hadn't thought about grandchildren. But I've thought long and hard about other things. I'm fifty, John. And up till now I've worked hard, looked after you all, and been a good Dad, haven't I?'

John's voice was tight with emotion. 'Yeah. Yeah, of course you have.'

'I've also put up with a helluva lot all these years, you know that's true, son.'

John was silent for a moment, then grudgingly said, 'Yeah.'

Ted spoke with the strength and certainty of a man who knows that he has someone who will love him, come what may.

'I know I'm being selfish, and it doesn't come easy to me, but I have to take this chance to be happy. I know I haven't been here long, but I can't believe how different this life is, how different I am. I'm relaxed, I'm comfortable with Rose all the time. And we have fun, we go to shows, we go dancing, we go visiting. She's got lots of friends and they've become my friends because they love her. And I love her.'

'You married my Mother, did you not love her?'

'In a way, but not like this. It happens, John, sometimes people marry the wrong person. And our parents taught us we had to make it work, stick with it whether you're happy or not. But I decided I couldn't face wasting the rest of my life with somebody who didn't make me happy, who didn't love me as I wanted to be loved.'

'If you hadn't met her . . . .' John said resentfully.

'But I did. Thank God.'

'And is that what I'm supposed to go back and tell my Mother, that you love somebody else and you're never coming back? I can't, Dad. I can't do that!'

Lynda put her arms round her husband, who bowed his head, trying to stop himself from crying. Then he became aware that there were other people on the beach, and he couldn't let them see him make an unmanly fool of himself like this.

'We'd better go. Come on, Lynda.'

Ted wasn't going to let his son just walk off. 'Yes, Rose will be waiting for us. But don't worry, lad, you won't have to tell Sheila. I've written her a letter for you to take home with you. Now, let's go and try to enjoy ourselves a bit. Life's too short, you know.'

Ted put one arm round his son's shoulder and the other round Lynda's and they set off again, walking towards the sound of a brass band playing 'I do like to be beside the seaside'.

CHAPTER TWELVE

Sheila didn't believe a word of what was in Ted's letter. She burned it, and put the contents out of her mind. She got on with life, went to church on Sundays and ignored the whispered conversations she thought she could hear going on behind her back. She planned for the future, bought a new double bed for Sylvia's room, ready for when she and Graham came to visit with the grandchildren. When Sylvia and Graham moved to Cheshire Sheila did, of course, feel very lonely. John wasn't much use to her as a companion, even though he came to visit several times a week. She especially missed being able to confide in her daughter. Sheila felt she really needed someone to talk to, but could think of no-one who would understand. She was surprised and grateful when she found Ellen Heywood coming to rescue her from her feeling of isolation.

Ellen made it seem nothing unusual, and certainly not a gesture of pity. She needed a new suit and several dresses for the summer and visited Sheila frequently for fittings, but whenever Sheila went to Kirkwood House to deliver the finished garments, she found she was also invited for afternoon tea in the Victorian conservatory at the side of the house.

Sheila loved sitting on the floral cushioned sofa warmed by the sun which always seemed to shine strongly enough to make the room comfortable. The atmosphere in the conservatory felt cosy but also exotic, with palms and ferns and pink and white azaleas. As the weather became warmer Ellen would open the elegant doors and the perfume of the rose garden would drift in on the soft summer breeze and make Sheila feel she was enjoying a brief stay in paradise.

Sheila, delicately holding a fine bone china cup and saucer, sighed with contentment. 'It's so lovely in here, especially with the roses.'

'Yes, it was my Mother's favourite room. It was she who planted the rose garden close enough to enjoy the scent from in here.'

'She'd be very proud of the way you look after it.'

'Geoffrey does most of the heavy work, I concentrate on the flowers.'

'I have a lot more to do in our garden now, but I enjoy it.'

'Well, that's the main thing. And you have your son to help you. I think Geoffrey is missing Daniel's help this year.'

'Is he enjoying living in London?'

'What young bachelor wouldn't?'

'I wish my son had remained a bachelor.'

'Yes, but young men can be very headstrong, especially when encouraged by a girl.'

'He was certainly encouraged. It's terrible to say this, I know, but I hope they don't have children. Like you, Ellen, I don't believe in divorce, but . . .'

'Sometimes it is the only way to prevent a life from being ruined. I think you're doing very well, Sheila, to cope with all this the way you are, keeping your dignity.'

Sheila sipped her tea slowly before she spoke again.

'It's very hard. People can be very malicious. I have to tell you it has helped me greatly, your taking me under your wing at church and, of course, I do enjoy making clothes for you, and I appreciate the income. My uncle left me some money, but at the moment I don't know how long it will have to last.'

'I'm sure your husband will come to his senses before too long. The seaside is all very well in the summer, but . .'

'Yes. All the same, I am so grateful that my Mother insisted that I should learn skills as a dressmaker as she did. I appreciate now how important it is to be able to support oneself.'

'My Mother was equally wise. She came from a very wealthy family but, once she was married, my father had control of her money, as was the custom in those days. That is, I came to understand, why she encouraged me to qualify as a music teacher and thus have the means to have at least a little financial independence.'

'Do you still take private pupils?'

'A few. I may also be teaching a little at a private school which has approached me. When Richard is at Grammar School he will spend less time at home and . . .'

'It's good when your talents are appreciated. And you are very talented.'

'Thank you. Music is one of my main interests.'

Sheila, wishing to impress, said eagerly, 'And mine.'

'Really? Then perhaps you would care to come with my friends and I to some concerts this autumn.'

'Oh, I'd be delighted to.'

'We are just a small group of ladies who venture out, sometimes as far as Manchester. We arrange transport between us. You will know some of them from church, and you certainly know Alice Smith.'

'Oh, yes, everyone knows Alice.'

'Yes. She wouldn't have been my first choice as a member of the group, but she has a way of asking.'

'Oh, yes,' Sheila, following Ellen carefully, again agreed.

'She was at school with me, you know, and my Father was both a client and a friend of Clarence Smith in their younger days. She does enjoy coming along with us.'

'Oh, I'm sure she does. Who wouldn't?'

'Well, I'll let you know when the next concert is.'

'Thank you.'

'And may I make a suggestion, Sheila?'

'Of course.'

'Have you thought about having a telephone installed? They are so useful when making arrangements, and also when one is in the house alone . . . .'

'You're quite right. Sylvia has mentioned I should think about having one.'

'They are quite expensive, but . . .'

'Necessary. My uncle wanted me to enjoy the money he left me, and I am obeying his wishes. I've bought new furniture, so that I was able to help out by passing my old furniture on to John and Lynda. John is very grateful, but I've seen that young madam pull faces when she thinks I'm not looking.'

'Young people like her have no taste, or appreciation of quality.'

'Exactly. It's been my one pleasure these last few months, buying new things. I don't mean I've been extravagant . . .'

'Of course not.'

'Though I have to confess to one purchase I'm embarrassed about. I've bought a television.'

'So have I.'

'Really?'

'Yes, it's in the small sitting room. I'm afraid I let Richard persuade me.'

'Well, it can be very educational. And in the evenings . . .'

'It will be a very good thing for you. And so will our concert outings.'

'Yes. Oh, yes, I'll look forward to those.'

'And I'll look forward to your next visit, Sheila. It doesn't always have to be a matter of delivering my clothes, you're welcome to call at other times, too. You must let me have your phone number when you have one.'

Sylvia was very pleased at the way her mother was taking pleasure in refurbishing the house and was also surprised at how willing she was to spend money. Graham was less reassured, but didn't have the opportunity to talk to John and Lynda on their return from Blackpool. He listened carefully to Sylvia's angry report of what she had been able to learn from her brother, and what he heard made him doubt whether Ted Stanworth would ever return to Milfield.

Although Graham was still in his twenties and wasn't yet, therefore, fully experienced in assessing people's reactions and motives, he had inherited some of his mother's perception, and certainly her listening skills. He was also used to adapting to circumstances, and had decided to accept that fate, or God's will, takes you where you are meant to go in life.

From an early age he had learned that it would be his elder brother who was the stronger man and would take over the farm, that his younger sister would always be his father's favourite, but that his mother loved them all equally. Graham had always known that, and also that she was always there to give him good advice when he asked for it, and to reassure him about his strengths. Graham was quietly satisfied with what he had achieved so far in the world, but in October, when he returned to his family home as the father of two baby sons, he allowed himself to become a very proud man indeed.

Enid wanted to make sure she was not absent from the room for long when her wonderful grandsons were there, and so had prepared plenty of cold meats, pies and desserts for the visit from her son's in-laws. Sheila had been disappointed that Sylvia and Graham were not staying with her, but had to accept that there was more room at the farm. As Sylvia's mother, she did expect to be Number One grandmother, and at first insisted on holding both of her grandsons at the same time; but the babies were not comfortable and so she reluctantly handed one back to Sylvia, who passed him on to Enid's soft, welcoming arms.

Harry tried to wait patiently for his turn for another chance to cuddle his grandsons. 'Good job you had two, Graham, or we'd have had these two Grandma's fighting over them.'

'Yeah, and Grandad is keen to get hold of them when he can, as well,' Sam teased his father. 'I'd rather leave it to the women, myself, what about you, John?'

John, piling his plate with Enid's roast beef and pork and stuffing pie, nodded, 'Too right.'

Harry laughed, 'Just you wait, you two, you'll think different when you become Dads. Of course, it'll be a while before we see that with our Sam, he's not even courting yet. I reckon you'll be next, eh John?'

Sheila, who seemed to have forgotten about the pain of Lynda's miscarriage, looked up from the child she was holding. 'They've only just got a house, they can hardly afford children.'

Enid smiled gently. 'You never can afford them, if you think about it, and you can't always choose when they'll arrive.'

'You can now. Have you not heard about this new Pill, Enid? I wish they'd had that when I was young and fancy free.'

'Harry, behave yourself,' Enid told her husband firmly, and turned to Lynda, whom she had observed had gone to look out of the window. 'Lynda, do help yourself, it's there to be eaten, you know.'

'Thank you.'

Graham, like his Mother, aware that Lynda was upset, joined in the conversation. 'It's good to have some time to enjoy just being married for a while.'

'Yes, you're young yet,' said Harry, 'have a bit of fun first, eh?'

Lynda fixed on a bright smile as she approached the table. 'Yes, I've promised John a motorbike for his 21st birthday next year, so we'll be able to go off and enjoy ourselves.'

'You're not getting a motorbike,' Sheila instructed her son and his wife firmly as she handed the now restless baby to Sylvia. She shook her head as she looked at Harry and Enid. 'They can't afford it. They wouldn't have any furniture if I hadn't been able to give them mine. There are a lot of things you need to buy before a motorbike, young lady. Ted and I never had . . .'

She stopped, suddenly remembering, but Lynda was too annoyed to notice.

'I've nearly saved enough for the deposit already, and I can pay it off so much a week.'

'You can't take on any more debt. You're already renting a television you can't really afford. And there was no need when you can come round and watch mine.'

'We need one of our own. And I will have the money to make the payments. I've made my mind up, I'm buying John a bike.'

'He won't want you to. Do you John?'

Sheila ignored her son's lack of response and carried on, 'John knows I don't believe in paying on 'the never-never'.

Lynda had had enough of being shunned and contradicted over the last few months, 'No, and you don't believe in having fun, either.'

'I beg your pardon!'

'You heard me. Your Uncle Freddie was right about you . . .

'My Uncle Freddie?'

John shouted at his wife. 'Lynda, shut up!'

'No I won't shut up. I've had enough of being told to keep quiet. It's time your Mother and your sister were told the truth.' She turned to Sheila and her daughter; 'When we saw Ted in Blackpool he said he was having more fun than he'd ever had in his life. No wonder he isn't coming back.'

It was as if a death had been announced. As if sensing the trauma, both babies began to cry. Enid held the child she was holding closer.

'It's time for their feed, isn't it, Sylvia? And no doubt they'll want changing. Shall we take them upstairs? Do you want to come and help, Sheila?'

Another silence followed the departure of the three women. Harry Laycock picked up a flagon of beer and slowly refilled the glasses of the other men in the room. Seeing Lynda alone and embarrassed after her outburst, he found her a way out. 'Oh, Lynda, our Jane wants to show you the litter of puppies our Judy's just had, don't you, love? If you want?'

Lynda was glad of the chance to breathe some cool air. 'Yeah, I'd like that.'

'They're in the barn,' Jane said, trying to understand why her Dad had sprung this on her. 'You can borrow Sylvia's wellie boots.'

'O.K.' Lynda, said, and headed for the door.

The men leaned back in their chairs, relieved to have the room to themselves.

'Women, eh?' Harry began. 'Not easy, is it, John?'

'No.'

'Especially if your Mother and your wife don't get on,' added Sam. 'Our Graham's lucky, Queenie likes Sylvia.'

Harry, who knew what doubts Enid had had over that marriage, and her views on Sheila Stanworth as her son's mother-in-law, concentrated on drinking his beer.

John had drunk enough to make him give way to his need to confide. 'My Mother didn't want me to marry Lynda. And sometimes I wish I hadn't.'

Harry had always felt sorry for the young girl. 'Nay, don't talk like that. She's a nice lass, a bit prone to say what she thinks, I suppose, but we all do that sometimes.'

'My Mum and Sylvia blame her for my Dad leaving. And like Lynda said, we can't see him coming back.'

Graham felt it was time to admit he'd come to the same conclusion. 'No, neither can I. It's a situation we'll all have to learn to deal with.'

'I'm still having to spend loads of time round at Stanhope Road, my Mother keeps finding me jobs to do. But it's worse when she comes round to our house, she always seems to find fault with something. I know she wants to help, but . . .'

'She's spent quite a bit of time at your place, hasn't she, Graham, helping Sylvia,' Harry pointed out, knowing that visits from Sheila weren't always easy for his son either.

'Yes.'

Sam, as usual, was unable to miss a chance to make mischief. 'You'll both have to watch it now she knows her husband isn't coming back. She might decide she wants to move in with one of you.'

Both John and Graham took a moment to absorb that idea. Then John held out his glass to be refilled. 'Lynda was so excited about getting me a bike.' Sam smiled. 'I expect you aren't exactly against the idea.'

'No.I'm mad keen to have one. But whether I will now, I don't know. It was going to be for my Christmas present as well as my 21st '

Harry shook his head. 'Oh, bloody hell, don't mention Christmas. That's another flaming minefield we'll all have to cross.

CHAPTER THIRTEEN

Dan Heywood found that by the beginning of 1964, through awkwardness or idleness, he had lost touch with most of his friends in Milfield, so when he came home to celebrate his 21st birthday in February he'd already declined his father's offer of having a party. He had, in any case, already celebrated with a party in London. It had been set up by the younger members of the hotel staff, and they'd danced till the early hours to all the Beatles and Rolling Stones hits.

There'd been a terrific atmosphere, as if everyone felt that there would never be a better time of their lives. Dan would never forget that party; it had proved to be a truly momentous occasion, for it was the night he lost his virginity. To be honest, he had only a vague memory of the pleasure but was rather chuffed, and a little relieved, when he found that the young woman he woke up with after the party was Sandra Burnett.

He had been aware of her for a while, she was a secretary and often came to the hotel restaurant with her boss who worked in the City and looked after the investment portfolios of some very wealthy clients. She was a very beautiful girl, not very tall but with a softly curvaceous body, short blonde curly hair and fluttery eyelashes. She also had a beguiling voice and a mischievous sense of humour, and had quickly become part of the group of friends Dan socialised with on his days off. They'd chatted a few times, but Dan had not imagined that she would ever be seriously interested in him.

Apparently, he'd underestimated himself as usual, because there he was that morning, in her bed. He'd been heading back to Milfield that day, so had only had time to kiss her and promise to see her as soon as he got back. On the train journey he tried to recover from his hangover, hoping the alcohol would have disappeared from his breath before his Mother could smell it. All the way home he kept thinking of Sandra, and wishing he could remember more of their night together.

His birthday celebration on the Saturday evening consisted of his favourite roast beef dinner, a wonderful birthday cake and some very restrained conversation. His 21st birthday inheritance from his maternal grandmother was discussed briefly, and his Mother gave stern advice about investing the money. He nodded and told them he was hoping to buy his own restaurant one day.

'Could be a good idea that, Dan,' Geoff enthused. 'People are getting quite keen on eating out these days.'

Ellen had little confidence in her eldest son as a business man. 'He hasn't the experience to make that kind of decision yet, he still has a lot to learn about the world.'

He attempted to defend himself. 'I'm learning fast.'

His mother looked doubtful and decided on another topic of conversation. 'Have you been taking advantage of the art galleries and museums?'

'Yes, on rainy days I go to The Victoria and Albert quite often.'

'And The National Gallery, I would hope.'

'Yes, now and again.'

Geoff could see his son becoming irritated by his mother's interrogations. 'You'll be short of fresh air, living in London. We'll have to go for a nice long walk while you're here.'

'Yeah, that would be great.' Dan smiled at his Dad.

Ellen continued her enquiries. 'What work are you doing at the moment?'

'I'm still working in the kitchen of course, but I'm also helping with the wine cellar. The hotel has a great wine list, mostly French, but also some white wines from Germany.'

'You must recommend some for us to try.'

'I think I'll stick to beer, talking of which, we ought to have a walk down for a pint in The Red Lion, see if any of your friends are there.'

'He has his London friends now, Geoffrey.'

'Good idea, Dad. You don't mind, do you, Mother?' Dan said, already getting up from his chair, and pretty sure she would have had enough of his company.

'If you must. Don't be too late, and don't drink too much.'

John and Lynda were in the Red Lion, chatting to some friends, but John left them immediately when he saw Dan and Geoff.

'Long time no see, Danny Boy! We missed you at Christmas.'

'Yeah, sorry, I was working. Busy time on the catering front.'

'I'll get you lads a pint, and it's a lager and lime for Lynda, isn't it?' Geoff said and headed off to the bar.

'How are you doing, mate?' John asked, putting his arm round Dan's shoulder. 'Still enjoying the bachelor life in London?'

'Yes. Having a great time. Thanks for your card,' he added, changing the subject as Lynda came to join them. 'My Mother gave it to me when I got home.'

'Yeah, sorry we didn't have your London address.'

'I bet your Mother pulled a face when she saw it,' Lynda giggled.

'Yeah,' Dan, remembering his Mother's revulsion, smiled at Lynda. 'Well, she would, wouldn't she?'

'Lynda said perhaps we should have got something a bit less cheeky, but . . .'

'No, it was a good card. Thanks, mate. I'll have to find a good one for you, get my own back.'

'Yeah. Not long now. Mind you, I got the key of the door last year,' John boasted.

'Yes, I heard you've bought a house.'

'The building society has, you mean,' Lynda put in. 'His Mother doesn't believe in buying things on 'the never-never' but she's all in favour of us having a big mortgage.'

John, who tried to avoid talking to Lynda about his mother, noticed that Geoff was having a laugh with some of his workmates at Earnshaw's who had come into the bar.

'I'd better go and help your Dad with the drinks.'

It was a long time since Dan had seen Lynda and he wasn't sure whether he was glad to be left alone with her. He tried to concentrate on making conversation and not staring too hard at her beautiful hair, and the soft curves of her body.

'You wanted your own place, though, didn't you?'

'Oh, yeah, couldn't wait to get away from the old bag. Mind you she still manages to cause trouble.'

'You are happy, though?'

Lynda looked into Dan's questing blue grey eyes but had to look away quickly.'

'Yes, of course I am. Are you?'

'Oh, yeah. Having a great time,' he repeated.

'Have you got a girlfriend?' Lynda asked, wondering why she felt such a need to know.

'Yeah. Of course.' Dan suddenly found he didn't want to think about his night with Sandra Burnett.

'Is it serious?'

'I don't know yet.'

'Who is she?'

'A secretary. John's 21st birthday would have been no better than Dan Heywood's, if it hadn't been for the motorbike which Lynda arranged to have driven up to the house with balloons tied to the handlebars. John was overjoyed and ran out to greet it, watched by some of the neighbours, who retreated with embarrassment when he turned to kiss his wife with gratitude and passion.

'I can't believe you managed to get it for me.'

'I said I would, didn't I?'

'Yeah, but it was a lot of money. Are you sure you . . .?'

'You're not going to spoil it by talking about money, are you? We'll get enough of that when we go round to your Mother's. Come on, let's have a ride before we go to your so-called 'birthday party'.'

Speeding over the moors with her arms clasped round John's waist and the wind in her hair was an exciting sensation. This was what she wanted, to feel thrilled in her husband's company, to feel free and to feel they could get away from Milfield and John's family.

When they eventually arrived at Sheila's house the back door opened and Sylvia and Graham, who'd been listening for the sound of the bike's engine, came out to greet them as they rode into the small paved area at the top of the back garden. They were slightly taken aback to see John in his jacket and helmet looking like a creature from another world. Ted and Rose had sent birthday money in advance so that John could buy the helmet, and Sylvia, with encouragement, and generosity, from Graham, had also given her brother money, knowing that he craved a black leather jacket.

Graham walked round the machine, admiring all its features. 'It's a smashing bike, you'll have some great times on this.'

'Thanks for the leather jacket, sis. And you, Graham.'

'Oh, is that what you bought with the money?' Sylvia said innocently, ignoring the smile between Graham and his brother-in-law.

'Do you want to come for a ride, Graham?'

'He can't.' Sheila stood in the kitchen doorway. 'Dinner's ready to serve. You said you wanted it for twelve. You'd better wash your hands after being on that thing.'

'Yeah.' John swaggered towards her.

'Twenty one, eh?' he said as she stood aside to let him through the door.

'Yes. Not my little boy any more. Happy Birthday,' Sheila said and kissed him on the cheek. 'I don't like that jacket. It's what those hooligans wear, what do they call them, Rockers? I don't want you turning into one of those.'

As usual the roast beef was excellent and well appreciated. Sheila had been glad when John had asked if they could eat at midday. She didn't want to sit at the table remembering the last birthday tea they'd had there. She'd even felt reluctant to make a birthday cake but tradition could not be ignored when your only son reached twenty-one years of age. She placed the cake on the table and handed her son a small box.

'I didn't expect a present, Mum. That was the deposit for the house. Key of the door, you said.'

'I know. This is the watch I bought for your Father. But he didn't want it, if you remember. No point in it going to waste.'

No-one seemed capable of breathing as John took out the watch.

'Thank you.' He held the watch in his hand for a moment, and then hesitantly fastened it round his wrist.

Lynda's voice rang out loud and bouncy. 'Twenty-one today! Twenty-one today! He's . .' and was joined for the rest of the birthday anthem by voices more relieved than celebratory. Sylvia, wishing now that they'd brought the children with them instead of leaving them to have their afternoon nap in Enid's care, tried to fill the silence which followed the singing.

'You'll have to start behaving like a grown up now, John.'

'I suppose so.'

'No more climbing trees and coming home with a big hole in your trousers. Do you remember that day he fell in the river and came home caked with mud and stinking, Mum?'

'Yes. You never think when they're that age that one day they'll up and leave you.'

'John hasn't left you, Mum. You see him nearly every day.'

'It's not the same once they're married. Just you wait till your two decide they don't need you any more.'

Graham didn't like the downward trend of an already sinking occasion. 'We're a long way from having to think about that while they're still in nappies! Did you have a birthday celebration at work, John?'

'Yes, Mr Earnshaw let us finish half an hour early, and he bought me a pint.'

'Then John had a few more with the lads,' Lynda laughed. 'He came home absolutely blotto.'

'Do you want to go for a drink tonight? My treat.'

John glanced at Lynda. 'Thanks, Graham, but I can't tonight.' He looked at his new, memory laden wristwatch. 'In fact, we've got to be going soon.'

'Going?' Sheila had expected them all to stay the whole afternoon. 'Where?'

'For a ride on the bike. He hasn't really been out on it yet,' Lynda lied.

Sylvia, who knew she and Graham needed to get back to the farm for teatime at the latest, was annoyed at her brother's selfishness. 'But Mum's expecting you to stay, it's your birthday, you should be spending it with her.'

'I have done. But I . . .'

It wasn't hard for Sheila to guess. 'You're going to see your Father, aren't you?'

'I have to.'

'There's no 'have to' about it!' Sylvia exclaimed. 'I don't go and see him.'

Lynda was ready for this argument. 'No, but you should. And you should take his grandsons. The poor man's heartbroken that you haven't let him see them.'

'He should have thought of that before he deserted my Mother! He'll never see them unless he comes back home to his wife. And even then, he'll be lucky if I let them have anything to do with a man as wicked as he is!'

Graham felt this was going too far. 'Sylvia!'

'I know you don't agree, Graham, but I can't help the way I feel.'

'And I can't . . .' John was close to tears. 'He's my Dad, and he wants to see me on my 21st birthday. And I want to see him.'

He grabbed his leather jacket and almost ran out of the house.

CHAPTER FOURTEEN

For the next year or so life chugged along in Milfield, following a routine of going to work, watching television and socialising at the pub. For Jean Clayton, though, life was no longer the same routine, she found herself going out a lot more than she'd ever done. It was hard to refuse Peggy Haworth's invitations to see a production by the local amateur dramatic society, or a musical in Manchester. It was not often that Jean was allowed to pay for tickets, even when she wasn't going as Gordon's 'date'. Peggy would get complimentary tickets or make some tactful excuse for paying for all of them. Similarly the clothes she gave to Jean were 'samples' given to her by clothing suppliers, and as Jean's wardrobe grew, so did her confidence.

Peggy gave her the mothering she'd never had, treating her as the beloved daughter-in-law she was determined Jean would one day become. Added to his mother's affection was the adoration she received from Gordon, flowers, chocolates, and especially his Valentine cards and presents were always everything Jean had dreamed of. She found it impossible to refuse any of this loving attention, and was beginning to wonder if she would be able to refuse when Gordon asked the question he was obviously preparing her for.

Sheila Stanworth's life was also becoming much more comfortable in every way. She took every opportunity she could to spend time in Ellen Heywood's social group, and found she was made welcome as a member of various groups and committees. She was also benefitting from connections which provided more clients for her dressmaking and millinery skills, particularly at the church, where many ladies of the congregation followed Ellen's lead as far as fashion was concerned.

By the spring of 1965 no-one she met at church or in town enquired about her absent husband. There were days, and sometimes a whole week when she could manage not to think about Ted, except when she was with her family, and even then there was an unspoken agreement that his name would not be mentioned. She visited Sylvia and Graham as often as they would allow, and brought home photographs of her grandchildren which she kept in her handbag to show to everyone, or displayed in silver frames on her sideboard and china cabinets.

She suspected that Lynda and John regularly went on their motorbike to visit Ted, but she was careful not to ask where they'd been. She did keep hoping that she might hear hints that Ted was tiring of life at the seaside, but nothing was said about their visits to Blackpool until the summer, when a photograph appeared in 'The Milfield Express'.

The caption was 'Local Beauty Wins Blackpool Competition' and John and Lynda weren't aware of it until Sheila slammed the newspaper down on their living room table one evening.

'Have you no shame?' she shouted at Lynda.

'Oh, hell.' John sat down slowly and turned the paper towards him.

'Look at her, look at your wife, flaunting her naked body.'

'I wasn't naked. I was wearing a bikini.'

'Oh, is that what you call it? You're as near naked as makes no difference. What were you thinking of, John, how could you let her do this?'

'I didn't let her. I knew nothing about it till she came back with the cup.'

'And the prize money. That's why I entered, it were too good a chance to miss.'

John thought he ought to try to make excuses for his silly wife, and made things worse.

'She didn't know it was going to be in the paper. It wasn't a big competition, it was in aid of a local charity that Rose's involved with. There must have been somebody from the Express in Blackpool last weekend.'

'Rose? That woman, do you mean?'

'Yes.' Involuntarily Lynda looked at the corner of the photograph where Rose was applauding and beaming up at Lynda. Sheila didn't miss the direction of the glance and peered more closely at the photo. Then she stabbed at it with her finger.

'And is that her? Is that the nasty piece of work who took my husband from me?' Sheila's voice was shaking now.

'I'm sorry, Mum.' John put his arm round his mother's shoulders as she sank down on the settee and began to cry. Sheila had begun at last to defy her parents and allow herself to cry more readily since Ted had left.

'Not half as sorry as I am. How can I face my friends at church now? I'd just managed to come through the shame of your Dad leaving me, they'd more or less stopped talking about him, and now this happens. It'll be all, 'Was that your daughter-in-law we saw in the paper?' and then they won't need to say any more. That picture speaks for itself. It's disgusting. Oh, what if the Bank finds out about it?'

John looked at her blankly. 'What's it got to do with the County Bank?'

'Are you so slow that you haven't taken it in yet? As a bank employee Graham and his family have to be beyond reproach. He can't afford to be embarrassed by this sort of thing.'

'They won't hear about it,' John reassured her, and hoped he was right.

Lynda was again wishing Rose had never told her about the contest. 'It's only a photo. Everyone will have forgotten about it next week.'

Sheila, clutching her handkerchief, glared up at her. 'Did you do this deliberately to show me up, to hurt me?'

'No. I did it for a laugh.'

'A laugh? It will be me who'll be laughed at - again.'

Tears ran down her cheeks once more, but now their source was more anger than shame as she asked in a bitter tone, 'Oh, John, why, oh why did you have to marry such a stupid, shameless girl?'

Lynda watched her husband's face grow white with anger, just as it had when he'd seen her on that catwalk parading her body for other men to stare at and lust after. They'd had a huge row about it that night, and Lynda's attempts to calm his fury had led to sex driven by his rage and a jealous need to prove possession. That was the night their child was conceived.

That summer Dan was invited to meet Sandra's parents who lived in Surrey, in a lovely old Georgian house not far from Richmond. It was, the elegant and slightly bohemian Mrs Burnett pointed out with a languid wave of her hand, in need of some repair and refurbishment, but Dan loved the atmosphere of the place. It seemed the kind of house which held echoes of laughter, and the aroma of coffee, and of wine poured into generous glasses; the garden furniture was bleached by the sun and worn smooth so it was no longer smart, but held out an invitation to the delights of long days in the sunshine. Dan was also astonished and delighted by the easy-going attitude of Sandra's parents towards him sharing a bed with their daughter, and their acceptance of him as her 'young man'.

Roger Burnett, unbowed by his somewhat precarious life in the City, and with the look of a watchful Roman soldier, was a keen tennis player who had been 'the golden boy' of the village near Oxford where he had been brought up. He and his wife, Laura, were only in their fifties but had lived their lives at such a pace, and with the help of so much alcohol and exotic experiments that they looked much older than Dan had expected. He was fascinated by their accounts of their travels, and amused by their other favourite topic of conversation, their daughter's adventures and talents. Sandra was a good singer and actress, and Dan had been enjoying spending time with the amateur dramatic and musical theatre societies she'd introduced him to, particularly when they encouraged him to sing.

'You're something of a star yourself, Sandra tells us,' Laura said as she poured another cup of coffee. Dan, relaxing in an armchair on the lawn which stretched between the house and the river, smiled shyly. 'Not really. I've no talent at all compared to Sandra.'

'No-one has any talent compared to Sandra,' Roger asserted proudly, stroking his daughter's arm. 'She's going to be a star one day, once she's had a bit more professional training.'

'You have a lovely voice, Daniel.' Sandra smiled at him in that way she had of making him feel more special than he'd ever felt in his life.

'It would improve if you had training, though. Why don't you and Daniel go for singing lessons together, darling?'

'It would be lovely, Mummy, but they're so expensive, and I can't ask you to . . . .'

'I could pay for them,' Dan offered eagerly.

'No, I couldn't let you do that.'

'Please. It would be wonderful, I wouldn't like to go on my own, but if the two of us went . . .'

Sandra clapped her hands with delight. 'It would be much more fun. Yes. All right. You've persuaded me.'

Her mother beamed with satisfaction, twisted her pale sand-coloured hair more securely on top of her head, and leaned back languidly in her chair. 'Why don't you take Daniel for a stroll along the river, one never knows how much of this sunshine we'll have. You should make the most of it.'

Dan's need of time alone with Sandra was a constant obsession for him, and made him jump to his feet immediately. The Burnetts nodded knowingly to each other as they watched the couple walking hand in hand out of the garden.

The first person Lynda wanted to tell about her fear that she was pregnant was Kathleen Kelly, because she wanted to find out if there was a way she could stop herself from having a baby. She didn't want a child yet, it wasn't the right time for her or John, or their marriage. Then she remembered what Kath had said to her once: 'whatever the circumstances, the gift of a child should always be welcomed'. Lynda, however, couldn't stop herself from secretly hoping that she would lose this baby. So she didn't confide in Kath until over two months had passed.

They were sitting in Kath's kitchen one evening having a cup of tea and had left Bernie snoring in front of the television set. John had again gone round to his mother's and Lynda had felt lonely sitting in the house on her own, so she'd gone for a walk and found herself on Bennett Street.

'I've missed twice now, Kath, so do you think I am pregnant?'

'More than likely. Are you pleased?'

'No. I wish I'd had the courage to go and ask about The Pill.'

'You might still have got pregnant, it's not 100% reliable. And it's much more natural to have babies – that's what men and women are for. A child is a blessing, Lynda.'

I know I should be pleased, but . . .'

'There's women who would give anything to be having a baby.'

'I know. But, I'm scared.' She suddenly felt tearful and was grateful for the comfort of Kath's embrace.

'What if I'm no good as a mother? I don't seem to be good at anything these days.'

'That's just your hormones talking – and your mother-in-law.'

'She won't think I'm fit to have a child. Oh, Kath what if the baby doesn't like me either?'

Kath laughed, and stroked her cheek. 'Don't be daft, Lynda! Your baby will love you, like nobody else has ever loved you before.'

'Oh, I hope so, Kath. And I hope I'll be good enough to be its Mother.'

She didn't tell John until October, until she was sure that this little life was really there. She thought afterwards that she had probably chosen the wrong moment to tell him. He'd come home after a day at work that had been even harder than usual, and he'd just sat down to read the newspaper after their evening meal.

'John, I've got something to tell you.'

'What?' he grunted, focusing on the piece of news he was reading.

'I'm going to have a baby.'

The newspaper was slowly lowered on to his lap, and he stared at her with a look of horror.

'Oh, hell. Are you sure?'

'Yeah. It's been three months.'

'But we've been so careful.'

'Except that once.'

He looked at her and then bowed his head, remembering with some shame how he had treated his wife that night.

'I suppose there's nothing we can do.'

'No.'

'I don't know what my Mother will say.'

'I do. That we can't afford it. And she'll be right for once.'

'Yeah.'

She saw then that fear in John's eyes, the fear that would become part of him and change him. They were already struggling to make ends meet sometimes, and she could see that John now felt the full burden of being a man who would have to provide for his family.

A week later Lynda had the opportunity to let her friends know. The occasion was Jean Clayton's engagement party, held in the snug, the cosy back room at 'The Red Lion'. It was more of an informal gathering of local women than an engagement party as Shirley Clayton hadn't offered to organise anything, and Jean didn't want the embarrassment of inviting people to her home.

For the same reason, it was doubling up as her 21st birthday party for her friends. Her actual 'coming of age' had been frugally celebrated a few days earlier in the Clayton household, and had been a big disappointment for Jean who had been hoping that her huge contribution to the care of the family would, at last, be shown real appreciation. When she went out with Gordon that evening, and he went down on one knee like the true romantic he was, and offered her not only a diamond ring, but a new life, she saw no option but to agree to marry him.

Jean was thrilled that there were 'bottom drawer' presents and a cake, the latter being donated by Annie, who was very fond of the young girl who worked so conscientiously alongside her in the shop. Shirley Clayton was keen to assist her daughter with the presents, looking after each one as it was opened.

'Oh, what good towels, we could do with some new towels, ours have got holes in them, haven't they, Jean? And what a lovely tablecloth - and napkins. Oh, aren't we posh!' she exclaimed as she held up the cream damask cloth which was one of the presents from Peggy.

'Yes, I'll keep them here for you, shall I, Jean?' Lynda offered, taking them from Shirley and firmly placing them in the pile she was guarding. She'd known Jean's mother long enough to be able to read her mind fairly accurately, and could see she was already having ideas about these items and doing calculations about their 'selling-on' value.

'Have you set a date yet, Jean?' Annie enquired.

'I've always wanted to get married in May, with all the blossom and spring flowers.'

'Ooh, lovely. And will it be a church wedding?'

'Oh, yes,' Shirley declared proudly, 'a white wedding and a sit-down do afterwards.'

Jean turned to her mother in surprise. 'Oh, I didn't think . . . . '

Lynda raised her eyebrows. 'Oh, been saving up, have you, Mrs Clayton?'

'No, but we'll manage something. And I'm sure Mrs Haworth, as mother of the bridegroom will want to . . .'

'Mum!' Jean's face was scarlet with embarrassment. 'We don't know what . . .. Me and Gordon haven't talked about the wedding yet.'

'We'll discuss it later, you and me, shall we, Jean?' Peggy suggested.

Shirley, suspecting immediately that she was going to be cut out of those discussions, tried to assert herself. 'She'll be having our Marilyn as one of her bridesmaids, the little love's really excited about it already.'

'Yes. And I'm hoping you'll be matron of honour, Lynda.' Jean turned to her friend. 'We promised each other, years ago, that we'd choose each other as bridesmaids, didn't we?'

'Yes, we did. But I won't be able to, love.'

'Why ever not?'

'I'm expecting at the beginning of May.'

'Oh.'

'I'm sorry, Jean. I wouldn't let you down for the world, you know that.'

'Bit of a surprise, Lynda.' Shirley said, watching her carefully.

'Yeah.'

'Is John pleased?' Jean asked.

'Yeah, of course he is.'

'And his Mother?' Shirley again.

Kath decided it was time to stop Shirley from looking for mischief. 'She'll be hoping for a little girl, I expect, having two grandsons already.' Kath raised her glass.

'To Lynda and John, and the little one.'

A few weeks later, on November 27th which, fortunately, was a Saturday, she was asking the same guests to raise their glasses again, but this time in her front room. She and Bernie had had to raid Grandma Kelly's old brown teapot to have enough money to buy the food and drink, but they'd felt they had no choice when they'd met John on his way to the football match the week before, and learned how little celebration of Lynda's coming of age was being planned.

'What do you mean, she's not having a party? It's her 21st !'

John couldn't look at Kath. 'I, we might have a few friends round to our place for a drink. She told me she definitely didn't want my Mum putting on a birthday tea for her, so I don't know what I can do, really.'

Kath shook her head. 'Why women marry men, I'll never know.'

'I'll show you why tonight,' Bernie put his arm round his wife, and received a sharp jab of her elbow in his ribs.

John was floundering now. 'I think Freda's got something organised at the café in the afternoon, but . . . .'

'You can't have a 21st birthday on a weekend and not have a party on the Saturday night. Leave it to me. Just you bring Lynda round to our place for a drink and we'll surprise her.'

'Oh, will you, Kath? That'd be great.' He took out his wallet and pressed some money into her hand. 'Here, take this towards the drink and that. Please.'

'O.K.'

He held on to her hand. 'I'm ever so grateful, Kath.'

'There's no need to be, I'm glad to do it. Your Lynda's the daughter of one of my best friends. Doreen, God rest her, would have wanted her to have a party. And we can't have it in The Black Bull, but we can make it as close as we can to that.'

Bernie raised an imaginary glass and grinned. 'Sounds good to me!'

Sheila came round to the house on the Friday evening with her present.

'Sorry to disturb you,' she said, looking disapprovingly at the remains of their egg and chip supper.'

'It's all right, we'd just finished.' John scooped the last two chips off his plate and swiftly cleared the table.

'I thought it best to bring it round this evening as you're working tomorrow. You can open it now, though.' She placed the large parcel on the settee.

'It's from me and Sylvia. We went to Manchester for it.'

Lynda unwrapped the dark blue woollen coat and looked at Sheila with gratitude.

'Thank you.'

John beamed at his Mother, and would have given her a hug if he'd known how. 'Thanks, Mum. It's just what she needed, isn't it, Lynda?'

'Yeah. I was freezing just wearing my mac, and it's too tight across the front now.'

'That's why we chose this wrap-over style. There's a bit of room for . . . .it'll see you through the winter.' Sheila opened the shopping bag she was carrying and took out a square tin. 'I've made you a cake.'

Still feeling guilty at having made sure she wouldn't be available to organise a celebration of her daughter-in-law's birthday, Sheila didn't look at the couple as she placed the tin on the table and repeated her well planned excuse.

'I'm sorry I can't do you a birthday tea but, like I explained, we had this concert booked a long time ago.'

'It's all right. My Mother's friend is putting on a party for me at her house. It was supposed to be a surprise, but I found out.' Her eyes shone as she looked at her husband.

'Oh. Which friend is that?'

'Kathleen Kelly. Do you remember, Mum, she's a nurse. She was at our wedding. It was her husband who played the piano.'

'Oh, yes. Well, I hope you have a lovely time. I must be going now. You'll be round on Sunday to mend the shed roof, won't you, John?'

'Yeah.' He glanced at Lynda, thinking of their precious Sunday mornings in bed. 'Might not be till the afternoon, though.'

'Well, don't leave it too late,' Sheila said, wishing she hadn't seen the saucy grin Lynda had given her husband.

The curtains in the large square bay window of the front room of the Kellys' house were rarely closed; anyone nosey enough to stare inside was always given a cheery wave and many a time beckoned inside for a drink. Anyone passing that night would have hoped to be invited to join in the fun among the bright lights, multi-coloured balloons and records played at full volume.

The large sandstone terraced house was a Victorian family home which had been bought as a bargain in the days when Kath and Bernie had been expecting to have at least four children. They'd never had, and never would have, the money to decorate it properly and all the repairs were done on a 'desperate fix' basis, usually by a friend of a friend who was happy to help out and satisfied with a very marginal profit.

Any visitors who noticed the faded wallpaper soon forgot it when they found their attention captured by the huge collection of black and white family photographs, and the brightly coloured pictures in cheap frames. Many of these were pictures of thatched country cottages or rascally mongrel dogs which had been saved from the lids of the large boxes of chocolates given to Kath and Bernie at birthdays or Christmas.

Not all of the guests knew Lynda but most of them were 'regulars' at the Kelly parties, and all of them had brought a few bottles of beer or a plate of food to be added to those set out on the large old table in the cosy living room. As soon as most of the guests had arrived Bernie set them running all round the house following clues for a treasure hunt which necessitated everyone huddling together to read clues and then, laughing at Bernie's daft and often bawdy sense of humour, charging off to the next bit of silliness. By the time the hunt was over, and someone was standing there clutching a prize which wouldn't look out of place at a fairground, there was no-one who hadn't got to know or renewed acquaintance with everyone else at the party.

Peggy and Gordon Haworth had been invited because of their connection to Jean, and because Peggy and Kath, through Lynda, had got to know each other at the café. Gordon was at first too shy to speak to any of the noisy crowd and was very hesitant about invading the bedrooms as Jean pulled him up the stairs on the hunt for clues. Then, as he saw kisses being stolen and bottoms being slapped he began to realise he was discovering a world where risqué seaside postcards came to life.

When Lynda suddenly landed heavily on his lap during the game of musical chairs, he slipped sideways off the chair and looked up to find Lynda in a heap on top of him.

'Will you look at that, Jean,' Bernie cried out. 'You thought you were marrying a nice quiet chap and it turns out he's a real Lothario. Let go of her, you dirty dog!'

Gordon leapt to his feet, waving his hands in a gesture of innocence and looked around to find everyone laughing at him.

'Leave him alone, Bernie,' Lynda pleaded as she scrambled to her feet and pulled down her skirt. 'Can't you see poor Gordon's dying of embarrassment? It was my fault anyway, I landed on him like a baby elephant, it's this bump of mine, sends me off balance.'

'Oh, God, are you all right, Lynda?' Gordon had forgotten Lynda was pregnant and was now petrified he'd harmed her.

'Yes, I'm fine, don't you worry. It's made of strong stuff, this baby of ours, isn't it, John?'

He put his arm round his wife and kissed her, suddenly pushing all his anxieties aside and feeling confident about his child. 'Yes, it's going to be a little belter.'

Kath took charge now. 'I think it's time it got fed – and the rest of you. The food's curling up at the edges next door, so get in there.'

Jean put a possessive arm round her fiancé's waist, and gave Lynda a disapproving look. 'Come on, Gordon, I'll get you a plate.'

Lynda sought out her friend later that evening when she saw her sitting alone in a quiet corner under the stairs.

'I'm sorry about the musical chairs.'

'It's quite all right,' Jean said in her 'prim' voice.

'It was an accident.'

'Yes. But you should be more careful, the condition you're in.'

'I know. It should be you having a baby, not me. You'd have more idea how to cope with it than I will.'

'Yes, I've had enough practice, looking after our Marilyn and Peter. I've had enough of looking after babies.'

'It'll be different when it's your own.'

'Will you shut up, I'm not even married yet!'

'Won't be long, though.'

'No.'

Lynda saw the doubt in Jean's eyes. 'You do want to marry him, don't you?'

'We're engaged, aren't we?'

'Yeah, but you're a lot younger than him. You haven't had time to play the field really.'

'I have. I've been out with quite a few, but . . . I've not met anyone as nice as Gordon. And his Mother's lovely to me.'

'Yeah, I can see she's very keen. But you're not marrying his Mother.'

Jean was beginning to get upset. 'Lynda, will you stop looking at me like that, and asking me all these questions.'

'I just want to know if you're sure Gordon's 'the one', truly?'

'Oh, if you mean the big romance, the handsome hero I dreamed about, no he isn't. You married him!' She jumped up and ran up the stairs.

Kath, taking an empty tray back to the kitchen, paused as she saw Lynda's shocked expression. 'What's upset Jean?'

'Me. When I married John. She used to have a big crush on him, you know. I thought she'd got over it. I should have kept my mouth shut, but I'm worried that she might be marrying Gordon for the wrong reasons.'

'And what would those be?'

'Well, because he makes a fuss of her, he's always buying her presents, him and his Mother. And because she's desperate to get away from that house and skivvying for her parents.'

'You can't blame her for wanting to do that.'

'No, but you should marry because you're in love with somebody.'

'And how long does 'in love' last with most couples? I've talked to Jean, she thinks Gordon is the best offer she'll ever get, and who are we to tell her any different?'

'She's only twenty-one, she's got plenty of time to meet somebody else. It's his Mother pushing this, wanting to see him settled.'

'Jean knows that, but she thinks the world of Peggy.'

'I know. She's even told me she's happy that she and Gordon are going to live with her after they're married. You'd think she'd know better than that after seeing what it's been like for me and John living with Sheila.'

'But it won't be like that, Lynda, not like that at all. Jean told me that she'll be happy to have a proper home, and that with Peggy and Gordon she feels like she's being looked after, cared for, for the first time in her life.'

'Oh. But, being Gordon's wife . . .And Peggy can't wait to be a grandma.'

'It's no use your worrying, Lynda. You made your decisions, and Jean's making hers, and she could do a lot worse than Gordon Haworth. Now how about you and John, and your baby?'

'We've found it hard, but I think we're both getting used to the idea. John's really uptight about how we'll pay for everything. Did your Bernie get worried like that?'

'My Bernie, worried about money? That'll be the day! He just believes in Divine Providence, and me having a steady job!'

'I haven't dared to start making a list of what we'll need. Like I said, it's all come at the wrong time for us, Kath. We can't afford to start a family really.'

'You never can, but you'll manage somehow, you have to.'

'Freda says she'll keep my job open for me till after I've had the baby.'

'Are you sure you'll want to go back to work?'

'No, but I think I'll have to, we've got a mortgage to pay and loads of work still to be done on the house. I'll be able to take the baby with me, there's a room at the back of the café. I'll have it making sandwiches and cups of tea in no time!'

'If it's a girl!'

'John wants a boy, and I do really.'

'Sorry to tell you, my darling, but you won't have much say in that! You get what God gives you!'

'Yeah. It's scary, you know. I've not come across many babies. I won't know what to do with it.'

'Don't you worry, your Auntie Kathleen will be there to help you,' Kath reassured her, placing her strong, loving arms round Lynda's shoulders.

It was Geoff who passed on the news about Lynda's baby to Dan during one of their phone calls. He'd been told by Annie about Lynda's pregnancy and had a feeling that Dan needed to know. Geoff suspected that his son still held on to a dream that one day, somehow, Lynda's marriage to John would end and she would marry the man who had been her first love.

He was right, and losing that dream made Dan vulnerable. When he came home that Christmas he brought Sandra with him.

'This is a lovely room, Mrs Heywood. So elegant.' Sandra, perched decorously on the edge of the Chesterfield sofa in Ellen's 'drawing' room, sipped her glass of sherry and smiled sweetly.

'Most of the furniture belonged to my parents and grandparents.'

'That's wonderful. We have quite a lot of furniture which was inherited, too. Quite valuable some of it, but it's the family connection which is important.'

'Yes.'

'I'm so thrilled that my engagement ring is a family heirloom.'

Geoff, who had been leaning back in his armchair contentedly observing Sandra's charms, sat forward anxiously, looking first at his son and then at his wife.

'You're engaged?'

'Yes, I've asked Sandra to marry me.' Dan turned towards his Mother. 'I came home to get my Grandmother's ring, the emerald one she left me to give to my fiancée.'

Ellen's tone was cold. 'You haven't asked permission, Daniel.'

He took pleasure in deliberately misunderstanding her. 'Yes, I did. I asked Sandra's Father two weeks ago.'

'He was delighted, and so was my Mother,' Sandra gushed.

Ellen scrutinised Sandra's face. 'This is very sudden.'

Daniel was glad his Mother's attention had been directed at Sandra, so that she didn't notice that his face went slightly pink at her comment. His engagement to Sandra had come rather more quickly than he had expected, and in fact he wasn't quite sure how it had come about, but he was proud that she'd agreed to become his wife.

Sandra smiled briefly at Ellen and then fluttered her eyelashes at Geoff. 'Not really. Daniel and I have been, together, for quite a while now. Surely you knew that?'

There was one of those silences often experienced over the years in that room. Then Geoff jumped to his feet and strode over to shake his son's hand. 'Well, Congratulations!'

Sandra stood up to receive his kiss on her creamy pink cheek. Ellen didn't move.

'We're very pleased for them, aren't we, Ellen?'

His wife said not a word, so he blustered on. 'I think there's a bottle of champagne in the cellar. Do you want to come and help me find it, Dan?'

Father and son disappeared together as fast as they could, as they had so many times in the past.

The wedding took place at Richmond registry office on Valentine's Day the following year, a romantic date but also one which enabled the Burnetts to suggest sharing the cost with the Heywood family, as it would also be Daniel's birthday. The bride wore an ivory satin suit with a skirt short enough to make Ellen raise her eyebrows.

CHAPTER FIFTEEN

There wasn't really room for three people in the small back bedroom at Beechwood Avenue, especially as Lynda was now eight months pregnant, but both Sheila and Sylvia wanted to make sure everything was properly organised. Graham had brought Sylvia to the house to bestow a Moses basket and a pile of bed linen and baby clothes. Once he and John had carried the things upstairs the two men had retreated downstairs to have a glass of beer.

'You sort out the linen, Sylvia, while I put the clothes away. John made a good job of painting this chest of drawers. I like white. It would have been better if they'd painted the walls white as well, yellow's a bit cold looking.'

Lynda eased herself down onto the small rocking chair which had been her grandmother's. 'I like yellow. I wanted it to be a nice sunny room. Do you like the ducks I've painted along that wall, Sylvia? I got Bernie to do me a stencil, he's good at things like that. He made me the set of shelves as well.'

'Yes, the ducks are quite good. Who's Bernie?'

'The husband of a friend of mine, Kathleen Kelly.'

'They're Irish,' Sheila informed her daughter, making it sound like an affliction.

Lynda was determined to remain calm. 'Kath's a midwife at the hospital. I'm hoping she'll be on duty when the baby comes.'

Sheila spoke as if addressing a slow-witted servant. 'You can't know when it will arrive. You'll have to have whoever's there at the time.' She smiled at her daughter. 'John was two weeks late, but you were born on the predicted date.'

'That's me, always on time. Graham compliments me on my punctuality. I think you could be early, Lynda, looking at the size of you.'

Sheila looked with distaste at Lynda's large bump. 'Oh, don't say that, I don't want it arriving before my birthday.'

'Have you decided what you want to do yet, Mother? We must do something special for your 50th.'

'Oh, don't say that number, it only upsets me. I don't want to be an old lady.'

'Fifty isn't old, is it, Lynda?'

'No. Thanks again for all this stuff, Sylvia. Especially that dress, I didn't think I'd have anything to wear at Jean's wedding.'

'Lynda's friend from school, Sheila reminded Sylvia, and then added, 'A family from The Clough.'

'Oh. Is it church or registry office?'

Lynda, feeling her friend was being judged, said defensively, 'It's quite a big white wedding actually. At St Matthew's.'

Sheila added importance to the date. 'On the 7th, the day before my birthday.'

In spite of complaining how she was dreading reaching the age of fifty Sheila had been mentioning the date of her birthday at every opportunity. She didn't miss the sarcasm as Lynda feigned surprise.

'Oh, is it on the Sunday, May 8th, your birthday?'

Sheila sniffed, and turned to her daughter. 'It's very good of you, Sylvia, to let John and Lynda have all these things. It will be a big help, especially in the circumstances.'

'I'll let you have it all back as soon as I've finished with it.'

'No rush. We're hoping we might not need it again. Two sons are quite enough.'

'Don't you want a little girl?' Sheila sounded disappointed.

'Sometimes I think it would be nice, but I don't really want to have any more children. You'll have to hope Lynda has a girl.'

'I don't care what she has, as long as she doesn't have it on my birthday.'

'I'll do my best not to inconvenience you.'

Sylvia, following Graham's guidance, didn't want antagonism to increase between her Mother and sister-in-law. 'So what do you want to do on your birthday? We can't have you catering for your own birthday celebration.'

'No. And there are too many bad memories bound up with birthday teas at my house now. I think I'd like to have a meal at a hotel. Somewhere really smart.'

Sylvia was relieved. 'Oh, that's a good idea. We could book a table at The Peacock.'

Sheila responded quickly. 'I've heard that Ashton House has an excellent menu.'

Lynda guessed whose opinion that was. 'Who told you that? Mrs Heywood?'

'Yes. Of course, it is rather more expensive than The Peacock.'

Sylvia's voice was bright and cheery. 'That's all right. It's a special birthday after all, and the four of us are sharing.'

This was the first Lynda had heard of it. 'Are we?'

'Yes, I've discussed it with John, that and the joint present.' Sylvia turned to examine the pile of nappies Lynda had arranged on a shelf. 'These are good quality nappies. Where did you get them?'

'They're one of the presents from the customers at the café. They had a whip round and bought me quite a bit of stuff.'

'Would you like me to show you how to fold one?'

'Yes, please. I haven't got a clue.'

Jean Clayton's wedding day was the happiest day of her life. Her white satin dress was brand new and trimmed with lace and pearls, and her tiara made her look like a princess. Everyone told her she looked beautiful and that the meal at The Peacock was excellent. She was living her dream all day, from having her hair done at the hairdresser's to driving away in Gordon's car festooned with ribbons and Good Luck horseshoes.

She noticed that her father's speech had had the benefit of a few glasses of whisky but thankfully he didn't make her blush too much. She did wish he'd remembered to mention that it was Peggy's generosity which had made the wedding and the reception possible. She wasn't aware of how her family, and the few guests her parents had been allowed to invite, were gently guided towards good behaviour by Peggy and watchfully supportive guests like Geoff Heywood. His wife, of course, had arranged a previous engagement, which everyone was glad about.

Lynda was desperate to go home and lie down but sheer will-power kept her standing outside The Peacock ready to shower her friend with confetti again before she got into the car. She was pleased to see Jean looking round for her.

'Where's Lynda?'

'I'm here, love.' She gave Jean a hug and kissed her on the cheek. 'Be happy, won't you?'

'Yes, of course I will. And you take care of yourself. I hope we're back from The Lakes in time for you having the baby.'

'Don't even think about that. You're on your honeymoon.'

She saw the apprehension on Jean's face and whispered. 'Don't worry, everything will be fine. Like I said, be happy.'

As soon as the car had driven round the corner Lynda asked John to take her home.

'But we'll miss the best part . . . '

Kath Kelly, who had been observing Lynda throughout the wedding, intervened.

'Bernie hasn't had a lot to drink, he'll take you home, or to the hospital. Which do you think?'

'I don't know.'

'Are you having contractions?'

'No, but my back aches, and I just feel I've got to go home.'

'O.K. I'll come home with you. I put cushions in the back of the van, so you won't spoil your suit, John.'

'Right, thanks. I need to wear it tomorrow.'

'What for?'

'His Mother's bloody birthday!'

Ashton house had been built by Hubert Ashton who had owned three cotton mills and who knew how to make money. His wife had known how to spend it, and they'd both been very proud of the imposing sandstone mansion they'd built for their family on a large plot of land in the leafy outskirts of Milfield. There was a Roman style marble-mosaic in the centre of the floor in the lofty, echoing entrance hall, and the darkness of the oak panelling of the interior was offset by the many large windows inlaid with panels of stained glass. After the war it had been converted into a hotel with a dining room large enough to cater for civic events and weddings and funerals. On Sundays the clientele were seated at tables arranged on the side of the room which faced the large garden, and Graham had managed to book one of the best tables by a window.

As Sylvia and Graham escorted her into the dining room at Ashton House everyone soon became aware that it was Sheila's special day. She was flutteringly, but determinedly, coy about which birthday she was celebrating, but very graciously accepted congratulations from some of the other guests in the dining room and the members of staff who were unfortunate enough to be in attendance that Sunday. As she and her family took their seats Sheila was delighted to see a small side table on which stood a silver ice bucket containing a bottle of champagne.

'Oh, you are spoiling me! I didn't expect all this!'

She noted every detail of the table setting with pleasure, and thanked the waiter in her most refined tone as he handed out the large silver and white menus and gave Graham a copy of the wine list.

'Oh, isn't he smart? You can tell he's properly trained. Oh, this is lovely. Look at this vase of flowers, and all these knives and forks. What are you having, Sylvia?'

'I don't know yet. We'd better wait for John and Lynda.'

'They should be here by now. I hope they're not going to be late on my birthday.'

Graham saw them crossing the foyer. 'No, they've just arrived.'

The hint of disappointment was quite obvious. 'Oh. Both of them?'

Graham, a little annoyed, glanced at his wife. 'Of course.'

Sheila, for the benefit of the other diners, waved prettily as she saw John and Lynda arriving in the doorway, but then gasped as she saw Lynda clutch at John's arm and then stand very still and open-mouthed. She and John stared at the small wet patch which had appeared on the floor at Lynda's feet, and John followed his wife as she scuttled towards the Ladies' toilets.

A few minutes later he reappeared in the doorway, and then came across to them in such a hurry that he almost knocked the glasses off one of the tables.

'It's Lynda. Her waters have broke.'

'Keep your voice down,' his mother hissed.

'They've called a taxi to take us to the hospital. I've got to go.'

'But what about my birthday? You can't miss my birthday!'

'I'll be back as soon as I can.'

Sheila sat there, her mouth opening and closing as fury and embarrassment vied for supremacy across her face. Graham stood up, took hold of the bottle of champagne and signalled to the waiter.

'Shall we open this?' he asked brightly, hoping to change the expression on his mother-in-law's face.

Every sound seemed to crash against the crazed white tiles of the hospital walls and bounce off straight into Lynda's body as she lay shivering on the rattling trolley which was shaking her along the draughty corridor leading to the delivery room.

John had run along behind the trolley but the door of the delivery room had been firmly shut against him. He sat on a hard wooden bench in the corridor and prayed that Kath Kelly would arrive before the baby did. He'd phoned her and she'd told him she was on her way. She'd previously arranged to swap shifts with her friend, Pauline, who also worked on the maternity ward. John was looking anxiously at his watch when there was a swish of starched uniform and a tall, solidly built staff nurse spoke to him with all the authority of a sergeant-major.

'Mr Stanworth?'

'Yes.'

'Your wife is quite comfortable.'

'Oh, thank you. How long do you think . . . . ?'

'You could have quite a long wait. I'd go home, if I were you.'

'Would you? You see, it's my Mother's fiftieth birthday, and . . . . '

'You don't want to miss the party. Quite understandable. Do you have a telephone number where we can contact you?'

'I'll be at Ashton House, and if I'm not there, I'll be at my Mother's. She's got a phone.'

'Well, give me the number and we can call you there. Off you go now.'

'I ought to ask Lynda if . . . ..'

'Your wife? She's rather busy at the moment. She's being well looked after, and it won't help her to see you looking worried.'

'Oh. Right.' He bent over the clipboard the staff nurse held out, and scribbled down his Mother's phone number. 'Thank you. Tell my wife that . . .'

'She'll be quite all right. We'll phone if there's any news. Now, if you'll excuse me.'

John watched her swiftly disappear into the delivery room and close the door. He hesitated again, staring at the grey metal door as if he might be able somehow to see through it. Then he looked at his watch once more, and hurried down the corridor to the exit.

Lynda, closing her eyes and gritting her teeth as the next contraction began, felt soft warm hands take her clenched fist and unfurl her fingers before holding her hand gently but securely.

'Take a deep breath and try to relax, Lynda, love.'

Lynda turned her head and her eyes filled with tears as she saw Kath's face, full of confidence and reassurance.

'Oh, thank God, you're here,' Lynda gasped and began to breathe through the contraction.

From then on Kath took charge of Lynda, aided by a trainee nurse who was very inexperienced but anxious to learn. The staff nurse had gone off duty, having checked that Kath was available to stay all night. Progress was slow, and painful.

'Where the bloody hell's John?' Lynda demanded as the transition phase started.

'He's on his way.'

'About bloody time! Running off to his bloody Mother's! What time is it?'

Kath waited till the end of the next contraction, and wiped away Lynda's tears before replying. 'Midnight.'

'Thank God! It won't be born on her bloody birthday! I don't want it having the same birthday as that old cow!'

Kath winked at the trainee. 'Language! What an example to set this child.'

An hour later, with the help of a bleary-eyed consultant and a pair of forceps, John and Lynda's baby daughter arrived. John was finally allowed into the delivery room and stood with tears streaming down his face, hanging on to Lynda's hand as if he'd never let go of it ever again.

Kath stood before them, holding the precious, beautiful baby swaddled in white cotton, and wishing Doreen could be there to see her.

'Here she is, your little girl.' She handed the baby to Lynda whose eyes were shining with happiness and love. 'What are you going to call her?'

John, looking in wonder at this child, this living, breathing little person, found he was stammering a little. 'We can't decide between Carol and Lyn.'

'Why not have both? You could join them together and call her Carolyn.'

'Oh, that's different,' Lynda smiled. 'I like that. Do you, John?'

'Yeah. I suppose . . . .'

Lynda kissed her child gently. 'Hello, Carolyn, love. I'm your Mummy. And that big, strong handsome man over there is your Daddy.'

When Lynda and the baby had been transferred the post-natal ward, John was told he should go home as mother and baby would need to get some rest. He didn't want to phone, so he went straight round to his Mother's and was pleased to find his sister was still there, and had also waited up with her to hear the news.

'We've got a little girl, 7lb 6oz.'

'Oh, lovely. A little girl, that's lovely, isn't it, Mother?'

'What are you going to call her?' Sheila asked.

'Carolyn.'

'Oh, that's a nice name, isn't it, Mum?'

Sheila had at first secretly hoped the child would be named after her, but had been told this wouldn't be the case. 'Yes. I thought Caroline, but . . .'

'It's near enough.' Sylvia and Graham had decided the birth of this child needed to be a source of harmony in the family, and might fill some of the emptiness in Sheila's life.

'So, little brother, you're a Daddy now.'

'Yeah.'

'You'll enjoy having a little granddaughter to make dresses for, won't you, Mum?'

'Yes, that will be nice. I'll start knitting some little pink cardigans and matinee coats now. I've only done white ones so far, but now we know it's a little girl . . .'

'It will be wonderful to have a grandchild just round the corner. You'll be glad of Mum's help, won't you, John?'

'Yeah. Yes, we will. Have you got anything to eat, Mum? I'm starving.'

'Of course. I'll cook you some bacon and eggs. A very early breakfast!' Sheila smiled with contentment as her son sat down where he belonged, at her table.

It was unfortunate that Sheila and Sylvia's first visit to the hospital coincided with Lynda's attempting to breast feed the baby. They both sat down on the chairs by the bed and looked first at each other, and then at anything they could see that wasn't in the vicinity of Lynda's bare breast.

'Oh, hello. I'm just having a go at feeding her. She hasn't quite got the hang of it yet.'

Lynda bent her head towards her child and tried to ease her nipple into the tiny mouth. 'Come on, sweetheart, give it a good suck.'

Kath, observing the two women sitting straight backed with disapproval at Lynda's bedside, came over to help as she saw the baby arch her back and cry out in frustration.

'Oh, Kath. She doesn't like it. I can't . . . .'

'I couldn't feed my two,' Sylvia admitted guiltily. 'They were a lot happier when I gave them a bottle.'

'You and John both did well on Cow & Gate. And it's much more convenient.'

'She just needs a bit of time and practice,' Kath said as she sat down next to Lynda, and gently guided the baby's head towards her mother's breast, easing the way into her mouth with her finger until there was a gentle sucking sound.

'There you are. There's a clever little girl.'

With the air of quiet authority which was so well known and admired in the hospital, Kath turned to the uncomfortable visitors. 'Would you like to go and get a cup of tea, and come back when these two have had some quiet time to finish this feed?'

Lynda wished she could have taken Kath home with her, and she did call in as often as she could to make sure mother and baby were making good progress. However, her own nine year old daughter, Jennifer, caught mumps, and passed it on to her brother, and so Kath was unable to visit Lynda for quite a while.

When she and Gordon returned from their honeymoon Jean came a couple of times to see Lynda, but was so nervous about holding the baby that the child cried every time she picked her up. There were days when Lynda, too, couldn't pacify the infant and on those days she came close to panicking. John, working as much overtime as he could, was only there in the late evenings or part of the weekends and he, too, having no experience, was unable to help much.

His daughter, however, decided that she was happy when in her Daddy's arms. Even when she'd been fretful all day, when John came home she'd smile at him or contentedly fall asleep. Lynda couldn't help feeling a little jealous, seeing her daughter show such a preference for her father. Most of Lynda's friends were still working and Sheila was her only regular visitor, and she, too, seemed to have a magic touch as far as her granddaughter was concerned. She found it very gratifying when the child reached out to touch her face or allowed her Nana to rock her to sleep, even later when she was teething.

The bond of breast-feeding and cuddles, and Lynda's natural talent for making the child laugh helped overcome Lynda's lack of confidence as a mother. For the first few months she enjoyed being at home and watching her daughter's every movement and expression. Eager to earn a bit of money, she tried taking the baby with her to the café, but it was too dangerous with all the hot food and drinks being carried around. She knew she and John didn't have enough money coming in, and had secretly started supplementing her housekeeping with money from her post office account.

Then one evening John announced he was going to give up his job at Earnshaw's and go and work on the assembly line at the local electronics factory.

'You can't do that, John. It'd drive you crackers sitting at a conveyor belt all day.'

'Some of my mates are doing it and earning really good money on piece work.'

'But you're an electrician, a good one, and you're happy at Earnshaw's.'

'Yeah, but they don't pay me enough, even with overtime. We're not managing on what I'm earning, and we're having rows about it.'

'Not all the time. And I am trying not to spend money.'

'I know. But, look at this bloody carpet,' he pointed at the faded carpet they'd inherited from the previous owners of the house. 'We can't have our little girl learning to crawl on a mucky old carpet like this.'

'I know. It's only the fleas holding hands across the gaps that stop it from falling apart,' Lynda joked.

'It's not funny, Lynda.'

'I'll give it a good scrub, it'll be all right for a while.'

'No, it won't! I don't want my child not having a decent home.'

'And I don't want my husband doing soul-destroying work, however much bloody money it brings in!'

'We haven't got a choice.'

'Yes, we have. I can go back to work. Freda's kept the job open for me. I can go back part time, a couple of days a week. I could do Fridays and Saturdays, and you'll be at home on Saturdays.'

'Two days won't make enough difference, moneywise.'

'All right, I'll do three.'

'What about Carolyn?'

Lynda already knew the dreaded answer to that one, and turned away so that John wouldn't see her tears.

'We'll have to ask your Mother if she'll be willing to look after her.'

Sheila wasn't just willing. She was delighted.

CHAPTER SIXTEEN

That first morning when she started work again at the café Lynda couldn't stop crying. She couldn't forget the sight of her child holding out her little arms as her Mother walked out of the door. She didn't tell John how upset she was, she told him it had been fine, no problem for either of them. It was certainly no problem for Sheila, she was happier than she had been for a long time. And she was a good grandmother, with all the skills needed to take care of the child, and she was proud to take her pretty little granddaughter out in her pram. When the child was asleep, Sheila spent time cleaning the house and doing the washing and ironing.

Lynda knew she should be grateful but the truth was, she hated it. She tried spending more time making sure the house was clean when Sheila was due to come and look after the baby, but that was precious time she wanted to spend playing with her daughter. In any case, Sheila made it clear that Lynda's standards weren't good enough and just did the work again. The kitchen was reorganised the way Sheila liked it, towels and bed-linen were folded her way, and even their clothes were re-arranged in the drawers and wardrobes.

'Where the hell has she put my clean nightie?' Lynda said, closing a drawer impatiently.

John was already in bed, waiting to cuddle his wife. 'Be quiet, we don't want to wake the baby. Come to bed, you don't need a nightie.'

'Oh, I see. Like that, is it?'

'It certainly is.' He pulled her close and began to make love to her. They'd learned to seize the moment swiftly whenever they had the chance, and the energy. It was the only time John was really happy these days, when he was wrapped in Lynda's love. He loved his daughter, too, but could never free himself from worrying about her and about her future.

He wanted to fall asleep straight away afterwards, but Lynda, looking at the clothes she'd scattered on the floor, and thinking that she'd have to put them away before her mother-in-law saw them, was still annoyed about Sheila's intrusions into their life.

'Why does she have to come into our bedroom at all? We've got no privacy,'

'Oh, go to sleep.' John didn't like his mother in their room either, but had faced the practicalities.

'Why does she have to take over everything? It's more like her house than mine sometimes, especially when I come home late, and she's sitting there having her tea with you. I feel like I'm the unwelcome visitor.'

'Lynda, I'm tired. She's only trying to help. You should be grateful. We couldn't manage if my Mother didn't help out like she does. We couldn't have bought the sidecar for a start.'

'I suppose you're right.' Lynda turned away from him with her secret.

She'd already broken her rule and dipped into her post office account to supplement the housekeeping money, and then she'd withdrawn a larger amount so that they could buy the sidecar. They had to have it to enable them to take the baby with them when they went out on the motorbike. Lynda had pretended she'd saved up the money her customers gave her as tips. The truth was that she'd bet some of her secret money on England winning the World Cup that summer and had blessed hat-trick scorer Geoff Hurst many times over as she'd counted her winnings. She and John could now set off again at the weekends for a day in the country, or at the seaside.

John, picturing his Dad's face, smiled. 'It's great that we can take Carolyn to see her Grandad.'

'As long as your Mother doesn't find out. Or your sister.'

John sighed heavily and pulled the blankets over his head.

Sheila had always loved the spring, watching eagerly for the appearance of the snowdrops, crocuses and daffodils. It had always been the time when she would join Ted in the garden, helping to clear away the dead leaves and any precocious weeds. For a long time after he left she had avoided going into the garden but now, eight years later she regarded the garden as hers. She had made a special corner where Carolyn was allowed to dig and plant seeds, and they spent many hours walking round the large garden at the back of the house, looking at the plants and feeding the birds.

Sheila realised that she was more fortunate than the child's parents, for she had plenty of time to devote to her. Sometimes she was even glad that she had no husband to take care of because it gave her more hours to spend with her granddaughter, and her grandsons. She went to Sylvia and Graham's as often as she could, of course, and she loved their two boisterous boys, but Carolyn was with her every week.

She knew that John and Lynda took her to see her Grandad; that had become obvious when Carolyn had brought her drawings home from school, and there had been a picture of her Grandad as well as the rest of her family. Sheila had at first been furious, and had been going to confront Lynda and John with their deceit, but then it had begun to entertain her, watching them trying to hide what was going on and looking guilty. And she had everything she wanted, lived the way she wanted, and she had Carolyn. The only time she missed having a husband was on occasions like Ellen Heywood's fiftieth birthday celebration.

Ellen, remembering the kind of soiree her parents used to hold to show off their elegant home, had organised a party at Kirkwood House, with a respectable number of well-chosen friends, including Sheila.

It was a much grander party than Geoff Heywood's fiftieth birthday celebration two years previously. That had been a small, formal celebration at home with just the family and a couple of friends. Dan had not enjoyed it, and, as usual, had asked himself why his father had chosen to marry this woman. He had concluded that Geoff's reasons, all those years ago, must have been similar to the ones which had led him to marry Sandra Burnett.

Geoff's employees, and the many customers who had become friends had arranged a surprise party upstairs at The Red Lion, and Dan had enjoyed that, sharing memories and laughter with many people he'd known all his life, but his Mother hadn't been there. Dan felt guilty about not coming home as often as he could have. He knew his Dad missed him and loved to see him, but being with his mother and brother always led to tensions and feelings of being the outsider.

He was finding this visit home even more uncomfortable than usual, partly because he had had to make an excuse for his wife not accompanying him, but also because his brother, now in his first year at university, seemed to be more arrogant and self-assured than ever. Richard had reluctantly left the freedom and unlimited pleasures of university life to return home for a couple of days. He had, of course, come to celebrate his Mother's birthday, but also with the intention of acquiring the extra money he needed to finance the summer in Paris he and his friends had decided was necessary to improve their French language skills. Dan suspected that his Mother had given her favourite son even more money, and it annoyed him that his brother, so blatantly always motivated by his own needs, could command all his Mother's attention and make himself the centre of her world.

'I'm getting a bit fed up with Richard giving his orders,' he complained to his father the day before the party.

'He just wants to make it a special occasion for her, like we all do.'

'We didn't have a big party for your fiftieth. She always gets more fuss than anybody else.'

'She needs it. And I always think it's harder for a woman, getting older. They think they stop looking beautiful.' He shook his head slowly and smiled as he confessed, 'She looks as good to me now as she did on our wedding day.'

Dan looked at his father in surprise. 'Is that why you married her, because she was beautiful?'

'It had a lot to do with it, I suppose. Better than marrying her for her money, which is what some people thought I was doing.'

'Dad, do you not sometimes regret marrying her? I mean, the way she treats you . . .'

'I know. I'm not saying it's been easy, being married to your Mother, but I made my choice. And I was brought up to believe that once you're married, you stay married, for better, for worse.'

'It's different now.'

Geoff caught the hardness in his son's tone. 'Is it?'

'Do you still love her?'

Geoff, who had almost never lied to his son, paused for a moment before answering.

'In a way. Perhaps if I'm honest, it's more the memory of the way I felt then. And we all like to pretend that everything's all right, that we've made a success of things, don't we?'

Dan, who had been guilty of such pretence for a while, kept silent.

'Your Mother needs to look good, tonight. She needs everyone to think that her life has been a success, and that includes being married to me. We can't deny her that on her special birthday. That's why I've agreed to sing for her at the party.'

'Sing?' Dan knew his father had a good voice, just from hearing him singing in the pub, but he couldn't imagine him singing at the party.

'It's supposed to be Richard's idea, but I know where it came from. It's a special song she wants, 'Always'. You remember, she used to like us to sing it when you were a young lad, our party piece. Has Richard not asked you to sing it as well?'

'He hasn't mentioned it to me. I expect he wants it to be his surprise.'

'I think he'd like to be the one performing, but . . '

'I'm the one who inherited your voice. Couldn't carry a tune in a bucket, our Richard.'

They laughed together for a moment, but then Dan couldn't stop himself from adding, 'It's the one thing even my Mother will agree I'm better at than he is.'

Ellen watched her tall, elegant son with his collar-length, wavy auburn hair and easy charm playing host to her guests, and sighed. He reminded her so much of her father that she felt her eyes warm with tears. She would not, she decided, succumb to the emotion of the moment, but concentrated instead on observing her guests admiring her antiques and highly polished family furniture. Later she listened to them chatting and marvelling at the delights of the buffet supper her husband and son had prepared. She congratulated herself on having organised a party which was obviously going to be talked about as one of the big events on the Milfield social calendar of 1971.

She had invited mostly friends from church and family friends, people like the Lawsons, the local solicitors, and she had also included some of her husband's friends, like Robert Horton, a builder who had only arrived in Milfield just over a year ago but was already investing in new properties, and looked as if he was going to be very important to the future of the town. It was gratifying to hear these people praising her home and her achievements, but she regretted having invited the vicar, who had held forth loudly, and at length, about love and fidelity and the example of her marriage to Geoffrey. It was rather tactless, she thought, that he should address his 'party sermon' to Sheila Stanworth.

At nine o'clock Dan, pouring champagne for the guests, watched his brother walk towards the table on which stood a large two tier birthday cake. Alice Smith, once she had eaten as much as she could manage of the food spread out on silver platters in the dining room, had taken up her position at the side of this table, ready to accept all the compliments about the cake's decoration of delicate, intricate lacework of white icing and the sprays of golden roses.

'Yes, it took me days and days to make them all. Roses are Ellen's favourite flower and the thistles on the sides, of course, are in memory of her parents, they were Scottish you know,' she explained to Frances Horton. Alice was keen to talk to the relative newcomer to Milfield and find out as much as she could about her and her husband, their background and financial status.

'Oh, do you know the family?' Frances, who had deliberately dressed in clothes expensive enough to make an impression, was keen to know more about the Heywoods, or indeed anyone else in the room who seemed to be well-connected.

'I was at school with Ellen,' Alice confided, in her 'special occasion' voice.

Sheila, standing behind her, was a little jealous of Alice's claims upon Ellen's favour, and chose to insert a little accuracy. 'Alice was in the first form when Ellen was a sixth form prefect. May I introduce myself, I am Sheila Stanworth.'

Frances smiled and held out her hand. 'Frances Horton. So pleased to meet you. I was going to seek you out. Ellen tells me you made that beautiful dress she's wearing.'

'Yes. I'm so glad you like it.' Sheila was beaming. She had heard about Frances, and her husband who seemed to be buying up any land which became available.

'Do you have a card?'

Sheila had been instructed by Ellen that this was just the kind of opportunity she must take advantage of. She was amused to see Alice's eyes open wide with astonishment as she watched her take a business card from her evening bag.

'Yes. Ellen insisted I should have some printed.'

'Thank you. I hope to go into business myself one day. Bob doesn't like the idea, of course, he thinks a woman's place is in the home. Men do like their food, and home comforts, don't they? '

'Yes, my husband . . . ' Sheila began, and then remembered. She turned quickly to Alice. 'You've excelled yourself with this cake, Alice.'

Alice smiled, and was thinking about making a comment about Sheila's absent husband when Richard placed himself beside them, next to the cake.

'Excuse me, ladies,' he said and nodded as they moved aside and he took centre stage.

Dan was still pouring the champagne and their father, who'd gone to bring Molly from the kitchen to make sure she was there for the toast, had only just come through the door when Richard tapped a coffee spoon on the side of a glass to demand silence. Ellen, who had taken care to be standing by the piano, where the light flattered best, turned and smiled modestly as if she had not expected this attention.

Richard's manly voice was strong with confidence. 'Ladies and gentlemen! As you know, we are here this evening to honour a great lady, my Mother, Ellen Heywood. I'm sure you will agree that she is not only very beautiful, but also a lady of culture and good taste. She is also a lady who knows the value of education and good manners, and who has encouraged me and my brother to have the same values. We thank her for that and for everything she has done for us. We are proud to call her our Mother, and I know my Father is proud to call her his wife. And your presence here this evening is proof, if proof were needed, that you are proud to call her your friend.'

He paused to allow a murmur of respect to wind its way round the room.

'Now, this elegant lady claims to have reached her half century, but none of us believe her because she looks far too young and is far too vivacious. However, as it is her birthday, if she will be good enough to come over here, we will be delighted to sing her the traditional song of celebration.'

Richard turned to beckon to Dan who hurried forward to light the five golden candles arranged in an elegant spiral on the cake. Ellen, her hands clasped prettily over her heart stood next to her youngest son and waited for her moment. Richard nodded to Clarence Smith who, as pre-arranged, had slipped into position on the piano stool, and now accompanied an enthusiastic, and in tune, rendition of 'Happy Birthday to You.'

During the three cheers which followed and the flurry of guests coming forward to congratulate Ellen once more, Richard whispered to his Father.

'Are you ready?'

'I'm not sure I can do it.'

'I thought you'd been practising,' was the irritated response.

'He has,' Dan shook his head. 'You shouldn't have asked him to do this, Richard.'

'I didn't have a choice. She's been going on and on about Grandfather, and how he used to sing that song, and dance with her. It would mean a lot to her, you know it would.'

'I know, but I . . .'

'You'll have to sing with him, Dan.'

'No.'

'Yes! You're the one who's had all the bloody singing lessons. I wish you'd brought your wife. I'm damned sure Sandra would have done it, if she'd been here.'

Dan tried not to flinch at the mention of his wife. 'All right.'

The guests were calling for a speech now, and Ellen paused and looked round the room until they were all silent.

'Thank you all so much for being here this evening, and thank you again for all your charming gifts. I wasn't sure I wanted to celebrate this birthday, but now I'm very glad I agreed to have a party. I'm very grateful to my husband and two sons for making all the arrangements.'

Alice, who knew how much Ellen had taken charge of this event, raised her eyebrows at Molly, who frowned at Alice's indiscretion. Ellen slowly looked around the room, at the deep red velvet of the curtains, her Father's high-backed leather chair by the fire, and the candles lit especially for the occasion in the silver candle sticks and candelabra which were family heirlooms. She took a deep breath. 'I am so glad to be able to celebrate in this house, which belonged to my parents, and which they named after the house they had owned in Scotland.'

She gazed at the piano. 'Some of you knew my Father, Richard Alistair Buchanan, and know how much he is missed. I have spent many happy hours in this room, listening to my Mother playing the piano, and my Father singing. It was another world, then, another life. I only wish I could recapture that, but . . . I have said enough. Thank you again.'

She stood for a moment to acknowledge the applause and seemed about to move away when Richard stepped forward and led her to the centre of the room.

'Mother. We have one more present for you. Ladies and gentlemen, this is a song my Grandfather used to sing.'

Clarence began, with a flourish, to play Irving Berlin's 'I'll be loving you always'. Geoff took a deep breath and steadied himself by holding on to the piano, but his voice was shaking and he knew he was about to make a fool of himself.

Dan stepped forward, put his arm round his father's shoulders and their voices blended together with warmth and strength as they sang the rest of the song. Ellen, graceful, elegant and happier than she had been for a long time, danced with her favourite son.

In July Dan came home again, this time for a few days. He arrived on a bright sunny day and, as he only had a small suitcase with him, he decided to walk home from the station. He'd chosen to arrive on the Tuesday afternoon when he knew his Mother would be at her bridge club. He'd only spoken briefly to his father on the telephone and Geoff, when questioned by Ellen, had only been able to relate that their son would be visiting for a few days, and that she could still go to her meeting as he would stay at home to greet him.

As soon as he saw Dan walking slowly towards the front door, alone again, Geoff knew there was a problem. He hurried to meet him, putting his arm round his shoulder.

'I'm really glad to see you. It's too far away is London. Sandra not with you?'

'No.'

'Just leave your case in the hall, I've got some sandwiches ready. We can eat in the kitchen as your Mother's not here.'

'I'm not really hungry, Dad.'

'Oh, I am. Tell you what, shall we take them with us and go for a stroll round the park? You look a bit pale, do you fancy a bit of fresh air?'

Dan looked round the hallway which always felt cold and unwelcoming to him and decided his father was right, he did need to be out in the sunshine.

His Dad had always appreciated the power of silence, the comfort of walking companionably side by side without needing to make conversation or answer questions. Whenever he had been in trouble as a young boy Geoff had taken him for a walk and just let him find the right moment to unburden himself.

Geoff had a favourite bench, up on the top of a slope leading down to the children's paddling pool and playground. Geoff never tired of watching children play. They sat there for a while, Geoff eating the sandwiches and Dan staring morosely at the trees. When he spoke it was as if he was speaking at a funeral.

'We've got divorced, Dad.'

'What?'

'Me and Sandra. We're divorced. I didn't want to tell you till it was all over and done with.'

'Oh. Oh, hell. A bit of a shock, that.'

'I know, I'm sorry.'

'You must be upset.'

'I was at first, but I'm not now. I'm just flaming angry.'

'What went wrong?'

'Everything. I've been taken for a ride, Dad. I've been an absolute fool. Everybody must be laughing at me.'

'Hold on. I don't get this. You seemed so happy. She was crazy about you.'

'She's a very good actress,' he said bitterly. 'In fact, she's gone to Hollywood.'

'Eh?'

'Yeah, it's like something you read about in a magazine, isn't it? This producer took a fancy to her and she decided it was her big chance. So Bye bye Daniel.'

'Could you not have gone with her?'

'She decided, quite a while ago, apparently, that being married would cramp her style. Fancy free is what she needs to be to make it over there, she reckoned.'

'Bloody hell. Then why did she marry you?'

'I think, I hope, she did really care for me, in her way.'

'Of course she did.'

'She liked my money, I know that. And so did her parents. They've nearly spent it all, my grandmother's money. And I just let them. My Mother will kill me.'

'Leave your Mother to me,' Geoff said, with much more confidence than he felt. 'You did try, didn't you? I wouldn't like to think . . .'

'Believe me, Dad, I've given her every chance. Too many chances. It wasn't just the money, it was the other men. You can only take so much.'

'Oh, hell.'

There was a long silence and Geoff watched his son staring at the children playing on the swings and rocking horse and clambering up the slide.

Dan took a deep breath before confessing, 'I begged her to stay, or to let me go with her, I'd forgive her anything, I said. I was driving her mad, trying to . . .'

Geoff put his arm round his son's shoulders, and felt him begin to tremble, as he continued in a whisper.

'In the end she told me something she knew I wouldn't be able to forgive. There was a baby. We would have had a child, but she got rid of it.'

There was nothing Geoff could say now. All he could do was watch his son cradle his head in his hands and weep.

A while later Geoff silently cursed himself for suggesting going to the park. There was only one way out from where they were sitting. They had to walk past the children's playground, and Lynda was there, pushing her golden haired daughter on a swing.

She saw them and swiftly lifted the child out of the swing and carried her towards them. 'Dan!' she yelled, 'Dan!'

He tried to just wave and walk on, but she ran after them. 'Wait, please . . .!'

He stood, ashen faced as she came up to him, laughing with the joy of seeing him.

'Oh, it is lovely to see you. It's been ages.' Then she saw the pain in his eyes and gently lowered her child to stand beside them, looking up at these adults with shy curiosity.

'What's the matter? Has somebody died?'

'No. Just my marriage,' he tried to laugh. 'How are you doing?'

'Fine. This is my . . . .'

'Yeah. I heard you'd had a little girl.'

'Yeah. Say hello, Carolyn. This is Mummy's friend, Dan. And his Daddy. You know his Daddy, don't you? You've met him at the café. He buys you ice creams, doesn't he?'

'Yes. Like my Grandad. Nana says I have too many ice creams.'

Geoff laughed and bent down to talk to the child, 'Oh, dear. Perhaps I'd better not buy you any more.'

'You can buy her as many as you like, Geoff,' Lynda assured him firmly.

The child turned back to her observation of the younger man, and her Mother's breathlessness. 'Are we going home now, Mummy?'

'Yes, in a minute.'

There were dozens of questions racing through Lynda's mind, many of which she couldn't ask.

She tried to calm herself. 'Did you say . . ? Are you getting a divorce?'

'Decree nisi last week.'

'Oh. I'm sorry. Will you be moving back to Milfield then?'

He paused, gazing at the woman he should have married. 'No. No, I don't think so.'

Geoff sensed his son needed some pride to hang on to. 'He's got a restaurant to run in London.'

'Oh, yes. Your Dad's told me all about it. I've got a café to run – in Milfield. Bit of a contrast, eh?'

Geoff saw the two of them looking at each other, and again gave his attention to the child. 'And this little girl is going to school in September, aren't you, Carolyn?'

'Yes,' she declared proudly. 'And I can read already. Can we go home, now, Mummy? I'm hungry.'

Geoff and his son stood and silently watched them walk away.

Freda had offered to open up the café the morning Carolyn started school, so Lynda could be there to hold her child's little hand as she walked through the gates of Beechwood school. The Victorian sandstone building stood in the centre of a yard where hop-scotch paving stones had been replaced by smooth tarmac, but some small areas of grass and daisies had been preserved.

There were also two old oak trees which scattered acorns for the children to collect and imagine into fairy cups and dishes. Lynda loved these reminders that this had once been a village school and that there was life beyond the desks and discipline of the classroom.

She was so glad that she and John lived in this area and so were able to send Carolyn to this school, but it didn't stop her from being afraid for her child. She couldn't shut out the unhappy memories of her own schooldays, and couldn't bear the thought of little Carolyn having to learn to survive as she had done. She felt the warmth of tears in her eyes, and her fingers tightened round her daughter's hand. Carolyn looked up at her.

'What's the matter, Mummy?'

'Nothing, Carolyn,' Sheila's voice replied as she arrived to join them.

'What are you doing here?' Lynda demanded, but her question was ignored.

Sheila crouched down in front of her grandchild, demanding all her attention. 'Look. Nana's brought you a bag of sweeties for you to share with your new friends at school. Shall we go in and say hello to Mrs Jackson.'

Sweets in one hand and Carolyn's hand in the other, Sheila led her and her Mother towards the main entrance where the headmistress, Mrs Jackson, and her teaching staff were waiting to greet the new pupils.

'Good morning, Mrs Jackson!' Sheila trilled. 'As promised, I've brought my granddaughter to see you.'

'Good morning, Mrs Stanworth. Good morning . . . '

'Carolyn,' Sheila prompted.

'Hello, Carolyn. Are you going to come to my school?'

Carolyn nodded.

'Oh, she's so like Sylvia. And I'm sure she'll be a pleasure to teach, just as she was at my old school.' Mrs Jackson took the child's hand from Sheila's. 'Say 'Bye bye to your Nana, and . . .' the headmistress seemed to notice Lynda for the first time, 'your Mummy.'

'Nana will come to take you home later,' Sheila informed Carolyn brightly. 'Bye bye.'

Lynda barely had the chance to kiss her child before she was led away. She tried to smile as Carolyn, waving reluctantly, disappeared among the crowd of bemused or panicking small children entering the education system.

'That won't help her, letting her see you upset,' Sheila said, grasping Lynda by the elbow and steering her firmly out through the school gate.

Lynda wrenched her arm away. 'Why did you come? I told you I wanted to bring her on her first day.'

'I know. But the school needed to see who'd be taking her home. And I wanted to introduce her to Mrs Jackson, so she'd know who Carolyn belonged to. I know her quite well as one of Sylvia's teachers.'

That was one of the reasons I agreed to your buying the house here, so your children would come to her school. Here's your bus coming.'

CHAPTER SEVENTEEN

Lynda closed the café early on Tuesday afternoons as it was half day closing for many of the shops in the centre of Milfield, and in the market hall. Jean worked part time for Peggy now, as well as three days at the Belmont Road shop. She'd set up a little routine of calling in to see Lynda for half an hour after she'd finished looking after Peggy's stall.

She'd also, since having money for the first time in her life, got into the habit of bringing a little present with her, usually something for Carolyn. This cold, wet miserable day in November she'd brought a miniature television for Carolyn's doll's house.

'Thanks, Jean, she'll love it.'

'I saw it in Mason's and couldn't resist it.'

'You always were mad keen on doll's houses.'

'Yeah. I never had one, though. But I used to like buying things for our Marilyn's, the one our Dennis made for her, thanks to you.'

'Yeah, I remember. Wait till you've got a little girl of your own, then you can get all the stuff you never had and play with it.'

'Not much chance of that,' Jean sighed, and then wished she hadn't spoken.

'Why? He's not gone off you, has he?'

'No, he's too keen if anything. But, nothing seems to be happening. Peggy wants us to go to ask the doctor about it, but Gordon . . . '

'Men can't cope with anything like that. Too embarrassed. We're not looking like having any more but we don't talk about it. Mind you, we couldn't afford it anyway. You should see the price of kiddies' shoes.'

'I thought Sheila bought Carolyn's shoes.'

'Not always. Likes to keep us guessing on that sort of thing, power mad, that woman. Still she does help out, that's the main thing.'

'I thought you were doing all right.'

'We still to have to save up for everything, it takes ages.'

Jean shook her head. 'You're never satisfied, Lynda, that's your trouble.'

'It's all right for you. You've only got to drop a hint and you get any new furniture you want.'

'Well, Gordon gets a discount. And we've still got a lot of his Mother's old stuff. I didn't get a house of my own like you did.'

'Think yourself lucky. It eats money does our house. The toilet's playing up now, and the bath's got a big crack in it so we might have to have a new bathroom, and we've no money for that, I can tell you.'

'Oh, will you stop moaning? You sound like my Mother!'

'God forbid! I'm sorry, it's not like me, is it? But sometimes it seems there's no fun any more. It's all bed and work for me and John, and I mean 'bed' as in going to sleep!'

Jean didn't want any more talk about that part of married life. She picked up their plates.

'Shall I get us another piece of that cake, and make us another cup of tea before you close?'

'Yeah, why not? Let's live dangerously! And why don't you come with me when I go to pick Carolyn up from school, and then you can give that television to her yourself.'

'O K.'

Jean had just gone into the kitchen when the phone rang. When she came back with the tea she found Lynda sitting on the stool next to the phone, and still clutching the receiver.

'What's wrong?'

'That was Rosie. Ted's died. About an hour ago.'

'Oh, my God. What happened?'

'He had a heart attack. They got him to hospital but it was too late.'

'You'll have to tell John. What are you going to do? Ring him at work?'

'No. I don't want to tell him on the phone. No, I'll tell him when he gets home. We can't do anything.'

'You'll have to tell Sheila.'

'She goes out on Tuesdays. And anyway, I think it's best if she hears it from John, not me.'

'Here, get this cup of tea down you. We'll have to go and get Carolyn soon.'

'Yeah. We'll have to tell her later.'

Lynda's face crumpled as she began to cry. 'I'm so glad we took her to see him, so she knew her Grandad. He was such a lovely man, was Ted. He loved me, and I loved him. He was a better Dad to me than mine ever was.'

Jean put her arms round her friend and held her close. 'Have a good cry now, love, before we go to the school. Good job it's raining, Carolyn might not notice if you've got tears running down your cheeks.'

John set off for Blackpool on his motorbike the next morning after he'd phoned Earnshaw's to tell them what had happened. He'd stayed the night at his Mother's after they'd spent the evening holding conversations made up of unfinished sentences which they launched through the heavy stillness which seemed to fill the living room.

'Oh,' was the only word his Mother had uttered in response to the news of her husband's death.

She'd been watching television and had been reluctant to turn it off when John had walked in and announced that he'd something to tell her. He'd put his arm round her, ready to hold her when she cried, but there were no tears. Earlier he'd sobbed for an hour, with Lynda holding him close and crying with him, and Carolyn clinging to them both, not understanding what 'dead' really meant.

John watched his mother sitting in her armchair, waiting for her to cry, but she simply stared at the blank television screen, with her hands clasped in front of her.

'Do you want me to phone Sylvia, or would it be better if you told her?'

'No, you do it.'

He was very relieved that it was Graham who answered the phone; he listened quietly and said he would break the news to his wife. John put the receiver down gently, as if afraid to make a sound. 'Graham's going to tell her.'

'We'll have to make arrangements for the funeral. You'll have to go and get him. I want him bringing home. I'm not having him buried over there. She's not having him. You'll have to go over there first thing in the morning.'

'I am doing. I've got time off work.'

'We're not having Hanson's. It was ridiculous what they charged for Uncle Freddie's.'

'It's the Co-op who's doing it, Mum. My Dad had it all arranged and paid for, just in case.'

'Oh.' She put her hands over her cheeks, clutching her face and staring at him with the eyes of a bewildered child. 'You'll go and bring him home.'

'Yeah.'

'I know you've been going to see him. And I know you've taken Carolyn.'

'Oh. I'm sorry, Mum.'

'And so you should be! But I don't blame you, I know it was her idea, that wife of yours, her and her secrets. But of course I knew. Do you think I'm stupid, that I didn't guess?'

'No.'

'I didn't say anything. I thought if I didn't cause trouble, he'd come back. I didn't want a divorce, I couldn't bear that, to be divorced. I thought he'd grow tired of her and come back.'

They both sat silently for a while, staring at the room which was full of memories.

There were still no tears, just a cold and bitter anger which twisted itself into her face.

'She's not coming to the funeral. You'll tell her she's not to come, won't you?'

John had not even thought about Rose wanting to be there, but had no doubt that his Mother was right.

'Of course, I will. Don't worry, Mother, I'll see to it. I'll do whatever you want.' He looked at the clock. 'I'd better go to bed, Mum. Early start in the morning.' He stood up slowly even though he felt desperate to be out of this room. 'Are you coming up?'

'Not yet.'

'I might not see you in the morning, I'll have to set off at . . . .'

'I know. You said.'

'Good night, then.'

'Come and see me as soon as you get back.'

He paused, beginning to realise that this was an ordeal that would go on and on. 'Yeah.'

As he crept out of the room and started to climb up the stairs his Mother turned and called out sharply.

'And tell that woman to, to make sure they put him in his best suit.'

Lynda had begged John to take the country lanes route to Blackpool, she didn't think he was in a fit state to cope with traffic. He was glad of the frosty morning air rushing past him as he rode along, he'd felt as if he hadn't had any air to breathe since he'd had the news about his Dad. He couldn't take it in that he was gone, that they'd never again walk through the fields together, or sit and chat over a pint of beer.

When Rose opened the door to him, she seemed smaller than he remembered, and suddenly the fifty-nine years which she'd always covered with a cheery smile and a touch of Max Factor, seemed to have grabbed hold of her face and dragged it towards old age.

'Sit down, love, I'll make you a cup of tea. You'll be hungry. I've got some sandwiches ready.'

His voice surprised him with its hoarse brusqueness. 'I can't stop long.'

'No. I understand that. You'll have a lot to do. There's quite a bit of paperwork to sort out, they wouldn't give it to me, because I'm not . . . .'

'No.'

'Sit down. Tea won't take a minute.'

He sat on the edge of the sofa covered in rose-patterned chintz and piled with cushions in all shades of soft pink. There were roses on the curtains, on the prints on the wall and even on the teacups in the china cabinet. He stared at the chair his Dad had looked so comfortable in and remembered him laughing and saying it was like sitting in a garden. At home Ted had been allocated a leather armchair with a straight back which his Mother had bought in a sale at Denton's, the high-class furniture store in the town centre. That was where he should have died, John suddenly thought, sitting in that chair, at home. This wasn't right, any of this.

Rose came and gave him his tea and sandwiches, but sensed that this wasn't a time for a chat and went upstairs to get the suitcase she had packed. She had hated every moment of taking Ted's clothes out of the wardrobe and drawers, and had hardly been able to see with her eyes filled with tears all the time. It was all too soon, too quick and she was angry that she was having to do it.

She'd decided she wasn't going to let them have everything, though. She wanted to keep, at least for a while, the clothes she'd chosen carefully for him, and as for the little presents and souvenirs of happy times together, well, she'd left them exactly where they were. She wasn't letting them go, or him.

John had eaten the sandwiches as fast as he could, and as soon as she came back into the room, he stood up, ready to leave.

'I've put your Father's things in the suitcase in the hall.'

'Right. I'd better be going now.'

She looked up at the tall, good-looking man who was the son Ted had been so proud of, and who was looking down at her now as if she were a stranger.

'He was a lovely man, your Dad. I was very lucky . . .'

'Yeah.'

She was hurt that he didn't want to talk to her. She picked up the large envelope she'd put out on the top of her writing bureau and held it out to him.

'His wallet and his watch, and papers and the address of the . . . where he is.'

'Thanks.' He stuffed the envelope inside his leather jacket.

'Ted made all the arrangements a while ago.'

'Yeah, Lynda said.'

'He told me that it would have to be Holy Trinity church. Will you let me know . . .?'

John picked up his motorcycle helmet and strode through the door. At the last moment he turned towards her, not looking into her eyes.

'You can't come to the funeral.'

Then he wondered why he should feel ashamed of forbidding this woman to go to his Father's funeral. This woman had taken his father away from his family for years, and had caused his Mother a lot of pain; that realisation had become a searing part of his grief and now was making him angry again. He wanted to hit out at this silly woman who thought life was all about roses. 'It wouldn't be right.' His voice was loud and harsh. 'He was my Mother's husband, not yours. You've no right to be there. You can't come. OK? Goodbye.'

He shut the door firmly behind him and she heard him crash the suitcase into the fancy wrought iron umbrella stand before he slammed the front door.

Ted Stanworth did not come home. He came back to Milfield but took up residence for his final days in the Co-op Funeral Parlour. A couple of years earlier he'd put everything in a letter which he'd given to Rose and had made a copy for her to give to his son. The letter had made his final wishes very clear, and he'd wept as he'd written it.

When John, his hands shaking, had had to show it to his Mother she didn't shed a tear; instead, she'd got up and had, with all her strength and fury and pain, begun to shove the furniture in her front room away from the walls and back into the space she had cleared for his coffin to lie in state among the lilies she'd bought.

The church was by no means full on the occasion of Ted Stanworth's funeral, but there was a respectable number, made up partly by his friends and former colleagues from the police force, and partly members of the congregation who felt sorry for the abandoned wife and family, and didn't want to see them suffer alone. Holy Trinity had been the family's church for many years and the vicar, after Ellen Heywood had had a quiet word with him, had taken care in his address to be discreet about the prolonged absence of this member of the parish.

Sylvia had at first refused to attend the funeral, but Graham was not going to let his wife live the rest of her life with that regret, and had gently persuaded her that she must be there, if only to support her Mother. When Sheila had decided the evening before the funeral that she wished to see her husband for one last time, she had informed her son and daughter that it was their duty to accompany her on her visit to the funeral parlour.

Graham had not intruded on that private family ordeal, but had been waiting outside to catch hold of his wife as she stumbled out into the dimly lit street, shaking with the shock of seeing the old man who had once been the broad-shouldered, patient and kindly man who had been her Daddy. After that, Sylvia could no longer hold back the feelings of guilt, regret and grief, and at his funeral she sobbed and clung to her husband's arm all through the service.

Sheila held on tight to her son, leaving Lynda to stand next to Graham, feeling as if she was on her own at the far end of the pew. She wasn't as alone as the small figure standing at the back of the church. Rose crept in just before the service began, but Lynda heard the quick tapping of her high heels on the stone paved floor, and made the mistake of turning to give her the comfort of a tearful smile. Sheila saw this, glanced behind her and instinctively realised who the woman was whom Lynda had acknowledged. She gripped John's arm even more tightly and gave her daughter-in-law a look of hatred she would never forget.

Rose hurried out at the end of the service and ran to hide behind the trees in the churchyard to watch the coffin placed in the hearse, ready to be taken to the crematorium as Ted had stipulated. Sheila stood in the church doorway receiving condolences, and then got into the black limousine which was to follow the hearse. As the funeral cortège approached the gate she saw a movement in the trees, and commanded the driver to stop the car.

Before John or anyone could stop her she got out of the car and marched across the churchyard. Rose saw her coming and froze. Then she stood there, helpless, as Ted's wife slapped her face and then beat her with her fists until she was pulled away by John and Graham. Sheila was shaking and sobbing as they led her back to the car where Lynda and Sylvia were standing horror-struck.

'Was that her?' Sylvia gasped.

John nodded. His sister looked at him accusingly. 'I thought she'd been told not to come. I thought nobody was going to tell her when it was. Did you tell her?'

'No.'

Sheila, still choking on her tears, broke away from Graham's arm, grabbed hold of the front of Lynda's coat, and said the words so closely into her face that Lynda could feel her breath. 'It was you, wasn't it?'

'I thought she'd a right to know.'

John recoiled from his wife. 'Lynda!'

Sheila almost spat at her daughter-in-law. 'Get out of my sight! She shoved Lynda away from the car. 'Go on, clear off! I never want to see you again.'

Lynda looked at the group of hostile faces and turned and ran out of the churchyard. She didn't look back at the car driving away but carried on in the direction she had seen Rose had taken. When she caught up with her they held each other tight, both of them trying to stop shaking.

'I'm sorry. I wasn't going to come, but in the end I just had to.'

'Ted would have wanted you there. Take no notice of them. Come on, let's get away from here. Did you come in the car?'

'No. I couldn't trust myself to drive, I came on the train and got a taxi to the church.'

'You'll need a cup of tea now.'

'Yes, I could do with one.'

'We could go to our house , but . . . . '

Rose understood. 'No. Is there a café near the station?'

'Yes. Come on, Rosie, love, we'll find a quiet corner and have a proper talk.'

They hardly said anything on the bus to the station. They felt conspicuous in their dark funeral clothes and were wary of any nosy passengers who might listen in to their conversation. The woman who ran the Station Café knew Lynda, and gave an understanding nod when she asked if they could sit at a table in the back room of the café, away from the other customers. Lynda, feeling ashamed that she didn't dare invite Rose to Beechwood Avenue, insisted on buying tea and sandwiches, and a cake each.

'Won't you have to go and get Carolyn from school soon?'

'No, Graham's going to take her up to the farm to play with her cousins.'

'Have you told her . . . .?'

'Yes, but she doesn't really understand, she doesn't realise that she'll never . . . .'

'No. I'm finding it hard to realise that. I've kept expecting him to walk into the room or walk up the street whistling. He was always whistling or singing.'

'He never did that here, not while I've known him anyway. You made him very happy, just remember that Rose.'

'Yes. I just wish he hadn't been somebody else's husband. How did she recognise me, though, at the funeral?'

'Perhaps she kept that photograph, you know, you and me in the paper when I won that contest.'

'Oh.' Rose tried to laugh. 'I expect she stuck pins in it, and who could blame her?'

'Rose, I'm sorry to have to ask, but John couldn't face asking you when he came over. He was too upset that day, but he wants to know. How did Ted die? We know it was a heart attack, it says so on the certificate.'

'Yes.'

'Was it sudden? I mean, would he have known anything about it?'

'No, it was in his sleep.'

'Oh, thank goodness for that. Was he having an afternoon nap?'

'Yes.'

'Ah, in that big comfy armchair.'

Rose turned a shade of pink bright enough for any of her namesakes. Lynda stared at her, and couldn't stop herself asking, 'In bed?'

Rose concentrated on slowly stirring her cup of tea for the second time, and her face turned from pink to scarlet as she whispered, 'Yes.'

Lynda knew she shouldn't be asking this question, but she'd inherited her Grandma's curiosity and lack of discretion about such matters. 'With you?'

Rose nodded.

Lynda's voice rose above the whisper she'd been trying to maintain. 'Do you mean you and Ted had been . . .?'

Rose looked furtively round the café as Lynda gave a shout of laughter and then put her hand over her mouth. 'Sorry! But . . .. Oh, my ' she burst into a schoolgirl fit of giggles.

Rose saw that no-one was close enough to be aware of the laughter, and soon she was laughing too, and then crying.

'I didn't know what to do. I had to get dressed. I couldn't have the ambulance coming before I'd . . .. He was gone, Lynda, I swear to you, he was gone. I checked him. I used to be a nurse, remember. Calling the ambulance a couple of minutes earlier wouldn't have made any difference. It was embarrassing enough having to tell them he wasn't my husband.'

'Oh, you poor thing.'

Rose reached out and took hold of her hand beseechingly, 'You won't tell anyone, will you, Lynda? Promise me, you won't tell anyone.'

'I won't. I promise. I'm so glad you told me, though. I've been so upset, but now I'll,' she began to laugh again, 'Oh, I'm sorry. I can't help it. I'll just remember he died with a smile on his face!'

'Lynda, stop it! Oh, what am I going to do with you?'

'You're going to be my friend, that's what you're going to do. You're not going to forget about us now Ted's not here, are you?'

'No, of course not. But I don't think John will want to see me again.'

'No, you might be right, there. But that won't stop me coming to see you.'

'He won't let you bring Carolyn.'

'He will. When he's had time to get over it. Anyway, you and me will see each other.'

'Yes. But I don't know how long I'll stay in Blackpool now. I'm dreading going back and being there on my own.'

'I'll come and stay with you.'

'You can't. You've got Carolyn and John to think about before me. I'll be all right. I'll probably go away for a while. I've a friend, Janet, who helps run a hotel in Cornwall. Me and Ted went there for a holiday, if you remember? She wants me to go and stay with her.'

'Oh, that would be good.

'Yes. We'd better go now, Lynda. I don't want to miss that train.'

Very few people were invited back to Stanhope Road after the funeral and there were several people there who didn't want to be. Geoff and Dan would have preferred to join Ted's friends and former police force colleagues who had decided the best place to celebrate his part in their life was The Red Lion. John knew that his Dad would have wanted 'a do' at the pub and would have liked to be there himself, but had not felt he could absent himself from the sombre gathering at what was now his Mother's house.

The letter which Rose had given to him that horrible day had contained some money and the instruction that it should be put behind the bar at The Red Lion, so that his friends could be his guests for one last time and raise a glass to him and the good times he'd had there. John had raised his glass silently to his Dad's memory when he'd called in a few days earlier to give the landlord Ted's money.

His Mother had disapproved, but not argued, when he'd insisted that some bottles of his Dad's favourite ale should be available at the house as well as cups of tea. He and the other men there were glad of it, none of them ever felt comfortable balancing dainty, flower-sprinkled china cups and saucers. He took refuge with Geoff and Dan Heywood and Graham in the living room, clutching glasses of beer and standing well out of the way as Alice Smith and her father flitted back and forth between the kitchen and Sheila's 'best room'.

Alice and Clarence had not been invited, but they always managed to be at any funeral to which they could manufacture the slightest connection. They had, however, received the advice from Ellen Heywood that, since they were there, they should make themselves useful. They'd taken over the tea-making from Sylvia and were now moving quietly and attentively around the house. As they offered the mourners the sandwiches and cakes which Sylvia and her Mother had set out on the best china that morning, Alice and her father both concentrated hard on absorbing any interesting bits of conversation they could manage to listen to.

Ellen sat with Sylvia and Sheila round the small table in front of the fire, glad of the warmth and cheer after the cold of the crematorium. It had caused comment at the church that Sheila's husband had chosen not to be buried in the churchyard as was customary. Alice placed cups of tea on the table and then pulled another chair towards the little circle, but they did not move aside to make room for her. Undeterred, as always, Alice leaned forward and joined in with, 'Nice to get warm after that crematorium, no warmer than being outside, was it? I prefer a burial myself. Unusual to get cremated.'

Sheila stated crisply, 'It was his choice.'

Alice helped herself to another sandwich. 'And he didn't come back here.'

Ellen gave Alice a cold stare. 'It's not always a good thing to have a coffin in one's sitting room, it can become a painful memory.'

Alice was not going to give up. 'Yes, but it is a sort of 'coming home'. And Ted did like his home, didn't he?'

Sheila sat up proudly. 'He loved this house, and his garden. There are so many wonderful memories here, aren't there, Sylvia?'

Sylvia's cup rattled in its saucer and she had to lower it on to her lap to steady it. 'Yes, and there would have been a lot more if it hadn't been for that woman!'

Ellen quickly looked at Sheila, wondering how they were going to stop this outpouring which they both knew Sylvia had been struggling to keep from everyone. Alice looked as if she'd just been given a surprise gift.

'She robbed my children of their Grandad, my boys should have had many happy hours playing in his garden like I did. He built me a sandpit, you know, and a little house.' She put down her cup and took another handkerchief from her bag to dry the tears which had become unstoppable since her father's death.

Alice never let an opportunity like this pass. 'He was such a lovely man. Always a real gentleman to me. Not like Henry Morton. He was the one who led him astray, wasn't he? Ted wasn't the sort you'd expect to go off with another woman.'

Sheila and her daughter looked at each other in despair. They'd known that Ted's absence was bound to have been talked about, but there was a difference between whispered rumour and this blatant tittle-tattle from Alice Smith.

Ellen was rigid with anger. 'I think you should go and make a fresh pot of tea, Alice.'

Alice knew she was being forced to retreat, but her father, always a skilful ally in their quest for gossip, had entered the room and had been hovering close enough to hear everything.

He stepped forward. 'Was that the woman you were, er, talking to in the churchyard, Mrs Stanworth?'

Ellen called him firmly to heel. 'I don't think we need to talk about that, Clarence.'

'No. I suppose not, but . . .

His daughter smiled up at him. 'Lynda seemed to know her, didn't she?'

Clarence was quick to follow her lead. 'Lynda wasn't at the crematorium, and she's not come back here, has she? Do you know where she went?'

Sheila's anger was still strong enough to push aside discretion about her relationship with her daughter-in-law. 'I neither know nor care!'

Ellen decided this conversation was not going to continue. 'Is that the piano your uncle left you, Sheila?'

Her hostess gratefully followed her gaze and let her eyes rest on the small, elegant Edwardian piano which had been part of Uncle Freddie's legacy. 'Yes, I don't really have room for it, but I'm hoping my grand-daughter will play the piano one day.'

Ellen smiled at her. 'Yes. A splendid idea. It won't be too long before she's old enough to start lessons.'

Clarence, whose income was always in need of a supplement, spoke up quickly. 'I'd be happy to teach her.'

'I think Mrs Stanworth would prefer her to come to me. Wouldn't you, Sheila?'

'Oh, yes.' Sheila suddenly saw a future after this awful day. 'I'm sure she'd love to have lessons with you, Ellen.'

'Good. We'll arrange it when she's a little older. Now I'm sure you and your daughter would be pleased to save Mrs Stanworth the task of washing up, wouldn't you, Clarence?'

Clarence took a deep breath. 'Of course.'

He and Alice bent down to retrieve the cups and saucers and took them to the kitchen. Before they began the washing up, however, they made sure they also collected up all the remaining sandwiches and cakes and filled the bag which Alice had brought to take them home in.

Clarence had spent most of his time in the kitchen or in the hallway, examining the treasures in the china cabinets, rather than staying with the other men in the living room. He had learned many years ago that he could never make himself accepted among the kind of men who were at ease in the local pub. He, therefore, was not privy to the piece of news which would have immediately moved Ted Stanworth's affair from the top of the list of topics valued highly by the Smiths, and the rest of the gossips of Milfield. The matter was discussed, albeit briefly, by the three men sitting round the table which had witnessed much of the unhappiness laid bare in the Stanworth household.

Graham, who always knew when to leave any kind of social gathering, had gone earlier than was necessary to collect Carolyn from school, and take her to the farm. Knowing that John would need to talk further about his Dad, he left him in the safe hands of Geoff and Dan Heywood, who had known and loved Ted, and could be trusted. They gave him hearty reassurance that his father was not someone to be ashamed of, and they had known Ted and his son long enough to give John the comfort of sharing many good memories. When it was getting towards the time for them to take their leave, John, to be polite, asked how Richard was enjoying life at university.

'A bit too much,' Dan replied, and when Geoff nodded his permission, he continued, 'he's been giving us a lot of problems to deal with.'

'Oh, getting drunk and spending money is he? I'd probably do the same if I'd had the chances he's got.'

Geoff bowed his head. 'It's a lot worse than that. There's this young French girl who's expecting a baby, and claims Richard's the father.'

'He denies it's his, of course, but . . . .you know my brother.'

Dan and John had had enough experience of Richard's wildness over the years to know he was capable of anything. Dan had even admitted to John that he couldn't bring himself to love his brother, but it was his duty to look after and defend him as much as possible.

'Will he have to marry her?'

Dan suddenly sounded much older than he ever had to John. 'No. He's sent some money. To, to take care of the matter.'

Geoff added quietly, 'I'd have loved a grandchild, whatever the circumstances. But, Richard . . . . But God forbid that his Mother should find out about this. You'll keep it to yourself, won't you, John?'

'Yeah. Of course I will.'

And he kept the secret, but one day wished he hadn't.

When Graham brought Carolyn home to Beechwood Avenue that evening he wasn't surprised to find that John was still at his Mother's. When she opened the door Lynda saw that Graham was a little startled to see her wearing a bright yellow skirt and floral patterned blouse.

'Sorry, is it a bit bright, what I'm wearing? I couldn't wait to take off my funeral clothes and I needed something to cheer me up, so I . . .'

Graham wanted to tell her it was fine, but he was wondering how John would react when he came home and saw his wife so colourfully dressed.

'Carolyn is a little tired, but she's had a lovely time, haven't you, Carolyn.'

'Yes. Auntie Enid had made fairy cakes and she gave me this magic wand to keep. Look.'

The child waved the silver and gold star with sparkling threads trailing from it.

'Lovely. I wish someone would give me a magic wand.' Lynda smiled ruefully at Graham. 'Now say thank you to your Uncle Graham for bringing you home, and run upstairs and put your pyjamas on. I'll be up to read to you in a minute or two.'

'Thank you Uncle Graham.' She paused at the foot of the stairs. 'I wish we had a car like Uncle Graham's. Why can't we get one?'

'We will do one day. Now, up to bed.' Lynda watched her little girl scramble up the stairs holding her fairy wand high in the air, and then turned to face her brother-in-law.

'Will you stay for a cup of tea? It's been very quiet here on my own.'

'You could have come round to Sheila's.' He winced as he realised that wasn't really true.

Lynda smiled with understanding. 'I didn't think I'd be welcome.'

'You didn't come to the crematorium. I would have thought you'd want to be there.'

'I did. But I thought Ted would have wanted me to look after Rose. I took her to the station. I couldn't let her go on her own, she would have got lost.'

She watched Graham take hold of the door handle, ready to leave, and put her hand on his arm. 'Please, listen to me for a minute, Graham. I only did what I thought was right, telling her and . . . . She was very upset.'

'So were Sheila and Sylvia.'

'Yes. I know. Has John said anything about me going off like that?'

'No. No-one's said anything.'

'Not worth talking about, am I?'

'I wouldn't say that.'

'None of them like me, do they? I can't seem to get anything right.'

She looked so lost, he gently took her hand from his arm and, as he held on to it, he saw she was blinking back tears.

'How do you do it?' she asked.

'What?'

'Belong. I don't belong in the Stanworth family.'

He tried to make a joke of what he knew was the truth. 'We're both 'the outlaws', aren't we?'

'Yes. But they accept you. They'll never accept me. And you have your own family that you belong to. I've only my brother who buggered off to Australia. Sorry, swearing again. John keeps telling me I swear too much. Not a good example for Carolyn. Will you stay and have a cup of tea?'

'Sorry, Lynda, I can't. I have to go and pick Sylvia up from Sheila's. I'll bring John back on the way home.'

'Will you?'

'If I can.'

'If she'll let you, you mean.'

His rueful smile confirmed that he understood Lynda's doubts. 'Goodnight.'

Lynda slowly closed the front door and locked it before going upstairs to see her daughter. This was Lynda's favourite part of the day, the time she spent tucked under Carolyn's pink duvet with her arm round her little girl, reading a story book. It was one thing she was good at, reading stories, making up different voices for the characters. Carolyn had always happily followed the routine of two stories followed by Lynda tucking her in and giving her a big kiss. Tonight, after the stories, there was a question.

'When's Daddy coming home?'

'He won't be long,' Lynda replied, hoping it was true. When she reached the bedroom door and lifted her hand to turn off the light another question came muffled by the duvet.

'Is Grandad not a naughty man now he's gone to heaven?'

Lynda drew in a sharp breath. 'Your Grandad was never a naughty man.'

'Nana said he was.'

'Your Grandad was a lovely man, the best Grandad anyone could ever have. You remember that, my little love, and don't let anyone tell you different. Now, 'night, 'night and God bless.'

'Night, 'night, Mummy,' Carolyn called and fell asleep so quickly that she didn't hear her Mother begin to cry.

Lynda still hadn't really stopped crying when John came home later that evening. He pretended not to notice. He'd refused Graham's offer of a lift and had walked home. He'd felt like going to the pub and getting drunk, but was still wearing his funeral suit, so instead he'd drunk the remainder of the beer he'd bought for the gathering at Stanhope Road. He was tired, irritable and wanted to go to bed, but he was also still angry with Lynda and didn't want to speak to her.

She knew by the way he took off his jacket and threw it over the back of the settee that he'd had quite a lot to drink. He went into the kitchen and found another bottle of beer. He didn't bother to look for a glass but came back into the living room drinking it out of the bottle. Lynda stood up and saw his look of disgust as he noticed her yellow dress.

'Do you want me to make you something to eat?' she asked tentatively.

'No. I've had plenty at my Mother's. Is Carolyn OK?'

'Yes. She had a nice time at the farm.' Lynda felt tired, and leaning against the table, she began to cry again. 'She asked me, - somebody's told her that her Grandad was a 'naughty man'. How could anyone tell her that?'

He was as perturbed as Lynda, but wasn't going to start criticising his Mother or his sister, both of whom, he knew, could have made that statement. 'What did you say?'

'That it wasn't true of course! There was nothing wrong with your Dad.'

'No. There wasn't. And if she hadn't come on the scene . . . .'

Recklessly Lynda snapped at him, 'And who's 'she' – the cat's mother? Her name's Rose, and if she hadn't 'come on the scene' your Dad would have missed out on the best nine years of his life.'

'And Sylvia's kids wouldn't have missed out on all those years with their Grandad!'

'That was Sylvia's fault, nobody else's. We took Carolyn to see him, she knows who her Grandad was.'

'Yeah. And my Mother knew we were doing that, she told me the other day, 'sneaking off behind her back' that's what she called it. You don't seem to realise how hard it's been for her all these years since my Dad walked out. But you don't understand anything you! How could you tell that woman she could come to the funeral? I told her straight when I went over there that she wasn't to come.'

Lynda stepped away from him a little, retreating from the force of his anger, but she wanted to defend her actions.

'She wanted to be there. Right from the start, when she phoned me to tell me that he'd died, she begged to be allowed to come to the funeral, to say goodbye to him properly. She made me promise to let her know when it was. So I phoned her. I had to, I'd promised.'

'You broke my Mother's heart, doing that. She never wants to see you again.'

'Well, she'll have to! I'm Carolyn's Mother, so . . .'

'More's the pity!' The words hit his wife as if he'd slapped her across the face. .

He knew it was a terrible thing to say but he needed to hit out at someone. And so did Lynda.

'Oh, the truth's coming out now, is it? You wish you'd never married me, don't you? Well, that makes two of us! You're always putting me in the wrong, you and that damned Mother of yours. Well, I'm not in the wrong this time. Rose Milner is a good kind woman who loved Ted more than your Mother had ever done – in every way! There were no bloody separate beds for your Dad in Rosie's house!'

'Don't be disgusting! You've no right to talk about my Mother like that. She was right about you, she always said you didn't know how to behave, and that you dressed like a tart. Look at you now, tarted up in that yellow dress like, like it was a day out in Blackpool not the day of my Father's funeral!'

'I put this on because your Dad said he liked it, it was like a bit of sunshine, he said.' She moved towards the door.

'I'm going to bed now because I can't stand to see that nasty, bad-tempered face of yours any more. And I'm going to follow your Mother's example for once. I'm going to sleep on my own! You can sleep in the spare room, or stay down here on the settee and cuddle that bloody bottle of beer!'

Three weeks later Lynda went to Blackpool on the early morning train. There had been a storm the day before but now the sea was eerily still, like a child keeping quiet when he knows he's been naughty. The pier was closed, but one of Rose's friends worked for the council and had managed to borrow a key for a couple of hours.

Rose carried the small urn which contained some of Ted's ashes and held it close to her heart all the way along to the end of the pier. The rest of his ashes had, as instructed, been taken by John on to the hillside overlooking Milfield and scattered along part of one Ted's favourite walks. Lynda had hoped her husband would ask her to go with him, but he didn't.

She and Rose stood with their arms round each other and shed tears as they watched Ted's ashes disappear into the sea.

'There's enough water down there without us adding to it,' Lynda quipped as she dried her eyes. 'What do you want to do with that?'

Rose took a clean yellow duster out of her pocket, and wrapped it round the small imitation marble urn before tucking it into her handbag.

'It was the only piece of yellow cloth I could find,' she said apologetically. 'Yellow was his favourite colour.'

'I know. Come in handy for polishing it as well,' Lynda laughed as she took Rose's arm and they retraced their steps, past the melancholy sight of the boarded up Fortune Teller's booth, kiddies' roundabout and candy floss stalls, to the entrance to the pier.

When they got back home Rose placed the urn on a small shelf tucked away by the side of Ted's chair.

'I suppose it's a bit morbid to keep it,' but I'll find the right place to bury it one day. Probably in Cornwall. I'm moving down there next week, Lynda.'

'What? That's a bit sudden, isn't it?'

'I know. But me and Ted had talked about it, and I can't bear to spend the rest of the winter here without him. I've sold the café, some friends of mine had always said they'd want it if ever I decided to sell, so . . .'

Lynda was devastated at the thought of losing her friend. 'Cornwall. It's a helluva long way.'

'Yes.'

'I won't see you again if you're going next week.'

'No. But you'll always be welcome to come and see me in Cornwall. You, and John if he wants to come.'

'I don't know if there'll be a 'me and John' for much longer.'

'Oh, no! Is he still not speaking to you because of me?'

'Not a word more than he has to, but don't you go blaming yourself.'

'It is all my fault, though, this trouble between you and him, and his Mother, of course. I feel so guilty, that I took Ted away from his family.'

'You didn't. I told you, like I told John, Sheila drove him away. She killed his love for her bit by bit over the years, like John's killing mine.'

'Oh, don't say that, Lynda. It'll come right. It has to, you have a child to think about.'

'I know, but I tell you something, if John had to choose between me and his Mother, it wouldn't be me that he chose. Now, let's have a cup of tea and some of your cream scones. I'll have to travel all the way to Cornwall for the next batch.'

'I hope you will be able to come and visit me.'

'I will one day, I promise.'

CHAPTER EIGHTEEN

It had all been arranged without a word to Lynda. Ellen and Sheila had agreed that Carolyn should begin taking piano lessons in January but it wasn't until the day before the first lesson that John remembered to tell Lynda about it.

'Piano lessons?'

'Yeah, I meant to tell you before but I forgot, with Christmas and that. My Mother's paying for them. It's a surprise for her, an extra Christmas present, but from her Nana, not Father Christmas. She's going to tell her when I take her round there tomorrow, and then I'm going to run them both up to Mrs Heywood's for the lesson.'

'Mrs Heywood's? She's not going to Ellen Heywood for piano lessons.'

'Yes, she is. I told you, my Mother's paying for it. Mrs. Heywood thinks she's about the right age now.'

'Oh, does she?'

'Yes. What's that look on your face for?'

'I don't want Carolyn to go there for lessons.'

'Why not? Anyway it's all arranged. Apparently Mrs Heywood offered last year when she was at my Mother's after Dad's funeral.'

There was a silence between them, the silence which had become a habit every time that anything to do with Ted's death was mentioned. Lynda had become anxious about her marriage since that day and had made herself learn to keep quiet and avoid any argument with John, for fear of what might be said in anger. She couldn't keep quiet about this issue, though.

'My daughter is not going to Ellen Heywood for piano lessons or anything else.'

'What are you on about? She's a good teacher, and she's offered lessons at half her usual rate, because my Mother's a friend. And my Mum's got that piano of Uncle Freddie's at her house so Carolyn can do her practice on that. I thought it was a good idea for her to learn to play the piano.'

'It is. But not with that woman.'

'Why not? We know her. She's Dan's Mother.'

'And that's why not. She treated me like dirt when Dan took me home to meet her.'

'That was bloody years ago, when we were just kids. You're not going to stop Carolyn having the chance of piano lessons over something stupid like that.'

'It wasn't stupid. It was the worst thing that's ever happened to me.'

'What? That she stopped you going out with her son, so you ended up marrying me instead. And that was the worst thing that ever happened to you. Is that what you're saying?'

She closed her eyes and wondered how she'd got herself into this argument. 'No.'

'Right. Well, Carolyn's starting piano lessons with Mrs Heywood tomorrow, then. And let that be an end to it.'

These days John seemed to enjoy being 'the master of the house' and, when he felt like it, the bedroom. Lynda could say nothing, she knew she was a long way from forgiveness for her part in Ted leaving his wife, and her friendship with the woman who had made him happy. So that was the end of the argument, and Lynda tried to tell herself that an hour a week spent with Ellen Heywood wasn't going to harm Carolyn. She couldn't rid herself of the terrible feeling that her daughter was being gradually taken away from her. She felt her child already spent too much time with Sheila, and now there was to be another reason for her to spend even more time at 'Nana's house'.

Lynda had even wondered if she should give up her job at the café, to prevent Sheila from being with her daughter so much, but she loved her work. They also needed the money, and Lynda was proud that she was helping to ensure that Carolyn would have the kind of future she herself had once dreamed of.

Secretly she admitted to herself that she also didn't want to be completely dependent on her husband for money, like a lot of women were. Sometimes she wondered if she should try to take more exams at night school to give herself more chance of going after a better job, but she wanted her evenings at home with Carolyn. And she knew John wouldn't take kindly to being married to one of these 'career women' she'd heard talked about. She found it hard to be patient, though, and to accept that, thanks to Sheila's influence, John insisted that everything like the television or the washing machine had to be saved up for.

John wasn't ambitious, he worried about money but didn't dare look round for a better paid job. There was little chance of anyone achieving any kind of management post at Earnshaw's, not with the two sons already being lined up to take over when Mr Earnshaw was ready to retire. John was happy to stay there with his mates, just as Lynda valued the social life of the café. And, for a time, Lynda had consoled herself with the thought that things were looking up, thanks to his Dad. John had inherited some money when Ted had died, and had been able to have driving lessons and buy a car. Lynda had got excited, thinking they would have some good times together, like they used to with the motorbike, only this time there would be their daughter to add to the pleasure.

Their first holiday after they bought the second-hand Austin A40 had been in North Wales, staying at a boarding house in Barmouth. Lynda had not been pleased when Sheila had invited herself along, but John had been relieved that Sheila was paying for the petrol and the room that she was sharing with Carolyn. Lynda tried to tell herself not to resent the fact that Sheila was the one who sat next to John in the car, claiming that she suffered from nausea if she travelled in the back. Lynda made the best of it, enjoying cuddling Carolyn and playing games with her to make the journey pass more quickly.

She couldn't stop herself laughing when, on the very first day, Sheila slipped and landed on the sand in an undignified fashion. After that Sheila decided that she preferred to look round the shops or sit in a deckchair knitting or reading 'The Daily Mail'. Lynda rejoiced that she and John were free to go off to the beach without her, and have a wonderful time with their little girl, building sandcastles, playing with the beach ball and paddling.

She was glad when Sheila also declined to join them on their trip to Shell Island, clambering around rock pools and having crabs and seaweed dropped in her lap by her grand-daughter was not her idea of a good time. Carolyn observed that her parents held hands a lot while they were on that magical island. She liked it when they held hands and kissed each other, but she was jealous too.

'Kiss me, Daddy! Kiss me!' she squealed, pushing her small body between them. John laughed, gathered her up in his arms and gave her a big salty kiss before striding across the rocks again and depositing her by a large rock pool.

'It's big enough for you to paddle in is this one.'

Carolyn looked doubtfully at the sandy depths of the pool. 'There won't be any big crabs, will there?'

Her father hitched up his swimming trunks and waded into the water. 'I'll go and check for you, little Miss Scaredy Cat.'

'I'm not scared, I'm just being sensible,' his daughter informed him. Lynda and John grinned at each other. 'I wonder where she learned that from? Not from her Mother, that's a certainty!'

He ducked as Lynda threw a clump of smelly wet seaweed at him.

They found a large flat rock and sat side by side watching their child become absorbed in exploring the pool and delighting in being able to lie down and splash about in the warm shallow water. Lynda leaned against her husband, pushing her shoulder against his and enjoying the feel of his strong muscular arm. She rested her head against his.

'I don't want to go back, do you? I want to stay here for ever.'

'It'd be nice. It's been good to get away from all that talk about strikes.'

'Oh, don't let's talk about work. Let's just think about you and me, and how happy we are. It's what we needed, this, to get away from everything, have some time together, get back to being a happy married couple.'

'Yeah.' He put his arm round her and kissed her tenderly. 'Just you and me.'

'And our little golden angel.'

They had stayed as long as they could, watching their child, and staring out at the sea, wishing they didn't have to go back to reality.

Back in Milfield life had soon gone back to boring routine again. It seemed to Lynda that other people were always out having a good time, whereas she and John didn't go out together very often, even on a Saturday night. They were mostly dependent on Sheila being available, and being willing to babysit, and she perfected the art of being so awkward about 'another favour' that it took away half the pleasure of the evening.

She'd been in one of her 'jealous moods' the following November, when John had broached the idea of her babysitting so that he could take Lynda out to celebrate her 30th birthday. After a hard and contentious day at work, he'd felt too tired to go through the routine of pleading with her, and finding out what reward she required this time, and so had surprised his Mother by giving up and going home. She was even more surprised, and very annoyed, when she found out that her son and his wife were going out to a party to celebrate, and wouldn't need her to babysit, because they were taking Carolyn with them.

It was Kath Kelly's idea that she and Lynda should have a 'joint 80th' party. Her birthday was also in November and she joked that it would save her an awful lot of embarrassment if they could disguise the fact that she was reaching the unwelcome milestone of fifty. It would help out with the finances too, she assured John, if he could buy some of the booze, and Freda had already offered to provide a fair bit of the food – on condition that she'd be asked to dance and not be expected to sit in a chair like an old lady!

It had been Kath's idea that they should bring Carolyn with them.

'She's eight, the little darling, that's old enough to stay up late for once. And there'll be other children there, little Steve Sheldon, our neighbour's son and a couple of other local kids Bernie's invited. You know what he's like, can't have a party without the excuse to play kiddies' games.'

Ever since the success of 'Waterloo' in the Eurovision Song Contest earlier that year, Kath had been dying for an excuse to wear satin and a dark curly wig. After some groans of 'Mother, you can't be serious!' she and Lynda had persuaded Kath's teenage daughter, Jenny, who had won prizes for needlework all through school, to make them 'Abba outfits' for their birthday suits. She'd also made an outfit for Carolyn, who danced around at the party until she was dizzy.

For the first half hour after the dancing started Bernie was happy to be the little girl's partner but now was getting out of breath.

'Let's go and have a sit down at the piano, sweetheart. Your Uncle Bernie needs a rest. You're a great little dancer, but you should have brought your boyfriend with you to dance with.'

'I haven't got a boyfriend.'

Bernie pointed over to where Steve Sheldon and a couple of other boys were surreptitiously pouring themselves shandies with a bit more beer than they were supposed to have in them.

'What about that one, our friend Stevie, will he do?'

Carolyn had already noticed Steve Sheldon and thought he was really good-looking, the kind of boyfriend she'd like to have, but she wasn't going to confess to that. 'No,' she said, but blushed enough to betray that it wasn't true.'

Bernie nodded with all the gravity he could muster. 'A pity, that. He's a nice boy, but he probably thinks you're too young for him anyway. It's my girl Jenny he has a crush on, but she no doubt thinks he's too young for her.' He sighed heavily. 'Ah, it's all very complicated and a little bit sad. So what do you say we play a happy tune on the old Joanna to cheer everybody up?'

Carolyn was thrilled to be treated in such a grown-up way, and to be given the chance to show off her piano playing skills. It wasn't the kind of piano playing she learned at Ellen Heywood's. She quickly learned a lot about 'boogie woogie' and twelve bar blues that night, and was soon having a great time joining in and helping to thump out tunes as she shared the piano stool with Bernie.

Kath, cradling a large glass of whisky, and sitting in her favourite seat by the window, nudged Lynda who was beside her, savouring a large glass of her favourite 'vodka and black'.

'That'll shake things up a bit in Sheila and Ellen's front parlours when she shows them what she's learned here tonight.'

'She'll probably not let on that she's learned it. She seems to know when to keep quiet about different things with different people. It worries me. I don't want her to become a devious little soul, it's not good that a child has to learn to be careful what she says.'

'We all have to learn that sometime, Lynda – especially when you're married,' Kath added with a laugh.

'Too true. I feel like I'm walking on egg shells half the time when I talk to John. It really gets me down. I mean, it shouldn't be like that, should it, not between husband and wife?

'Nothing and nobody is perfect, Lynda. I've learned that in my life if nothing else.'

'Yeah, but you and Bernie are happy and enjoy life. You know how to have fun, like tonight, everybody's having a good time because of you two.'

'Well, I'm glad about that. But it's not always been plain sailing with me and Bernie. Many a time he's felt like catching the ferry back to Ireland, and many a time I'd have packed his bag for him. But sometimes, you know, you just have to learn to be satisfied. This is a good life we've got, Lynda, but it's not the one I dreamed of having. All you can do is your best, and then just hope your kids get the future they want, and marry the right person.'

Lynda saw that Kath was watching her daughter who was trying not to look bored while listening to the boy who had been pursuing her all evening. He had long floppy hair and a touch of acne, and was propping his arm against the wall and leaning in towards Jenny in what he thought was a seductive pose.

'Your Jenny won't be short of offers. She's a lovely girl.'

'Yes. There's plenty of lads who want to go out with her, but she doesn't seem very interested. Concentrating more on her A levels.'

'Good for her. I wish I'd been able to stay on at school. Plenty of time to get a fella later.'

'Yes, but what worries me is that she says she's after one with money.'

'Well, if she finds one, give her this piece of advice from me. Get his ring on her finger before she goes to meet his parents. If I'd done that before I let Dan take me to meet his damned Mother, she'd have had to give in.'

The vehemence in Lynda's tone startled Kath. 'That still hurts, doesn't it? But it's all in the past, Lynda. Isn't it?'

Lynda fixed on a bright smile. 'Yeah, of course it is. But you tell Jenny, that's what she'll need to do. Promise, you'll tell her.'

'OK, I promise, but I know very well she won't listen to me.' She took another good drink of her whisky. 'Your children can make you feel small, you know, when they become teenagers. Jenny told me there's no way she's going to be like me, spending her life making do and never having enough money.'

'I've that to look forward to, then, Carolyn being a teenager.'

'You have indeed, so enjoy yourself while you can – like your friend over there.'

She gestured with her glass to the centre of the room where Jean Haworth, after losing track of how many Martini and lemonades she'd drunk, had boldly asked John to dance with her.

At Kirkwood House everyone looked forward to Carolyn's piano lessons, and the little girl was always quite excited at the thought of what she might experience at the large old mansion which was so different from other houses she had visited. At first she'd just had her piano lesson after school, and had then been collected straight away and taken home to her Nana's for tea, but Ellen became very fond of the pretty, well-mannered child. She began sometimes to invite her to come on a Saturday for her lesson, when they could spend more time together.

Carolyn thought the house was like a castle and she was fascinated by everything she found there. On her very first visit she had at once focused on the cranberry glass epergne which was the centrepiece of the display of crystal and silverware on the sideboard. With its tall central vase and three dainty posy bowls, all shaped like ice-cream cones it seemed like something a princess might have, or a film star.

She had kept glancing at it, and at the end of the lesson she slipped down from the piano stool and walked straight across the room to point at the delicate glass ornament.

'Is that a vase?'

'Yes, a kind of vase, you put flowers or sweets in it. You won't touch it, will you? It's very old and very special. It belonged to my Grandmother.'

'Oh, have you got a Nana as well?'

'I used to have but she's no longer with us.'

'Where is she?'

'In heaven.'

'Oh. Like my Grandad. Do you not put flowers in it?'

'No.'

'That's a shame. It would look even prettier with flowers in it.'

'Yes, I expect it would.'

'Do you think that in the summertime we could pick some flowers from your garden and put them in the little vases?'

Ellen smiled, and later that year they did pick flowers and arrange them in the posy bowls; delicate flowers like lily of the valley and later pink and white sweet peas.

They developed the habit in the colder months of making little expeditions to various rooms in the house. It amused Ellen to answer the child's innocent questions and to see the wonder in her eyes when she explained the history of the many treasures on display or lying long-forgotten in some of the nooks and crannies.

The visit now always ended with afternoon tea, with special 'fairy' cakes which Molly took delight in making for the little girl. Geoff came home early if he could, to enjoy the child's company, and that of his wife, for Ellen seemed always at her best on these occasions.

'How is she doing with her piano playing?' he enquired one afternoon after he'd returned from driving Carolyn home, and he and Ellen were enjoying another cup of tea.

'Quite nicely, though I'm afraid she'll never make a concert pianist.'

'That doesn't matter, as long a she's enjoying it.'

'Exactly. And I feel she gets more from coming here than just the piano tuition.'

'I'm sure she does.'

'She's a very clever little girl, it's a pity there isn't the money to send her to a private school, but she's bright enough to succeed anyway.'

'She's a pretty little thing, too, and she's got a lovely sense of humour.' He hesitated, but then his sense of justice drove him on to say. 'She takes after her mother a lot.'

Ellen immediately changed her tone. 'Do you think so?'

Geoff sighed, realising that, as usual, it had been only a temporary illusion, this compatibility between him and his wife.

'Of course she does, you can see it as well as I can, but you don't want to. Carolyn could have been our grand-daughter if you'd given Lynda half a chance.'

'Really, Geoffrey, that's all far too long ago to even think about.'

'I think about it a lot, every time I see our Dan looking unhappy. He'd have had a different life if he'd been allowed to marry Lynda Collins. And he'd be living in Milfield for start.'

'Not necessarily. That young lady was very ambitious at the time, I seem to remember, with fancy ideas about going abroad.'

'She was just a kid. And anyway you didn't have any objections to Richard 'going abroad'.

'That was to help his career. And I'm sure he'll come home eventually. When I spoke to him the other day I had the impression that he was already thinking about it.'

Geoff nodded. 'I thought he might be.' And he knew the reason why, and the embarrassment which Richard's behaviour had caused his older brother, but none of that could be divulged to Ellen.

Richard Heywood had graduated in 1974 with a double honours degree in French and German. His Mother was very proud of him and displayed his graduation photo in a large silver frame on the piano. Geoff was also proud, and relieved, that Richard had managed to qualify for a degree. It later became clear that the degree wasn't of a high enough level to qualify him to achieve his ambition of working as an interpreter in Brussels, and Richard had had to spend several months sitting at home applying for top-flight jobs and again 'borrowing' quite a bit of his parents' money. After a plea from his father, it was Dan who had managed to find his brother a job, with a wine-merchant he knew in London, who imagined Richard's language skills would be of benefit to his company.

Recently, however, it had been discovered that cases of wine were disappearing from various shipments and so it was not long before Richard returned home. The reason he gave was that he had arranged to go into partnership with an old school friend, Dave Cooper, who had set up as a trader in expensive second-hand cars. Ellen was persuaded to provide Richard's share of the capital investment needed but made sure that the legal documentation was dealt with through her solicitor. It was on his visits to the solicitors' office that Richard met Jennifer Kelly, and found that her cascade of silky dark brown hair and her softly curved body quickly became the main focus of his thoughts and fantasies.

Jenny noticed him too. Richard didn't favour the current fashion in clothes, he'd always found that women were more impressed with the dynamic image of a formal business suit and white shirt. Jenny felt the power of that every time he walked into the office, and it made her heart beat faster. However, considering herself wiser than her nineteen years, she determinedly set herself the task of not falling for his charms.

Her Mother had warned her of the dangers of men as handsome and confident as Richard Heywood, men who found they could have any woman they wanted, and didn't see any reason to deny themselves the pleasure. Jenny, by now, had a lot of respect for her mother's opinions; she also knew that her mother, in almost every aspect of her life, had had to resign herself to being disappointed and 'making the best of it'. Jenny loved her Dad, and admired her mother's loyalty, but had long since decided that she would do better for herself. She'd also witnessed what had happened to girls she knew who had been unwilling to ask for 'The Pill', but had been persuaded to 'go all the way' and had ended up pregnant.

Jenny knew Richard Heywood presented a danger to her, but she couldn't help fancying the challenge of resisting him, and flattering herself that she might be the one woman who could change him. For several weeks she politely turned down his invitations to go for a drink with him, to go for a ride in his sports car, but when he invited her to go to the opening of a French restaurant, the first in Milfield, she told herself there was no harm in going for a meal with someone.

Going to Paris was on the list of achievements that Jenny had begun to draw up as a teenager, but she was still a long way from saving enough money for such a visit. 'The Paris Restaurant', according to the feature in the local paper, guaranteed that it would offer a first glimpse of that experience, and young Jennifer Kelly was hungry for experiences like that. She bought a new dress, which at first glance seemed soft and demure but which had a neckline that had made Kathleen Kelly shake her head.

The restaurant owners had modelled its interior on the luxury of a famous restaurant in Paris, but they had been commercially aware enough to limit the menu and to satisfy the Milfield customers' expectations by playing accordion music and Edith Piaf quietly in the background. Richard had taken care to book one of the intimate alcoves where candlelight was reflected in the gold-framed mirrors and deepened the red velvet of the cushions which offered an overwhelming temptation to relax your body against them.

Richard in a well-cut suit and a dazzling white shirt leaned back in his chair and let his gaze rest briefly on the cleavage of her dress before smiling as he saw his attention had made her blush. He had a deep voice and spoke in a seductive tone which made the words apply to much more than the large, elegant menu. 'You can have anything you like. Don't hold back.'

He was amused to see the blush deepen as she retreated behind the folds of the menu, and then laughed as she gasped, 'It's all in French!'

Raising the collar of his jacket and leaning across to her like a conspirator, he whispered, 'It's a French restaurant,' and was gratified to hear her giggle.

'Shall I choose for both of us?'

'Yes, please,' she replied, and loved him for looking after her without adding to her embarrassment. He chose the pate de campagne followed by chicken chasseur - deliberately avoiding things she wouldn't know how to handle, like the whole artichoke with vinaigrette dressing and the lobster. He could teach her about those, and many other things, later.

'Now, Jennifer Kelly, how is it that you've lived in Milfield all your life, yet I've only recently come across you?'

'I don't know. Perhaps I've been hiding from you,' she teased.

'That's cruel. Making me suffer all these years without you.'

'You don't look as if you've suffered. I'm sure you've had lots of girlfriends.'

He was taken aback, but entertained by her willingness to be so forthright. It was such a contrast to the other girls he'd dated, many of whom had been devious in their attempts to push him towards buying a ring.

'I've had several, I'll admit, but none as pretty as you.'

She laughed. 'Richard, I've enough Irish blood inside me to know blarney when I hear it.'

'Tell me about that, about your parents.'

'They're both Irish, from Galway. My father's a carpenter and joiner and what he loves best, apart from my Mother, of course, is shaping a piece of wood with his hands, or bashing out a tune on our old piano.'

'Like my father with his bread dough.'

'He owns his own business, though, that's something my Dad will never do.'

'And why is that?'

Jenny had been brought up to be open and honest, and Richard had a way of making her feel she could confide in him.

'He just hasn't got it in him, he's too soft, he'd never charge people enough money. Still, he likes the work he does, even though he doesn't earn enough.'

'Money isn't everything.'

She laughed. 'No, but it helps!'

He poured her another glass of wine. 'Yes, you're right. You're like me, aren't you, you appreciate the pleasures the world has to offer.'

'Yes. I do.'

'Nothing wrong with that. And what about your Mother, she's a nurse, you said.'

'My Mother's a hard worker and a great one for looking after people, and throwing parties.'

'They sound like very nice people, I'll have to meet them one day.'

Jenny's heart leapt at this overt suggestion that their relationship had a future. Richard was very different from the other young men she'd been out with, but she knew he was the kind of man she'd been looking for. He made her feel excited and safe at the same time. But when she tried to imagine him in her parents' house she felt apprehensive, he'd see the shabbiness of it all and would laugh at her father's simple view of the world. She resigned herself to just enjoying a few dates with him and then watching him walk away, especially when all she was willing to offer in return was a cuddle and a goodnight kiss or three.

It was the Queen's Silver Jubilee in 1977 and Sheila talked about it a lot, and made sure that Carolyn shared her enthusiasm. Lynda didn't join in; the main event that year, as far as Lynda was concerned, was her daughter starting at senior school. Lynda felt Carolyn's childhood had gone past too quickly, and it had come as a shock when her tall, slim, fair-haired eleven year old daughter, had stood before her in her new school uniform.

Lynda tried to kiss Carolyn goodbye at the gate of Milfield comprehensive school, a two storey building with a blue and silver frontage which seemed to have more windows than walls. Carolyn moved away swiftly as her mother leant towards her.'

'No, Mummy. Look, I told you, nobody else's Mother has come.'

It wasn't quite true, there were a couple of parents standing by the gate waving anxiously as their children, nervous, and conscious of the stiff newness of their navy and gold school uniform, walked away from them. Lynda and her daughter had argued about taking her to school on this first morning at 'senior school' and Lynda had won for once, but only because John had, as usual, felt tremendously protective of his child. Carolyn had sulked all the way there, protesting that she would rather have walked. She'd got out of the car hastily, having noted how shabby the old A40 was compared to the other cars which parked briefly to drop off their passengers in front of the school.

Sheila, on Ellen's advice, had not attempted to be there and was content to wait for Carolyn to come home to her house, which was closer to the school than Beechwood Avenue.

'I was so embarrassed, Nana,' she complained as she began to give her account of her first day.

'Well, never mind. Now change out of your uniform and I'll make us both a cup of tea. I've made a chocolate cake to celebrate your first day, and meat and potato pie, your favourite.'

'Oh, thanks. Can I have a piece of cake now?'

'Please may I have . . .'

'Please may I have a piece now?'

'Yes, a small one, when you've changed out of your uniform.'

Sheila had paid for most of her granddaughter's school uniform, and it had given her great pleasure to feel the quality of the school blazer, which was the most expensive item, and see how smart Carolyn looked. Lynda had gone with them but had only been allowed to buy the shirts and sportswear. She hadn't argued because Earnshaw's had put John on a three-day week again and she'd do anything to stop him worrying about money.

By the time they'd had their evening meal Carolyn had told her grandmother all about the other girls in her form, some of whom she already knew from Junior School, and about her form mistress, Miss Thompson.

'She's my French teacher as well. I'm in the A Stream for French. That's the top stream. She's worked in Paris as a translator for an engineering company, and used to walk past the President's palace every morning on her way to work.'

'Really. That's very good. We'll have to go to Paris together when you've learned to speak French.'

'Oh, could we? That would be fantastic.'

'We'll open a special bank account and put some money away each month especially for our trip to Paris. Now, piano practice before your Mother comes for you.'

'Do I have to? I'm really tired.'

'Just ten minutes today then.'

They went into the front room and Sheila sat contentedly watching her granddaughter who everyone said was a credit to her.

CHAPTER NINETEEN

Jenny was heartbroken when, after a month or so of showing her what life could offer outside the world her parents lived in, Richard Heywood had gradually stopped taking her out. He wasn't used to not being able to persuade a girl to get into the back of his car and satisfy his needs. There were plenty of other girls who were more obliging when he dated them, and sometimes Jenny happened to see him with these other women. He observed how unhappy she looked, but he was still annoyed that she'd said 'No' to him and so never gave any sign of any regret.

But he found he couldn't forget Jennifer Kelly and her big brown eyes, and after a while he no longer felt satisfied with the easy pleasures on offer elsewhere. He asked Jenny out again, and eventually persuaded her to satisfy his curiosity by taking him home to meet her parents.

He was nonplussed to find that he was not immediately made particularly welcome. They were wary of him, knowing his family background was so different from theirs, and also having heard rumours about his reputation. But Richard Heywood liked a challenge and had worked hard to acquire the famous charm which won over allies and customers, and which could easily be adapted to winning over people like the Kellys. He also found that he enjoyed being in their home which was, after the awkward first visit, very welcoming, and so comfortable and easy-going that it became a haven he was always glad to escape to.

He was becoming increasingly irritated lately by his Mother's disregard of the fact that he was now a man. She expected to have her orders obeyed even more than she had when he was a little boy in short trousers. She was, as always, obsessed with having an influence on everything he did, and he was tired of arguing with her over the way he was spending her money. He knew there was a solution to this, he could get hold of money of his own. One day, when she refused his request for a loan to expand his business he went straight round to the Kellys' house to see Jenny.

Kath and Bernard were out at a 'pie and peas supper' and Jenny was in the kitchen about to make a ham and cheese omelette, and immediately invited him to eat with her, and tell her what was troubling him.

'I can't take much more of her expecting me to discuss everything I do. And then I have to listen to her putting the opposite point of view. She just loves to win an argument.'

'Perhaps she's bored. Not enough excitement in her life. Or perhaps she just thinks she's helping you.'

'I don't need that sort of help. What I need is somewhere I can sit and relax after a day's work, and have a good meal without having to feel I should be grateful for it.'

'Perhaps it's time you had a place of your own.'

He paused as she stood up and came to collect his empty plate. He watched the quiet, gentle movements of her body and mused that what he needed now was another glass of wine and then to take this woman to bed with him. He made his decision.

'You're right. I need to cut the apron strings and move into a home of my own.' He took the plates from her, put his arms around her waist and pulled her down on to his lap. 'How about it?'

'How about what?'

'Becoming my wife. Making a home for us both. Let's face it, it's the only way I'm going to get my wicked way with you!'

She laughed and tried to get up but he pulled her closer.

'I mean it, Jenny. I'm serious. I want to marry you. I need you.'

She'd imagined this for so long, but not like this. She'd fallen in love with him, and in spite of all the doubts which kept whispering in her head, she knew that love was strong enough to overcome them. But she thought that he was proposing to her because it was an idea which appealed to him at this moment.

'Richard. Don't. It's not fair. You need me now, but you'll change your mind tomorrow.'

He beamed at her. 'You're going to say 'yes', aren't you?'

He was happy and confident, the way she loved to see him.

There was no doubt that Richard Heywood was the kind of man she had always dreamed of marrying, and she realised she didn't want to let him go home and change his mind, or have it changed for him. Trying to keep her voice steady, she smiled at him and asked, 'To what? You haven't asked the question.'

He took hold of her hand and kissed it. Then he lifted her gently away from him and went down on one knee, in the traditional manner, albeit on the kitchen floor.

Taking both her hands in his, he looked up at her beseechingly, 'Will you marry me?'

'Do you love me?'

He laughed. 'Of course I do. Do you love me?'

'Very much.'

'So will you be my wife?'

'Yes.'

He lifted her off her feet and swung her round in a dance of triumph.

Kathleen Kelly had kept her promise and had passed on Lynda's advice. And Jenny had listened, but was terrified when Richard took her to meet his parents that Sunday afternoon. Kath and Bernie had been told on the Saturday, as Richard had delighted Jenny, and Kath, by formally asking Bernie for his daughter's hand in marriage.

Bernie had been sprawled in front of the television waving his fist and berating the jockey who had, according to Bernie, fallen asleep in the final furlong. He'd been startled when Richard had quietly entered the front room with a purposeful expression on his face. Bernie had quickly fastened his trousers which he'd undone for comfort to accommodate the extra helping of Kath's steak and kidney pie he'd enjoyed earlier, and leapt to his feet when he realised what was happening.

'Well, I never. You're wanting to marry her? That's a turn up, we never thought you'd . . .' Then, catching sight of his wife and daughter appearing in the doorway, he quickly continued, 'I'm very pleased, and of course I give you my permission.' He winked as Jenny came towards him and he put his arm around her. 'Not that I have any choice, Richard, you know what these women are like. Good thing I bought those extra bottles of Guinness, isn't it, Kath? We'll have to have a toast. Guinness all right for you, Richard? We haven't got any champagne at the moment.'

Richard had made sure there was a bottle of champagne in the fridge at Kirkwood House that Sunday, and was determined it would be opened that afternoon. He loved a drama and was excited at the consternation he was going to cause. Jenny, dressed in her smartest suit, and wearing her grandmother's silver shamrock pendant for luck, was trembling and holding on to his hand as if they were edging their way along a cliff.

Ellen and Geoff Heywood were sitting at either side of the fire, Geoff snoozing and Ellen doing 'The Sunday Times' crossword. Richard had taken Jenny out for Sunday lunch, and had made sure they'd both had enough wine to help them withstand the opposition they knew was coming.

'Mother, Father, this is Jenny, Jennifer Kelly, who is going to become my wife.'

Geoff looked at them slightly bleary-eyed, but Ellen's eyes were as sharp as an eagle's.

'I beg your pardon?'

Richard held out Jenny's left hand to display the neat emerald and diamond ring she'd chosen two weeks earlier. 'This is my fiancée Jennifer Kelly.'

Geoff struggled to his feet and held out his hand to Jenny. 'Pleased to meet you. This is a surprise, isn't it, Ellen?' He turned to his wife who slowly set aside her crossword, and clasped her hands firmly in front of her, making it clear she was not going to get up and welcome this visitor.

'It is indeed. You've kept this very secret, Richard. Why is that?'

'I wanted to surprise you. We've seen the priest and set the date, 9th September.'

'Priest?'

'Yes, You'll never guess what his name is, Father O' Neill – Oh kneel!; get it? Isn't that hilarious? He's a very nice chap.'

'So this young lady is a Catholic?'

Jenny found it hard to speak. 'Yes. My parents are Irish.'

Ellen looked at her son. 'Irish, and Catholic.'

He returned her look with one of arrogant determination. 'Yes. A lovely family, you'll have to meet them.'

Geoff saw Jenny was leaning on Richard and looking up at him apprehensively. He smiled at his future daughter-in-law. 'Of course. We'll look forward to it. Do sit down.'

'I'll go and get that bottle of champagne I put in the fridge.'

Geoff tried to laugh. 'I wondered what that was doing in there. All organised, isn't he, Jenny?'

Jenny smiled at him gratefully and hoped that Richard would not be away long.

Ellen spoke again. 'We were not aware that Richard was seeing any young woman in particular. Have you known each other long?'

'Nearly two years. We went out for a while and then stopped, and a few months ago we started seeing each other again.'

'And now, apparently, you're getting married?'

'Yes.'

'We've met before, haven't we?'

'Yes. I work at Lawson and Broadbent's, the solicitors.'

'Ah, yes. You're a clerk there.'

'A secretary.'

'And your parents?'

'My Mother's a nurse and my Father's a joiner and cabinet-maker.'

Geoff could see that Jenny was becoming more and more anxious. 'And are they pleased about you marrying Richard?'

'Yes, very.'

Ellen's tone was sardonic. 'I'm sure they are.'

There was then a silence which unnerved Jenny, and she sighed with relief as Richard strode back into the room carrying the bottle of champagne. Geoff hurried over to a cabinet to get four glasses, but was halted by Ellen holding up her hand.

'Just a moment. Before we go any further with this, may we know if there is a reason this wedding is to take place so soon?'

Richard opened the bottle of champagne. 'Do you mean, is there's a shotgun involved? No, Mother'.

He grinned at Jenny whose face was scarlet, as she echoed his answer. 'No.'

'Then I think we should talk about whether . . ..'

'The arrangements, Mother. Certainly.' He waited for his father to bring over the tray of glasses. 'I thought we'd see if Ashton House was available for the reception.'

Ellen looked coolly at Jenny. 'And are your parents able to pay for your wedding, as is the custom?'

'They've been saving up for it for a long time.'

Richard saw the battle was commencing, and, confident that he would win, poured the champagne. 'And we Heywoods will pay our share, of course.'

Ellen looked at him. 'Will we?'

Richard 'Yes.'

'I thought you needed all your money to expand the business, Richard.'

'I'll have my inheritance from my grandparents for that, it's due to me as soon as I marry.'

Ellen nodded her head slowly. 'I see. I still think it would be preferable not to marry so soon. You've hardly had time to . . ..'

Geoff, knowing too much about Richard's finances, realised that there was more than one reason for this wedding. 'It might be better to wait a bit. We've no objections to you, Jenny, of course, but . . .'

'Daddy, do be quiet. I have given Jenny my word that we shall be married, in September, and that's the end of it, whether you like it or not. Now shall we drink this champagne before it loses its fizz?'

Ellen, whose money enabled her to take charge of many of the arrangements, managed to make their wedding quite a low-key affair. Richard was allowed to invite Jenny's parents to Kirkwood House and they were treated with great courtesy, especially by Geoff who saw how nervous they were. Bernard hardly said a word, but had plenty to say when he got home, once he had satisfied his desperate need of a bottle of Guinness and an unbuttoned collar. Kath had skilfully fought only the battles she had worked out that she could win, and in the end achieved her aim, for her daughter to have the white wedding she'd dreamed of.

Jenny wasn't sure about having a hen-night, but her Mother seemed a bit depressed after all the hassle of arranging the wedding under the shadow of Ellen Heywood's narrow-eyed disapproval, and a few terrible weeks looking after young Steve Sheldon. His violent father had walked out for good just over a year ago, sending a chorus of 'good riddances' echoing round the neighbourhood. Steve's mother, Maureen, had seemed relieved at first but then hadn't talked much, and had become even more reclusive than before. A few weeks ago Steve had returned home after treating himself to a day out with his mates and found that, after writing a note to say she took the blame for everything, and apologising for one last time, his mother had allowed herself the luxury of a peaceful eternal sleep.

Kath and Bernard had helped the fifteen year old organise the funeral and then had moved him into their home, insisting that they needed a lodger, a replacement son now that their Kevin was packing his bags to go to stay with his uncle in America.

Kath was glad of the night out, the chance to put on a favourite dress and a pair of shoes not designed for working in. They weren't a big crowd, just a couple of Jenny's school-friends and a few more of Kath's friends but, led by Kath and Lynda, they made plenty of noise. They'd booked a table at 'The Star and Garter', a large pub which had a small space which could be used as a dance floor.

Lynda had bought a new dress from Grattan's catalogue, which John and Sheila didn't approve of. John had grumbled about the cost, until Lynda had pointed out that she was only spending the commission she earned from being a Grattan's agent. Jean, who'd been invited because Lynda told Kath she needed cheering up, wore a dress which Peggy had insisted on giving her when she'd closed her market stall a couple of years earlier. Peggy had died two months ago, after more than a year of fighting the legacy of forty Senior Service cigarettes a day.

Following Lynda across the small dance floor to join the small group of women gathered in the pub, Jean was reminded of the teenage years she'd spent seeing men turn and draw a deep, lustful breath as they watched Lynda saunter past them. The corners of Jean's mouth drooped as she realised that she was still doing the same as then, tagging along because Lynda had got her invited. She watched the faces light up with laughter as they approached the hen-party and Lynda demanded, 'Where's Ellen? Don't tell me you didn't invite her! No? Ah, what a shame. I was really looking forward to seeing her strutting her stuff across the dance floor!'

She'd set them off laughing and they had a good night, sticking to lager and lime and cider as they were all short of cash but nevertheless getting tipsy enough to let their hair down. Even Jean managed to smile and join Kath and Lynda in half an hour of dancing round their handbags.

They were just about to move off the dance floor for a drink and a sit down when a self-assured, good-looking guy in his thirties, with dark, wavy shoulder length hair eased his way into the group and started to dance up close in front of Lynda. Catching the warning look on Kath's face, Lynda backed away from him, said, 'Thanks but no thanks,' and followed her friends back to her table. The man looked for a moment as if he was going to follow her, but then shrugged, beckoned to the younger man watching from the bar and the two of them headed out of the pub.

'Who was that? Somebody you know, Kath?'

'Tony Randerson. His father-in-law is Ralph Bentham.'

'As in Bentham & Co. where Bernie works?'

'Yes. Randerson has been brought over from Manchester and put in charge of the new Milfield part of the business. And that was Craig Earnshaw he was with.'

'Oh, I thought I'd seen him somewhere before.'

'Bernie says Earnshaw's are after the electrics contract at Bentham's. Big business now they've gone into doing kitchens as well as renovating houses.'

'And that fella's married to Bentham's daughter? He didn't look married.'

'No. His wife's away a lot apparently, goes with her father on cruises and that since his wife died.'

Jean leaned forward to get in on the conversation. 'Cruises. They must have some money. Is that what your Jenny is doing for her honeymoon?'

'No, they're going to the South of France. Our Jenny's always wanted to go to Nice and Richard fancies Monte Carlo.'

Lynda was delighted as well as envious. 'Fantastic, isn't it? Your Jenny getting a taste of the good life. '

Jean picked up her glass and gazed into it sorrowfully. 'That's what I thought I was going to have, the good life, but it's back to square one for me.'

'What do you mean?' Lynda asked.

'We've had to sell the house to pay off Peggy's debts and her nursing home fees. We're moving to a little terraced house on Bridge Street.'

'Bridge Street?'

'Yeah. And there was I thinking I'd moved up in the world.'

'Oh, hell, I am sorry, Jean.'

'So is Gordon. He's really upset about it all. Finding out there wasn't the money he thought there was, and having to move out of that lovely house. I've told him I don't mind. But I do.'

Kath sighed and drained her glass. 'That's marriage for you. Ups and downs. I'll get us all another drink, shall I? Drown our sorrows. Or do you want another dance first?'

'I'm not dancing next to that lot.' Lynda pointed towards a group of young girls who had taken over the dance floor. 'I wish I was their age again.'

Kath paused as she collected up their glasses. 'Really?'

'Yeah. If I had my life over again . . . .'

'What would you change?'

'Everything.'

Jennifer Kelly had the wedding she had dreamed about ever since she had played with the 'bride doll' her Mum and Dad had bought for their little girl one Christmas. Kathleen watched the ceremony through a mist of tears and held Bernard's hand tightly as he sobbed and made a sodden mess of both the white handkerchiefs she had made sure were in the pocket of his new Burton's suit. She was relieved that he had at least managed to keep control of his emotions while he escorted his beloved daughter down the aisle and, a little shakily, handed her over to the man who Kath hoped to God would be a good husband.

Kath prayed hard at the wedding, for herself as well as her daughter. She prayed that she'd live long enough to see her grandchildren, and she prayed she'd have the strength of will to refuse treatment for the ovarian cancer which had stealthily invaded her body. She was mad with herself for thinking it was just middle age making her stomach swell up and then being too busy to take any notice of the symptoms. It was too late now. She'd made her decision almost straight away after they'd told her how bad it was. She'd hidden herself away to cry and when she felt like she was losing control completely, she'd grabbed hold of the strong, loving hand which was her faith. Kath had decided it would be for the best if she told no-one, especially not Bernie, who she knew didn't have the strength to go on this particular journey with her.

Throughout the day Jenny managed to avoid looking at her future mother-in-law, for she didn't want Ellen's down-turned mouth to be part of the memory of her wedding. Lynda, on the other hand, watched Ellen Heywood nearly all the time, rejoicing in her obvious displeasure. As the wedding party came out of the church she even managed to get close enough to speak to the sour-faced mother of the bridegroom.

'Nice to see your Richard getting to marry the girl he wants, not like Dan, eh?'

John saw the way Ellen turned her back on Lynda, and the distaste and fury on her face.

'What did you say to Mrs Heywood? Looked like you were causing trouble.'

'I just said Richard was lucky to be marrying a lovely girl like Jenny. Nothing wrong with that, is there?'

'No. Dan will be glad to see him married as well, with his record.'

'What do you mean?'

'Well, Richard's always had a reputation with women.'

'There's plenty of fellas you could say that about.'

'Yeah, but not like Richard Heywood. Most blokes will do the honourable thing and get married when . . . .'

'When what?'

John hesitated, realising he was talking about a secret. 'Nothing.'

'No. It's not nothing. Tell me.'

'No.'

'What are you doing? Keeping secrets from me now? There shouldn't be any secrets between us, we're husband and wife, or doesn't that count for anything?'

'All right, all right! But it's just between you and me. Dan and Geoff asked me not to tell anybody.'

'What?'

'When Richard was in France he got a girl pregnant.'

'Oh, hell. Why didn't he marry her?'

'I don't know. He told his Dad and . . .'

'What?'

'They sent money over.'

'Oh, typical. His Mother thinks money can buy anything.'

'She doesn't know about it.'

'So Richard, who's just married my best friend's daughter, has secretly got a child with another woman!'

'No. The money was for . . .'

'He made her get rid of it?'

'I suppose so.'

'Oh, God, no! Why didn't you tell me. We've let Jenny marry him. Why didn't you tell me?'

'I thought about it. But it was too late. She'd still have married him anyway.'

'No, she wouldn't. Her Mother wouldn't have let her, not after a sin like that. And Jenny wouldn't have wanted to marry him if she . . .'

'She might have. He's got money - that counts for a lot with some people. You can tell she loves all this, and the kind of life he can give her.'

'She didn't know he was a bastard like that. Oh, you stupid man! You should have told me! I could have warned her.'

'Don't you bloody call me stupid! And it's too late now, so shut up about it!'

There was only a relatively small number of 'selected' guests at the reception at Ashton House, but later on that day in 'The Red Lion' the party that the Kellys had invited their friends to was packed out. Dan was glad to get away from the funereal atmosphere at Kirkwood house, and to make it clear to his Mother that he was proud to be part of 'the Kelly gang'. When he arrived at The Red Lion he headed straight over to John and Lynda.

'How are you doing?'

John stood up straighter and smiled at his old friend. 'All right. Good to see you mate. It's been a while.'

'Yeah. You'll be seeing me a bit more often from now on, though.'

'Oh? How's that.'

'I'll be coming home more regularly, and one day for good. We're keeping it quiet, he doesn't want any fuss, but my Dad's got a heart problem. I need to keep an eye on him, and help out a bit if I can.'

'Oh, I'm sorry to hear about Geoff, but it'll be good to have you round more. We'll have to go out for a drink sometime.'

Lynda laughed, with little humour. 'Wonders never cease! My husband offering to go out.'

Dan saw the look John gave his wife. 'Let me get you both a drink. A pint and a Vodka and black, is it?'

'No. I'll get them. You stay where you are,' John insisted and strode towards the bar.

'Sorry,' Lynda apologised. 'I shouldn't have been so sarcastic. It's just, he's turning into an old man. All he wants to do is sit at home and watch tele, and save money.'

'Well, it's a tough time on the work front, especially for someone like John. He's never really been 'a union man.'

'No. He hates these strikes, just wants to get on and earn his money. His Mother keeps going on about this Margaret Thatcher, how she's talking sense. She's a bloody Tory for God's sake!'

'I know. My Mother thinks she's marvellous.'

'She would!'

'I saw you have a word with her at the wedding. What did you say? She looked like she wanted to kill you.'

'Only that it was good that at least one of her sons had been allowed to marry the right woman.'

'Richard . . .'

'Got what he wanted.'

'He always has done.'

'He doesn't deserve Jenny. I hope to God he makes her happy.'

'He will.'

'You make sure he does.'

Dan saw Lynda was close to tears. 'I will, as much as I can.'

'No. I mean it. You look after her.'

'What's the matter?'

'John's told me. About the girl in France.'

'Oh.'

'I want Jenny to be happy. For Kath's sake, as well as her own.'

'I'll look after her, Lynda, love. I promise.'

She looked up at his gentle, loving face, and blinked back tears. 'People have a right to be happy, Danny. We would have been, if . . . '

Lynda moved close enough to feel the warmth of Dan's body, and close enough for him to breathe in her perfume and feel her sweet breath on his cheek as she whispered softly.

'I'm glad you're coming home. It would have been great, you and me.' She paused, but couldn't stop herself. 'Still could be.'

He swiftly moved away. 'You're married.'

She stood very still for a moment, feeling both disappointed and ashamed. Then she tossed her head and tried to laugh. 'Oh, yeah. I forgot.'

When John came back with the drinks, Lynda gulped down almost half of hers before making the excuse that she needed to powder her nose. As she closed the door of the 'Ladies' she found she was shaking and close to tears. Then she heard someone sobbing in one of the cubicles. She tapped at the door. 'Hello. Who is it? Are you all right, love?'

There came a muffled 'Yes, I'm OK' in a voice she knew too well.

'Kath? What's up? It's me, Lynda. Come out of there.'

Slowly Kath opened the door and when she saw Lynda's open arms she almost fell into them. Lynda held her tight, shocked to see this woman who was always so strong shuddering and trembling.

'Tell me what's wrong? This isn't just the wedding, is it?'

'No.'

Lynda wondered for a minute if Kath had also found out the truth about what kind of a man her son-in-law really was.'

'Did you not want her to marry him?'

'No. And yet I did, in a way. It's what she's always dreamed about, Lynda. Who are we to say what's right for our children?' And I couldn't have stopped her anyway.'

'No.'

Lynda thought perhaps that would have been true even if Jenny had known the secret she'd just heard. She decided there was no point in raising even more doubts for Kath now, and also remembered there was more that Kath was having to deal with.

'Oh, I get it. You're losing both of them at the same time, with Kevin buggering off to his uncle in America as well next week. It's too much. Tell him not to go.'

'I can't. I won't do that to him. He has to have his chance, and he'll do well there.'

'I know he will. And I thought you were glad your brother's offered him a job.'

'I am. But . . . .Lynda, I'll never see him again!'

'Of course you will. You'll save up and go and see him, or he'll come back to show off with all the money he'll make.'

'No. You don't understand.' Kath began to gulp for air as the tears came pouring down her cheeks again and the look in her eyes told Lynda how desperate she was.

'Tell me.'

'No. I've made up my mind. I can't tell anybody.'

'Kath, my love, whatever this is, you know you can tell me if no-one else. And you know I can keep my mouth shut when I need to.'

Kath looked at this beautiful, resilient young woman and knew that if there was anyone she could confide in, it was Lynda. And she realised now that she had to talk to someone or go mad.

Jean, annoyed that Gordon had refused to get up and dance, was watching Bernard dancing with Carolyn. When she saw Lynda had left the room she went over to join in and, as she'd hoped, Carolyn soon persuaded her Dad to dance with them as well. Gordon Haworth sat quietly observing this, trying not to feel jealous, and wishing he didn't feel so unwell. When Lynda and Kath, with eyes dabbed with cold water, and lipstick and powder newly applied, forced themselves to join in Jean drifted away and sat down sullenly next to her husband. He sighed, and let his undeserved feeling of guilt come to rest on him once more. Jean deserved to be happy after the tough times she'd had in her life. He'd made her happy, or at least he hoped he had. Now there was that sadness within her again.

The next record was 'My Girl', a slow number. Gordon wondered if he could manage to dance to this one, and when he saw the look of longing in Jean's eyes as she gazed across the dance floor to where John Stanworth was dancing, a little reluctantly at first, with Lynda, Gordon decided he had to dance with his wife. He was rewarded with a smile and held her closer, and still had his arm round her as he began to lead her off the dance floor.

Then came the unmistakable opening chords of 'Jail House Rock'. Gordon felt a moment of panic as Jean squealed with delight as always when she heard Elvis Presley. She pulled her husband back to the centre of the dance floor. 'Oh, it's Elvis, we've got to dance to this one,' she insisted. They began to jive, but not in time to the music.

'Come on, Gordon, get with it,' Jean urged him.

'I can't.'

She was annoyed. 'What do you mean, you can't?'

Then her husband fell to the floor and lay there, fighting for his life.

He lost that fight. Lynda went with Jean in the ambulance and stayed with her in the desperation of that night and the days and weeks which followed. She helped Jean with the funeral, and she helped her move out of Peggy's grand semi-detached and into the little terraced house on Bridge Street. The hardest thing to bear was Jean's huge feeling of guilt.

'I didn't really love him, Lynda. I hope he didn't know. Oh, he was such a good man. I hope he didn't know.'

Lynda held her friend in her arms as if she were a child, and helped her believe what she needed to believe.

CHAPTER TWENTY

Everyone was glad when 1978 with its strikes and 'winter of discontent' finally shuffled out in bad-tempered disgrace. The New Year was welcomed by everyone and celebrated as usual at the Kellys' house. Those who could remember it, and those who couldn't, all agreed that this New Year's Eve party was the best ever, with even more dancing, laughter and daft behaviour than usual. Only Lynda knew the reason for Kath's extra determination to have a good time and make that night, and every day if she could, one that her loved ones would remember, and that they would bless her for the memory.

Carolyn became a teenager in May, so Lynda felt she had an acceptable excuse now for finding her relationship with her daughter getting worse. They rowed about practically everything – even politics when Carolyn had joined in Sheila's celebration of Margaret Thatcher becoming the first woman to be elected as Prime Minister. But what hurt Lynda most was Carolyn's increasing criticism of everything about her, from her cooking to the way she dressed.

It was, of course, orchestrated by Sheila but also Carolyn had become part of 'a smart set' at school, a group of girls who were as bright as she was but who had much wealthier parents. Both Lynda and John struggled to enable their child to keep up with the standards these girls set for clothes and outings.

Lynda earned extra money at the café by opening later on some days and taking bookings for parties in the evenings. When Freda had died last year Lynda had been worried that Duncan would sell the café and that she might be out of a job, but to her surprise he had left her alone, letting her run the place as she wanted. She assumed that as long as she was making money for him he was happy to let her get on with it.

There was another birthday in May, but this time in the Heywood family. Ellen had not been too pleased that Jenny had become pregnant early enough after the honeymoon to make people pause and add up the number of months, but Richard's daughter was such a beautiful child that all negative thoughts were swept aside. Ellen left the nursery duties to Jenny's mother while she made the important decisions, like naming the child Alexandra in honour of her late father, and insisting that the child would become a member of the Church of England. Jenny and her mother fought hard to resist both of these demands, but Richard supported his mother, and so they had to content themselves with the knowledge that the child would have their love and guidance, and all their inherited strength.

Kath was only working two days a week now, giving the excuse that she wanted to help Jenny with the baby, which was true, but also she was finding work a struggle. She could ignore the pain more easily, though, when she was cuddling her grand-daughter, and she rejoiced that the child had brought her daughter close to her again.

'I don't know how I'd manage without you, Mum,' Jenny declared one day when little Alex had demanded what seemed like non-stop feeds and nappy changes.

'Oh, you'd manage all right,' Kath replied, knowing that soon Jenny would have to. 'Has Richard got the hang of nappy changing yet?' she enquired, trying to make it sound like a casual question.

'No. He's just one of those men that can't cope with that sort of thing. He does play with her, though. But he finds it hard that she takes so much of my time, and he thinks I should be giving up the breast-feeding.'

'It's too early for that.'

'I know, but he needs me to go out with him to dinners with clients, that sort of thing. There's one next week. If I can leave her a bottle, do you think you could babysit?'

Kath didn't hesitate, every moment she spent with the baby was precious, and she knew that Jenny was anxious to keep her husband happy.

It seemed as if becoming a father had not been in Richard's plans when he married. Jenny didn't say much, but Kath had the suspicion that this marriage wasn't as Jenny had imagined it would be. She had confided her worries to Lynda one evening when Bernard had gone off to the pub, to give them the opportunity for what he called 'women's talk'.

'You'll keep an eye on her after I'm gone, won't you?'

'Oh, don't talk like that, Kath.'

'And you'll help her take care of my grand-daughter. Oh, Lynda, I never thought I could love anyone more than my own children, but little Alex has stolen my heart away even more than they did. Promise me, you'll not let her, or her mother, come to any harm.'

Lynda made the promise – not knowing that it might be impossible to keep.

Lynda wished that she could be as close to her daughter as Kath was to her Jenny. There were moments when Carolyn would seek comfort from her, when she'd fallen out with her friends, or when there was a teacher she didn't get on with, but for the most part Lynda felt her daughter was moving further away from her. She felt this very strongly when Carolyn made it clear she didn't want her Mum and Dad to go to the parents' evening in July.

'Are your friends' parents going?' John enquired.

'Some of them, I suppose.'

'So we should go.'

Lynda had so far ignored her daughter's reluctance to have them meet her teachers . The first year parents evening had been a low key affair, simply introducing parents to the new world their children had entered, and John and Lynda had been very impressed. For Lynda it was very important that Carolyn was treated well by the teachers, but Carolyn didn't always respond well to her questioning.

Sometimes she was willing to talk, especially to her Nan and her Dad, about her work, but as she entered her teens she became impatient with her Mother's need to know about her life at school. She developed what Lynda referred to as 'attitude', and the parents' evening that year brought clear resistance to her parents being involved with the school. Lynda wasn't going to be put off.

'What time does this parents' evening start?'

'I don't know why you want to bother. I've told you what subjects I'm doing next year.'

'What time?'

'Six o'clock.'

'Oh, right. I'll try to close early. I should be able to get there by quarter to seven.'

'You don't both have to be there. I'll take my Dad. There's no need for you to come.'

'What's up? Are you ashamed of me or something?'

They both knew the answer. Carolyn shrugged her shoulders and sighed, and went up to her room.

It was a hot day and the customers sitting at the tables outside the café lingered to enjoy the soothing rays of evening sunshine. It was seven o'clock before Lynda got the bus to the school and she'd had to run to catch it so she had perspiration running down her cleavage by the time she'd hurried down the drive to the school entrance. Heads turned at the sound of her high heels as she took a few steps into the dining hall, where the tables had been set out for the encounters between the parents and the teachers, who were trying to match names to faces and comments scribbled on reports late at night.

Carolyn and John were sitting with the English teacher, Mr Conroy, whose good looks meant he had no problem retaining the attention of the girls in his classes. Carolyn saw her mother arrive, and saw her wave, but turned her back and prayed that the interview with Mr Conroy would end quickly.

'Whew! Sorry I'm late,' Lynda apologised, breathlessly but still loud enough to echo round the room.'

Peter Conroy looked up at the beautiful, shapely woman beaming down at him and brushing strands of golden curls from her damp forehead. He stood up and, as Lynda leaned across the table to shake his hand, both John and Carolyn noticed his eyes being drawn momentarily to the soft, glistening flesh which threatened to escape from the plunging neckline of the thin cotton dress she'd chosen that morning as her coolest option for work. Carolyn closed her eyes in shame and embarrassment and John scowled at his wife.

'You should've got changed!' he hissed as Mr Conroy gallantly went off to fetch another chair.

'Didn't have time!' Lynda hissed back before sitting down, crossing her legs and then, seeing John's look, tugging her skirt down a bit.

'So, how's she doing? And which teacher are you?'

'This is Mr Conroy, Carolyn's English teacher,' John informed her in the voice he used on the rare occasions he spoke to his employer.

'I was just telling your husband, Carolyn is doing some excellent work. Her essays are always beautifully written . . .'

'She takes after me, I always wrote good essays. She reads a lot as well, like I do – when I have the time.'

'That's very good. It makes a lot of difference.'

'She'll be able to get to university, won't she?'

'Well, it's early days, but . . . '

John saw that Carolyn was glancing round and wincing as she saw other parents looking across to see where these forthright questions were coming from. He pushed back his chair and held out his hand to the young man who seemed mesmerised by his wife.

'Well, thank you very much for your time. '

The teacher stood and held out his hand. 'Pleased to meet you both.'

By the time they had shaken hands Carolyn had fled as far as the door.

'Hey, Caro, wait for us!' Lynda called out, causing her daughter to disappear round the corner.

'I'm walking home with my friends,' she informed them when they caught up with her. 'If they're still speaking to me after they've seen what kind of Mother I've got! I didn't know where to put myself in there. Don't you ever come to a parents' evening again!'

'Bloody hell! What have I done now?'

'Why can't you be like my friends mother's? Why can't you talk quietly and wear nice clothes like they do?'

'Because I haven't got the bloody money for a start! It all goes on you, in case you hadn't noticed!'

'Lynda, leave her alone. Wait for me outside.' John steered his wife towards the door and then turned back to their daughter. 'We'll see you at home, love. Don't be too late.'

John wanted to give her a peck on the cheek but she was keeping a distance between them and he realised that here, in her school, she wasn't his little girl any more.

He found Lynda standing by the entrance wiping away a tear which had refused to be held back. 'I thought she'd be walking home with us. I was looking forward to it. The three of us together, just for once.'

'You must be joking. Not after the way you embarrassed her in there.'

'Not you as well!' Lynda cried. 'What do you mean? How did I embarrass her?'

'Shush! By talking as loud as that, for a start. And wearing that bloody short skirt and that blouse that shows everything you've got!'

'It doesn't! And like I said I didn't have time to go home and change. And it's been boiling hot at work today, what was I supposed to wear?'

'Something decent, like the other Mums were wearing!'

At the beginning of November they let Kathleen Kelly come home from hospital. Lynda spent every moment she could at the house on Bennett Road, keeping the place clean, making Bernard have something to eat, and talking and singing until Kath drifted off into a sleep she didn't want to wake up from. The last few weeks of her friend's life were some of the hardest Lynda had ever lived through.

Kath had been right about Bernard not being able to cope with her illness and Jenny, too, was in despair and seemed to have no support from her husband. Lynda was there to hold on to them, to take over the phone when they could no longer hold back their tears as they told Kevin his mother was dying, and to watch them weep as they held her hand for the last time. Her arms were round them as they walked behind the small narrow coffin of the woman who had added brightness and laughter to everyone's days.

Lynda had cried, too, that day, but it wasn't until New Year's Eve that her grief crashed over her like a tidal wave that carried away all her strength. She had stepped out into the street as she had so often with Kath on that night. to look up at the moon and stars, and to ask God to bless the year to come. There had always been a surge of hope, a breath of new beginning, but this night there was only darkness. She staggered back into the house, shaking and sobbing.

John, who'd been about to go to bed, paused at the foot of the stairs.

'Whatever's the matter?'

'Hold me, John, I need you to hold me.'

He wrapped his arms around her and let her cry for a while, but then his need for sleep got the better of him and he persuaded her to go up to bed.

'It's as if I'm grieving for my Mother as well as my best friend,' she sobbed as she lay by his side. 'Kath was the only one who understood me, who I could really talk to.'

'You can talk to me,' John muttered, but they both knew that wasn't really true.

January 1980 was even more miserable than usual in the Stanworth household that year, because there was no money left to spend. Every spare penny had been set aside for months to pay for Carolyn to go with her friends on the school skiing trip in February. John and Lynda had both been relieved when Sheila, who, as usual, had made them wait, had eventually offered to buy her grand-daughter a ski jacket and salopettes. She went with them to wave to Carolyn as she set off in the coach from the school gates. It was a cold, wet evening, and Sheila scurried back towards the car before the coach had turned the corner. She was already sitting in the front seat, waiting to be driven home when Joanne Draper stopped Lynda and begged her to go for a drink with her.

'Is it all right if I go, John? She's on her own.' They'd both heard that Joanne's husband had left her after Christmas.

'Yeah. If you want to. I'd better get my Mother home, she looks frozen.'

'I won't be late,' Lynda said, but he didn't hear her, he was already obeying the impatient signal from behind the car window.

They went to the pub round the corner from the school and found a quiet corner, well away from the group of parents who had walked away from the coach loudly discussing their own holidays abroad.

'You know Keith's left me and the kids.'

'Yeah. Bad news travels fast round here.'

'Oh, it's not bad news as far as I'm concerned. He's gone back to his Mother's where he belongs.'

'What about the kids?'

'Well, as you know, Tracy's just gone off on this ski trip and our Mark's with his Dad and Grandma for a few days.'

'Must be lonely for you.'

'Yeah, it is. But it's better than being shouted at or sitting there in silence waiting for the next row to start.'

'Are you going to get divorced?'

'I don't know. It's a big step, isn't it? But I just couldn't stand it any more. I'm not having the life I wanted.'

'You and me both! I said that to my friend, Kath, but she said you get the life you choose and you stick with it.'

'Not if you made the wrong choice and it's making your life hell. You've got a right to be happy, surely? I haven't been happy for years, and it got to the point I was so bored with living with him that I could scream.'

'I know what you mean. John's only thirty-six but he's already turning into an old man. And it's like I don't exist sometimes. He never even looks at me these days, unless he wants, you know.'

'Tell me about it!'

'There's no romance.'

'And no satisfaction either.'

'No. I get so fed up. He hears his Mother and our Carolyn criticising me and never says a word. He just sits there worrying about losing his bloody job. Worrying about money, all the time. There's always something Carolyn wants, like this bloody skiing trip. I feel so bloody miserable.'

'Why don't you do what I've done, leave him?'

The question silenced Lynda. She realised she'd said too much to Joanne and she remembered Kath saying that being fed up wasn't a good enough reason to throw away a marriage.

'No. I've too much to lose. And I'd better go now, or else I'll have no home to go to.'

Her conversation with Joanne had frightened her, she didn't want to be on her own, she would make her marriage work, as Kath had advised. On the bus home Lynda decided that she would take advantage of Carolyn's absence by putting the romance back in her relationship with John. They'd just lost the habit of seeing each other, she decided, just got each other sort of 'out of focus'. They needed to find their love, their passion for each other. John had seized the offer of some overtime, so he'd be late home the following day. She'd get home before him, cook them a special meal, wear a dress that would make him remember why he'd wanted her so much.

She even bought candles and had the table set and the meal ready before he arrived home. She stood by the door and put her arms round him as he walked in wearily.

'What's all this?'

'I thought we'd have a romantic evening, while there's just the two of us. You go and get changed, I've put a clean shirt out, and I'll light the candles.'

'Don't be daft.'

'It's not daft, it's romantic.' She coiled her body round him and kissed him. For a moment she felt him respond but then he slumped away from her.

'I'm tired, Lynda.'

'Oh, don't spoil it. Look, I've even got us a bottle of wine.'

'How much was that?'

'Does it matter?'

'Of course it matters! When will you learn not to go spending money daft like that?'

They ate the meal in silence. Lynda defiantly opened the bottle of wine but when she offered to pour him a glass John sullenly refused to share the pleasure, so she drank it herself. When she'd finished her meal she got up, grabbed her coat and, slamming the front door behind her, tottered unsteadily to the end of the street to catch a bus to 'The Star and Garter' where she knew Joanne would be having a drink and hoping she'd turn up.

All the way there Lynda tried to remember Kath's advice but all she could think about was John's coldness. It seemed to her that there was nothing to look forward to. There didn't even seem to be any hope of anything good happening. And then, with tears in her eyes, she allowed herself at last to acknowledge the truth that she knew she had buried deep down inside her. She wanted her marriage to end. But it couldn't. There was too much to lose, nowhere to go. No choice but to stay.

It was chance that Tony Randerson was in 'The Star and Garter' that night, but chance that had been given a helping hand. He'd never forgotten the beautiful, desirable young woman who had turned him down, and whenever the opportunity had arisen, he'd called in at the pub in case she might be there again. He was there that night with Andy Slater, an old school mate from Manchester. Andy travelled around selling insurance and looking for women who needed company, like Joanne Draper. He and Tony had already bought her a drink and were entertaining her in a quiet corner. Andy was glancing round, wondering who he could find for Tony, whose wife was away, when Lynda walked in. Joanne spotted her immediately and waved.

'Over here, Lynda!'

Lynda hesitated, a glass of vodka and black and an hour of sympathy from Joanne was what she'd come for, not to spend an evening with two strangers.

'No, I'll see you some other time,' she said and turned to walk away but Joanne hurried across and took hold of her arm.

'Don't go. They're OK these two, I'm having a real good laugh. Come on, just for half an hour, a bit of fun. It's what we both need. Don't spoil the party!'

Joanne always had been good at pleading. Lynda sighed and followed her back to where the two men were waiting. Lynda became aware as she walked towards them that she was being watched and admired. It was what she needed, that excitement she used to feel at Saturday night dances.

'This is my friend, Lynda.'

The two men stood up and politely held out their hands. Andy introduced himself and moved so that Lynda would sit next to his companion.

'Tony Randerson.' His hand was warm and he smiled and held on to hers firmly. 'I think we may have met before.'

'Have we? I don't remember.' He knew she was lying but smiled again and waited until she sat down. 'May I get you two ladies a drink?'

The two men were well practised in being good company, and Lynda soon found herself relaxing and laughing, and flirting. Andy was proud that Tony was his friend and told them all about him and his company.

'Did you see that red sports car parked outside? It's Tony's – a birthday present.'

'From my wife.'

'She must think a lot about you.' Joanne was surprised that Tony had mentioned his wife, and so was Andy. Lynda was disappointed, though she knew she shouldn't be.

'Where do you live?' she asked.

'Langridge Hall, at Calderwood.'

'Oh, very nice.'

'Do you know it?'

'We've been past it loads of times, it looks a beautiful old house.'

'It is. You'll have to come and visit us sometime.'

'Thanks. Might take you up on that one day. I've always wondered what it was like inside.'

'She's always been nosey, like that.' Joanne was feeling a little annoyed with herself for having missed the chance of flirting with this obviously wealthy man.

'You could come and have a look now, if you like. My wife won't mind, and I'll give you a lift home afterwards.'

'No.'

'I thought we were going on to The Fiesta Club. We haven't been there yet, have we Lynda?'

'No. But I don't want to be out that late.'

'I'll take you, Joanne,' Andy said, pulling her close. 'The night is young. And I bet you're a great dancer.'

'I am! I was hoping they'd put on some music here, but they obviously can't be bothered.'

'Right, that's settled, then, we're off!' Andy declared, holding up Joanne's coat. She swayed a little as she stood and allowed him to put it caressingly round her shoulders. They disappeared quickly, as Andy had told Tony they would.

Tony stood up and bowed gallantly. 'Your carriage awaits, my lady.' Lynda found that standing up was a struggle. She hadn't noticed that the drinks Tony had been buying her had double shots of vodka in them.

'No, I'll be all right. I'll get a taxi,' she said, and then realised she didn't have enough money.

'Now, I wouldn't be a gentleman if I didn't take you home. And I'd love to show off my car. Have you had a ride in a Mercedes before? It's quite an experience.'

'I've seen them in films.'

'Well, now's your chance to be a film star.'

If it hadn't been for her coat, she thought later, she'd never have gone with him. He held out the navy blue woollen coat that had seen too many winters, and which her mother-in-law had chosen, and the poverty of her life swept over her as she thrust her arms into the frayed lining of the sleeves.

She must have passed out for a while in the luxury of the soft leather passenger seat, but when she roused herself she realised that they were heading out of town.

'I thought you were taking me home.'

'Yes. We're nearly there.'

'No. I meant my house.'

'Oh, you said you wanted to see my home, Langridge Hall.'

'Did I?'

He stopped the car outside the main entrance and watched her gaze in wonder at the chandelier in the entrance hall. He led her gently into the lounge and on to the large, softly cushioned sofa in front of the fire. He decided against offering her a drink, he didn't want her to pass out again.

She was still gazing round the room in wonder when he began to kiss her neck and then her breasts as he skilfully moved his hands over her body. She felt herself shudder with pleasure, she had never been caressed like this. She allowed herself to be eased down against the velvet cushions; she felt as if she was floating on warm clouds, and all the surface of her body was tingling and shimmering with breathtaking sensations. Then she felt his hands tearing at her clothes and the whole weight of him on top of her. She took hold of his shoulders and tried to push him away.

'No!' she screamed.

He laughed.

She was still shaking so much that she couldn't fit her front door key in the lock. John heard her and let her in.

'Where have you been?'

'With Joanne. I'm going straight to bed.'

She staggered past him but she had been too dazed to fasten her coat properly and it fell open to reveal the dress which had been ripped away from her breasts.

'Lynda! What's happened?'

She tried to lie, to make up a story, but she couldn't. When he held her in his arms she sobbed and clung on to him. And when he asked her questions the truth stumbled out and gradually he moved away from her.

'You got in his car and you went to his house. You must have known what he was after.'

'He said his wife would be there.'

'Oh, yeah, taking you home to meet his wife. Is that what you thought, you stupid bitch?'

'I don't know.'

'And you let him . . .'

'No! I screamed but I couldn't stop him. I think I passed out.'

John hit her and called her a bloody slut. And she knew she deserved it, but she still wanted to hit him back, to tell him it was his fault as well as hers. Then he sat down and wept, and she knew he wouldn't hit her again.

She went upstairs and had a bath, tears streaming down her face as she scrubbed her skin till it felt as if it was burning. She'd heard John come upstairs but knew he wasn't sleeping. She opened the door to their room.

'I'll sleep in Carolyn's bed.'

'Yeah, you do that,' he snapped.

They both got up early the next morning, neither of them had really slept. John didn't want to speak to her, he just stared across the table with anger and hatred in his eyes.

'We have to talk John. Carolyn will be home in a couple of days, we can't let her . . .'

'No.' 'He shook his head slowly from side to side, and his face became ugly. 'You're bloody disgusting, do you know that?'

'Yeah.'

'And him. I'm going to find him and belt the bloody life out of him.'

'No.'

'Why not? Because he'll say you asked for it? That he thought it was what you wanted

'Yeah. That's what he'll say. But there's another reason you mustn't go after him.'

'What? You don't want him hurt?'

'No. I do want him hurt, I want him dead! But if you . . . it'd cost you your job. He told me that when he drove me home. He's Bentham's son-in-law and Earnshaw's get a lot of work from . . . .'

'I know that!' he snarled.

So they told no-one, but there was one person who found out. Carolyn. She sensed that something had happened as soon as she came home, but she knew instinctively that it was another of those things that wouldn't be talked about. She was frightened to see her father so depressed and her mother so quiet, so when, late one night she heard them having a row she crept on to the stairs and listened.

She pieced together the snatches of sentences she heard, and it was enough to make her realise it was the most disgusting, shameful thing that had happened and that her Mother was to blame.

She knew this had to be kept secret, but it was a secret she couldn't cope with alone. She knew she couldn't speak to her parents about it, but she had to tell someone, and the only person she could possibly share this with was her Nan.

Sheila held her while she cried, and assured her it would all be all right, and that no-one but the four of them would ever know.

'We'll just have to get on with our lives and try to forget it ever happened. But you must tell nobody else, Carolyn. Do you hear me? Nobody. Ever.'

The following evening, when Carolyn was away on a school theatre trip, Sheila went round to Beechwood Avenue and added to their pain.

'I'm sorry, but I had to tell you that she knows.'

John buried his head in his hands and wept. Sheila couldn't bear to see her strong, handsome son destroyed like this. She turned to Lynda, clenching her fist and then stabbing her finger at her.

'And you. You are nobody in this family from now on. Do you hear me? All I ever wanted was someone to look after my son, to love him and to make him happy. But he married you, you disgusting piece of trash! You don't look after him, you don't make him happy. And you don't love him. And now you go and do this to him. I'll never forgive you. And neither will he. And neither will your daughter!'

Lynda heard all these terrible truths, turned away and, taking her shabby raincoat from the peg in the hall, slowly walked out of the house into that cold dark night. She walked for hours in the rain, keeping to the dimly lit side streets of the town, not wanting to be seen. She found herself standing at the corner of Bennett Street, but couldn't bring herself to walk past Kath's house. She turned towards the main road, watched car headlights flashing past, and wondered what it would be like to step out in front of a fast-moving car.

There would be many times like that in the next few years, and many nights when she walked the streets rather than stay in the house and be bowed down by those accusing looks and silences. There was no-one she could confide in. Jean was her close friend again, grateful for all the support Lynda had given her since Gordon's death, but Lynda knew that Jean's friendship and loyalty had its limitations. Jean wouldn't be able to stop herself from passing judgement, and finding Lynda guilty of betraying all the good fortune which she had had and which Jean had never enjoyed. But she still went round to Jean's house some evenings so that, for a while, she could feel a little safer in the cosiness of the small terraced house which Gordon had made sure would be a lovely home for his widow.

One night, walking through town she came across Joanne Draper. She was relieved when Joanne, boasting that Keith had come back to her, seemed to have completely forgotten that night in 'The Star and Garter'.

The café and hard work were Lynda's lifeline. She could be Lynda Collins there, a woman who had more than shame in her life. She made good money organising children's parties and engagement parties, and even 'hen nights' for those women who preferred a more genteel environment than pubs and clubs. She enrolled for evening classes, to build up her business skills, anything rather than spend time at home.

She also acted as babysitter for Jenny Heywood, which annoyed Ellen but as it was something she didn't wish to do, she didn't interfere. She and Jenny became good friends, despite the age difference – as if inheriting the bond between Lynda and Kath. In July 1981, with little Alex cuddled in Lynda's arms, they watched the Royal Wedding together;

Carolyn had decided she would prefer to watch the golden pageant on the large television at one of her wealthier friend's houses, and Ellen didn't want to risk having the occasion interrupted by the demands of a lively small child.

'Diana is so beautiful. Such a lovely bride,' Jenny repeated as the royal couple waved from the balcony. Jenny heaved herself into a more comfortable position. 'I feel such an ugly great lump.'

'Rubbish! You're one of those women who positively bloom when they're pregnant.'

'Richard doesn't think so. Oh, he is going to kiss her.'

'Very good of him!'

'Lynda, don't be like that.'

'Sorry, but he's never struck me as a good catch, old Charlie Boy.'

'Everyone told me Richard was 'a good catch', Jenny said ruefully.

'They're all 'a good catch' till you marry them and have to share a bed with them.'

'Yeah,' Jenny sighed, suppressing thoughts of Richard's rough attentions.

'Still not good, eh?'

'No. Especially when he's had a drink – which is most nights.'

'You need to tell Dan. Get him to tell Richard he's got to stop.'

'No. He wouldn't be able to do anything. Ellen won't hear a word against Richard, Dan knows that. And if Richard thought I'd said anything, he'd make me pay for it.'

'But you can't let him . . .'

'I'll be all right. It helps being able to talk to you about it. It'll be better when this baby arrives.'

'I hope it's a boy. Perhaps he'll leave you alone once him and his mother have got an heir to carry on the name of the illustrious Heywoods!'

'Yes. Oh, they're going in now.'

'Yeah, the fairytale bit is over, married life starts now. I hope you'll be happy, Diana. And I hope you have more luck with your mother-in-law than I did.'

Jenny laughed. 'And me!'

Little Alex's sister was born in October and was christened Katie, a form of Kathleen which pleased her mother. Richard and Ellen this time had no strong opinions as to the child's name, and didn't even try to conceal their disappointment that she wasn't a boy.

Like Bernie, their Grandad Heywood was overwhelmed with love for both his little girls and spent every moment he could with them. But the following year, on a hot summer day in the bakery, Geoff Heywood had a heart attack and died.

Lynda went to the funeral service, standing on her own in the shadows at the back of the church. Ellen didn't notice her, she was aware of nothing that day, except that she had lost the husband who had managed to love her. The last time she had spoken to him had been when they'd quarrelled over her determination to change their will. Geoff did not usually argue with her, but this time he had stood his ground, insisting that, for once, both of their sons should be treated equally. He had even shouted at her, but she had ignored how upset he was and had walked out, not giving a thought to what the consequences of the row might be.

The knowledge that she might have been the cause of his having a heart attack, and the realisation that she had never shown any real love for him, was tearing her apart. It was a feeling of guilt that she would never speak about, but she would always carry the pain of it in her heart, and accept it as punishment.

Lynda sent Dan a card full of love and sympathy, and happy memories of his Dad, but she didn't have chance to talk to him until a week or two after the funeral. He came very early one morning with the delivery and accepted her offer of a cup of tea so eagerly that she realised his need to sit and talk.

'I'm so sorry about your Dad. He was a lovely man.'

'Yeah.'

'I did come to the funeral. I was at the back. I didn't think your Mother would want me there. You saw John and his Mother.'

'Yeah. I gather things aren't good, between you and . . . '

'And my so-called family. No, it gets worse not better. My daughter hardly speaks to me these days.'

'Well, she's a teenager and she's studying for exams. It's a tough time.'

'Yeah. For all of us. Thank God I have this place to come to, it keeps me sane this café. I'm happier here than anywhere.'

'And you've made a big success of it.'

Dan blessed his father for the smile on Lynda's face. When he'd gone through his Dad's files at the bakery, he'd found a letter from Geoff about buying the café, and instructions that he was to look after Lynda as far as possible.

'And what about you, Dan? Are you all right?'

He was relieved to have the chance to talk to Lynda. She loved him and would never betray him. She was the one person he had always felt he could trust.

'Yes. Upset about my Dad, of course, and I'll miss him like hell. Unlike some people,' he added bitterly. 'Our Richard has been horrible. All he's interested in is my Dad's money. Which is, of course, mostly my Mother's now.'

He leaned back and raised his arms in a gesture of despair.

'She's changed her will. Practically all her money will go to Richard now as he and his family are the future of 'the Heywood dynasty'! That's what she told me yesterday. How does she think that makes me feel?'

'She's a cruel woman.' Lynda hesitated for a moment, this was not the time to tell Dan more bad news, but she didn't know when she would get another chance. 'And her son takes after her.'

'What do you mean?'

'I'm sorry, Dan, love, but I've been wanting to speak to you about this for a while. I have to tell you, for the sake of Jenny and the girls. Do you know that Richard has been hitting her?'

'No. Oh hell.'

'It happens mostly when he's been drinking. Jenny says she doesn't want me to tell you, but she does. She's frightened of him, Dan. Will you have a word with him? Or even better, with your Mother, she has more power over him than anyone.'

'Yeah. I will.'

Watching Dan walk away, even more bowed down with sorrow than when he came in, Lynda hated herself. But she was so worried about Jenny.

CHAPTER TWENTY-ONE

To everyone's surprise, Carolyn announced that she would go with them to the New Year's Eve party to welcome 1984. It was to be the last party at the Kellys' house, and would also be a joint early birthday party for Steve Sheldon, who would be twenty-one, and Bernie himself, who would be sixty in the January. What Bernie hadn't told anyone, except Jenny, Kevin and Steve, was that it would also be his farewell party.

It had been a very hard decision; it would break his heart to only see his little grand-daughters on occasional visits, but Bernie had decided, as Kath had always known he would, to return to his beloved Galway. He'd even managed to get Charles Earnshaw, who'd always enjoyed Bernie's racing tips, to give him his pension early.

John had ordered a taxi for seven thirty and he and Carolyn were in the front room watching out for its arrival when Lynda came down the stairs wearing her new imitation leopard skin coat over her red satin party dress.

'What on earth is that you're wearing?' groaned Carolyn.

'My Christmas present to myself. Don't worry, it's not real fur.'

'Anybody can see that a mile off. And what have you got on underneath?' Carolyn enquired sarcastically. 'Something equally tasteful I suppose.'

'Of course. You've heard the expression all fur coat and no knickers, haven't you?'

'Stop it, you two. The taxi's here.' John glanced at the coat as he went to open the door, but made no comment.

Her appearance caused a different reaction when Bernie greeted them.

'Well, look at you! What a Glamour Puss! And is that my favourite dress you're wearing as well?'

'Thought I'd give an old man a treat!'

'Less of the old, I'm in my prime, as you well know! Just like your husband here.'

Lynda couldn't resist a dig. 'Oh, I wouldn't be too sure about that.'

Bernie avoided seeing the expression on John's face and moved quickly to take Carolyn's smart leather jacket. 'And the lovely Carolyn. I'm delighted you could come, my darling. Perhaps you and I will have a chance to tinkle the ivories together later?'

'I'd like that, Bernie. And Happy Birthday!' Carolyn gave him a kiss on the cheek.

He beamed, and then, seeing Steve was now standing close by, grabbed him by the arm and said,' 'Thank you! And it's this young man's birthday party, too. Does he get a kiss as well?'

Carolyn laughed and dodged away, aware that the sight of Steve Sheldon's handsome face, with eyes which seemed always to hold a glint of laughter, had made her face glow a deeper shade of pink than the blusher she had applied to her cheeks.

Steve, who hadn't recognised this beautiful young woman as the kid who used to play the piano with Bernie, stepped up close to her.

'I'll settle for a dance, instead. Carolyn, is it?'

'Yes.' She felt a little breathless, feeling him so close.

'I'm Steve Sheldon.'

'I know.'

'Can I get you a drink?'

'Yes, please.'

'And you won't forget about the dance, will you?' He placed his arm lightly but possessively across her shoulders as they made their way into the dining room where the bar had been set up in its customary place.

John followed them, but Lynda remained in the hall with Bernie for a moment and they watched the young couple walk away.

'Well, now,' Bernie speculated. 'And wouldn't that be lovely? Your daughter and our adopted son.'

'Yeah. Yeah, it would. But she's all set to go to university, you know. John's Mother's even picked out which one, with the help of her friend Ellen Heywood, of course!'

'Still in control, are they?'

'Yeah. I still don't know quite how it happened, Bernie, but they've completely taken my daughter away from me now.'

'Now, don't you go believing that. No-one can change the fact that you're her Mother. You were the one who brought her into this world.'

'Yeah, me and Kath between us. So let's go and drink to that happy memory. Our Kathleen, eh?'

'I'll drink to that any day of the week!' He put his arm round her waist. 'Come on, girl, you and me have got some partying to do!'

The party had been going full swing for a couple of hours when Jean Haworth saw John enter the front room again with another pint of beer. He stood by the fireplace, watching his wife dancing with Bernie. She was sitting alone as she didn't know many of Bernie's friends, even though, as Lynda's friend, she'd been to several of the Kellys' parties. She waved to John and beckoned him over to sit beside her.

'Are you not going to dance?' she enquired, hoping that he would ask her.

'No, I'm too old for dancing,' he responded, only half joking.

'Don't let Lynda hear you say that.'

'She already has. But I'll give you a twirl in a minute if you like,' he offered gallantly. 'We'd better make the most of tonight, eh, with it being the last party.'

'Yes, I'll miss coming here, but not as much as Lynda.'

'No.'

'She was really upset about Kath going. I was still coming to terms with Gordon and everything, I don't think I realised . . .'

'No. Neither did I.'

'She'll miss Carolyn when she goes to university. You both will.'

'Yeah. My Mother's got it in her head Carolyn should go to London, but it's too far away.'

'And too expensive.'

'You're not kidding! She wants to study law and economics or something.'

'Crikey. She'll be joining the posh people then.'

'She already has. I'm surprised she's not out with her well-to-do friends tonight.'

'She's always thought a lot of Bernie. They've had some fun on that piano! Oh, here he is now, is he going to make a speech?'

'Looks like it. That dance will have to wait.'

Jean smiled at him, and tried not to look too disappointed.

Bernie carefully placed his beer glass on the mantelpiece and then stood very still, waiting for all his guests to shuffle around until everyone had managed to get a place to sit or stand. He also checked that his clean handkerchief was in his trouser pocket.

'I thought I'd better do this while I'm still capable, because if there's one night I'm bound to get drunk, it's this one.' He paused, and took a deep breath, to ward off the tears already threatening to make a fool of him as they always did.

'First of all, I'd like to thank you all for coming, especially Kevin for travelling all the way from America to see his old Dad. And before I forget, thank you for bringing the food and booze like you've always done.'

He paused to beckon Steve to come and stand beside him.

'As you know, we're here to celebrate my birthday, and retirement, but also the twenty-first birthday of this young fella, Steve Sheldon, who we've known since he was a nipper. Steve has also been my apprentice and mate at work, and has, Kath and I agreed, become a member of the family. He's a fine young man – well, he's bound to be, I taught him all he knows! So can I ask you to raise a glass and wish him Happy Birthday.'

'And you, Dad!' Jenny and Kevin moved forward, starting the singing of 'Happy Birthday' as their friends brought in the two cakes they'd been hiding and which now blazed with candles.

Steve put his arm round the shoulders of the man who had been better than a father to him, and they both leaned forward to blow out the candles.

When the cheers died away, Jenny and Kevin stepped forward to present Steve with the wristwatch the Kellys' and his workmates had bought. Steve, not daring to look at Bernie, thanked everyone and then gave Bernie a hug that told him everything.

Kevin and Jenny stepped away for a moment and then brought out a large parcel.

'Before we give this to Dad, which is, as you know, a present from all of us here, and my Mam who is up there keeping an eye on us.'

Bernard took the white handkerchief out of his pocket. 'Yes, she gave me strict instructions to have this with me, because she knew I'd need it. And I do!'

He mopped at the tears which he could hold back no longer.

'Before we give him his present,' Kevin continued,' there's something he's asked me to tell you – because he knew he couldn't manage it himself. There's a lot of good memories in this house, many of which you all share with us, but it hasn't been the same since we lost our beloved Mam, and now my Dad feels it's time for him to go home to Galway.'

He waited until the shock had breathed its way through the room. 'So this is a farewell party, too, but don't be too sad. Wish him health and happiness, and plenty of time to enjoy these. Go on, you can open it now, Dad.'

A child at Christmas couldn't have matched the look of wonder on Bernie's face as he unwrapped the set of golf clubs.

'Oh, how long have I dreamed of owning my own golf clubs? Oh, thank you, thank you all from the bottom of my heart. And like Kevin said. Don't be sad. Just remember the good times. And don't forget us, because we'll never forget you. And I'll come back and visit whenever I can, I wouldn't desert my grandchildren, would I? And it's been a wonderful life. You've all been wonderful, the best friends as man could have. And now, and now, will you all clear off and get yourselves a drink, while I sit down and have a good old howl into this hankie!'

Carolyn didn't go home with her parents. Bernie sent the younger guests off into town to finish their New Year celebrations and in the early hours of the morning Steve Sheldon walked her home. When the Victorian town hall clock had solemnly marked the start of the New Year he had kissed her, and Carolyn had fallen in love. When he kissed her again at the corner of Beechwood Avenue she nestled in the warmth of his love and knew that this was the man she would marry.

She also knew she wanted to go to university and so made herself be sensible. She went out with Steve, but only at the weekends and she didn't want anyone to know, but Steve wasn't having that.

'Are you ashamed of me, or something?'

'No, of course not. I love you, you know that.'

'Yeah, and I love you. And I'm so proud to be your fella, I want to tell everybody. Don't you understand that?'

'Yes, but I'm afraid . . ..'

'Don't be afraid. Don't be frightened of anything. Just be happy.'

He held his arms open wide and gave her that smile that she couldn't resist. 'O K.'

The following Saturday, when they'd met in town, Steve put his arm round her waist and steered her towards the market and the café.

'Where are you going?'

'We're going to have a cup of coffee.'

Before she could protest Carolyn found herself pushed gently through the door of the café.

Lynda was so surprised she nearly dropped the tray of dirty crockery she was carrying.

'Hiya, Mrs Stanworth. Could we have two coffees please?'

Lynda stood very still for a moment, stunned at the sight of her daughter walking into the café, a place she'd avoided for years. Then she beamed with happiness and hurried back behind the counter.

'You certainly can. On the house!'

'No, you're all right. I'm paying.' Steve, who had never been short of pride, put his hand in his pocket and placed the money firmly on the counter. Lynda knew this wasn't a time to argue.

'Two coffees, it is,' she confirmed and poured the drinks while trying to decide what she could say that wouldn't annoy or embarrass her daughter.

Carolyn chose a seat in a corner by the window, and tried not to notice that she was being smiled at by several of Lynda's regular customers. Steve, before sitting down, turned and waved to them all, 'Good afternoon.' Carolyn had her hands clasped tightly in front of her. He smiled at her with that confidence she found so exciting, reached out, took hold of her left hand and kissed it before placing it on the table and holding on to it firmly. Lynda, her hands shaking a little, brought the coffees over.

Steve pulled out another chair. 'Have you got time to join us for a couple of minutes?'

Lynda hesitated and then sat down.

'Are you having a coffee as well?'

'No.'

'Oh, is it that bad?'

Lynda, who had teased Steve since he was in short trousers, immediately pretended to clip him round the ear, 'Don't be cheeky, you!'

Carolyn stared at them in horror for a moment and then found herself smiling as she saw them grinning at each other.

'Bit of a surprise for you this? Me and your Carolyn,' Steve commented, feeling much less assured than he sounded.

'Yeah. A nice surprise, though. How long has this been going on?'

'It's a song, isn't it, that?' quipped Steve, who, for years, had had no choice but to listen to recordings of American crooners at Kath and Bernie's. He softly sang the refrain.

Lynda smiled and turned to Carolyn. 'He's talented, isn't he, this boyfriend of yours?' Then, taking a chance, 'He is your boyfriend, isn't he?'

Carolyn blushed, 'Yes.'

Lynda, as usual, didn't manage to stop herself. 'Is it serious?'

'Mother!'

Steve saw Lynda wince, and then grow defensive. 'Well, you've never said anything!'

'No. Sorry about that, Mrs Stanworth. And it is serious. Very. Isn't it, Caro?'

Carolyn didn't say anything but Lynda took a deep breath as she saw the love in her daughter's eyes as she gazed at Steve Sheldon.

They stayed for about half an hour, and no-one seeing the three of them sitting there would have thought that there was anything unusual going on; but for Lynda it was as if the sun had come out on that dull January afternoon. For the first time for years, she had chatted and laughed with her daughter. As the young couple left the café, there was a question Lynda had to ask.

'Carolyn. Can I tell your Dad?'

'Yes.' There was no hesitation. Carolyn didn't want to be the one to tell her father there was another man in her life.

Lynda couldn't wait to share the good news with John, to have something positive to say to him, to have something they could talk about. Four years had done little to remove the misery and the silences which had filled so many hours in that house which was supposed to be their home, the cosy setting for their married life together.

It was still a marriage, in that they lived together, ate together, slept together. Occasionally they had sex; you couldn't call it making love because, for Lynda, each time was an ordeal of remembering the nightmare and the guilt of that night four years ago. John at first was aware of her tension and numbness, which he interpreted as a lack of response, and it made him brutal, which reminded her even more of Tony Randerson. Then, as the months passed, John chose to ignore her reactions and eventually he didn't even notice how still she was, how tightly she closed her eyes.

But they were still married, and Lynda wanted it to become, at least on the surface, a relatively happy marriage. She longed to move beyond the pretend normality and to have what she called 'proper conversation', and here, at last, was something they could really talk about together. So she burst excitedly into the living room that evening.

'Guess what, John!'

As always, he was watching the television, but had set the table ready for their usual Saturday night supper of fish and chips.

'What?' he muttered, not taking his eyes off the screen.

'Our Carolyn's got a boyfriend!'

He turned round. 'A boyfriend? What's this, another of your tales?'

'No. She's going out with somebody.'

'I don't believe you. She hasn't got time for boys, she's concentrating on her exams.'

Carolyn had, of course, been out with boys before, but only briefly, and she'd managed to keep any knowledge of these passion free, fleeting relationships from her parents.

'She's got time for this one. She brought him to the café, or rather, I think it was him who brought her.'

'She brought him to meet you?' John was anxious now.

'You'll never guess who he is.'

'I don't care who he is, he'd better clear off! Our Carolyn's too young to have a boyfriend.'

'She's as old as I was when we got married. You can't expect her to be your little girl for ever.'

'I know that.'

'Do you?'

John, not wanting to have this conversation, turned his attention back to the television.

'Aren't you going to ask me who it is?'

He sighed and turned off the television. 'I suppose you're going to tell me, whether I want to know or not.'

'It's Steve Sheldon.'

'Oh.'

'Good, isn't it? Somebody we know. Better than one of those lads with the sports cars that her mates go out with.'

Carolyn rarely brought her friends to the house, and she told her parents as little as possible about her social life. She would have been appalled at how much her mother knew about her friends, but Lynda was careful to listen discreetly to any useful gossip passed on by her customers at the café.

John was still looking obstinate and gloomy. 'I think we should put a stop to it.'

'Don't be daft. Since when have we been able to make our Carolyn do what we want? She'd only go on seeing him in secret. Better to have it out in the open. Well? Don't you agree?'

'I suppose so. But I don't like it.'

'Well, get used to it, because I've invited him round for his dinner next Sunday.'

Ellen Heywood had been quite ill that January and found she was unable to recover as quickly as she usually did. She'd found herself feeling very lonely since her husband had died and was glad when Sheila Stanworth telephoned to ask if she might call that Thursday afternoon.

They were discussing their favourite topic, Carolyn's future, when Ellen's new housekeeper, the third since Molly had died, brought in the tea tray and deposited it next to the sandwiches and cakes she'd already set out.

'You've forgotten the hot water, Mrs Thomson.'

'Again,' Maggie Thomson shook her head and smiled. 'I'll get the hang of it one day. Sorry. Won't be a minute.'

The two women sitting by the fire watched her waddling her way back to the kitchen, and Sheila responded with sympathy to Ellen Heywood's raised eyebrows.

'Not good at the finer points but she is a very good cook.'

'Oh, well . . .' The sound of the doorbell interrupted Sheila's comment.

'Shall I answer that for you?'

'If you would.'

Mrs Thomson returned just as Sheila reluctantly led Alice Smith into the room.

'Oh, shall I fetch another cup and some more cake?' she enquired before stepping forward to place the pot of hot water next to the teapot.

'You've just called in with my library books, haven't you, Alice?'

'Yes, but, . .' Alice clutched the carrier bag of books to her barely perceptible bosom. 'But I've time to stay for tea, if you're offering.'

She quickly put down the books and began to take off her coat. Mrs Thomson watched her, and turned to her employer with a wry smile.

'Is that a 'yes' then?'

Ellen nodded, not particularly pleased to have Alice intruding on what had promised to be a pleasant afternoon.

Sheila quickly resumed her position opposite her hostess, in the centre of the small sofa which had been moved to replace the ancient leather armchair which had been Geoff Heywood's favourite. Alice was always keen to sit close to the fire, and headed towards the small sofa but Sheila made no sign of moving along to accommodate her.

Alice's eyes glinted at Sheila before, with a hint of petulance, she plonked herself down in the centre of the other larger sofa which faced the fire, but which was much more removed from its warmth. However, it did have the benefit of also being close to the delights of the afternoon tea, which Alice had calculated would be served just before her arrival.

'I managed to find all the books you asked for, Ellen.'

'Thank you very much.'

'They're long dark days this time of year, aren't they? Nice to escape into a book.'

'Yes.'

'I like autobiographies, film stars mostly. Of course, they don't tell you everything, but I suppose everyone has to have some secrets.' She smiled at Ellen, who, never quite sure how much Alice Smith knew, concentrated on pouring the tea.

Sheila graciously received the first cup, and stirred it delicately before turning condescendingly to Alice.

'Do you not work at the bakery now, Alice?'

'Yes, but not every day. There's not as many cakes to do, just the occasional silver wedding or 50th birthday. There's no wedding cakes at this time of year, unless there's a shotgun involved, of course!'

Ellen didn't smile, so neither did Sheila.

Alice always carried a collection of titbits of information in her head and, on occasions such as this, made a selection from them, just as if she were drawing out of a dark velvet bag a slip of paper with a 'truth or dare' inscribed upon it. She structured her conversation carefully.

'I expect your Carolyn's reading a lot of books and stuff at the moment, with her mock A-level exams coming up.'

Ellen gestured elegantly towards the sandwiches and cakes. 'Do help yourself, Sheila. And you, Alice, of course.'

Alice immediately loaded her plate with salmon sandwiches and then, noticing that there was only one of them among the selection of cakes, added her favourite fresh cream chocolate éclair to her plate. Sheila, with much ceremony, selected two dainty salmon and cucumber sandwiches before responding to Alice's comment.

'Yes, she's studying very hard. I hope she gets the results she wants, the teachers keep telling them it's vital to do well in the mock exams. Is that right, Ellen?'

'It is usually a good indicator of the actual A-level results. But I'm sure Carolyn will do well.'

She and Sheila ate fastidiously for a few minutes, both noting how quickly and eagerly Alice attacked the treats she'd piled up on her small china plate.

'Do have another salmon sandwich, Sheila, before they all disappear.'

With a satisfied smile, Sheila delicately took the last sandwich.

Alice, fully aware of their attitude towards her, carried on eating for a while before asking a question which Ellen had answered weeks ago when Alice had visited her.

'Is she wanting to go to college?'

'University,' Ellen corrected her.

'Yes,' Sheila replied proudly. 'And Ellen has kindly been advising her about which university to apply for. She'll need to work hard to get the grades, of course.'

Ellen nodded reassurance. 'I'm confident she will.'

Alice licked a sliver of salmon from her middle finger. 'Let's hope she doesn't get distracted, eh?'

Ellen countered this firmly. 'She won't.'

Alice, bit into another sandwich, and then waved it airily as she approached the climax of the little drama she was eagerly creating. 'A certain young man seemed to be distracting her a great deal in a dark corner of the library.'

Sheila, who had been enjoying a Savoy fresh cream sponge, sat bolt upright. She knew Carolyn had gone to the library that afternoon.

'What young man?'

'Steve Sheldon.' Alice turned to enlighten to Ellen. 'He's a joiner and cabinet maker, works with Jenny's Dad. You know, he's the boy that your daughter-in-law's parents took under their wing.'

Ellen shook her head. 'I know very little about the Kellys' friends.'

'Your John will know him, Sheila. I expect Carolyn met him at one of those parties at the Kellys' house that Lynda used to take her along to. I've done cakes for them sometimes, when they could afford it. The Kellys have always been big friends of Lynda's. If Carolyn has to have a boyfriend, I expect Lynda's glad it's Steve Sheldon.'

Sheila was appalled. 'He is not her boyfriend. Carolyn hasn't got a boyfriend. She would have told me.'

'Do you think so?' Alice gazed at the chocolate éclair before biting into it, and then stuck out her tongue to catch the cream threatening to escape down the corners of her mouth.

Ellen decided it was time to end Alice's little tale. 'You must have been mistaken, Alice. And now, if you don't mind, I'm feeling rather tired.' She rang the bell on the wall next to her chair. 'Mrs Thomson will see you out.'

Sheila picked up her handbag, but Alice, disappointed to be denied a further selection from the tea tray, continued eating, determined to savour both every last scrap of the éclair, and every moment of the consternation she had engendered.

'I wasn't mistaken,' she said, as she licked the last streak of cream from her forefinger. 'It was your Carolyn, Sheila, and Steve Sheldon. And he is her boyfriend. And it's quite serious by the look of it.'

'You have too much imagination, Alice.' Ellen stood up, waiting for her to go.

'No, I haven't.'

'Ah, there you are, Mrs Thomson. Will you see my visitors out, please?'

'Goodbye, Ellen. And thank you.' Sheila stood up and was about to move towards the door but a discreet signal from Ellen indicated she should delay her departure until Alice had gone.

'You're very welcome. Goodbye, Alice.'

Mrs Thomson opened the door a little wider but Alice hadn't finished yet, and paused before making her grand exit, and declaring loudly. 'I know canoodling when I see it. And I know that when a young couple can't take their eyes, or their hands, off each other, it's serious. Whether you two like it or not!'

When they heard the front door close Ellen asked Mrs Thomson to bring a fresh pot of tea and invited Sheila to sit down again.

'We must put a stop to this, Sheila. Carolyn needs to concentrate on her A levels.'

'You think Alice was right, then?'

'Yes. But I didn't wish to give her the satisfaction. Alice may be too fond of tittle-tattle but she's usually very careful to base it on fact.'

'I'm so upset that I had to find out from Alice. I should have been told. Wait till I see Carolyn!'

'Teenagers like to have secrets. Do you think her parents know?'

'They wouldn't have told me if they did. At least Lynda wouldn't. I'm afraid Alice might be right about her being pleased if Carolyn is going out with this friend of the Kellys. Has Jennifer ever said anything about this Steve Sheldon?'

'No. She's never mentioned him, but she doesn't talk much about her family.'

'She just feels lucky to have joined yours, I expect.'

'No doubt. But she has a lot to learn about our way of doing things. So, you'll have a word with Carolyn?'

'I certainly will.'

'We both know the dangers of her getting involved with someone like that.'

'Yes. It makes me shudder just to think about it.'

'Quite. We can't have our young lady's life ruined.'

That danger was a constant presence in John Stanworth's mind when his daughter brought Steve home for Sunday lunch, and it made him silent and watchful as they sat round the table together. His wife's behaviour was the opposite, Lynda was livelier than she'd been for a long time in her own home.

'Hiya, Steve! Hope you don't mind lumpy gravy,' had been her greeting as Steve had entered the living room behind Carolyn.

'I'm just glad to be here, Mrs Stanworth. And it smells wonderful.'

'My cooking's rubbish compared to Kath's, but you're as welcome here as you always were in her house.'

'Thank you.' Carolyn saw Steve's eyes fill with gratitude and then was amazed as she watched and listened to the young man she loved exchanging affectionate banter and happy memories with her Mother.

She also observed her Dad, after sharing a couple of beers, gradually begin to talk to Steve, and later enter into a long analysis and commiseration over Milfield football team's recent defeats.

'Let's hope they win next Saturday, it'll be the last match I go to with Bernie.'

'You'll miss him.'

'Yeah, it'll feel strange being there without him cursing and swearing next to me.'

Steve quickly made the offer, 'You can come with me and my mates, if you like.'

'Oh, I don't think . . .'

'We'd be glad to have you with us. And it would be nice to be with Bernie at his last match. I won't promise to behave myself, mind! Or watch my language!'

'Neither will I, especially if we get a referee like the one we had last time.'

'Right. You're on. I'll see you and Bernie there next Saturday, and I'll introduce you to my mates. I'm sure they'll be happy for you to join 'our gang'. Shall we go to your Nan's now, Caro. You said she'd be back from her 'lunch with the ladies' about two o'clock, didn't you?'

'Yes, but . . . '

John shared the hesitation in his daughter's eyes. 'You're taking Steve round to your Nana's?'

'Yes, if that's all right, Mr Stanworth. I'd like to meet her.'

'And I'm sure she'd like to meet you!' Lynda exclaimed, laughing to herself. 'But just one thing before you go, Steve. I think we've known you long enough to get rid of this 'Mr and Mrs Stanworth' malarkey. John and Lynda will do, won't it, John?'

'Yeah, of course it will.'

'And he'll have to come again, won't he?'

Carolyn had almost forgotten that her Dad had a sense of humour, and she listened wide-eyed as he said, 'Yes. It's been good having another bloke in the house. I need all the support I can get, Steve.'

Their visit to Sheila's didn't last very long. There was the politeness of a cup of tea, but the chocolate cake she had made was only brought to the table when Carolyn, desperately trying to get her grandmother into a better mood, had said how much she looked forward to that traditional Sunday treat.

When Sheila received a phone call the young couple took the opportunity to escape and Steve, holding Carolyn firmly by the hand, angrily walked away from Sheila's front door as fast as he could.

'Steve, slow down,' gasped Carolyn, struggling to keep up with him.

'I'm sorry. Is she always like that?'

'No.' Carolyn had never seen Steve so annoyed. 'She'll come round when she gets to know you better.'

'No. She's no intention of getting to know me better. You didn't hear what she said when you went upstairs.' He fashioned a fairly accurate impression of Sheila's tone, "You must stop seeing each other immediately. It's very wicked of you to try to spoil Carolyn's future." And when I said I loved you, she didn't believe me. "Young men like you are only interested in one thing where young girls are concerned!"'

Carolyn was so embarrassed and ashamed that she couldn't bring herself to speak. She held his hand tightly as they headed for the park and a walk in the winter sunshine.

'She made it sound dirty, and it's not dirty, you and me, it's wonderful. Isn't it, Caro?'

'Yes.'

'She didn't give me a chance. She just looked me up and down and decided I wasn't good enough. She did the same to your Mother.'

'Did she?'

'Yeah, that's what I've heard from Bernie. Your Mother used to tell Kath everything, you know. And who's this Mrs Heywood?'

'My piano teacher. I told you about her.'

'She seems to have a lot of say in what your Nan thinks.'

'They've been friends, well, sort of friends for a long time. Please don't be so angry, Steve. They both mean well, they both think a lot about me. It's very important to them that I go to university and . . . .'

'It's important to me as well. It'll be terrible when you go away, but I wouldn't want to do anything to stop you having that chance. God knows I wish I could do the same. I want you to go, even though I'm scared to death you'll meet somebody else at university and . . .'

She stopped and stood in front of him, holding both his arms and making him look into her eyes. 'I won't. I love you, Steve. And I always will.'

She kissed away his anger and fear and, with their arms round each other, they walked on till they reached Bennett Road.

Bernie's friends had all been inviting him round to see them before he left for Galway, and tonight he was going to another of what he called his 'last suppers'. He'd made some sandwiches for Steve and Carolyn and had placed a box of chocolates on the table by the television. He went off to see his friends, and wished the young couple a happy evening in the warmth and comfort of the soft and shabby cushions of the Kellys' old settee which, Bernie boasted, had seen more than its share of kisses and cuddles.

CHAPTER TWENTY-TWO

Dan's new assistant phoned in sick on Valentine's day so that morning Dan had to deliver the bread round the shops in Milfield, including the cafe. He didn't want to stay long and refused Lynda's offer of a cup of tea.

'What's the matter? You usually have time for a cuppa. I haven't seen you for ages. Is everything all right?'

'Yes, of course it is.'

'Did you have a good birthday on Sunday? You got my card, didn't you?'

'Oh, yes. Thanks. We had Sunday lunch at our place as usual, and Jenny made me a birthday cake.'

'That'd be a change, you've always had to make your own.'

'Yeah. It was really nice of her, and it was a very good cake. My Mother turned her nose up at it, of course.'

'How are Jenny and the kids? I haven't seen Jenny for a while, come to think of it.'

He started to leave. 'They're O.K.'

She stepped between him and the door. 'I've always been able to tell when you're lying.'

He glanced across the square, checking that there was no-one else about. 'One of the reasons you haven't seen me is that I've been waiting for this black eye to become less noticeable.'

She looked closely at his face. 'Oh, yeah. Who gave you that?'

'My so-called brother. I got him on his own to tell him he had to leave Jenny alone. I told him if he didn't stop I'd make sure Mother found out what a bastard he is.'

'Not that she'd believe you!'

'He told me to mind my own business and that he'd do what he liked in his own home. He laughed about it, as if he took pleasure in hurting her.'

'So you hit him.'

'Yeah. We had a fight and he beat the hell out of me, just as he used to do when we were kids. I don't know what to do, Lynda. Jenny won't let me go to the police, and if I did my Mother would never speak to me again. I feel terrible about it all.'

'You did your best. All you can do now is persuade Jenny to go in for a divorce.'

'Yes. That's what I think, but it's not going to be easy. How are things with you? Anybody sent you a Valentine?'

No, but me and Jean are going to have a slice of one of your Valentine gateaux later on. I've invited her to drop in for a cuppa when she's finished her shopping. It's always hard for her is Valentine's Day, remembering how Gordon used to make a fuss of her.'

'Yeah.'

'But apart from the lack of Valentines, everything's great. You know our Carolyn's going out with Steve Sheldon . . .'

'Yeah, my Mother's going mad about it.'

'Nothing to do with her! He's a treasure, is Steve. We have such a laugh, him and me. And he's made such a difference to our Carolyn. And John gets on well with him. So we're all a lot happier at our house. Apart from Sheila, of course. She and Carolyn are hardly on speaking terms these days. Which, I have to say, suits me down to the ground!'

Steve and Carolyn had already had a row about the party that Belinda, one of her wealthy school-friends, was holding that night to celebrate the end of the mock A-level exams as well as Valentine's Day. Belinda had seen Steve out with Carolyn and had insisted that she bring her good-looking boyfriend to the party with her so that they could all meet him.

When Carolyn had been reluctant to accept the invitation, Steve had accused her of being embarrassed that he wasn't like the 'sports car set' most of her friends went out with. There was still this tension between them when they arrived at the party, and Belinda, whose boyfriend had dumped her the previous day, decided it would be entertaining to seduce Steve.

She managed to slip double shots of her father's whisky into Steve's glass as she poured him several beers during the early part of the evening. He made the mistake of humouring her as she flirted with him, thinking she was just having a bit of fun, but then he found her draping herself over him in a way which couldn't be misunderstood. Carolyn couldn't believe how jealous she felt, and had the urge to yank Belinda away from him.

Instead she called out, 'Steve, we're going now.'

'No, don't be silly, Carolyn,' Belinda protested. 'The party's hardly got going yet. Steve and I are just getting to know each other.'

'Yes, I can see that.' Carolyn handed Steve their coats. 'Are you coming, Steve?'

'Yeah, sure,' Steve's speech was a little slurred and he hung the weight of his body on Carolyn's shoulders as he helped her on with her coat. 'Mmm, you smell good.'

'Come on.'

Steve gasped a little as he breathed in the cold night air. 'There's the bus.'

She pulled him back. 'No, I don't want to go home yet. And you need a walk. Let's go to your flat, you haven't shown it to me yet.'

'It's a bedsit, not a flat. I can't take you there, Caro.'

'Yes, you can. Come on.

They walked for a while and then caught a bus to Brennan Street. A week ago Steve had finally moved out of the Kellys' house and taken his own few possessions and the pieces of furniture Bernie had given him to the bedsit over a greengrocer's. It was small, damp and shabby, and badly in need of new curtains and a coat of paint, but it was the only available accommodation he could afford. He'd not allowed anyone to see it, and had assured Bernie that it was fine.

The smell of rotting vegetables followed them up the stairs as Steve fumbled in his pocket for the key. He saw Carolyn flinch as she walked into the room, catching the heel of her shoe in the smelly, threadbare carpet.

'I told you, it's a dump.'

She saw the shame and misery in his eyes.

'Oh, Steve. It must have been bad enough for you, saying goodbye to Bernie, but having to move in here as well . . . '

'Yeah.'

'You poor love.' She put her arms round his neck and laid her cheek against his shoulder, but he didn't draw close to her. She lifted her head and saw the deprivation he felt as he looked round the room.

'Bit of a contrast to your friend, Belinda's mansion, isn't it?' he commented bitterly.

'Put the fire on,' she said and looked round for somewhere to sit. There was a rickety wooden chair and a divan bed which Steve had covered with a curtain from Bennett Street. She sat on the edge of the bed.

He made two mugs of tea, and offered the tin of chocolate biscuits Bernie had given him. They sat there in silence for a while.

'I don't know why you're going out with me, Caro.'

'Yes, you do!' she said, giving him a playful nudge before nestling against him.

'I've got no money.'

'Yeah, but you've got things that money can't buy.'

'You sound like Bernie.'

'It's true, you've got loads of talent, you're good-looking, and you've got charm. My friends were really impressed with you – well, the ones with any sense were.'

'They live in a different world to us, though. It's all about what car have you got, where are you going for your holidays, . . .'

'Who are you sleeping with?' Carolyn thought, but didn't say it out loud. She'd decided she wouldn't take Steve to another of those parties, it had scared her to see Belinda offering herself to him. She knew most of her friends slept with their boyfriends, and knew they laughed at her for being a virgin. She'd been shocked at the jealousy and fear she'd felt when she'd seen Belinda with Steve, and it had made her want him so much.

'I don't blame you for wanting what they've got, Caro. I dream about it myself. If you don't come from a family with money, you've only got yourself to rely on. I don't mind working hard, but the only way to make real money is to have your own business, and I'm determined to do that one day. Then I'll be able to give you everything. I'll make it, Caro, big time, and then we'll get married.'

Carolyn held her breath, he was talking about marrying her. She hadn't thought he would do that so soon. She was so astonished, and excited, that she heard herself acting like a fool and joking about it. 'Will we? You haven't asked me, yet!'

Steve got off the bed and knelt down on the greasy carpet.

'I'm asking you now, Caro. I promise to love you for ever, to keep you safe, to make you happy. Will you marry me?'

She panicked. 'I can't, not yet.'

'But will you, one day?'

'Yes. I will, Steve. I love you.'

He took her in his arms, and she remembered how she'd felt when he'd been in someone else's arms that evening. She clung to him with a passion increased by jealousy.

'I love you so much.'

'And I love you, Steve.'

And she realised that their love for each other was the most important thing in the world. Her love for him, and her need to be sure of him for ever took over her whole being. When they kissed there was no resisting the love and passion that was all that mattered in that moment.

Three weeks later she knew she was pregnant. She tried to tell herself what she had read in the agony columns of magazines, that women often miss a period or have it come late, but she was never late. She kept the terrible secret to herself for another month, but by mid April she was sure. On Easter Sunday she and Steve went for a walk in the hills above Milfield and she told him she was expecting his child.

For a minute he felt as if he couldn't breathe. 'Wow. Are you sure?'

'Yes. It's two months now.'

'But you don't look . . .'

'I've put on a bit of weight round the middle but no-one would know looking at me. What are we going to do, Steve?'

'Get married.'

She loved him so much in that moment. There had been no hesitation, he would marry her. It was the right thing to do and it was what he wanted. It was what she wanted, too, but she knew it wasn't that simple.

'We'll have to tell my Mum and Dad. Oh, Steve, what will they say?'

'That I should have been more careful. Or rather, I shouldn't have got you into bed with me in the first place.'

'We've been so good. It was only that once.'

'That's all it takes apparently. I'd heard that but never believed it before now. Come on, let's go and tell your Mum and Dad and get it over with.'

They were sitting in the front room, John was reading the Sunday paper and Lynda the latest Josephine Cox paperback. She closed the book when they entered.

'Did you have a nice walk, love?'

'Yes, we went up as far as Lane End Farm.'

John put down his paper and smiled. 'That was one of your Grandad's favourite walks, you can see for miles.'

Lynda saw that her daughter's eyes were filled with tears.

'Whatever's the matter, love?'

Steve put his hand on her shoulder and gently moved her towards the settee. 'Sit down, Caro.' Then he stood up tall and faced them.

'We've got something to tell you. We're having a baby.'

After a moment of silence John groaned. 'Oh, no!' Then he turned on his wife. 'What did I tell you? I said this would happen! But, oh, no, leave them alone, you said. Let them be happy. Don't say anything, let them just get on with it! Well, they got on with it all right!'

'John, shut up! Can't you see she's upset!'

Lynda went to sit next to her daughter and put a protective arm around her. 'Don't worry, darling, it'll be all right. It'll be lovely. A little baby.' She hugged her daughter and tried to make her laugh. 'Hey, I'll be able to enter those Glamorous Grandma competitions!'

'Don't talk stupid!' John snapped at her. 'Don't you realise what's happened here? Everything's shot to pieces! She'll have to leave school. No chance of university now. All those things she's always talked about doing, they're gone! What's she going to do now? Bloody sit at home and change dirty nappies!' He jumped up, grabbed hold of Steve by the coat collar and almost lifted him off his feet. 'And what about you, you little bugger? What are you going to do?'

Steve experienced a flashback to one of those terrifying moments with his drunken father, and the terror of his childhood swept over him.

'Dad!' Carolyn cried out.

John released him, and Steve took a deep breath and gave John that steady look of his which told everyone they were dealing with a man. 'I'm going to marry your daughter.'

An hour later, when Lynda had made them a cup of tea and they'd all calmed down, they were so engrossed in discussing practicalities that they didn't see Sheila look through the bay window and then enter by the front door.

As if some intuition had taken hold of her, Carolyn had just had a frightening thought.

'Oh! How will I tell my Nan? I can't tell my Nan!' She began to cry again.

'Tell me what?'

There was a silence. Then Lynda stood up and faced her enemy.

'She's going to have a baby.'

The decision came fast and sharp. 'No, she's not!'

'Yes, she is.' Lynda contradicted her firmly. 'Sometime in November.'

'What is she, then, two months gone? Right.' Sheila turned and took a step towards her grand-daughter, huddled small in the corner of the sofa. 'Listen to me, Carolyn. You will not have this baby. You will get rid of it.' Sheila's voice rose almost to a scream. 'Do you hear me? Get rid of it!'

It was Lynda who, after the Easter holidays, went to see Carolyn's headmistress. She was glad that, on a sudden impulse, she had bought herself a smart navy trouser suit in the January sales. Mrs Howell, a tall, sharp-eyed, immaculate woman, was also wearing navy, but with the added elegance of a silk scarf she had bought herself in Paris. The headmistress was extremely annoyed to learn that one of her star pupils would not be adding to her school's university successes. Lynda understood why Carolyn had been so afraid of entering that study bearing such disappointing news. At the beginning of the interview Mrs Howell was icily polite, and very strong in her view that it would be better if Carolyn left school as soon as possible, to save herself embarrassment.

'No, she's not leaving till June. And she won't be embarrassed because, if we're careful, nobody will find out till after she's left. She's very slim, as you know and she'll only be just over three months gone by the time she finishes her exams. We'll just have to make up some reason for her to be excused P.E. and Games and no-one will be any the wiser.'

'I'm not sure . . .'

'I am. My daughter needs to stay on at school. She's not leaving early like I had to. She's got to attend all her lessons and take all her exams. She has a right to do that, and she needs to get those A-levels to have a chance of having a career. Now, do you have any problem with that?'

Mrs Howell had many problems with it, but was experienced enough to realise that the path of confrontation with this particular parent would only lead to a lot of unpleasant publicity.

Lynda had taken the afternoon off, leaving her very capable assistant, Debbie, in charge of the cafe. After she'd been to the school she called in at the cafe on her way through town, to have a cup of coffee and check that everything was OK. She was surprised to find Jean there, treating herself to a cream tea.

'Oh, Lynda, I'm glad you're back, I was hoping to see you. I'm celebrating. I've got a new job!'

'Oh, lovely. What is it?'

'I'm going to help Frances Horton run her new dress shop.'

'Oh, you'll enjoy that. Congratulations!'

'Aren't you going to stay and celebrate with me?'

'No, sorry, love, I can't. I've got to go and see Ellen Heywood.'

'Ellen Heywood? Why on earth are you going to see her?'

Lynda looked round the cafe and decided it was too public a place to give Jean the news. 'I'll tell you later.'

Lynda hadn't been to Kirkwood House since that horrible night all those years ago when she'd been a frightened teenager. She was older now, but still felt a shiver of that memory. She was not afraid, though, because she had come to defend her daughter and her unborn grandchild. Carolyn had been to see her grandmother several times to plead with her to change her mind about the baby but always came home upset.

It was clear that Sheila had strong and unwavering support on this matter from Ellen Heywood, who was equally appalled that her dreams for her protégée were threatened by this unwanted child. Lynda had held Carolyn in her arms so many times in the last few days, listening to her grieve for the future she had lost, but most of all sobbing at the loss of her grandmother's love and respect. Whatever she thought of them, Sheila and her ally Ellen Heywood were important to her daughter, and she wasn't going to allow these two women to bully Carolyn any longer.

Ellen, engrossed in her newspaper's condemnation of striking miners, was annoyed to see Lynda striding into her drawing room with such determination and confidence. She had almost refused to see her visitor, but she, too, remembered her victory the last time Lynda Collins had dared to enter her home.

'Do sit down.'

'No, thanks, I'm not staying long. I've just come to tell you that you, and Sheila, have got to stop trying to bully Carolyn into having an abortion.'

Ellen drew herself up haughtily.

'I have a right to my opinion, and so has Sheila, and we both agree that having a child at this age, and in these circumstances would ruin her life. Your daughter has ambitions and dreams, and this . . .'

'I know she has, and she won't have to give them up, she'll just have to postpone them.'

'You're very naive if you think that.'

'And you're very cruel, you and my bloody mother-in-law!'

'I see your manners and language haven't improved.'

'Oh, shut up. You are cruel, both of you. How could either of you even think about making Carolyn have an abortion? She wants this child more than anything.'

'Does she? Or is it you who wants it?'

'I want it, of course, I do. Who wouldn't want a grandchild? But it's Carolyn we're talking about, and her instinct is to have this child. She loves it already, she feels it's part of her. It's her child, her baby, and she loves it, she's its Mother. You must understand that.'

'Must I?'

'You've got two children of your own, you should. Anyway, what I've come to tell you is that I've had enough of you. You make out you care about Carolyn, but you only care about her fulfilling your dreams.'

'Let me tell you something. If you had taken better care of your daughter she wouldn't be in this predicament. You encouraged this young man, and were too stupid to think of the consequences. You're not fit to be Carolyn's mother. And you're certainly not fit to be this child's grandmother.'

'That's funny. That's exactly what my mother-in-law said to me. Just think, that could have been you – my mother-in-law, and this baby you're so keen to get rid of could have been your great grandchild, if you hadn't stopped Dan marrying me.'

'He had a lucky escape.'

'Did he?'

'You wouldn't have made him happy.'

'I'd have done better than that ex-wife of his.'

'We're not talking about Daniel, we're talking about Carolyn.'

'Yes. My daughter. And she's going to have this child and I'm going to be its grandmother.'

'Oh, yes. I heard about that. The Glamorous Grandma - in a bikini no doubt. What a disgusting idea.'

'Disgusting, am I? I'll tell you what's more disgusting – killing an unborn baby. You call yourself a Christian, what would Jesus think about that?'

Ellen had struggled with that question and had not found an answer. Lynda watched her enemy shift her eyes and knew she was winning.

'Our Carolyn is going to marry Steve Sheldon. And you and my damned mother-in-law are going to give her your blessing – though God knows why it should mean so much to her.'

'Carolyn should not be marrying the likes of Steve Sheldon.'

'Why not? He's a good man, and he's going to marry Carolyn in June, we've already booked the registry office. And it will be lovely. And there'll be none of this shame that you keep going on about. After all, she won't be the first to get married quick, will she?'

Ellen rose to her feet and stared coldly at Lynda.

'I think you should leave now.'

'I'll be glad to. But you listen to me first. Carolyn is going to have this baby, because she wants to have it. And she's going to have a beautiful child. And you are going to accept that, and not give her any more grief. Or I promise you, you'll regret it.'

'Good for you, love,' John said when Lynda told him about her confrontation with Ellen Heywood. 'It's none of that woman's bloody business.'

'No, but your Mother listens to her like she was a female Moses with the Commandments in her handbag.'

'It sounds like you might have put a stop to them giving our Carolyn such a hard time.'

'I'm surprised Carolyn keeps going round to see your Mother.'

'She's her Nana.'

'Yes, but you wouldn't think it at the moment. Did you know she's told Carolyn that she won't be at the wedding?'

'She said she wouldn't be at ours, but she turned up.'

'Only because Graham went to fetch her at the last minute.'

'Well, there'll be no 'last minute' this time. I'll make sure of that. I'll go round and tell her she'll be there, or else!'

Lynda gave a little laugh, and the words 'I'll believe that when I see it' were written clearly in the look she gave him.

The wedding took place on a sparkling sunny day at the beginning of June. All of Carolyn's family were there, John had been to visit Graham and Sylvia to tell them the situation – which they already knew of course, from a lengthy agonisingly tearful phone call from Sheila. Graham, well aware that money was tight, volunteered to bring the bridegroom to the ceremony in the Ford Sierra Ghia which had been his present to himself on his promotion to assistant manager.

Ellen Heywood had been invited to the wedding but declined to attend. Dan was there, and drove the bride to the ceremony in the Ford Granada which Richard had obtained for his Mother. Dan also gave the couple a three tiered wedding cake. It had been decorated by Alice Smith with an exceptional enthusiasm fuelled by the satisfaction that all her predictions about the couple had come true. Since her father's death she had taken over his small, discreet but lucrative sideline of fortune telling in their front parlour.

Lynda and Carolyn had managed to find a wedding dress which almost completely disguised the presence of the newest member of the family.

Bernie, as well as travelling over from Ireland to be Steve's best man, had bought both himself and the bridegroom a new suit.

Steve was so proud of his beautiful bride and everyone said that they'd never seen a couple more in love. Sheila sobbed and whimpered all the way through the ceremony and half way through the small celebration afterwards, until she realised that everyone was ignoring her. It was many weeks, though, before she called at Beechwood Avenue; she could not face the thought of 'that young man' living there and sharing a bed with her grand-daughter. Lynda and John had moved into the back bedroom, letting the newlyweds move into the larger room at the front of the house, so that later on they would have enough space for the baby's crib.

They made sure that the young couple didn't suffer as they had when they'd had to live at Ted and Sheila's, and in fact the household was more relaxed and harmonious with Steve living with them. There was the occasional row, mostly caused when Lynda and Steve decided it was time they had a night out. John went with them to the pub sometimes but Lynda and Steve were so in tune with each other that he often felt like the odd one out.

Carolyn, increasingly aware how little money she and Steve had, usually refused to go with them but she made an exception when she received her A-level results. They went to 'The Peacock Hotel' as a special treat and Steve, relieved as well as proud, proposed the toast.

'To my beautiful and very clever wife, Carolyn. Congratulations!'

They all raised their glasses, and John, looking round, repeated loudly enough for everyone in the lounge to hear, 'Two As and a B. Well, done, love.'

Belinda Taylor broke away from her group of very fashionably dressed companions, and greeted Carolyn. 'Oh, hi there, is that what you got? I only managed a B and two Cs but it's enough to get me to Reading Uni, away from home and close to London so it'll do me nicely! You've given up on the idea of university, I gather.'

'Yes,' Carolyn said quietly.

'For the time being,' Lynda interjected.

'Oh, really? But you're . . .' Belinda smirked as she fixed her gaze on the large bump Carolyn was trying to cover protectively with her cardigan.

'Having our baby,' Steve declared proudly, 'but that doesn't mean she can't have a career as well one day.'

'Of course,' Belinda agreed with smooth scepticism. 'Well, good luck, with everything, Caro, and I hope you'll be very happy.'

'We will,' Steve assured her. 'Goodbye, Belinda.'

John watched her slink away. 'Who the hell was that?'

'Belinda Taylor, the one who told everyone at school that I was pregnant.'

They all fell silent, remembering the misery and shame that revelation had inflicted on Carolyn. 'She's right, though. I might as well have not taken my A levels. I should have been going off to university like she is.'

'We'll find a way to make it up to you love. You'll have a better career than her and any of her stuck up friends. We'll look after the baby and you . .'

'No,' Carolyn said firmly. 'I want to look after it myself. It's my job, I'm its Mother.'

Lynda tried not to read too much into the way Carolyn made that statement. 'Ok then, I'll work instead. Money's always useful. I'll help you, Carolyn. I'll be there, whenever you want me, come what may. I promise,' she said, and it was a promise she meant to keep.

The next day Carolyn went round to Stanhope Road to tell her Nan of her success. Sheila had been anxiously waiting for her to come, and this time there was no stiff formality and constant look of disapproval.

'I'm delighted for you, my dear,'

Sheila almost stepped forward to kiss her grand-daughter but could not bring herself to come into contact with the large expanse of stomach which harboured within it the cause of so much anguish. 'I'm very proud of you. I'm also very sad that you're not going to university, but . . .'

'It'll be all right, Nan. I've got my A-levels, I'll be able to get some more qualifications for a career later on. I just want to concentrate on the baby now.'

'Yes. Yes, of course you do. We all do. I've been thinking about it. Would you like me to knit some baby clothes?'

'Oh, yes please, that would be wonderful. I'm not good at knitting and Mum . . .'

'Hasn't a clue. Right, I'll start straight away, it will have to be white, of course, until we know whether it's a boy or a girl.'

'White would be lovely.'

'Have you decorated the little bedroom as a nursery again?'

'No, not yet. Steve and my Mum are going to do it next month I think.'

'Well, they don't want to leave it too late, babies can decide to arrive early.'

'Mum's hoping it will be late, she says it would be a lovely fortieth birthday present.'

Sheila had no interest in talking about Lynda, but forced herself.

'Oh, is she forty this year? How time flies. Of course she won't be expecting much of a fuss, not with the baby due around then. Have you bought anything for the baby yet, a pram or a cot or anything?'

'No, we're waiting till the room's ready, and till we've got some money saved up. We spent more than we intended on the wedding, but like my Mum said, you only get married once.'

'If you're lucky. Well, I might be able to help out a bit there. Perhaps we can start going shopping.'

'That would be great. Thank you, Nana.'

Sheila went round to see the newly decorated nursery and offered to make the curtains. She talked to Steve very politely, and even managed to laugh at some of his jokes. She was very careful at first, but gradually began to assert herself in the old way and took control of whatever she could. Lynda didn't like it, but when she complained about her behaviour to John he told her she was being over-sensitive. Steve was more sympathetic as he also had to suffer Sheila's snide remarks. He found it hard to take sometimes, and he and Lynda would spend an hour in the pub whenever they could, trying to think up strategies for dealing with Sheila.

Steve even tried to warn Carolyn what was going on.

'Your Mother's getting pushed aside, Carolyn, can you not see that? Sheila always wants to be top dog, and you let her.'

'You don't understand, Steve, it's just her way. She only wants to help, to be involved. And she's been lonely ever since she lost my Grandad. She never got over him walking out on her and going to live with that woman. It was terrible for her, and my Mum was partly to blame for him going.'

'He was going anyway, Lynda said, he'd been thinking about it for a long time.'

'You've only heard my Mum's version. I know you get on well with my Mum, and I'm glad - but you don't know everything about her. She . . . .Oh, I can't tell you, and I don't want to think about it. But you must understand that really it was my Nan who brought me up, taught me how to behave, who looked after me. My Mother was at work most of the time when I was growing up.'

'It wasn't her fault she couldn't stay at home and look after you herself. She needed to go out to work to . . .'

'Yes, I know, to earn money, but she also enjoys it, a lot. She always seemed to be happier out than being at home. I don't want our marriage to be like my Mum and Dad's, Steve. I want us to be happy, and part of that is me staying at home to look after you and our child.'

'While your Mum goes out to work.'

'Yes! She's OK with that, she thinks that's the way it should be.'

'All right. If she's happy and you're happy, that's fine. But we'll have to keep an eye on Sheila.'

Little Michael Sheldon was born at two o'clock in the afternoon on Thursday 15th November, several days before Lynda's 40th birthday. Steve dashed home from work and drove his wife to the hospital in John's car. He phoned Lynda who tore off her apron and ran, leaving Debbie to deal with the order she'd just taken. Steve and Lynda weren't going to phone Sheila till after the baby had arrived, but Carolyn had promised to let her know as soon as she went into hospital; so the three of them sat in a row on the uncomfortable grey plastic chairs in the maternity unit.

The nurse came out of the delivery room. 'Are you the father?'

'Yes.'

'Come and put a gown on and I'll take you in straight away, this baby seems to be in a hurry to get here.'

Steve steadily and calmly held on to his wife's hand all through the birth, but when their son was placed in his arms tears streamed down his face and he couldn't speak. Steve Sheldon's world changed in that moment and he felt he would never experience such joy again. He looked down at Carolyn who was smiling at both of them with the joy of knowing that she had a beautiful healthy little boy, and that she couldn't have chosen a more loving father for him.

The nurse, an experienced midwife, stepped out into the corridor.

'She can have one more person in to see her and the baby.'

Sheila stood up to go with her, but Lynda moved quickly past her. 'I'm her Mother.'

'Well, come on in, then, Grandma.'

To Lynda it was the best moment of her life when she walked into that delivery room and her daughter held out her hand. 'Hello, Mum. I'm so glad you're here.'

'So am I, love.' Lynda kissed her on the cheek, a pleasure she'd been missing for too many years, but which was welcomed by Carolyn nowadays.

'Would you like to meet your grandson? He's called Michael.'

Carolyn nodded to Steve, who gently handed over the tiny human being who was so precious. Lynda cradled him tenderly in her arms. 'Hello, Michael,' she said softly. 'I'm your Grandma, and I love you.'

On the Monday Steve and Carolyn were allowed to bring their baby son home. John and Lynda, and Sheila all went to the hospital in John's car and met Steve there. When they had completed the paperwork, Steve and Carolyn brought little Michael to the entrance and they all set off together across the forecourt.

Steve had to go back inside for the bag he had forgotten and Lynda waited for him. When he returned Lynda pointed to John and Carolyn, and Sheila walking towards the car park. They watched Sheila take the baby from his Grandad.

'Just look at her, insisting on being the one to hold him. She wants him all to herself. That's the child she wanted to get rid of, but I don't suppose she'll remember that.'

Steve put his arm round his beloved mother-in-law's shoulders and drew her close to him.'

'Forgive and forget, Lynda. That's what Kath used to say.'

'Yeah.'

'You've got a grandson, Lynda. And you've got your daughter back.'

'I hope so.'

'And you've got me as your son-in-law. You can't get luckier than that!'
She gave him a playful shove. 'You cheeky monkey. Come on!'
Lynda began to run after her grandson and the rest of his family. 'Hey, wait for me,' she shouted for all to hear. 'I'm his Glamorous Grandma!'

LIZ WAINWRIGHT

'The Girl who wasn't Good Enough' is set in the North of England, where I was born and brought up. I first started writing when I was a young Mum with two small children. I entered a novel writing competition in a magazine - I didn't win, but it taught me to type!

When people ask me where it all comes from, this writing, I tell them I have this special software - it's called 'my imagination'. There's reality and experience in the background though; for example, when I was young we lived in a run-down pub not unlike The Black Bull.

My characters do most of the writing for me, they become voices in my head and take on a life of their own. They're no angels, and they get into the sort of relationship situations which fascinate me. They make me care about them; they make me cry, and they make me laugh. I hope they'll do the same for you.

www.lizscript.co.uk

Printed in Great Britain
by Amazon.co.uk, Ltd.,
Marston Gate.